D1103805

THE ELEPHANT
KEEPERS' CHILDREN

Peter Høeg

The Elephant Keepers' Children

TRANSLATED
FROM THE DANISH
BY

Martin Aitken

HARVILL SECKER
LONDON

Published by Harvill Secker 2012

2 4 6 8 10 9 7 5 3 1

First published with the title *Elefantpassernes børn* in 2010
by Rosinante, Copenhagen

First published in Great Britain in 2012 by
HARVILL SECKER
Random House
20 Vauxhall Bridge Road
London SW1V 2SA

www.randomhouse.co.uk

Addresses for companies within The Random House Group Limited can be found at:
www.randomhouse.co.uk/offices.htm

The Random House Group Limited Reg. No. 954009

A CIP catalogue record for this book is available from the British Library

ISBN 9781846555848 (hardback)
ISBN 9781846555855 (trade paperback)

The translation has been sponsored by the Danish Arts Council Committee for Literature

STATENS
KUNSTRÅD
DANISH ARTS COUNCIL

MIX
Paper from
responsible sources
FSC® C016897

Typeset in Sabon LT Std by Palimpsest Book Production Limited
Falkirk, Stirlingshire

Printed and bound in Great Britain by
Clays Ltd, St Ives plc

For Awiti, Adoyo, Ajuang, Apiyo, Akinyi and Karsten.
For Stine and Daniel.

In case you wish to befriend an elephant keeper, make certain to have room for the elephant.

OLD INDIAN SAYING

FINØ

1

I HAVE FOUND A DOOR OUT OF THE PRISON. IT OPENS OUT onto freedom. I am writing this to show you that door.

You might ask how much freedom he thinks he's entitled to, this boy who was born on Finø, the island they call Denmark's Gran Canaria, and in the rectory to boot, with its twelve rooms and a garden as big as a park, and not only that but born into the midst of a father and mother, an older sister and older brother, and grandparents and a great-grandmother, and a dog, all of which sounds like an advert for something expensive but a worthwhile investment for all the family.

And while there might not be that much to see when I look at myself in the mirror, being the second smallest in the seventh class of Finø Town School, and on the skinny side too, there are many older, heavier players on the football fields of Finø who can only watch as I sail by like a surfer on the wind and feel their hair stand on end when I let fly with my lethal right foot.

So what's he complaining about? you might ask. How does he think other fourteen-year-old boys feel? And there would be two answers to that.

The first is that you're right, I shouldn't complain. But when Father and Mother disappeared and things became complicated and hard to explain, I discovered there was something I'd forgotten. I'd forgotten, while everything had still been bright, to seek to discover what will always endure, what can really be relied on when it starts to get dark.

The second answer is the hardest. Take a look around. How many people seem happy to you? Even if you have a father with a Maserati and a mother with a mink coat, as we had in the rectory once, how many people actually have anything to cheer about? Isn't it okay, then, to ask what can set a person free?

Now you might say that as far as the eye can see the world is full of people who'll tell you which direction to choose and what to do, and that I'm just one of them, and in a way you'd be right, though in another this is different.

If you ever heard my father give a sermon at Finø Town Church before he disappeared, then you'll have heard him say that Jesus is the way. My father can say that so beautifully and effortlessly you'd think we were talking about the way down to the harbour and that we'd all be there in a minute.

If you'd heard the service from a stool next to the organ, as played by my mother, and if you'd remained seated afterwards, she would have told you that music was the future. She plays and speaks in such a way that you would have already booked your first piano lesson and be on your way to spend your life savings on a baby grand.

If, after the service, you'd come back for coffee on one of those occasions when my favourite uncle, Jonas, who goes bear hunting in Outer Mongolia and has a stuffed bear standing in his hall and who has now become a union man, was staying with us, then you might have heard him say at some length that what really gets the ball rolling is having confidence in yourself and devoting your life to organising the working classes, and he says this not just to wind up my father, but because it's something he truly believes.

If you ask anyone at my school, they'll tell you that life doesn't begin till after ninth class, since that's when most of the children of Finø move away to board at the high school or begin vocational programmes in Grenå.

And finally, in a different direction altogether, if you asked the residents of Big Hill, which is a rehab centre just west of Finø Town, all of whom were substance-abusers by the time they were sixteen, if you ask them straight out, one on one, they'll tell you that even though they're totally clean and deeply grateful for their treatment and are looking forward to starting a new life, nothing even comes close to the long, mellow high you get from smoking opium or shooting heroin.

And I'll tell you this: I'm certain all these people are right, including the residents of Big Hill.

That's something I learned from my older sister, Tilte. One of Tilte's talents is that she can believe all people are right and yet at the same time be wholly convinced that she alone knows what she's talking about.

All these people I've mentioned, what each of them reveals is the door to their own favourite room, and inside that room is Jesus, or the songs of Schubert, or the national achievement test after ninth class, or a stuffed bear, or a steady job, or an appreciative pat on the back; and many of these rooms are, of course, fantastic.

But as long as you're in a room, you're inside, and as long as you're inside, you're a prisoner.

The door I'll try to show you is different. It doesn't lead into another room. It leads out of the building.

It wasn't me who found the door, I'm not cut out for that. It was my older sister, Tilte.

I was there when it happened, it's two years ago now, just before Mother and Father disappeared the first time. I was twelve and Tilte was fourteen, and even though I remember it like it was yesterday, I didn't realise that was what she'd found.

Our great-grandma was staying with us, she was making buttermilk soup.

When Great-Grandma makes buttermilk soup she stands on two stools placed on top of each other so she can reach to do the stirring, and she does that because she was born small and because her spine has collapsed six times since then and she's become so stooped that if she's to be in that family ad I was talking about before, they're going to have to take care what

5

angle they take the picture from, because that hump of hers is as big as an umbrella stand.

On the other hand, many people who've met Great-Grandma believe that if Jesus ever returns one day it could easily be as a lady of ninety-three, because Great-Grandma is what's called omnibenevolent. That means she's so kind she has room for everyone, even people like Karl Marauder Lander and Alexander Beastly Flounderblood, who was dispatched by the Ministry of Education to take charge of Finø Town School, and who you'd have to be his mother to love, and even that might not be enough, because I actually saw him collect his mother from the ferry once and she didn't seem to have much time for him either.

Nonetheless, no one should underestimate our great-grandma. You don't get to be ninety-three and survive several of your own children and a six-time spinal collapse and the Second World War, as well as being able to remember the end of the first one, without something special keeping you going. I'll put it this way and say that if Great-Grandma were a car, the chassis has been falling apart for as long as anyone can remember, but the engine purrs as if it were straight from the factory.

When it comes to words, though, I'd call her reserved. She hands them out like they're boiled sweets and there aren't many left, and maybe there aren't when you're ninety-three.

So when all of a sudden, without turning her head, she says: 'There's something I want to say,' we all fall silent.

'We' being my mother and father, my older brother Hans, Tilte and me, and our dog, Basker III, a fox terrier named after the book about the hound of the Baskervilles. He's called 'III' because he's the third of his kind since Tilte's been around, and she's insisted that every time a dog dies and we get a new one we give it the same name, just one number on. Every time Tilte tells people who've not enjoyed the pleasure of meeting us before what the dog is called, she always says the number, too. They're usually lost for words, maybe because it makes them think of the dogs that died before Basker, and I think that's actually why Tilte insisted on the name, because she's always been more preoccupied with death than kids normally are.

Now, as Great-Grandma seats herself in her wheelchair and prepares to speak, Tilte leans over the kitchen counter and lifts her legs off the floor, and Great-Grandma wheels up beneath her. Tilte always wants to sit on Great-Grandma's lap when there's something she has to say, but Great-Grandma's become frailer, and Tilte's heavier, so now they do things this way, Tilte lifting herself up and the world arranging itself beneath her so she can curl up in the lap of her great-grandmother, who at this point is already smaller than her.

'My mother and father,' Great-Grandma says, 'your great-great-grandparents, weren't exactly young when they married, they were in their late thirties. And yet they had seven children. Just after the seventh was born, my mother's brother and his wife, my uncle and aunt, died, smitten with the same influenza, the Spanish Flu. They died almost together, leaving behind them twelve children. My father went to the funeral in Nordhavn. After the ceremony there was to be a council at which the family were going to divide the twelve children between them. That's the way it was done back then; it was ninety years ago and it was all about survival. It took two hours by horse-drawn carriage to get from Finø Town to Nordhavn, and my father didn't arrive back until evening. He came into the kitchen, where my mother was standing at the stove, and said: 'I took them all.'

My mother looked up at him, full of joy, and then she said, 'Thank you for your confidence, Anders.'

When Great-Grandma finished telling us this, the room fell silent again. I don't know how long that silence lasted, because time had stopped. There was too much to absorb for anyone to think. It was like everyone had given up. We needed to grasp what had occurred inside Great-Grandma's father when he saw those twelve children at the funeral and felt himself unable to tear them apart. And most of all we needed to understand his wife at the moment her husband arrives home and says: 'I took them all.' There's no hesitation there, no going to pieces and wailing at the thought that we have seven children of our own, which can seem bad enough by itself if you think of the three of us in the rectory with our two bathrooms and one for guests, but all of a sudden they've got nineteen children.

At some point, when everything's been quiet for I'm not sure how long, but definitely a long time, Tilte says: 'That's how I want to be too!'

We all thought we knew what she meant, and in a way we did. We thought she wanted to be like the father, or like the mother, or like them both, and be willing to take on nineteen children if it ever became necessary.

And she did mean that. But she meant something else, too.

Before she said it, during the long silence, I think Tilte discovered the door. Or became certain of its existence.

Before I start, I'm going to ask you something. I'm going to ask if you can recall a moment of your life at which you were happy. Not just in a good mood. Not just content. But so happy that everything was totally one hundred per cent perfect.

If you can't recall a single moment like that, then obviously you're in a bad way. Which makes it all the more important I reach you with this.

But if you can recall only one, or better still several, such moments, then I'd ask you to think about them. It's important. Because that's when the door begins to open.

I'll tell you about a couple of mine. There's nothing special about them. I'm telling you to make it easier for you to identify them in your own life.

One such moment was the first time I got picked for the Finø AllStars, who play against teams from the mainland in July. The list was read out by the first team coach, whom we call Fakir on account of him being bald and built like a pipe cleaner, and because his mood all year round is like he just got up after sleeping on a bed of broken glass.

No one under the age of fifteen had ever been picked before, so it came out of nowhere. He read the list out loud and my name was on it.

For a brief moment I couldn't tell where I was. Was I outside or inside my body? Or maybe both places at once?

Another moment was when Conny asked if I wanted to be her boyfriend. She didn't ask me herself, but sent along one of her ladies-in-waiting called Sonja. I was on my way home from school and Sonja came up beside me and was like, 'Conny told me to ask if you wanted to be her boyfriend.'

For a moment there it's like someone pulled the plug out: are you floating or standing on the ground? You don't really know. And that sense of floating isn't something you imagine, the whole world as you know it is completely changed.

There's another situation with Conny. This goes right back to when we were about six years old and in kindergarten together. In all of Finø Town there are maybe three hundred children and only one school and one kindergarten, so in a way we were all of us at school and in kindergarten together at some time or another.

The kindergarten had been given these enormous wooden beer barrels by the Finø Brewery, and they'd set them down and chocked them up and put floors in and little doors and windows so they could be used for playhouses. Inside one of those barrels I asked Conny if she would take her clothes off in front of me.

You might ask where I found the courage, since normally anyone would think I'd be too afraid even to ask the way to the bakery, and I'll admit that this really was one of the times I surprised myself the most.

But if at some point you happen to meet Conny, you'll understand that there are women who can bring out the most extraordinary things in a man, even if he is only just past his sixth birthday.

She didn't say anything in reply. Just began ever so slowly to undress. And then when she was completely naked, she raised her arms and turned just as slowly to face me. I could see the down on her skin. The barrel enclosing us was round like a ship or a church, and it smelled of all the beer that had seeped into the wood over a hundred years. And I felt that what occurred between Conny and me was to do with the entire world that surrounded us.

The last moment I'll tell you about is also the most low-key. I'm a small child, three years old maybe, because we had just got Basker II and he's climbed up into my parents' bed where I've been sleeping too. I slide down onto the floor and push open the French windows and go outside into the garden. I think it must be early autumn, the sun's low in the sky and the grass is cold as ice and biting at my feet. Between the trees are big spiders' webs, and their threads are hung with dewdrops like a million tiny diamonds all glittering at once. It's very early and the morning is fresh and new and impossible to reproduce, as though there's never been a morning like it before and there doesn't have to be a copy because this one will last for ever.

At that moment the world is completely perfect. Nothing needs to be fixed, and there'd be no one to do it anyway, because there are no people, not even me, there's nothing else but the joy. It's all so very brief, and then it's over.

I know there are moments like that in your own life. Perhaps not the same, but similar.

I'm trying to make you aware of the seconds just before you realise how special the situation is and then begin to think.

Because the moment the thoughts come, you're back in the cage again.

That's part of what's so depressing about the prison. It's not just made of stone and concrete with bars in front of the windows.

If it were, it would all have been so much easier. If we were confined in the ordinary way we would surely have found a way out, even two such timid souls as you and me. From Grenå or Århus we would have got hold of a couple of hundred grams of that pink powder they put in the jet motors of the model planes when Finø holds its Grand Kite and Glider Day. And we would have found a rust-free pipe with a bung at each end, and we would have drilled a little hole in the pipe and put the powder inside and inserted a fuse from a New Year's firework into the hole, and we would have blown a great big exit in the wall, and they wouldn't ever have seen us for smoke.

But that wouldn't be enough. Because the prison, which is the life of every single one of us and the way we live it, this prison is not simply built of stone, it's also made of words and thoughts. And we are all of us involved in building and maintaining it, and that's the worst part of the whole thing.

Like that time Conny asked me out via Sonja. Right after the first second passed, right after the shock of it had turned the world around, it all snapped back again, and it snapped back because I thought: Can this be true? She means me, and not some other Peter? Why me? And supposing it is true, am I at all good enough for her? How long will it last? And if it does last, as I hope and pray it will, it's still got to end sometime, surely?

'And they lived happily ever after.'

I never liked that ending.

Father was the one who read to us in the evenings, to Tilte and me and Basker. Whenever the fairy tale ended with 'And they lived happily ever after' it always gave me a sense of discomfort I felt unable to account for.

Tilte found the right words for me. One day, she can't have been more than seven years old and I would have been five, she said: 'What does "ever after" mean?'

'It means until the end of their days, until they died,' Father said.

Then Tilte said: 'Were their deaths dignified?'

Father went quiet. Then after a while he said, 'It doesn't say.'

Then Tilte said, 'What happened next?'

I know where Tilte got it from, that thing about the deaths and whether they were dignified. She got it from Bermuda Seagull Jansson, Finø's midwife and undertaker rolled into one. That's the way it is – with the island being so small, a lot of people need to be two or three things at once, like Mother, who is the organist and churchwarden and advisor to the agricultural machinery rental firm all at the same time.

Tilte often talked with Bermuda and had even helped her put bodies in coffins. So that's where she got it from.

But that still doesn't explain everything. Try to imagine: you're sitting there with a seven-year-old girl and you've just read a fairy tale, and the idea behind them living happily ever after is for the story to have a happy ending and for the children to now be in the mood for going to sleep and to look at their family and feel secure in the belief that their mother and father and themselves and the dog are going to live happily ever after too, even if it is such a very long time indeed. And then there's this girl aged seven, Tilte, who asks if their deaths were dignified.

When Tilte said that, I understood why I had never really felt comfortable about those endings. I hadn't ever been able to think like Tilte, I didn't even have the guts. But there was something I'd sensed. That even if they did live happily ever after, what happened when they got to the end of their days?

That may be where the fun stops.

Now I'll tell you what happened to us. Not so much because I want to talk about us, but to help me remember when the door was open so I can show it to you.

I can't help you out through the door, because I haven't really gone through it myself yet. But if we can find it and stand in front of it often enough, you and me together, I know that one day we'll be able to walk through it and out into freedom.

It's never too late to gain a happy childhood.

That's something Tilte and I read once in the library, and I always loved that sentence. But don't think about it. If you think, you'll come to a halt. And then you'll say it doesn't make sense, because your childhood has already gone, and what's gone was like it was, and nothing can change that now.

Instead, you should let the words remain inside you: it's never too late to gain a happy childhood.

I think that's true. But sometimes it can be a problem.

Still, Tilte says there's no such thing as problems, only interesting challenges.

So I'll say that one of the interesting challenges of gaining a happy childhood began on Good Friday, on the square called Blågårds Plads, in Copenhagen, Denmark.

2

WE'RE WAITING ON BLÅGÅRDS PLADS IN COPENHAGEN, WE being Basker, Tilte, me and our older brother Hans, and we're waiting in a black-lacquered carriage drawn by four horses, and for that we can thank Hans. Assuming, that is, that we would wish to thank him at all.

Most of the population of Denmark, or at least the tourists of Finø, think my brother Hans looks like a prince in a Danish fairy tale. This they base on his being one metre and ninety centimetres tall and having blond, curly hair and blue eyes, and being strong enough to unhitch one of the horses from the carriage, turn it on its back, lay it down on a table and tickle its tummy.

But because Tilte and Basker and I know Hans, we think he looks like a grown-up baby, too.

The strategic midfield of the Finø AllStars may never have had a more formidable general. But off the pitch, with no ball to occupy his attention, his gaze is permanently fixed towards the stars, and anyone in that state will show a tendency to fall over the furniture.

Now he has moved to Copenhagen to study astrophysics, which also has to do with stars, and here he has taken on a part-time job driving a horse-drawn carriage, and Tilte and Basker and I have come to visit him for Easter while Finø Town Church is in the hands of a visiting pastor on account of Mother and Father making their annual trip to La Gomera, a wannabe Finø in the Canary Islands.

I don't know if you're familiar with Blågårds Plads. Personally, this is my first time here, and to begin with the square seems rather ordinary. It's warm in the sun and cold in the shade. There are still some piles of snow left over from winter, and there's a church with a number of people in front of it. As a clergyman's son one is always pleased to see customers in the shop. Sitting on a bench in the sun are three men in their prime of life, which they spend drinking Carlsberg Elephant beer. Behind our carriage, a greengrocer is standing outside his shop staring at a crate of lemons that have survived the winter thanks to the five daily prayers he directs towards Mecca, and in front of us is an old lady on her way across the street with a case of cat food balanced on her Zimmer. So the only unusual thing is the question of why a tourist wealthy enough to pay five thousand kroner online in advance for an hour and a quarter's carriage ride through the city's historical centre should have chosen to depart from Blågårds Plads, and besides that there's the issue of where he might be, since he should have been here ten minutes ago and has not yet turned up.

Then Hans' mobile phone rings, some sentences are exchanged, and after that our lives are completely different.

'It's Bodil,' says the voice at the other end. 'Are Peter and Tilte with you?'

Bodil Fisker, known to all as Bodil Hippopotamus, though short and slight of stature, requires no introduction. She is the municipal director of Grenå Kommune, which includes Finø and the islands of Anholt and Læsø, and everyone knows her. Hans has no need to put her on speaker phone, not that she's loud, she keeps within a normal range, but her voice is the penetrating kind that can reach out into the furthest corners of the globe. And it's not only her voice, it's the entire way she is, and all that stuff about the spirit of God moving upon the face of the waters could have been written about Bodil Hippopotamus.

But what truly moves upon the face of everything is Bodil's attention, not her actual self. A municipal director is not a person one meets in the flesh, but someone with people below her, who in turn have people below them, and they're the ones you speak to on the phone. I have seen Bodil only once, on an occasion I would prefer not to dwell upon, but which nevertheless I must tell you about presently. Bodil calling us in person is a sign that something is terribly wrong.

'Tilte, Peter and Basker are here,' says Hans.

'Did your mother and father leave an address?'

'Mother left her mobile number, that's all.'

'When are you due back?'

'We have one trip to make before I return the carriage.'

'Call me when you're on your way home. On this number.'

Then she hangs up.

Tilte turns her head and looks me straight in the eye. And I know why. She wants to remind me of something. That at this moment there is still a chance.

I have hesitated to tell you this. But now I'll say it straight out.

Tilte and I have discovered that the door is open not only in happy moments. It is open, too, in moments of dread. Exactly as you learn that someone is dead or has got cancer or has disappeared, or that Karl Marauder Lander – known by all on Finø as the eighth of the seven plagues of Egypt – has got up at four in the morning to be the first at the gull colonies where we gather eggs in May, which is okay because the gulls, the herring gulls and the lesser black-backed gulls only begin to sit on their eggs when there are three, so the nests that contain three we leave well alone. But at the very moment you discover that Karl has emptied the nests and the world is about to collapse around you, at that moment the door is open.

And now I shall tell you what Tilte and I have discovered one must do: one must reach inside and feel. The moment the shock kicks in there's this very unusual, very special feeling inside and all around you, and that is what you must reach into and feel. It is there just before the tears come, and the despair, and the customary depression, and the giving up, and the decision that if Karl can get up at four in the morning, then you can get up at three or two, or even not go to bed at all so as to be sure of getting there first. During that brief moment when your normal

16

instincts are gone and new ones have yet to appear, at that moment there is an entry.

This I remember on Blågårds Plads, and I listen inside and sense that the shock has caused the door to open.

After that, things happen so quickly it's all we can do to keep our snorkels above water, and this is even true of Tilte.

The first thing is that Tilte says what all of us are thinking.

'Mother and Father have disappeared!'

The next is that Blågårds Plads begins to change.

3

DO YOU KNOW WHEN THE WAY YOU'RE FEELING SORT OF rubs off on those around you, like on the way they look? One minute Blågårds Plads is all okay, without necessarily being worthy of preservation by UNESCO and attracting five million tourists to Copenhagen. The next it looks like a place people come crawling to in order to die. The group in front of the church look like a funeral procession. Once they've finished their beer, the three men on the bench will lie down and wait to expire, and they won't have to wait long. The greengrocer's lemons turn out to be composting, and the old lady with her Zimmer and her cat food looks at us as if we're driving a hearse and she's going to ask if she can see the deceased one last time.

Then I say: 'Bodil's frightened.'

We all heard it, and in a way that's the scariest part. All of us heard something in Bodil's voice that can only be understood in one way: that she has run into something bigger than herself.

And then the singing begins.

It comes from inside the church, and the voice is female. She must be using a microphone, and Blågårds Plads is at the same time a funnel that amplifies sound. The song is a foreign hymn and swings gently like gospel music.

The words are inaudible, but it doesn't matter as long as the voice is there. It is a voice big enough for us to park our whole carriage inside, and it is so warm that we would not be cold for one second, not even on a winter's day, and so cosy that we would gladly run the risk of a parking ticket, because we would never want to leave ever again.

For a brief moment, it lights up Blågårds Plads. It puts the greengrocer's lemons back on the trees, it makes the men on the bench consider joining Alcoholics Anonymous, and it causes the old lady in front of us to let go of her Zimmer and prepare to dance the fandango.

It prompts Hans to get to his feet, Tilte to stand up on the seat, and me to move up close to Hans and elbow him in the side so that he will lift me up to see, the way he has done ever since I was small.

A procession emerges from the church. I can see several clergymen in chasubles, a lot of people dressed in black, and in front of them walks the lady who is singing.

At first one wonders how someone so small could possess such a large voice, and then one thinks that she is not a person at all, because it seems like a long green dress is floating of its own accord, and above it a green silk hat like a turban with nothing in it. Then the dress turns and a face becomes visible, her skin is light brown like the stone of which the church is built, and that is what makes her face disappear.

Then she looks towards us, and as she holds the final note she takes off her golden, high-heeled shoes, removes her green turban, allows it to fall to the ground, and grabs a bag from a person standing next to her. In her hand she is holding a wireless microphone that she places on the ground, and then she lifts up the hem of her dress and begins to run. She runs towards us on her bare feet, over the snow and past the men on the bench. And before she is halfway across the square I can tell that she is the same age as Tilte or slightly older, and that she can do the 400 metres in under a minute.

As she reaches the carriage, she leaps like a grasshopper onto the box next to Hans, and even as she is still suspended in the air, she yells: 'Drive! Now! I'm the one who booked you!'

The procession is in disarray outside the church, people are shoved aside, two men in suits break out of the crowd and start running towards us. We know, all four of us, that they are after the singer. And we know, too, that we are on her side. I'll tell you straight out why. She could have been a child pornographer or an abuser of animals, but with that voice I would have tried to save her anyway, and I know that Tilte and Basker feel the same way.

But we need Hans, and for a brief moment we have no idea if he is up to the job.

Regrettably, Hans has yet to discover women.

Which is all the more embarrassing given that women have long since discovered him. When he stands in for Finø's harbour master in June and July and finishes cleaning the toilets at about eight o'clock every night and is done collecting mooring fees from all the boats, at least three of the sweetest girls of summer will be waiting to take him for a walk. But taking Hans for a walk is easier said than done, because no sooner have they begun to amble than Hans begins to swirl around them as though he's on the lookout for something from which to protect them, or a big puddle he can lie down in so they can cross without getting their feet wet.

The trouble is my older brother was born eight hundred years too late. He belongs to a chivalrous medieval age and considers all women to be princesses who may be approached only gradually by means of slaying dragons, for instance, or lying face down in puddles.

But the girls of Finø attend tae kwon do lessons and move to Århus when they are sixteen and take a year out as exchange students in America when they are seventeen, and if they should ever meet a dragon they would want it to be their boyfriend, or else they would pull it apart and write a biology report about all the pieces. So Hans has never had a girlfriend, and now he's nineteen, and his future prospects are less than bright, to say the least. Now, too, he stands gawping like some creature on which Finø's nature warden is about to perform taxidermy, until Tilte yells at him: 'Drive, Hans, you dolt!'

That wakes him up. Tilte yelling and two men halfway across the square in a full sprint definitely ticks all the boxes, and perhaps it seems to him like he really is saving the princess.

Now that I have spoken disparingingly of my older brother, even if only between the two of us, I need to add that he has a way with horses. Every year from April to September, Finø Town is closed for traffic with the exception of ambulances and delivery vehicles, and instead we drive the tourists around in horse-drawn carriages and small electric golf buggies. We charge two hundred and fifty kroner for the trip from the harbour to Finø Town Square, and Finø Town looks even more like a postcard, and the island, if we are to be honest and forthright, is transformed into a one-armed bandit in the middle of the blue Kattegat.

So everyone on Finø can drive a carriage, but none like Hans. Hans drives like he was aboard a sulky on the trotting track at Århus. Perhaps it has something to do with the horses always knowing that if they don't cooperate they'll be turned over onto their backs to have their tummies tickled.

He never uses the whip, not even now, but simply clicks his tongue and flicks the reins so our four horses leap into motion like wild rabbits and Blågårds Plads nearly vanishes into the horizon behind us.

Now the two men in suits make a mistake. They veer off towards a big black BMW with diplomatic plates that is parked in front of the library, and at once they are inside and accelerating away from the square.

Under normal circumstances they would catch up with us in an instant. But these are not normal circumstances, because Blågårdsgade is a pedestrian street, closed to motor vehicles.

Strictly speaking, it is closed to horse-drawn carriages, too. But in every Dane there resides a yearning for the days when Denmark was still a land of agriculture and the King rode through the streets of Copenhagen on horseback and everyone kept livestock and slept with the pigs in the kitchen to keep warm and because it was so nice and cosy. So as we come towards them at full trot, people step aside and send us friendly smiles, even though Hans is urging on the horses as if we were part of a rodeo.

But when the black BMW appears, popular sentiment turns. I'm familiar with it from Finø Town, because when all the streets are pedestrianised as they are in the summer, something nasty rises up inside people when they see a car that's not supposed to be there. It doesn't help that the BMW displays the mark of the diplomatic corps – in fact, it only makes things worse – and what happens then is that people begin to close in on the car and prevent it from moving.

Now Hans looks back over his shoulder, and then comes the stroke of genius that proves quite exceptionally that my brother can retain an eye for the ball even off the pitch, because now he careers off to the left down a side street.

It's a one-way street and we're going the wrong way, there are cars everywhere, and for a moment we appear to be heading for a catastrophe. But when people see us in our horse-drawn carriage, it's as if all road traffic legislation is suddenly suspended. Perhaps it's because horse-drawn carriages are so diverting, maybe people think we're parading new high school graduates around as is the custom, even though it's only April, but the school year does seem to be getting shorter all the time. Whatever the reason, cars and bicycles pull into the side, some pull up onto the pavement, not one of them blows its horn, and then the street is cleared and we can get through.

The BMW sweeps around the corner. The two men inside have escaped the adversity of Blågårdsgade, and now they smell blood.

But it doesn't last long. A carriage of new high school gradu-ates moving against the traffic is one romantic exception, but a BMW is in obvious contravention of the law. So now it is swal-lowed up by other vehicles and bicycles and pedestrians, all of them cursing and blowing their horns with all their might.

At that point, the only thing we know about the two men is that neither of them is likely to be our sprinting songbird's father or uncle, for they are both as white in complexion as Finø asparagus. And we know that their 200-metre dash is deserving of respect.

That respect is now enhanced, because they have abandoned their vehicle in the middle of the street, have battled their way free of the massive unpopularity that enveloped them before, and are once more in pursuit.

If, like me, you have ever allowed yourself to be enticed into stealing pears or dried dab in the gardens of Finø by friends of dubious character, then you will know that when people become old enough to buy a house and grow pears and dry fish in the garden, they have usually lost the ability to propel themselves faster than what at best might be called an energetic shuffle, and besides losing the ability, they have also lost interest. Especially when they happen to be wearing a suit, because personally I have never seen anything in a suit move faster than a brisk trot.

But that doesn't apply to the two men who are after us. They are what I would call older people, perhaps even forty, but their sprint is awesome. So all in all a rather gloomy picture begins to emerge of a future in which we are about to arrive at a major thoroughfare with a lot of traffic, which means we shall have to come to a halt, thereby giving the two men a chance to catch up with us, and I really don't want to think any further than that.

Tilte and I have drawn up a theory that your first impression of a person is crucial, before you find out how much he or she earns and whether they have children and a clean record with the police, before that there's a first impression that's kind of naked.

If I'm to follow that instinct, then I'm glad that as far as I can see neither of the two men who are now approaching is Conny's father, because they're not at all what a prospective son-in-law such as myself would be aiming for. Though their hair is short and they're both clean-shaven and drive a BMW with diplomatic plates and are awesome over the short distance, they don't resemble people who are out looking for reasonable conversation or a game of ludo. What they look like are people who want things their own way and who couldn't care less if they left a couple of dead children and the corpse of a dog in their wake.

In this rather bleak state of affairs, Tilte suddenly barks: 'Stop here!'

Hans makes a sound and the horses draw to a halt as if they just walked into a brick wall.

We have stopped next to a small park with tables and benches in the sun. On them, people of all kinds are seated. Mothers with children, young people our own age playing basketball, pensioners, kids with shaven heads and safety pins stuck through their lower lips who are sitting around contemplating their future, perhaps thinking of joining the police. There are men and women who are suntanned and tattooed and who have arrived at that crucial point in their career-planning where they must decide whether they should roll their next joint now or leave it for another fifteen minutes.

Tilte is standing up in the box. She waits for a moment until she has the attention of the entire park. Then she points directly back at the two men.

'Honour killing!' she bellows.

Tilte is only a tiny bit taller than me, and slightly built. But her hair is thick and curly, and the same colour red as a letter box. She has extensions, too, and if you add to her hair what some would call her aura of military leadership, you will have some idea as to what happens now.

Reality once again begins to change. It is suddenly obvious that we are driving a bridal carriage, that Hans and the girl are the newly-weds, Tilte is the bridesmaid, I am the page boy, and Basker is the bridal dog. It is also clear that the two men rapidly approaching are prospective murderers bent on preventing young love from prevailing.

This abruptly brings Nørrebro's history as a working-class district of the city into prominence. It's a subject we have only touched upon in school, on a day when my intellectual curve was not at its apex, so its details aren't particularly clear to me, and it's hard to say how many of the people taking in the sun in the park one would justifiably call industrial workers, if one were to be exact about it. But we learned at school that if the Danish working class holds one image dear, it is that when love is true, young people must be permitted to follow their hearts, and that image rises to the surface now and becomes visible. Another thing is that the BMW and the suits cast an air of capitalism over the two men, a state of affairs that in Nørrebro may quickly prove detrimental to the health, and then there's Tilte's charisma. Everyone in the park can sense that she is a sovereign queen calling to arms, and deep, deep down the Danish people have always cherished their royal house.

So what happens is that a barricade is extended across the road, consisting of mothers with prams, kids in baggy jeans and hoodies, and men and women who are not to be messed with. Their backs, which are turned towards us, exude warmth and protection, and their fronts, which are facing the other way, say that one more step and the two gentlemen in suits will be afforded the opportunity of witnessing an historical event, namely the reintroduction of the death penalty in the Nørrebro district of Copenhagen.

Tilte sits down again, Hans flicks the reins and the four jet-black horses leap forward like kangaroos. Far behind us I can see our pursuers once more picking up speed, but this time they are fleeing, away from us and their firing squad, back to whatever is left of their BMW.

We cross a main road and continue along sun-drenched streets, and so powerful is the effect of what has happened and what Tilte has said, that for a moment we have forgotten all about what might have happened to Mother and Father. We are just happy on behalf of Hans and his divinely beautiful bride, and cars honk their horns in congratulation and we wave back.

We pass a large square and follow a street lined with trees, and then our singer says: 'This is where I get off.'

From her bag she has produced a pair of running shoes, which she is now wearing, and a sweater she has put on over her green dress, and she has placed a scarf over her head and managed to dull some of her starry lustre, though only slightly so, for it is forceful and enduring, and quite frankly I will still say, between

25

you and me, that were it not for the fact that I had sworn eternal devotion to Conny and moreover firmly believe that an age difference of more than two years between lovers is tantamount to cradle-snatching, then I, too, would be in immediate danger of falling in love with her.

So now we all look at Hans.

It makes no real sense to say that Hans had been bowled over by a woman, because every second of the day he is not merely bowled over, but knocked for six by the very fact that women even exist. And yet I will say that even though I have seen him look quite ridiculuous so many times and in so many different ways when confronted with a girl, this time completely demolishes all previous records. He is utterly dazed by that first, naked impression that Tilte and I have drawn up our theory about, so dazed that he is transformed into a cuddly teddy, helplessly gazing at this dark beauty with his big watery-blue eyes.

Tilte takes charge.

'What's your name?' she asks the girl.

'Ashanti.'

And then she adds: 'You've all been wonderful.'

'We know,' says Tilte. 'And now you can do one of two things. The first is that you can keep all that wonder and put it away inside your heart to treasure like a pearl and carry it with you until the day you lie upon your deathbed.'

I don't know why Tilte always has to bring death into everything, but that's the way she is.

'And the second?' asks the girl.

'The second,' says Tilte, 'is that we give you Hans' phone number. With two admirers like yours, you could be needing help again in a hurry.'

The girl whose name is Ashanti looks at Tilte.

'They're bodyguards,' she says.

She gets out her mobile.

'They looked like prison guards,' Tilte says.

'That's the problem,' says Ashanti. 'When it gets hard to tell the difference.'

You can hear that somewhere deep within her perfect Danish resides a foreign dialect, rather like if you were to bump into a coconut palm in the woods of Finø.

Tilte gives her Hans' number and she adds it to her contacts. When she looks up again we all think she's going to climb down from the carriage. But first she gives Basker a kiss, me a kiss, Tilte a kiss, and finally she presses her lips to Hans' lifeless body, a kiss that lasts just a moment longer than all the others. And then she climbs down and floats away.

Some people take daylight away with them when they leave. After she has gone, everything seems that much darker, and then reality returns with the phone call from Bodil Hippopotamus and the certain knowledge that Mother and Father have disappeared.

4

WE'RE WAITING IN THE COURTYARD OF HANS' STUDENT residence facing the Fælledparken. The street outside is all sunshine and traffic and church bells pealing and people going to buy milk and newspapers at the twenty-four-hour store, an abundance of life. But in our own immediate space everything is bleak.

'They'll be here in a minute,' says Tilte.

'No one's going to take you away,' says Hans.

Perhaps all of us have other people inside us, but I do know that inside my older brother lives someone who wants to protect us. It's not often that person appears, but when he does, all readings go off the scale and things begin to tumble. The best restaurant in Finø Town is down by the harbour and is called The Nincompoop, and on several occasions Hans has passed by the place, swirling around some girls who are taking him for a walk, and from out of The Nincompoop three or four young men have appeared who have taken it into their heads that the perfect conclusion to a hearty five-course meal with a selection of fine wines during an idyllic holiday break in surroundings of natural beauty and historical significance would be to beat the living daylights out of some of the locals, and they have been under the impression that Hans and his girls were just what they were looking for. But at the very moment they launch their attack, something occurs inside my older brother. The bashful, warm-hearted young man we all know and love disappears and instead a natural disaster takes his place, and before you know it two of the young men are swimming around in their own blood, another is grovelling on the ground among the parked bicycles, and the fourth makes a getaway in a cloud of dust.

That's the side of Hans that appears now. But Tilte shakes her head.

'We'll be needing you on the outside,' she says.

And then comes a pause, and in the pause is silence. All four of us know that we are now to be separated, and that life is about to get hard. We say nothing, yet in the silence I sense something about Tilte and Hans.

Parents are okay, of course, even ours. But if there were an exam that adults needed to pass before being allowed to have children, how many would actually succeed, if we're to be honest about it? And the ones who did, would they not merely scrape through? Even though Tilte claims that there is nothing about my upbringing that cannot be rectified by two years in borstal and five years of therapy, I would nevertheless venture to suggest that if my mother and father were ever to have passed that exam, someone would have to have taken pity on them first.

But with brothers and sisters it's different sometimes. It may be hard to explain, but there in the carriage I sense something very clearly. So of course Tilte looks me straight in the eye at that same moment.

You have to be careful with the word love. It's a word that so easily can slow you down, and it can make a botch of that curling shot with the inside of the foot. Nonetheless, I must use it now, because it's the only word that fits, and that being the case means the door is opening and there's a chance of catching just a glimpse of freedom.

In order to make it perfectly clear what I mean, I'd like to insert a comment about how we discovered that love and the door are connected. In actual fact, it was Tilte who discovered it, and it happened in the kitchen of the rectory.

I don't know what your own family is like, but in our house we all have to get up so early, and there are so many lunches to pack, and so many lessons at school, and so much homework, and so much football afterwards, and so many people paying visits to the rectory, not least because my mother and father service all three of Finø's churches by turn, that in the day-to-day run of things you can get the feeling that Hurricane Lulu is wreaking havoc in the Kattegat and has moved into the rectory with us for good.

But then what can happen is that the wind dies down, usually on a Friday or Saturday, and at once the waters are calm and a brief opportunity arises for us to realise that our being a family is not merely theoretical fancy, and when such a moment occurs it tends to do so in the kitchen, and it was at just such a moment that we made the discovery.

Father was preparing food. He says that's the way he relaxes, though when he's doing it you'd be forgiven for thinking he was a butcher on piecework. He says, and even believes, that the food he makes is the same he enjoyed in his childhood home in Nordhavn, in the northern part of Finø, of which he speaks as though it were drenched in sunlight and tears of happiness, even though we actually met his mother, our grandmother, before she died, presumably of pent-up gall. We stayed with her, and are therefore able to completely rule out the possibility that she had ever been capable of preparing food.

Nonetheless, my father does on occasion succeed in contriving delicacies of a sort with his old meat press and recipes for dishes from medieval Finø, and at this moment, as what I am telling you about is happening, he is preparing duck rillettes, and pig's feet in jelly as stiff as a Leca block.

Mother is sitting at the table with a pair of nippers and a soldering iron, a watchmaker's magnifying glass, a computer, microphones and an oscillograph, and she is constructing an opening mechanism for the larder that is to work by means of speech recognition. Seated on the bench beside her is Hans with his star map. Next to him, keeping an eye on everything, is Tilte. Beneath the table, Basker lies wheezing as though he has asthma, which he hasn't, but he has the oxygen intake of a greyhound, and he likes to listen to the sound it makes when he breathes.

And seated in the good chair is me, if you can imagine me as

I was then, a small boy, rather delicate and refined, though at that moment simply immersed in being a part of all the nice things going on around me.

It's one of those moments at which you might venture to believe that you belong to a family.

Then something happens that at first seems quite innocuous.

Mother is setting the computer to recognise our voices, and while she is doing so, she is also humming the first verses of 'Monday in the Rain on Lonely Avenue'.

It's one of Mother's favourites. She treasures Bach and Schubert, but what really moves her is 'Monday in the Rain', so for us it's the most natural thing in the world to hear this old Danish evergreen. The risk is that you take it for granted. And for that reason the whole family is given a little jolt when Tilte suddenly says: 'Mother, does that song have special significance for you and Father?'

Silence descends upon the kitchen. Mother clears her throat.

'When I was nineteen,' she says, 'my friend Bermuda, whom you all know, encouraged me to enter the annual talent competition at the Finø Hotel. I practised for three months, and when the big day arrived Bermuda and I went along together. I took the stage wearing a raincoat and a pill-box hat, and sang "Monday in the Rain on Lonely Avenue". I'd even choreographed a little dance to go with it. The lights were rather glaring, so it was only in the middle of the last verse I got the feeling that I wasn't in a talent competition at all. After I finished, I discovered it was the annual meeting of the North Jutland Clergymen's Association.'

For two whole minutes, we remain respectfully silent. And then Tilte speaks.

'I hope you got your own back on Bermuda.'

'I was about to take my revenge at that very moment,' Mother replied. 'But then something happened. Your father came up to me. It was the first time I ever saw him.'

'What did he say?' Tilte asks.

Mother returns the soldering iron to its holder. She puts the reel of tin solder down in front of her. And then she moves aside the magnifying glass.

'He told me how happy I would be. How wonderful my life was going to be with him.'

We sit with that for a moment. We know it's true, because that's the way Father is. He believes he is exhibiting the most heartfelt Christian sympathy by telling people that the experience of their lives is in store for them, if only they get to know him a little better.

Now Mother rises to her feet and approaches Father. To his credit, he blushes, and despite what one might think, and what many of us believe, he thereby demonstrates that he possesses humility. He looks into Mother's eyes, and the jellied pig's feet are consigned to oblivion.

'And do you know what, Konstantin?' my mother says. 'You were right.'

Then she kisses him, and in one way it's deeply embarrassing for all of us, and in another we can be glad no one else is here to witness it.

Until that moment, everything that has happened has been rather commonplace and under control, and within the range of what you could observe in any number of Finø families on a good day. But at the very moment Mother releases Father and is about to step back to the table, Tilte speaks.

'Listen.'

What then occurs is hard to describe, though it does involve all six of us listening for a moment. Not to things being said or done, but to what is at the core of it all. And for a few sensational seconds, everything begins to float: the rectory, the storks on the roof, the larder, even the jellied pig's feet have become weightless, and inside that weightlessness the door is opening.

And then we can keep it up no longer. Intensity of that kind is like training for a run. You must build up your form slowly. So Mother sits down, Father sticks his head back into his duck rillettes, Hans turns his gaze to the stars, and Basker has a renewed attack of asthma. The spell is broken.

But once you've realised what happens if you lean into love, you will never forget it, ever again.

And that is what returns to me in the courtyard of Hans' student residence when I sense how good it is to have a brother and a sister, and Tilte looks me in the eye.

Then we hear an engine.

It is a minibus with tinted windows, and even before it turns into the courtyard we duck.

It parks behind us.

'They'll be looking for a taxi,' Tilte whispers, 'not a horse-drawn carriage.'

She's right. The three individuals who climb out of the vehicle give the carriage and the horses only cursory glances, and then they go inside the building.

The two in front, a man and a woman, are plain-clothes police officers.

Every other Friday in the summer season, the Finø ferry, besides the usual six hundred tourists, deposits two plain-clothes police officers onto the island to reinforce the local constabulary, and among six hundred tourists those two police officers stick out, in their own inconspicuous way, like two tree frogs on a fish rissole. So we are in no doubt, even now, as to what is afoot, and all of it is basically as we had expected. The real surprise is that the woman who follows them in is Bodil Hippopotamus.

We abandon the carriage and reach the black minibus in an instant. That's another good thing about brothers and sisters: when you really need them, you find you can play together as a team and everyone knows their position.

We pull open the door. There's room inside for seven, and in the back is a cage for dogs, and five of the seats have bottled mineral water in the holders.

'They'll be taking Peter and Basker and me,' says Tilte. 'We can be sure of that. So you'll have to go now, Hans. Stay with a friend and keep your head down. Petrus and I aren't really rated in their book, we're still childen to them, so we'll stand a better chance of finding out what's going on.'

All four of us can see there's no alternative. Hans climbs onto the box of the carriage. His teeth are clenched and he's on the verge of despair. He looks back at us one last time, then clicks his tongue and the carriage is away.

5

THE CORRIDOR OF THE STUDENT RESIDENCE IS EMPTY AND on the door of his room Hans has affixed a map of Finø and an even bigger one of the firmament. The door is closed.

Tilte opens it and we step into a combined cloakroom and kitchen from where a door leads into the bathroom and another into the living room. We open that one with caution.

Bodil Hippopotamus is sitting in an armchair. The two police officers are searching for something and it's not something they've simply mislaid, because they've removed Hans' books from the shelves and most of the contents from his cupboards and now they look like they're about to pull apart his bed.

Tilte gets out her mobile and snaps a couple of photos of the police at work, and then the phone is back in her pocket.

Bodil sees us first and beckons us over to the armchair, because that's the kind of person Bodil is, seated on top of her throne, and people have to go to her.

'How nice to see you,' she says. 'Where's your brother?'

She opens her palms so you can put your little hand in hers.

'He's in the basement putting his bike away,' says Tilte.

'We're unable to contact your parents. We've no reason to believe they're anything but safe and well, but we can't find them. So now I shall have to ask you something. They told the parish council they would be in Spain, on an island called La Gomera. Is that what they told you as well?'

'We'd very much like to answer your question,' says Tilte. 'But before we do, we need to know why you should think they aren't where they say they are.'

I know nothing about hippopotami. But I think that in the great mudbath of all things, the hippopotamus is one of the animals that is boss. This would be true of Bodil, too. She tightens her grip on Tilte's hand.

'I'll ask the questions to begin with,' she says. 'Have you arranged with your parents that they should phone you?'

'We'd very much like to answer that,' says Tilte.

As she speaks, she slips her phone into my pocket.

'But first,' she goes on, 'we need to ask you about something that concerns us, and that is whether you're in possession of the proper documentation.'

Bodil frowns.

'We have the documents required by the social services to take you into our custody,' she says. 'Under what we call Paragraph Fifty.'

'That's not what I was getting at,' says Tilte. 'I was thinking of the warrant required to enter my brother's room and search through his belongings.'

Now a silence descends. And the police officers realise they're up against something here.

'What we're afraid of,' says Tilte, 'on your behalf, is that this should get into the papers. That it should become a story, substantiated by the photographs I've just taken.'

Bodil and the female officer lunge at Tilte and grab hold of her all at once. But the telephone is with me and I'm nearly through the door.

'Petrus has the phone with the pictures on it,' says Tilte.

The male officer has a look in his eye.

'I play a lightning right-wing,' I caution him. 'Before you reach me, I'll be away as if I'd dissolved in front of you.'

The three adults have ground to a halt. I sense their indecision. And I sense something else as well, which is that they are under pressure and are afraid of something.

'You'll never catch Petrus,' says Tilte. 'He'll go to the papers and you'll be on the front page. *Police and municipal director remove children from rectory home without requisite authorisation.*'

Bodil gathers herself magnificently. You don't get to be municipal director without what Tilte calls strategic intelligence.

'We're doing this for your own good.'

'And we're grateful,' Tilte replies. 'But we need more transparency. Why do you think Mother and Father aren't in La Gomera?'

Bodil is on her feet now.

'They never left the country,' she says.

'Do the police keep an eye on all Denmark's clergy?' asks Tilte.

'They've been keeping an eye on your parents.'

6

THEY'RE NICE TO US IN THE MINIBUS.

Bodil asks why Hans is taking so long putting his bike away and nearly has a stroke when Tilte tells her that was just a fib and that we have no idea where he is now. Bodil then tries to call his number, but he doesn't reply. After that, she calls another number and tells someone that we're with her but that Hans is gone, and the voice on the other end says something that calms her down, and then I delete the incriminating photos on Tilte's mobile and everyone breathes a sigh of relief.

It's a peaceful ride. They let me sit with Basker in my lap. He's more a person than a dog and won't sit in the cage. They stop at a service station and buy us sandwiches and sweets, and the mood is bearable until we get there.

And where we get is the landing strip at Tune, near Roskilde. They run flights here to Finø with several daily departures in the tourist season.

Most people get to Finø by ferry from Grenå, which first puts into Anholt to send a handful of bewildered tourists ashore. They have no idea what could have been in store for them if only they had remained on board. After Anholt, the ferry sails on to Finø, and the final hour of the crossing affords the passenger the clear sense that he is now on his way out of the Kattegat and sailing towards the North Atlantic, so anyone prone to seasickness and whose finances so allow will tend to go by air.

The landing strip at Tune is situated in a woodland clearing and comprises a shed with large panes of glass inserted into it, and a strip of tarmac extending seven hundred and fifty metres. On days without scheduled flights it's lent out to the local youth club, whose custom-built skateboard ramps can be rolled away if air traffic should wish to land. For this reason, aircraft servicing Finø are small, single-engined Cessnas requiring only short distances for take-off and landing.

But that's not the kind of plane that's waiting for us, because this is a military Gulfstream, camouflaged, with twin engines and two pilots, and the only occasion on which an aircraft like this ever comes to Finø is when a member of the royal family is on it and wants to visit.

We climb out of the minibus and stand looking at the plane. Bodil seems to sense from our posture that we are politely curious.

'Grenå Kommune,' she says, 'will do everything in its power to provide the best of care for children and young people in difficulty.'

'I know,' I say. 'But isn't this a bit over the top?'

A look of weariness spreads across Bodil's face. That's the moment Tilte chooses to borrow Bodil's mobile.

'I want to call my brother,' she explains. 'Only there's no battery left on mine.' Bodil hands her the phone and I'm the only one to notice that Tilte accesses the list of recent calls and takes a long look at it, notes something down in her phenomenal memory and then presses a number that predictably fails to answer, whereupon Bodil's phone is returned to her and we all climb on board the plane.

Access to the runway is through an empty waiting area, and on a large noticeboard some flyers have been put up, one of which makes me stop.

It is a poster advertising a series of concerts to mark something that is surely of importance, but which I fail to notice, because the picture accompanying the text reaches out and grabs me by the throat. It's Conny's face, and she's smiling at me.

Tilte touches my arm, and I return to the world.

* * *

As we take off, my dear sister leans towards me.

'Do we know anyone called Winehappy?'

I shake my head.

'That was who Bodil called,' she whispers. 'I got the number from her phone.'

Then she gives my arm a squeeze, and I feel I know you well enough now for me to be quite frank and tell you why. It's because the person I love has left me.

Now you might say so what, and perhaps add that a third of the world's population is in the same boat. Indeed, the world's population consists of one third yearning for the person who left them, one third yearning for the person they have yet to meet, and one third who are with someone they never fully appreciate until all at once that person leaves them and they find themselves consigned to group one.

But that's not exactly how it is with Conny and me. In a way, Conny hasn't left me at all. She has been sucked away. By fame.

Two years ago, a film was being shot on Finø. It was one of those films for all the family, and because the girl who was supposed to play the bright and irresistible younger sister fell ill, Conny was brought in and ended up stealing the show and being offered a role in another film, and then three more, and now she has been in seven films in the space of two years.

I know exactly what it is about Conny. She can condense her aura and her energy on command.

All of us are able to condense our energy. But for most people it's something of which they are unaware, and when it happens it catches them off guard, like an abrupt feeling of elation or annoyance, or the sudden awareness that the goalkeeper is off balance with his weight on the wrong foot, and if you put your entire soul into taking a long shot at goal he won't have a chance. Normally, it's not something under your control. But with Conny it's different, and that's what she exploits on screen. In the first six of her films, she played a little girl with pigtails and a spark of vandalism in her eye. In the seventh, she played a young girl with a boyfriend. Whose name was Anton. In the film. And she spoke his name the way she used to speak mine. The way that's so impossible to describe. But it was different from the way she spoke any other name. I used to save her phone messages and play them back just to hear the way she spoke my name.

Until that film. When I saw it and heard that she had assumed control of that way of speaking a name, I knew that I had lost her. And then I stopped listening to all those old messages.

After the second film, Conny's mother moved her off to Copenhagen. Conny and I never really knew what hit us. The first film was fun. Then came the second, and suddenly she was gone. It's been eighteen months now.

Since then I've seen her only once. It was a day I came out of school and there she was waiting for me. We walked down to the harbour. Our usual walk. There's a long jetty that extends out between the beach and the dock, and you can walk along it sheltered from the wind and stop to look back on the town. She had changed. She was carrying a shoulder bag like you only ever see in adverts, and wearing a pair of earrings you don't even see there. We walked close together, but it felt like the whole harbour was between us and no bridge could ever be built. I could feel she had to be going, and I thought I was about to die. Eventually, she took hold of my shirt with both her hands and gripped it tight. 'Peter,' she said. 'This is something I have to do.'

And then she was gone. I haven't seen her since. Apart from in the cinema, on the screen. And now I can't even see her there any more, because of that last film and the thing about Anton.

Tilte knows all this. She knows what goes on inside a person when he encounters his lost love looking at him from a poster. That's why Tilte gives my arm a squeeze. And then we're in the air.

41

7

I WOULD LIKE TO EXPLAIN EXACTLY WHERE FINØ IS SITUATED.
Finø lies slap in the middle of the Sea of Opportunity.

If you collected all the songs that have been written about
Finø, for the purpose of dumping them all in the recycling bin,
a very good idea indeed, you would need to hire a lorry. An
articulated lorry with a trailer. Many of those songs can be found
in the Danish Book of Song, and all of them may be divided into
two groups.

The first group contains all the songs in which Finø is depicted
as a tiny pearl in a foaming ocean against which the brave little
island battles to hold its own.

The second group takes the opposite view, that Finø is an infant
child sucking its toes in the arms of its mother, and the sea is the
mother.

These are songs that beg the question whether people who
write patriotic songs take drugs before they put pen to paper.
Because on Finø half the population makes its living fishing
langoustines and turbot to sell to the tourists, or servicing the
tourists' boats at the Finø Boatyard, or sailing the tourists out
to the colonies of seals on the Bothersome Islets, or selling suntan
lotion and beachwear and *café au lait* at forty kroner a mug from
The Nincompoop's decking on the beach by the harbour. And
the rest of Finø's population makes a living out of doing the hair
and fixing the teeth and changing the nappies and intravenous
drips of the half who service the tourists.

So the sea is no longer either a threat or a mother to Finø.

The sea is a tombola from which we pull out a winning ticket every day all through the summer season. And it is also a gigantic playground and a sports facility for the children and young people of Finø, except for the two in every school year who are afraid of water.

Alexander Flounderblood, the ministerial envoy to Finø, once coerced Tilte into putting up her hand in class, which is a thing Tilte has never been happy about. She finds it humiliating and believes that if a teacher wants to know if she knows the answer to a question, he or she ought simply to ask her straight out, so now they've given up asking altogether, Alexander included. Nevertheless, he tried his utmost all through his first year, and on this particular occasion he asked: 'What is the sea called that surrounds Finø?' And he insisted that Tilte put up her hand so that he might ask her if she knew the answer.

'It's called the Cat's Arsehole,' Tilte told him.

Alexander Flounderblood nearly fell off his chair and gave her a look that could depopulate vast areas of land, but Tilte had consulted the etymology of the Kattegat in the *Dictionary of the Danish Language*, and nothing he said could ever change it.

But then Tilte told Alexander that the Cat's Arsehole was perhaps not the most suitable name, and that the most appropriate would be the Sea of Opportunity.

The people of Finø have turned it into a saying now. If anyone asks where Finø is, we tell them: 'Slap in the middle of the Sea of Opportunity.'

We descend now towards it from out of the clouds, its waves are trimmed with white foam, the wind is at fourteen metres per second, and our approach makes the blood run that much faster through the veins of Tilte and Basker and me, which is just as well, because now Bodil Hippopotamus says: 'You'll need to put on these little blue wristbands like last time.'

There they are in her hand, three wristbands, each consisting of two nylon strips holding what looks like a watchface of blue plastic, and now the police officers, whom we have been told are

43

called Katinka and Lars, snap the wristbands shut with a special tool that looks like a pair of tongs.

The watchface contains no watch. What it contains instead is a small, though rather powerful, radio transmitter and two tiny batteries. At Big Hill there's a large board on the wall, the same as they have at the police stations in Grenå and Århus. On the boards are tiny lamps, each with a number corresponding to a transmitter. In that way, the whereabouts of those proudly sporting blue wristbands will always be known by the social services and by the police.

So blue wristbands are given to thugs on parole who are serving four-year sentences for knocking the life out of seven people all at once. And they give them, too, to women doing time for mistreating their husbands, and who have been told by the police to maintain a distance of one and a half kilometres from the place where their beaten husband and his new girlfriend now sit and cower.

And they give them also to those residents of Big Hill who begin to let themselves into the houses of Finø Town by means of a crowbar.

But blue wristbands are not what they give to ordinary kids accustomed to walking around at will.

Bodil knows that, and so she speaks with what I would call false levity, as one might imagine she would do if, to pluck a couple of examples from the Bible, she were telling Job that all he's got is a rash and it'll be gone in the morning, or assuring Noah that it's only a shower.

'Remember,' she says, 'that we are here to look after you, no matter what.'

It's obvious that Bodil belongs to that large group of adults who feel ever confident that children will understand subtlety. I now undermine that confidence.

'This *no matter what* . . .' I say. 'Tilte and Basker and I are not quite sure about it. Does it mean: *Even if your parents never come back?*'

That puts the wind up her, but because she has her seat belt

44

fastened for landing and cannot sneak away or step out onto the wing, the only thing she can do is look us straight in the eye.

'Of course they'll come back,' she says. 'Of course they will.'

And then, for the first time, hard pushed, and at the very last gasp, Bodil produces an utterance straight from her hippopotamus heart.

'But we are worried,' she says.

8

THE BIG HILL REHAB CENTRE LIES ABOVE FINØ TOWN, ON THE slopes of the hill known as Big Hill, whose peak, at one hundred and one metres above sea level, is Finø's most elevated location.

Tourists who chuckle at the name Big Hill and who intend to do so in the vicinity of Tilte or Basker or me are advised to ensure adequate dental protection and to pay any such instalments as may be outstanding on their life assurance policies. We people of Finø are tender souls and rather sensitive as to how our home is perceived by others.

But any chuckles that might be expelled soon die when you see the view from Big Hill. Once standing on the top, no one has ever been less than deeply moved. I've seen men in leather jackets bearing the insignia of motorcycle gangs, men with shaven heads and flames tattooed across their necks and throats, and with sawn-off shotguns holstered on their Harleys, who have burst into tears and wept on seeing the view from Big Hill.

What people find so moving is the vastness of it all, and vast-ness is always so hard to explain. But from the top of Big Hill you can take in all of Finø, all twelve kilometres from Finø Town in the south to the lighthouse on the northern point, and surrounding it all as far as the eye can see is the Sea of Opportunity, which makes Finø look almost like it's in suspension, green in a dark blue firmament of sea. Just to give you my take on what could be included alongside those patriotic tributes in the Danish Book of Song.

It is this view Tilte and I now have in front of us as we stand on the patio of the rehab centre called Big Hill.

And now Tilte puts her arms around me from behind.

You should always be cautious when it comes to allowing others to touch you. To name one example, touching is history for me as far as my mother is concerned. I'm fourteen now, and in eighteen months I'll be off to boarding school for a year, and when I come back I'll be leaving home altogether.

So my mother is rather mixed up when it comes to touching, and her confusion comes from her not being able to grasp that only a moment ago, in her terminology, you were her baby, and now you're fourteen and have been left by a woman and are the first team's top scorer and under suspicion of once having smoked a marijuana cigarette, though nothing was ever proven.

So Mother doesn't know if she is entitled to embrace me or whether she must send in an application, or else simply forget all about it and avoid the situation entirely, unless I take pity on her and put my arms around her like she were the child and I the adult.

It's different with Tilte, she knows inside her how much she is entitled to, which is quite a lot, and so now she puts her arms around me from behind.

'Petrus,' she says.

When Tilte addresses people like that she means something by it. Once, when Mother and Father had been arguing and visitors arrived, Tilte received the visitors outside before ushering them in and presenting Mother and Father with the words: 'This is my father and my father's wife of his first marriage.'

Father has only ever been married once and that's to Mother, so needless to say we were all rather taken aback. Later, when Mother and Father asked Tilte what she meant, Tilte told them that one could never be sure how long a marriage would last, especially when it had entered the violent phase.

For that reason, a long time passed before Mother and Father argued again.

When she calls me Petrus I need to be all ears, because that's what she often calls me when she wants to make me aware of the door.

And then we stand completely silent for a moment. We listen to the silence, even though it makes no sound. It's like that happy childhood I was talking about. You must never let your mind dwell on it, because if you do it'll be gone for good. All you should do is listen. Listen to what makes no sound.

The silence lasts only for a moment and is broken by someone's cheery voice.

'Tilte, my little bluebell! And Peter, scrumptious little Peter! You look marvellous!'

We turn towards the voice.

'Rickardt,' says Tilte. 'You look like a rent boy from Milan.'

Which is the Count to a T.

9

COUNT RICKARDT THREE LIONS IS SPORTING HIGH-HEELED cowboy boots of genuine snakeskin, and yellow leather trousers that cling to him like the skin of a banana. He is wearing a snow-white shirt, which is open to the navel to allow the beholder a full look at his gold chains, as well as to note that he is so skinny it looks like he lost his appetite years ago and never got it back again.

Which is actually what happened. The first time we met Rickardt, he was being treated for a heroin addiction that had taken away his appetite, as it does with most everyone. Finding something as good as heroin is a bit like falling in love, because it means you've got no time to attend to such trifling needs as hunger.

Now he's clean and a qualified addiction therapist. What's more, he's bought up the whole rehab centre and put himself on the board of directors. He could do that because all rehab centres in Denmark are privately owned and because he really is a count and has inherited more money than would ever normally be healthy for a former heroin addict to be anywhere near.

His inheritance has also allowed him to indulge his passion for clothes and thereby to develop his tastes from the bizarre to the outrageous. Today, for instance, he is wearing something on his head that could only be described as over the top, even for him. It is a swimming hat with holes cut in it, and tufts of his hair protrude from the holes, and in between the tufts are electrodes flashing green and red.

'There's a neural scientist with us today,' he tells us. 'We're in the middle of an experiment. My brain has caused something of a stir.'

The first time we met the Count was just after Mother and Father came home with the Maserati and the mink coat.

From having been a home in which we were given porridge to eat one day a week and fish, which is basically free on Finø, on two of the other days, we had entered a period in which the rectory overflowed with milk and honey. On my birthday I was given five crisp one-thousand-krone notes, as were Tilte and Hans in case they should feel overlooked, and that morning we all went out and drank hot chocolate on the decking of The Nincompoop, and when we got home our money was gone.

All the doors and windows were locked, there were no signs of a break-in, and yet our money was gone.

We're all different when it comes to being tidy. My brother Hans, for instance, trusts in cosmic disorder, so his room looks like the Big Bang just went off and everything is still chaos. Tilte's room is rather more orderly, but since her style is extravagant and she owns enough clothes to start a theatrical wardrobe, and over fifty pairs of shoes and two dressers full of cosmetics and earrings, plus a walk-in wardrobe with rails suspended on wires from the ceiling and crammed with her dresses and feather boas, one still gets the feeling of having suddenly landed in the bazaar in *Arabian Nights*.

I'm tidy. If you're born into a family like mine, in which, no offence intended, you're the only one besides Basker who's normal, then tidiness is the only option. It's for your own good.

So I like things to be in their proper places, and one such proper place is my window sill where all my medium-sized trophies, like Player of the Year and the Kattegat Championships, are kept on permanent display. But on that particular day the trophy for Finø FC's annual summer tournament wasn't quite where it was supposed to be and there were fingerprints on it, which are always going to show up clearly on polished brass.

50

And in the garden below the window lay a small, rectangular piece of green plastic. We showed it to Mother, who explained to us that it was an adjustment wedge for the double glazing, and she took hold of the wooden frame that holds the pane in place and it came away in her hands and revealed to us that someone had done some very neat work with a crowbar.

So at twelve o'clock precisely, when we knew they would all be having lunch at the rehab centre, Tilte and Hans and Basker and I walked over to Big Hill and went inside. That was before they began to keep the doors locked, and we had the trophy with us and let Basker have a good sniff, and then we began to go through all the rooms systematically. We found the money in the third room, or rather Basker did. It wasn't even hidden away but lay in an unlocked drawer in a wardrobe containing two hundred ties on pull-out racks.

So when the Count returned from lunch we were sitting waiting for him in his room. He remained standing in the doorway, and then he said: 'How nice to see you.' Whereupon Tilte replied: 'Likewise. And nice to see our money again, too.'

That was our first encounter with the Count, and after some initial difficulties and minor misunderstandings of the kind that are bound to occur when you've just nailed your interlocutor for breaking into your house and stealing fifteen thousand kroner, it was very pleasant indeed. We told him about life on Finø, and the Count told us about his childhood in a castle in northern Sjælland with a moat around it and room enough to sleep two hundred and fifty guests at once, and he told us about how his parents had given him his own flat when he finished boarding school at Herlufsholm, and about how he immediately sold it and spent the proceeds on Ketamine, which he explained to us was a bit like LSD, only more fun, and that you inject it and two minutes later you find you've been catapulted through the top of your skull and out into space.

I sensed a tremor of excitement run through my brother Hans at the mention of being catapulted into space.

Every day for a year, the Count went tripping away on Ketamine, and when all the money was spent he discovered he was homeless. Fortunately, this coincided with the start of the mushrooming season, which prompted him to move into a tent in the woods. And there, so he told us, lived tiny elves who gathered psilocybin, which is just as good as mescaline, for him and then when the weather grew cold and he moved into a stairwell in Nørrebro the elves brought him small portions of heroin, and chocolate milk and valium, and so it was he was able to survive until finally he got arrested and was given a sentence and shipped out to Finø.

By the time we left the Count late that evening we had become friends and each of us had given him a thousand kroner, and as we walked off down the driveway he stood in the window and sang for us.

He's kept up the singing ever since. Every fortnight or so he appears on the lawn of the rectory wearing a pink suit, perhaps, with white polka dots on it, and brandishing an archlute, which is a musical instrument that looks and sounds exactly like it came from outer space, and there he will sing for us for half an hour or more. The Count is bisexual, so of course he's in love with Tilte and Hans like a rat is in love with two pieces of cheese, and to begin with I had some explaining to do whenever I had friends round and they heard the Count with his archlute and noticed how every now and then he would lift one hand from the instrument so as to conduct the tiny blue people he says populate the space beneath our veranda and who always provide his accompaniment. But now we're used to him, and Tilte says, in the quiet, unassuming manner for which she is celebrated, that having your own kingdom involves having to be nice to subjects of many different kinds, and gradually the Count has become almost like a member of the family.

Tilte now tests how far he has come in that process.

'Rickardt,' she says, 'isn't this a wonderful view?'

The Count nods. He thinks the view from the patio of Big Hill is wonderful, too. Especially now that it's been improved by Tilte's presence.

'I see there's a guard on duty at the gate,' Tilte says. 'That's new since last time we were here. I'm sure it must give the residents and staff a sense of security.'

The Count nods.

'And those white sensors,' says Tilte, 'the ones on top of the garden wall. I suppose they register if anyone climbs over the wall, and that will give you a sense of security, too. Am I right?'

The Count nods.

'Then there's these blue wristbands we've been given,' says Tilte.

The Count rocks slightly on the balls of his feet.

'Would you not say, Rickardt, that Petrus and I are locked up like a pair of pigs on a factory farm, even though we have yet to see a solicitor or a magistrate?'

The Count says nothing.

'And there's our room,' Tilte continues relentlessly. 'Spacious and with such a view anyone would think we were at the finest of hotels. Not to mention being in the company of such good friends. On the one side we've got Lars, who was with us on the plane. And on the other we've got Katinka, who was also with us on the plane. Lars and Katinka. Wouldn't you say, Rickardt, drawing on all your experience, that they look like police officers?'

'They're only staying for a couple of days,' says the Count.

A lot of people have been wondering why a multi-millionaire like the Count would buy up Big Hill and condescend himself to work. But for me and Tilte it's plain. It's because most of the residents have depth.

Among Danes at large, even on Finø, a great many people, adults and youngsters alike, though perhaps especially the former, hold the opinion that of all the humiliations and insults to which they have ever been subjected, life is by far the worst. This doesn't apply to the residents of Big Hill. Not one of them has escaped losing everything in the world, and for that reason they seem to recognise that once a year, at least, one perhaps ought to be slightly glad to be alive.

It is this spirit that so attracted the Count, and it is why he leans towards being on the side of the residents, and right now, standing here in front of Tilte, the side of the residents is a decidedly dodgy side on which to be.

'Rickardt,' says Tilte 'we know that Basker is a lively dog. And Petrus is a troubled child. But would you say that two plain-clothes police officers plus electronic tagging plus Big Hill, which is guarded like a prison camp, were necessary measures to provide for their care?'

The Count says he was thinking the same thing himself.

Tilte pauses rhetorically, as they would say in Finø's Amateur Dramatic Society.

'Imagine the headlines, Rickardt.'

That's something Tilte learned from our great-grandmother on an occasion to which I shall later return, and you can tell she's becoming more practised because it sounds more ominous and more inevitable than it did in Hans' student accommodation.

'*Count aids police in illegal detention of clergyman's children.* How does that sound, Rickardt?'

The Count doesn't think it sounds good at all. Substance-abusers who have got clean and own hereditary titles and a castle and two manor farms and five hundred million kroner tend to be rather sensitive about their good name and reputation.

So now we're at the crux of the matter.

'We need your help,' says Tilte. 'We need to get out of here for a while. We need to find out if Mother and Father have left something behind in the rectory.'

At this moment, the Count's existence is in the balance. His voice is a hoarse whisper.

'Visitor to see you,' he says.

We stride across the patio of Big Hill. Residents are lounging in the sun wearing swimming hats with wires sticking out, and we nod and smile at them and are far too polite to point out that with headgear like that they look like they weren't blessed with brains to take readings off in the first place.

To be exact, only Basker and I stride. The Count tries to see

54

if he can propel himself forward and wring his hands together and fall down on his knees in front of Tilte all at once.

'It's out of the question,' he says. 'Don't even ask. I can't help. I'd lose everything.'

Now I step in between them. It's a technique Tilte and I have been developing. She's the tormentor, whereas I'm more like a nurse.

'You could fetch a pair of sharp scissors,' I suggest. 'So we can lose the blue wristbands.'

The Count is mute. Tilte takes his hand. I take the other.

'You'll never get through the gate,' he says.

We look down towards it. At the lowered barrier, the keen guard, the closed-circuit cameras, the wire fence. It's enough to make Houdini despair.

'Rickardt,' says Tilte, 'what do the Knights of the Blue Beam say? About that door.'

'There's no door,' replies the Count. 'Keep on knocking.'

Rickardt Three Lions is the leader and founder of the Knights of the Blue Beam, which is a lodge of spiritual seekers meeting every Tuesday at the manor house called Finøholm, where they while away the time with tarot cards and numerology and trying to get in touch with the dead by means of Rickardt's song and dance, and all of them clad in costumes that make the swimming hats of neural research pale in comparison. But whoever thinks that such an assembly under the leadership of the Count must surely be a matter for the secure psychiatric ward of Finø Hospital would be wise to keep their lips sealed and their heads down when Tilte and I happen to be around, because Rickardt is our friend and, like I said, as good as family.

'That's very beautiful,' says Tilte. 'No door, but keep on knocking.'

We help each other to keep the Count moving along and to exude optimism in his direction. And in that mood we step from the patio into the main hall, only to stop dead in our tracks. Because seated at the table in front of us is one of the greatest obstructions to any hope one might ever entertain of a brighter future for humanity: Anaflabia Borderrud, Bishop of Grenå.

10

MANY PEOPLE IN OUR SITUATION WOULD HAVE SEIZED UP and been rooted to the spot, able only to stare into the face of capitulation. But not us. No more than an instant passes before communication between brain and body is re-established and we approach the table with long, gliding steps.

'Ms Borderrud,' says Tilte. 'How nice to see you!'

Anaflabia Borderrud is one of the very few people we know who makes an imperative of standing on ceremony. So Tilte is off to a good start. And yet we are aware that in this situation a good start is so very far from sufficient.

Physically, Anaflabia is as tall as our brother Hans. But her gaze is not fastened on the stars, it is fixed on whoever she happens to be speaking to, and it is a gaze that could easily be put to use at the Finø Sawmill to split open hardwood logs. And besides that, she gives the general impression of being utterly unwilling to listen to any more nonsense.

But listening to more nonsense is inevitable, especially once you've become acquainted with our family.

Anaflabia it was who presided over proceedings in the ecclesiastical court initiated by the Ministry of Church Affairs to investigate my father, and its complete acquittal of him was tarnished only by Anaflabia's own dissent.

So when Tilte says how nice it is to see her, we can be certain that the pleasure is entirely our own.

'I am here by chance,' says Anaflabia. 'With my secretary, Vera.'

I don't know if the Bishops' Association stages a Christmas

revue, but if it does they should refrain from casting Anaflabia Borderrud as the lead of anything they might wish to put on for their seasonal amusement. Tilte and Basker and I have never witnessed a poorer performance than her attempt to convince us that she's at Big Hill quite coincidentally – and that includes the annual *Landlubber Revue* in Finø Town's community hall the last Sunday in June, which otherwise has the reputation of being as dire as anything ever gets in the world of amateur dramatics.

'I understand they're looking for your parents,' Anaflabia says. 'I'm so sorry.'

Basker growls from underneath the table. What he senses is that it may well be true that the Bishop is sorry our parents are missing, but what she is more sorry about is that the matter has necessitated her crossing to Finø, which she in no way considers to be Denmark's Gran Canaria, but more like a cross between Alcatraz and Papua New Guinea, an outland populated by convicts, headhunters and their offspring. That's what Basker senses and it makes him growl.

'But why are you all here?' asks the Bishop.

You can't tell by looking at us, but it's a question that makes a profound impression on Tilte and me and Basker.

It's not because Anaflabia Borderrud would find it inappropriate for us to be incarcerated at Big Hill. In fact, if it were up to her, there would be patrolling Rottweilers and bars at all the windows. Rather, it's because she so obviously has no idea what we're doing here. And that indicates to us there's something Bodil and the police haven't been telling her.

Now Tilte leans across the table towards the Bishop and her secretary, Vera, who is only barely old, which is to say about thirty, though as hard as an unshelled walnut. Tilte lowers her voice to a whisper.

'I'm here to visit Peter.'

'Is he a substance-abuser?' the Bishop whispers back.

At least, she thinks she whispers. But her voice cannot disguise its years of training in the vaulted interiors of cold stone churches, and even when, as now, her voice is lowered, one is made to wonder if her technique was ever employed by characters of the New Testament in cases where there were dead who needed to be wakened.

Tilte nods. Her face is solemn.

'And forced into crime, too,' she says.

Anaflabia and her secretary seem not to be surprised. For them, this is information only to be expected. I, however, am astonished, and temporarily out of order.

'But isn't he too young to be a resident here?' Anaflabia asks.

Tilte lowers her voice still more.

'In particularly acute instances,' she whispers, 'where addiction is considered to be particularly serious, and where the acts of crime that are committed . . .'

The Bishop nods. 'Looking back, it's no wonder,' she muses.

Vera the Secretary nods as though she were looking back, too.

'I was thinking,' says Anaflabia, 'that while I was here I should take the opportunity of paying a short visit to the rectory. But it seems the police have sealed it off and locked the doors.'

She lowers her voice to a volume that would still be audible in a football stadium.

'I was going to see if your parents had left any clues as to their whereabouts, something that might be useful in tracking them down and getting in touch with them again. So that we might deal with this without the police being involved.'

For people who think deeply about existence it strikes me that big surprises always seem to arrive in clusters. If clusters can arrive at all.

Even before I have begun to digest the pack of lies Tilte has just delivered concerning my person, the shock of it all is at once superseded by a sense of honour at being seated here with two of the truly great female strategists. It's clear that what the Bishop wants is what she succeeded in achieving the last time she was here: she wants to avoid a scandal. And in order to find inspiration for her project she wishes to tear the rectory apart in search of evidence.

It's what Tilte wants, too, though for entirely different reasons.

Bishop Anaflabia Borderrud casts a glance at her watch with a movement she tries to conceal. At that moment, the door of the room opens and a voice booms out, 'Well, I never! What a fascinating coincidence!'

11

I DON'T KNOW IF YOU'VE HEARD OF THE PHILOSOPHER Nietzsche. I have to say that he has yet to appear on the curriculum for the seventh class of Finø Town School, and perhaps one should be thankful. At least if the photograph on the front cover of the book of his that Tilte and I found at the library is anything to go by. It shows Nietzsche with a moustache like a broom and a look in his eyes that suggests the man may well be a genius but he'd need to run into an exceptionally good day just to be able to button his own trousers.

The man now standing in the door is the spitting image of Nietzsche except that his moustache is white and he's as bald as an egg, which makes you think that God didn't have a single hair left by the time he'd finished doing the moustache.

'Well, indeed,' he reiterates. 'What spieth my little eye? Familiar faces.'

Tilte and Basker and I rise. Tilte curtsies, I bow and Basker begins to growl, compelling me to give him a kick with an outstretched foot like a ballet dancer's.

By outrageous coincidence – so outrageous that we cannot for a moment assume it to be coincidence at all – we find ourselves standing before one of the very few people with whom you are guaranteed to get very far indeed by calling him sir. And who is he? This is a man renowned well beyond the borders of Denmark. This man is Professor Thorkild Thorlacius-Claptrap, consultant physician and head of the Department of Neural Research at Århus New Regional Hospital.

Like the Bishop of Grenå, Thorkild Thorlacius-Claptrap is a family acquaintance. He headed up the small group of forensic psychiatrists who conducted the extensive mental examinations of Father and Mother that resulted in both of them being declared more or less normal, an outcome that was a clear precondition of Father being able to resume his position of pastor following what had happened, which I am awaiting the opportunity to tell you about as soon as the events with which we are concerned begin to level out.

Next to Thorkild stands his wife, whom we also remember from that same occasion, she being his secretary, and, I might add, one of his warmest female admirers.

Anaflabia Borderrud claps her hands together in glee, thereby once and for all consigning any remaining hopes of an acting career to the grave.

'Thorkild,' she exclaims. 'Fancy seeing you here!'

Thorlacius takes a seat, the Count hovering behind his chair. Rickardt Three Lions is blessed with an open face of the kind that can be read by anyone exactly as though it were a children's book. At this moment it says that he is afraid of what Tilte and I are up to, that he is rather self-conscious to find himself occupying the same room as such major players as these, and that more generally he has absolutely no idea what any of this is about.

'This young man . . .' says the Bishop to Thorlacius.

Her voice drifts away as though she is searching through her memory for my name, only to find it has been erased by the time that heals all wounds.

'This young man has been admitted here to be treated for addiction. His sister . . .'

Again, she searches, and this time her memory comes up with something, perhaps because a couple of years is hardly sufficient to suppress the recollection that is Tilte.

'. . . Dilde,' says the Bishop. 'His sister Dilde is here to pay him a visit.'

The Count emits a sound as though he were gargling

61

mouthwash. Thorlacius sends him a look replete with profess-ional psychiatric interest. Tilte and I send him a look replete with the threat of extensive physical harm. It's enough to keep him quiet.

Everyone is speaking in what they think are quiet voices, obviously out of consideration for me. It's like they all assume my substance abuse has made me deaf, or at least hard of hearing.

Thorlacius fixes his gaze upon me. It is the gaze of Nietzsche. I remember that he's also a hypnotist and has had Mother and Father in hypnotherapy a few times. I should also mention now that of the group of three psychiatrists who conducted my parents' examinations, it was the two others who declared them normal. Thorkild was in dissent.

'Indeed,' he says. 'Things are clearly amiss. Can you see it, too, Minna?'

'Goodness, Thorkild,' his wife exclaims. 'You're right, it's so very clear!'

I find it romantic when married couples stay together for years and years. For instance, I'm very fond of the pair of storks on the roof of the rectory, the same pair that keep coming back. I think, too, that my mother and father have done well to stick it out for twenty years in each other's company, especially when you know them and are their children and have to put up with them and therefore know how much it takes.

But to stand by a man like Thorkild Thorlacius for any period of time must surely involve miracles of the same calibre as those in the New Testament. And not only does she stand by him, she kneels and considers him a demigod and a gift to humanity.

'Personality disorder,' says Thorlacius. 'Inevitable. Family back-ground like that. The girl's stronger. Tough as boots.'

Tilte sends him a look that bodes ill for his future.

'I'm intending to pay a visit to the rectory,' says Anaflabia. 'Perhaps it might interest you to come along, Thorkild? Cast a professional eye over the place.'

There's always a little pull inside when finally you get over the dunes and find yourself looking out across the sea. And only now does this entire conspiracy reveal itself to Basker, Tilte and me in all its artfulness.

Anaflabia Borderrud has travelled to Finø to hush up what she fears may turn into a new scandal involving our family in a prominent role. And with her she has brought Thorkild Thorlacius, just as she did the last time, so that he may illuminate the psychological aspects. Together, they hope to sweep Father and Mother and Hans and Tilte and Basker and me under the carpet, and after that they will sit on it until they are certain no one is left breathing, which will take very little time indeed, since both are on the portly side of ninety kilos. I recognise two masters at work and feel almost reverential.

Anaflabia clears her throat.

'Unfortunately,' she announces, 'the rectory has been sealed off by the police.'

And then I give a start, because now I understand why she has come to Big Hill. Not to see us. But because she needs help entering the rectory.

Tilte nods.

'I know a way in,' she says. 'But it's impossible to explain. I'll need to go with you . . .'

12

WE'RE ON OUR WAY BACK ACROSS THE PATIO. AND LET ME tell you: we are a group of many conflicting emotions.

If, for once, I may begin with myself, then I would say quite frankly that I am panicking at the thought of Tilte leaving me and Basker on our own in this place. For the Count's part, I can tell that he is at a complete loss for words, and that his aura prompts Thorlacius to scrutinise him closely and with some expectation, as though he feels certain that the Count's swimming hat may be about to register a genuine result.

The Bishop seems stricken by doubt. Not religious doubt, or the kind of everyday hesitation that might preceed breaking into a rectory, because in both cases it's clear she feels certain that the Lord is on her side. What she doubts is presumably the wisdom of taking Tilte along with them in the car. Can anyone be sure that whatever is wrong with our family isn't catching?

Vera the Secretary moves keenly and with great agility, as if she were the batman of some legendary field commander making his way through hostile, uncharted territory. And Minna Thorlacius-Claptrap proceeds with a gaze of adoration fixed upon her husband.

Now the Professor throws out his arm in a sweeping gesture towards the swimming hats and turns to the Bishop.

'I have taken the opportunity of conducting an experiment. We are very close to localising a gene for substance abuse. It gives rise to a minor defect in the brain.'

To claim that the Bishop exudes profound interest would be inaccurate. What she does exude is that she already has plenty of brain-damaged individuals from Finø to be getting along with.

But from two years ago we know Thorlacius to be both a great orator and a great scientist, relentless in his quest for new insight. So now he turns to the Count.

'What's the prognosis for the boy?' he asks, gesturing in my direction. 'Can he be cured? Shouldn't we run him through the scanner for you?'

Count Rickardt's predicament is a difficult one. Insurmountable, even. He gazes beyond the Professor's shoulder and waves his hand about.

'It's the little blue men,' he explains. 'They live under the patio. I'm calling them closer.'

Now comes a sudden and unexpected occasion to recall the old adage that even if there is no door one should keep on knocking. Because it transpires that opportunities still remain for Anaflabia Borderrud in showbiz. And that's because the prospect of little blue men running around between her toes prompts her to make a sudden and surprisingly athletic leap into the air.

Thorkild remains standing. He scrutinises the Count intensely and one can sense that his wildest expectations as to the gene for addiction and its attendant brain damage are about to be surpassed.

It is in this situation of acute chaos in front of goal that Tilte strikes.

'I need to take some luggage with me,' she says. 'It's rather heavy, I'm afraid. Perhaps the Professor would care to help me?'

In other circumstances, this mention of heavy luggage would most likely have aroused Thorkild's and the Bishop's suspicion. But at this moment, both are distracted. The only thing Thorkild has understood is that a young woman has asked if he would care to help her carry something heavy. He straightens his back.

'You are addressing a long-standing member of the Academical Boxing Club,' he says.

He seems imminently close to removing his jacket and rolling up his shirtsleeves to display his biceps. But then Tilte raises her hand to stop him.

'How sweet of you, Professor. Would you come to my room in ten minutes?'

13

WHEN TILTE CLOSES THE DOOR OF OUR ROOM BEHIND US I fold my arms over my chest. I'm not the type who lets the sun set on his anger, and in the space of the last half-hour Tilte has tarnished my otherwise spotless public image and made motions to leaving me.

But the reason I don't complain is that Tilte presses her finger to her lips.

'Lars and Katinka,' she whispers. 'Did you sense it, too? The cupids are at play.'

In case you don't know what cupids are I can tell you that they're these chubby little angels they used to put on greeting cards in the olden days, and at this moment Tilte is holding two of those cards in her hand.

Many people on Finø believe that Tilte lost all interest in worldly love when she was abandoned by Jakob Aquinas Bordurio Madsen, who received a calling and went to Copenhagen to become a Catholic priest and spend the rest of his life in prayer and abstinence. But we who know Tilte in private realise that in spite of all adversity and disappointment she remains a romantic at heart and is so very fond of films in which love prevails and the couple sails off into the sunset in a pink gondola to music as gooey as dual-component epoxy. Sometimes I think that what Tilte has against all that happily-ever-after stuff is basically that she thinks the perspective is too short and that love that lasts only fifty or sixty years is a joke, because what really counts is eternity. As devoted as she is to helping people get over being abandoned, she's equally enthusiastic about spotting love affairs before even the prospective lovers themselves know what's going on, and then giving them a nudge to get them started, and that's why she always carries a stack of those greeting cards that she's waving about in front of me now.

Before my incredulous eyes, she draws a heart on each of the two cards.

'I'll give this one to Lars,' she says, 'and tell him that Katinka wants to meet him under the big acacia tree in the park. You give us two minutes, and then give this one to Katinka. And tell her the same thing. With all the boyish credibility for which you're known.'

'We've got seven minutes,' I say, 'before the Professor's here.'

'Some people have changed the course of their lives in seven minutes,' Tilte replies.

If we'd had more time, and if I'd been less shaken, I would have asked her for concrete examples of who exactly had ever changed the course of their lives in seven minutes, but now Tilte takes me by the arm and draws me over to the open window.

'There's another thing,' she says.

The windows of the rooms on either side of our own are open to let in the delightful spring air. From inside comes a gentle clicking sound. Tilte pulls me away from the window and closes it.

'They're at their computers,' I say. 'Writing a report. About us.'

Tilte nods.

'Petrus,' she says, 'if we could get them out of their rooms in such a hurry they forgot to switch off their computers, would we not be giving young love between officers of the law a well-deserved boost? And would we not be able, in so doing, to take a peek at what the archives say about us, and about Mother and Father, too?'

I withdraw to our room as Tilte knocks on Lars' door and hands him the greeting card of the cupids with the heart on it, and I can honestly say that until this moment I have always had my

68

doubts about Tilte's theory of falling in love. Such doubts are now firmly put to shame. Because at the very instant Tilte returns, we hear Lars in his bathroom, and through the wall the finer details are lost to our ear, but it is clear to us, nevertheless, that he is simultaneously doing something along the lines of blow-drying his hair, brushing his teeth and applying eau de cologne to his armpits, all in less than thirty seconds, and then he is out of the room and on his way down the corridor as if he was about to retake his entrance exam for police college.

So with the other card in my hand, I knock on Katinka's door.

From Leonora Ticklepalate, who is a close friend of our family and a member of Finø's Buddhist community, and who moreover runs her own business offering services in the field of *Sexual–Cultural Coaching*, I am aware that many men may be deeply moved by the sight of a woman in uniform. Here, in private, and between the two of us, I would like to admit that I am one of them.

I once brought the subject up with Conny and asked if she felt the same way, only with boys, and she pursed her lips pensively and said that to find out she would have to ask me to put on the uniform her older sister wears in her capacity as junior assistant in the reception area of the Finø Brewery. Regrettably, we were unable to clear up the matter to any satisfaction, because no sooner had I put on the uniform, which consisted of a red jacket, red skirt and high-heeled shoes, and switched on all the lights in the room so that Conny might form a clear impression, than her parents walked in through the door, and though I endeavoured to explain the situation, I fear that some nagging doubt lingered on in their minds which I never wholly succeeded in exorcising before Conny went away.

So when Katinka opens the door in plain clothes I feel rather disappointed.

Jeans and a sweater aren't enough on their own to make Katinka look like a civilian or even resemble an ordinary woman. She still reminds you of someone who can drive a forklift and step in to lead a team of roadworkers at a moment's notice. But when I hand her the cupids and tell her that Lars is waiting for her under the acacia tree, the look on her face makes me afraid she's about to hit the deck, and I feel sure that training in the anti-terror corps is the only thing that keeps her upright. Then her cheeks begin to flush and I think about blood clots and strokes, and a moment later she's hell for leather off down the corridor.

She leaves the door wide open. Tilte and I can see her computer. It's on.

And not only is it on, but the document it displays, itemising what Tilte and Basker and I have been doing until this moment, is wide open for anyone who might care to look.

On the screen are the words: 'Contact established with Bishop Anaflabia Borderrud and Professor Thorkild Thorlacius-Claptrap. Both persons informed by Police via Ministry of Church Affairs as to KF's and CF's whereabouts being unknown, though have received no further information.'

KF and CF are obviously Konstantin Finø and Clara Finø, our father and mother respectively. The words on the screen confirm what we have already guessed, namely that the police and Bodil Hippopotamus are in possession of knowledge so confidential that they are unwilling even to reveal it to such old and intimate friends as Thorkild and Anaflabia.

Besides that, we note two things.

The document is curiously entitled *The Floaters*. It is a name neither of us is able to connect in any immediate way with our family.

Then there's the signature. The signature is interesting. Katinka has written her name. And beneath it she has added the words: *Police Intelligence Service*.

Obviously, it's flattering in a way to learn that the authorities have deployed their very best officers to look after us. Yet at the same time it's hard not to find it rather disturbing. Babysitting normal, well-functioning kids like Tilte and me can hardly be in the job descriptions of the nation's intelligence services.

Footsteps sound on the stairs above us, cautious and stealthy.

70

We open the door and Rickardt Three Lions hands us a pair of kitchen shears.

The moment we snip the blue wristbands, more footsteps appear, not cautious or stealthy this time, but athletic and spritely, presumably the result of time spent skipping in the gym of the Academical Boxing Club. But before Thorkild Thorlacius gets as far as knocking on the door, we are already back in our room.

Tilte closes the door soundlessly behind us. She takes the wicker basket containing extra bedding, empties it and stuffs the duvets and the pillows under the bed. And then she gestures for me to get inside.

I don't believe it. I want to die standing up, not to expire and be discovered in a picnic basket.

'Petrus,' Tilte whispers, 'we're getting out of here, all three of us, and the only way we can do it is by them taking me out because they think I'm a visitor, and taking you out because they don't know you're there.'

There is a knock on the door, and Tilte gets this imploring look in her eye.

From our studies of spiritual and religious literature on the Internet and at the Finø Town Library, Tilte and I have learned that all the great religious figures recommend turning down the warrior's pride and turning up the will to cooperate. So all I can do is jump into the basket and curl up in a ball at the bottom. Tilte puts on the lid, the door opens, and Professor Thorkild Thorlacius says: 'Is that all? Leave it to me!'

And then he lifts me up and carries me away.

The basket softens all sounds. But I can tell from the Professor's breathing that the honourable members of the Academical Boxing Club possibly spend more time drinking cognac and smoking cigars than skipping and beating the daylights out of punchballs. And then to my consternation I hear that we have now encountered the Bishop, because her voice comes through loud and clear,

71

and if there had been room in the basket the hairs would have stood up on the back of my neck.

'We should check what's inside,' she says. 'Leaving a place like this.'

But then comes Tilte's voice. Utterly cool, yet cautioning.

'I would advise you not to, Ms Borderrud. It's a Finø monitor lizard.'

For you to understand what happens now, I must provide you with some brief information concerning the animal and birdlife of Finø.

Before Tilte and I came to the aid of Dorada Rasmussen, who is in charge of the local tourist office, providing her with much-needed assistance in order to improve the tourist brochure the office puts out every year, Finø could boast of a comparatively rich fauna without necessarily being in the same league as Mato Grosso.

We approached the job by first securing the photographs that were taken when a killer whale drifted past Finø in a state of confusion and later beached in Randers Fjord. Then we found the photographs Hans had taken seven years before during a particularly severe winter when the Finø Rescue Station and the Forestry Commission were deployed to capture a polar bear that had drifted south on an ice floe from Svalbard. By the time we got that far, Dorada had grasped the full scope of our vision and unearthed the film that had been shot when her Amazon parrot escaped its cage and settled in the copper beech in the tourist office garden with the national flag of Denmark, the Dannebrog, waving in the background. We edited out the next sequence, in which the parrot was torpedoed and filleted by a local goshawk, and made colour prints of the stills, putting together a whole new brochure that made no direct reference to Finø being Scandinavia's own New Zealand with a polar climate and a tropical paradise on one and the same island, but the photographs spoke for themselves. In the middle of it all, Tilte borrowed a traditional costume from the Finø Local History Museum and split the seams so Hans could squeeze into it, and then we took a picture of him in short trousers and long stockings and shoes with silver buckles and hair blowing in the wind, and underneath we wrote: *A resident of Finø on his way to church in typical local costume worn to this day.*

We rounded things off with a picture of my giant python, Belladonna, taken in the Tropical Zoo at Randers, because we had given Belladonna away when she reached two and a half metres and no longer wished to make do with rabbits, preferring live pigs, which Mother wouldn't have in the rectory garden.

The brochure was a huge success. It reversed a declining market and since then people have been coming in droves.

The most immediate knock-on effect was that Tilte and I were compelled to mete out corporal punishment in the playground of Finø Town School, since a number of myopic individuals insisted that our brother Hans looked like a village idiot in that photograph of him wearing local costume. Furthermore, our brochure seems to have given rise to some uncertainty among the wider population as to the exact nature of Finø's flora and fauna.

It is this uncertainty Tilte now turns to our advantage by saying that what is in the basket is a Finø monitor lizard.

And what happens now is that the Bishop pulls back her hand and performs another one of those leaps that could win her a place in the Århus Ballet if ever she should tire of being a bishop.

'My younger brother brought it with him,' Tilte explains. 'But Rickardt says it's too dangerous to have on the loose.'

I hear the Count gargling his mouthwash again, and then the basket is lifted, more respectfully this time, carried down stairs and along corridors and eventually placed in what must be the boot of Thorkild Thorlacius' Mercedes. People get in, and all I can do is hope that everyone is present: the Professor, his wife, the Bishop, Vera the Secretary, Tilte and Basker. The engine starts and the car rolls forward. Words are exchanged with the guard at the gate. And on this, one of the darkest days of our lives, Tilte, Basker and I are suddenly on our way out into freedom again – though I must hasten to stress that it is a kind of freedom that is highly restricted and almost totally inside the building and wholly unfree in respect of the infinitely greater freedom all this is actually about.

14

THE RECTORY IS SITUATED DIRECTLY OPPOSITE THE CHURCH,
only a kilometre or so from Big Hill, a trip that takes ten minutes
in a horse-drawn carriage, fifteen minutes on foot and a couple
of minutes at most in a Mercedes. Yet these two minutes are
entirely full of what I can only refer to as drama.

The first thing that happens is that I feel a sneeze coming on.

I don't know what kind of treatment Thorkild's New Regional
Hospital offers those unfortunate enough to suffer from asthma
and dust mite allergy, but I would certainly hope they warn against
curling up in a ball at the bottom of a wicker basket.

At this point, as I struggle to hold in a sneeze, Anaflabia
Borderrud says: 'It would be best if we could explain this in terms
of mental breakdown on the part of your parents. Last time,
we were able to pull through. But many of us bear wounds that
have yet to heal, wounds that continue to bleed and which mustn't
be picked at.'

To which Tilte replies by expressing her complete agreement,
because, as their children, we feel that way, too.

'The police seem to believe that something criminal is afoot,'
says the Bishop. 'We would look very dismally upon it, in the
Diocese and in the Ministry of Church Affairs.'

Tilte says that we children couldn't agree more and declares
us to be fully in line with the Ministry.

'But if the matter were to be explained as the result of breakdown,' Anaflabia goes on, 'or depression, something requiring
hospitalisation . . . That's why I should like to inspect the rectory.

Thorkild will assess the situation, drawing on his professional expertise. His words will weigh heavily in the final outcome. But we must locate your parents before the police do likewise. The Professor and I will take it from there. What was your impression of your parents, prior to their disappearance?'

'It's very hard for a daughter to concede,' says Tilte. 'But I think the word *unbalanced* would be the most appropriate.'

If Tilte hadn't said that, I'm fairly certain I would have been able to hold back my sneeze. And I would have done so simply by adhering to the profound guidelines for attaining freedom that one may find in all spiritual systems and which invariably involve trying to listen inwards as one asks oneself: Who is the individual who feels he must sneeze? Or: From which source within the consciousness would the sneeze be perceived, if it should transpire?

But one must face the fact that consciousness training is a phenomenon that requires mental acuity, at least to begin with, and at this moment, when I hear what Tilte is saying, I am utterly lacking in it, and with those words she thereby joins the long line of candidates for greatest traitor in world history, along with Judas, Brutus and Karl Marauder Lander, who besides those gulls' eggs has cleared several of my chanterelle locations in Finø Woods, and I haven't even mentioned yet how one time, together with Jakob Aquinas Bordurio Madsen, he duped me into getting up on stage to join the Mr Finø contest.

You could never get me to subscribe to the view that our mother and father are unbalanced. Certainly not. Firstly, the inherent lunacy of one's parents is a matter that belongs in the department of well-guarded family secrets that ought never to be divulged to anyone. And secondly, at the time of their departure, Mother and Father had in no way exceeded their average level of madness.

So the shock triggers the sneeze.

Not even Anaflabia could give height to a leap initiated from a seated position in the back of Thorkild's Mercedes, but I hear her make the attempt regardless and bang her head against the roof.

And at that moment, mercifully, we are there. The car stops, and everyone piles out.

'We must remove the basket,' says the Professor. 'It can't be left in the car without supervision, I've just had the interior done.'

The basket and I are lifted from the car and placed on the ground with great caution, my sneeze and Tilte's warning still salient.

Then all around me is silence. It lasts perhaps a minute, and then the lid is raised.

'Petrus,' whispers Tilte, 'do you remember when we drove to the lighthouse and back?'

I glance up and note that we are alone and that darkness is falling.

Tilte's question is superfluous and she knows that, because neither of us could ever forget it. We took the Maserati, Tilte worked the foot pedals and changed gear, and I steered. It would be a rather vast understatement to say that our drive to the lighthouse and back was Tilte's way of saying sorry to me after she and Jakob Bordurio and Karl Marauder had duped me into getting up on stage in front of twelve hundred people in the belief that I was to receive Finø FC's Player of the Year award, whereas actually I had unwittingly joined the annual Mr Finø contest. This was an occurrence that left me not merely wounded but traumatised, and it was to make amends for it that Tilte lay down on the floor and operated the pedals.

'This will be easier,' says Tilte. 'Thorkild's Mercedes has automatic transmission and you should just about be able to see through the windscreen. I suggest you remain in the basket and slowly count to five hundred. Then drive the car into the lane and return here.'

And then she is gone. Normally, my pride, which I mentioned earlier, would forbid me to work with Tilte on a purely need-to-know basis. But our situation is desperate and fraught with danger, so I curl up in my basket, pull the lid back on and begin to count while thinking about all the advantages enjoyed by the dead of the Finø Town Churchyard in their cool, spacious and above all dust-free coffins.

When, like me, you're an enquiring soul, meaning that you never miss an opportunity to feel for the door, then much of what others would consider to be idle waiting time may be filled with meaning. And that is what happens now, because I haven't even reached one hundred before I hear dragging footsteps approaching. Someone spits. And then my basket receives an almighty kick.

Many in my position would have groaned. But I remain quite still. Perhaps you're familiar with the expression *Know your lice by the way they walk*? Well, in this particular instance that saying is apt indeed. I know my louse by the way it walks.

Then a hand is inserted beneath the lid. It's too dark to see if the hand is stained with blood. But I know that it most certainly is stained by the juice of the chanterelles that Karl Marauder Lander, our neighbour's abominable snowman of a son, has stolen from my possession.

So there's no reason for me to wait. I pop up like a jack-in-the-box and hiss: 'Looking for something, Karl?'

For Anaflabia's sake, I hope Karl Marauder Lander keeps well away from her audition at the Århus Ballet, because otherwise the competition will be fierce indeed. The leap Karl performs is rare, so rare that one fears he may never return to earth again.

But return he does, and hits the ground running, as soon as his feet touch. If you know the saying that fear sprouts wings, then you'll have a rather accurate picture of Karl on his way down Rectory Lane.

When a boy loses his parents he is in need of comfort, and some of that comfort may derive from watching Karl disappear into the horizon.

As I devote myself to savouring this feeling, footsteps sound again from behind.

Many a person would have panicked at the thought that it might be Vera or the Bishop approaching through the darkness and that now we have been discovered and Tilte's plan, whatever it may have involved, has been foiled. But I keep my cool and remain standing, because once again, without yet having seen him, I know my louse by the way it walks.

I would like to take this opportunity to present Alexander Beastly Flounderblood, the ministerial envoy to Finø, because he

77

plays a small but important part in these events, and it is he who now approaches.

Alexander Flounderblood has been posted to Finø by the Ministry of Education as a replacement for former headmaster Einar Flogginfellow, popularly known as Fakir. Einar was a dearly loved and highly respected headmaster, but seen from the mainland he was making a nuisance of himself, not only on account of his being chairman of the Breakaway Party, which has a seat on the Grenå local council and is committed to working actively for the secession of Finø from the Kingdom of Denmark in order that the island may be recognised as a sovereign state with its own foreign policy and rights of self-determination as to whatever may be of value within its subsoil, but also on account of his being chairman and high priest of the local branch of the association called Asa-Thor, whose members offer sacrifices to the ancient Nordic deity at every full moon on top of Big Hill. Yet still there are many who believe that Einar could have continued in his position had he not at the same time been the first-team coach of Finø FC and firmly believed that sitting on one's backside for thirty-odd hours a week was acutely damaging to the health of anyone under the age of eighteen. And since the teachers of Finø, all of whom were born here, were in whole-hearted agreement with Einar's viewpoint, much of our time at school was spent playing football and swimming in the sea and going on trips to the Bothersome Islets, and delightfully little time was spent in the classroom, and eventually the Ministry of Education and Grenå Kommune dispatched an expedition whose objective was to mete out appropriate punishment.

It did not comprise Thorkild Thorlacius-Claptrap and Anaflabia Borderrud, but rather Alexander Flounderblood in the company of selected thugs, and I have to say that the results they achieved are pretty much of the same calibre.

Though he has only just passed his thirtieth birthday, Alexander has already completed his post-doctoral dissertation and the look in his eyes says that life is a long cross-country run and that he is anticipating a hard, steep climb and intends to come first. How he managed to reach this stage in his life remains a mystery to us, but it certainly hasn't benefited his motor functions, because when he walks he somehow adds extra lift to each step he takes, and this lends him a gait that might be appropriate for someone performing in a circus, but which seems rather rash if, like Alexander Flounderblood, one happens to be on near-permanent display for a couple of hundred children and youngsters, all of whom believe that when Einar Flogginfellow was deported, the golden age of their childhood went with him.

This gait it is that I now hear approaching from behind.

My keen sense of hearing is renowned on Finø, so long before Alexander Flounderblood appears in my field of vision, which at this point remains restricted by my still standing with the lid of a wicker basket on my head after having sent Karl Marauder so emphatically on his way, I hear that he has with him his Afghan hound, called Baroness.

I readily admit to never feeling quite as natural and relaxed with Alexander as one should in the company of one's teachers. But such uncertainty may be offset by seeking refuge in the polite manners one has been taught at home, so now I lift the lid and bow as well as a person who happens to be standing in a wicker basket is able.

And then I say: 'Good evening, Dr Flounderblood. Good evening, Baroness.'

On those rare occasions on which the first team loses a match, Einar Fakir will often comfort us by saying that as long as you've done your best, you can never ask for more. So I have no reason to blame myself even now. But one's best may sometimes be insufficient, for example in this instance, because although the look Alexander gives me may be taken in any number of ways, it most certainly does not point towards him ever wishing to adopt me should my parents fail to return.

At the very moment he passes me by, Tilte taps me on the shoulder.

'Petrus,' she whispers, 'time to be off.'

15

I CANNOT CLAIM TO BE IN POSSESSION OF A VALID DRIVING licence. But I have passed my cycling proficiency test and like most other people I do possess at least some driving experience, having driven a tractor and a soapbox cart, and a golf buggy and a horse-drawn carriage, and Mother's and Father's Maserati, so when I climb in behind the wheel of Thorkild Thorlacius' Mercedes it feels like I'm at home in my own room. And I must admit it's a treat with all this brand-new interior and automatic transmission.

The perfect situation would be if only I could see through the windscreen, because on that account Tilte was too optimistic. But then you can't have it all, and so I comfort myself with the thought of how often I've heard Mother say that driving a car is a matter of intuition rather than vision, and I can see the sky and part of the wall surrounding the rectory perfectly well.

The key is in the ignition. I start the engine and roll carefully along the lane and around the corner.

I have every reason to believe that the coast will be clear as I make the turn and that Alexander Flounderblood has long since gone. So imagine my surprise when the top of his head suddenly appears in my field of vision.

I manage to avoid him and Baroness, but though I am driving at a snail's pace they must surely be startled, because they leap aside as though their lives depended on it, and in a way I'm thankful there's no time for me to return the glaring looks they undoubtedly send in my direction.

The reason there's no time is that when I swerve to avoid them I catch a glimpse of Karl Marauder Lander through the side window, which means that since I've straightened my course again he must now be directly in front of me. So my only option is to press hard on the horn in order to alert him.

A lot of good things have been said about Mercedes cars. Now I feel able to add to the list that the horn ranks right up there alongside the foghorn of the Finø ferry. Moreover, the sound it makes is amplified as it reverberates against the garden walls along the lane. So now Karl appears again because he has once more felt compelled to leap into the air, providing further evidence of his exceptional powers of vertical propulsion.

I stop the car and get out.

Neither Karl nor Baroness nor Alexander has yet found their feet. This is one of those situations that clearly demand some reassuring gesture, so I wave to them as though to demonstrate that things are under control, and then I lock the car remotely, in part because the most sensible policy when Karl Marauder's around is to lock everything that isn't bolted to the floor, and in part to demonstrate that I am also in complete charge of the vehicle. And after that I jump over the wall into the garden of the rectory.

16

WHEN I LAND ON THE LAWN I SEE THREE THINGS THAT CANNOT easily be explained.

The first of these is that the long ladder has been taken from the outhouse and leaned against the gable-end of the rectory. On its own, this would seem reasonable enough, as the rectory's cellar is so deep that the ground floor is actually almost a first floor, and the window of Tilte's room, at which the ladder has been placed, corresponds in terms of height to what normally would be considered the second floor.

Rather more difficult to comprehend is the fact that four people are on their way up the ladder. Uppermost and at the window is Professor Thorlacius, then comes his wife, in turn followed by the Bishop of Grenå, and finally, almost halfway up, Vera the Secretary, who is making a cautious ascent.

The sight of all this prompts the immediate thought that none of the four has climbed a ladder in a good many years, if at all, and for that reason they are under the impression that a ladder is a sort of stairway capable of accommodating several individuals at a time.

The third thing I see is the most difficult with which to reconcile myself. Crouched behind the big rhododendron in front of me are Tilte and Basker, and beside them, in a little huddle, are Finø Town's policeman, Finn Metro Poltrop, affectionately known as Finn Flatfoot, and his police dog Titmouse.

Experts claim that dogs resemble their owners, or perhaps vice versa, that dog-owners resemble their dogs, and it does seem to be rather a neat theory. For instance, I find that Basker in many ways resembles everyone in our family, including Great-Grandma. Flounderblood and Baroness are definitely a case in point. They could even be man and wife. And the theory fits Finn Flatfoot and Titmouse just as well, because Titmouse isn't your everyday police dog in terms of breed. His more specific origins would be a matter for genealogical research, but like Finn he has hair falling down into its eyes, wears a beard and is rather corpulent, and like Finn he loves all kinds of food, but especially my father's. Finn Flatfoot weighs in at one hundred and fourteen kilos and says he's proud of it, and to keep his weight up he frequently stays for dinner at ours.

Like Finn, Titmouse is a friendly creature whose forceful impression derives mostly from his appearance. Both are unkempt and chronically unshaven, and look like something that stepped out of Borneo's jungle, but behind the frightening exteriors beat two hearts of gold.

And yet I would never personally venture to tease either Titmouse or Finn Flatfoot, just as I would never stick my head into a hive of bumble bees, because even the fluffiest exterior may conceal a sting that could have you howling with pain. Although Finø is a quiet place in the winter, members of the fishing community have nonetheless been known to take it into their heads to clear The Nincompoop's cellar bar of all inventory, and in such cases Finn and Titmouse have been on the scene within minutes. I have witnessed them step forward to face twenty-five fishermen who have just trashed the place leaving only powder behind, and after a moment the fishermen have paid for the damage and offered their apologies and sloped off into the night with their tails between their legs.

So now, as ever, I'm glad to see Finn Flatfoot though I've no idea why he might be here, or why he and Tilte, and Titmouse and Basker, might be hiding in the bushes, and so I join them.

Finn gives me a pat on the back. His hand is like one of those spades they use for digging ditches.

'Have you seen them before?' he whispers.

'They're from Big Hill,' Tilte whispers back.

'They're older than the usual crowd,' Finn whispers again.

'One said she was a bishop. And another said he was a professor,' Tilte whispers back again.

Finn watches intently.

'The brain goes out when the weed goes in,' he says.

And now I see what the world looks like through Finn Flatfoot's eyes. Whereas before I saw four pillars of society on their way up a ladder on important business, I now see what Finn Flatfoot and Titmouse must see, which is four criminal substance-abusers about their shadowy deeds in the darkness. I begin to pick out the awe-inspiring contours of Tilte's strategy. My thoughts drift to our religious studies, from which we have learned that all the great spiritual figures point out that to a very great extent the world is made of words.

'Shouldn't they be stopped?' Tilte whispers.

Finn shakes his head.

'We're waiting for two things. Firstly, for them to break open a window. That makes it burglary and caught red-handed, section 276. And secondly, we're waiting for John, because I've just called him. This lot are the violent sort.'

John the Saviour is with us a moment later, like a shadow in the night, but a shadow of the kind cast by a brewer's dray, because that's about the size he is. Ordinarily, he's in charge of Finø's rescue services, which is to say the lifeboats and the fire station and the ambulance service, as well as the Finø Security Corps, and if I were to describe him in brief I would say he was a friend of the family and a man you would want by your side in any situation other than the Annual Spring Ball for the benefit of Finø FC, because no one has ever seen him wear anything other than overalls and ambulance-coloured safety boots size 52 with steel toe-caps.

Meanwhile, Professor Thorlacius has managed to open Tilte's window and has half his corpus inside her room, thereby now technically guilty of breaking and entering, even though Tilte and I know that her window is only ever pulled to and never locked. Now Finn Flatfoot and John the Saviour and Titmouse step forward out of the bushes and give the ladder a gentle shake.

Whoever has stood on a ladder with someone shaking it from below will know that keeping a cool head in that situation requires at the very least an ice pack, something which is on hand only rarely whenever you're up a ladder. The four individuals on this one roar in unison. And Vera the Secretary is the first to come tumbling down.

I'm not sure how a bishop's secretary is used to being received, but I think in the fading light I glimpse a slight sense of surprise on her face as John and Finn whirl her round and snap on a pair of handcuffs.

'Release that woman immediately!'

Anaflabia Borderrud has raised her voice, and it is a voice of such authority as would prompt army battalions to lie down on their backs and wave their arms and legs in the air.

But Finn Flatfoot and John the Saviour are men who have stood face to face with hurricanes without it affecting them in the slightest, so the only thing that happens is that the Bishop of Grenå, too, suddenly and perhaps for the first time in her life is placed in handcuffs.

Now John and Finn shake the ladder again as one would shake a pear tree, and they make ready to catch Minna Thorlacius-Claptrap in their arms as though she were ripened fruit falling from that very tree.

'Thorkild! Help!'

Her cries bring the Professor to the window of Tilte's room and back down the ladder again with all the assurance of a man used to putting things in their place and making sure they stay there.

Standing on the lower rungs of the ladder he seems to realise that he now must attempt to talk sense to the broader population.

'I am Professor Thorkild Thorlacius-Claptrap of Århus New Regional Hospital,' he announces.

'A pleasure indeed,' says Finn Flatfoot. 'And I am the Metropolitan of the island of Finø.'

Finn Flatfoot is a clever man, but his cleverness is more the shrewd kind than the sort of thing you learn at school. My guess is that he would not know what a metropolitan was if it weren't for Tilte, who gave him the nickname because it's so close to his real name, Metro Poltrop, and because Tilte says he has the looks and aura of a metropolitan, which is a kind of priest with authority in the Eastern Orthodox Church. And Finn is fond of Tilte and fond of the new word, so that's at least part of the reason why it suddenly crops up here.

'I can explain the entire matter,' says Thorkild. 'We are conducting a psychiatric and theological appraisal of the rectory.'

'Beginning by entering second-floor windows,' adds Finn.

It is a detail the Professor chooses to ignore.

'I can explain everything,' he says. 'And I can provide you with the necessary identification. My car is parked over there.'

The Professor steps out into the throng. Finn and John remain at his side. He makes a sweeping gesture with his hand in the direction of where his Mercedes is supposed to be and where only the wicker basket remains.

The Professor is flummoxed to discover that his car is gone. But the great scientists are never defeated, they seek new avenues.

'We have transported the girl,' he says, 'Dilde here. She has been visiting her brother, a substance-abuser and criminal serving a term of mandatory treatment up there.'

He points towards where he thinks Big Hill lies, but has seemingly lost all sense of direction, so what he points towards is actually the cooperative supermarket and behind it the old people's home. Finn and John consider him intently.

'We have transported the girl and the reptile,' the Professor continues. 'The Finø monitor lizard.'

He indicates the basket and, as though to provide final, impenetrable evidence, lifts the lid. He and Finn and John peer into the emptiness inside.

And now Thorkild notices me.

'The boy!' he exclaims. 'The addict, passing himself off as a lizard!'

John the Saviour and Finn Flatfoot exchange glances.

'There's alcohol involved here, too,' says Finn Flatfoot. 'Drugs and alcohol together. I've seen it before. It's like injecting air into the brain.'

The Professor's face changes colour and becomes what technically would be referred to as purple. Finn Flatfoot grips his arm with one hand and reaches into his pocket for a pair of handcuffs with the other.

Now again something happens that must prompt us all to revise our opinion of the Academical Boxing Club and revert to our initial theory that what goes on behind its doors must be at the highest level of competitive sport. Because Professor Thorlacius now delivers a punch to the stomach of Finn Flatfoot that no one could ever dig out and dust off unless in possession of some considerable years of training.

Finn carries a lot of upholstery in his one hundred and fourteen kilos. But one hundred and twenty would have stood him in better stead given that the wind is now knocked right out of his lungs, forcing him down onto his knees.

Then John the Saviour is upon the Professor. From the dire fate of Finn Flatfoot he has learned a valuable lesson and covers his more vulnerable parts accordingly, whereupon the Professor is cuffed.

'Always watch your back,' says Tilte.

She says so because John has now straightened himself up as though after a successful rescue operation, but he has forgotten all about Minna Thorlacius-Claptrap, who now lends further weight to my experience that married couples are often so tightly knitted together as to comprise a commando unit, and now Minna strikes John from behind like a missile while expelling what sounds to me like a battle cry originating in some Japanese martial art.

The last thing I see is that the Bishop and Vera begin to run, cuffed hands behind backs, away from the scene of the crime.

Hardly a wise strategy, but one can understand them. When the feeling arises that the world is going to the wall, all of us are bound to feel the impulse to leg it.

And then Tilte's hand touches my arm.

'They'll be put into custody in the new detention house,' she says. 'That's what Finn does with drunks. We've got twenty-four hours.'

17

THERE'S SOMETHING SCARY ABOUT HOW QUICKLY LIFE CAN seep away from a house once it's been abandoned.

Of course, the rectory has not been abandoned, but it's been a week since we left, and the place is already different. In the hall is what looks like a bill the postman has pushed under the door, and the envelope is already yellowed. The pendulum clock above the bench is still ticking and everything in my father's study appears untouched. The light there is the same as ever, flooding in through the great windows and the patio door, and allowing Tilte and I, even now as the sun sets, to see everything clearly. From inside my mother's study comes the hum that is always present in a room containing a grand piano, so in a way nothing is changed. And yet these rooms are already becoming lifeless.

I remember sensing the same thing once when I returned from summer holiday, and it was there again another time when we had all been away visiting someone. And most of all it was there during the two months in which Mother and Father were held in custody and we were looked after by our great-grandmother, who had threatened Bodil Hippopotamus with her knuckleduster when Bodil wanted to put us away in a children's home in Grenå. When those two months had passed, the rectory was at death's door, and it took most of a week to revive it. That's what it feels like now.

In this grave state of affairs, Tilte and I are seated, each on our own sofa, staring at each other without speaking, taking a deep breath before we search through the house in which we were born and have grown up, in the hope of finding a clue as to our parents' whereabouts.

And in this brief pause, I would like to say a few words about Tilte.

I don't think you'd be able to find many tourists, and probably not a single resident of Finø, who would consider Tilte to belong to that large group of people normally referred to as mortals. By far the majority would think of her more as a minor deity.

This is a theory that builds upon events such as a talk Tilte had with her teacher one parents' evening when she was in the fifth class of Finø Town School, at which I was present because Father was tied up preparing candidates for confirmation and I was under constant supervision following an unfortunate incident involving Karl Marauder Lander. In the car I heard Tilte say: 'Mother, this evening the teachers will complain about me, and it's because they feel squeezed by the breadth of my personality.'

This she said in earnest, meaning every word, and when we arrived at the meeting the teachers said that Tilte was an attention seeker, no matter that she had an important role to play in class and was always helpful to her fellow pupils, and they said that her absenteeism was becoming a serious problem, even by the school's own comfortably loose standards, this being before the authorities launched their insidious attack on Einar Flogginfellow Fakir. And when the teachers had finished, they looked at Tilte, expecting her to apologise for being absent all the time and perhaps even to admit that we had spent the entire spring term collecting gulls' eggs. But the only thing Tilte said was: 'You can never get too much of a good thing.'

She said this without smiling and with complete dignity. And it is episodes of this nature, however small, that have made the people of Finø think so highly – too highly, perhaps – of my sister Tilte.

It is extremely important that you consider the world in a clearer light. Because if you do not, you perhaps might not grasp that this thing about finding the places that conceal a way out into freedom from more constrained reality is a matter not only for the godlike or the similarly exceptional. It is a matter also for likeable and engaging individuals, and for ordinary sorts like you and me.

So now I will tell you about Tilte's grief so that you might better understand her and realise that she is in part just like the rest of us.

Eighteen months ago Tilte and Jakob Aquinas Bordurio Madsen became a couple.

I know what you're going to say. You're going to say that of all the stupid names you have ever heard in your life and which fill the hearer with an overwhelming sense of pity for the poor individual whose parents named him such when he was but a defenceless infant, among all those names Aquinas Bordurio Madsen takes the biscuit. And yet there is a perfectly natural explanation: Finø has always faced the world. In days gone by, its two shipyards constructed some of the nineteenth century's fastest schooners and tea clippers, and in general the people of Finø are accustomed to their men striking out as Vikings and ordinary seamen, ship's captains and stowaways, and women likewise have ventured out as shield-maidens and stewardesses, cooks and missionaries, as well as occasionally in more Mata Hari-like capacities. Returning from these journeys, the people of Finø have often been accompanied by men and women of diverse ethnic origins, and in that manner the island has been enriched by a variety of odd-sounding names, of which Aquinas Bordurio Madsen is but one example, that regrettably and yet so inevitably leave one no choice but to lie in the dark, tossing and turning and unable to fall asleep if one has heard them uttered even a single time.

And many different religions found their way to Finø in the same way. Jakob's family are Catholics and Jakob always carries a rosary around with him, which he turns and twirls between his fingers while saying his Hail Marys inside, and he prays without interruption and is famed for his fingers never pausing with that rosary of his, not even when he won the ballroom dancing final at Ifigenia Bruhn's Dancing School, which is situated on Finø Town Square.

This, of course, is a detail one should bear in mind when assessing the state of Jakob's mental health, i.e. that he is a competitive ballroom dancer who says his Hail Marys, and that he has taken part in at least a couple of major crimes against humanity, such as when he and Karl Marauder secretly ushered three classes onto the gallery of the parish community centre at a point in time when Simon the Stylite and I had taken off our clothes and were in the process of investigating the inherent spiritual possibilities of soft soap, a matter to which I shall presently return. However, it will not explain what happened between him and Tilte, because Jakob is a person who, in all the years we knew him and watched him grow up, despite certain flaws in his character, also was able to demonstrate many human qualities. At one point, for instance, he formed part of Finø FC's first-team attack, playing on my left side, and some of his finishes were of such quality that I and a great many others have been willing to turn a blind eye to his six national championship titles in ballroom dancing, a form of movement we members of Finø FC look upon with the same kind of pity with which a mother looks upon her sick and bedridden child.

In spite of all this, he suddenly received a calling.

I shall now explain exactly what a calling involves. But first I must relate to you the extent of Tilte's and Jakob's feelings for one another in order that you may comprehend the full scope of the disaster: Jakob and Tilte were happy.

Tilte had been happy before, with previous boyfriends, but in a different way, because those boyfriends were manageable. With them, she was happy in the way Basker is happy with his doggy friends, and that is by being on top of the hierarchy. Even the most bloodthirsty hound on Finø, which is to say John the Saviour's Greenland husky called Count Dracula, whose face will remind you of a white teddy bear but who carries around with him two court orders for his destruction and wears two muzzles all at

once when John takes him for a walk on his chain, even Count
Dracula would wet himself if Basker one day should feel a split-
ting headache coming on, so with that kind of standing it's an
easy matter indeed to love all other dogs, if we are to be frank
and even if it does reflect poorly on Basker.

But with Tilte and Jakob it was different, and this was plain
to anyone who saw them on the street. Of course, they were in
love and went about gazing dreamily into each other's eyes, giving
you these dreadful flashbacks to some of the poems my older
brother Hans composes. But at the same time, they were like best
friends and on different sides all at once. Which is impossible to
explain, but it was pure love.

They were together for six months, until Jakob received his
calling. One day when he was crossing the bridge from the swimming baths west of Finø Town where he had taken on a holiday
job as a lifeguard, he heard a voice inside him telling him to leave
Finø and travel to Copenhagen, there to take steps to become a
Catholic priest, never marrying, and living the rest of his life
alone.

Two months later he was gone.

I don't know about your own neighbourhood. But here on Finø
people often receive callings by which God or Buddha or an
avatar or four angels speak to them and give them orders or
good advice. I have never personally had such an experience. But
if it happens one day, then I shall do everything I can to make
sure I know who the sender is. Take Count Rickardt Three Lions,
for example. He turned up at the Finø Amateur Dramatic Society's
auditions for *The Merry Widow* with his eye firmly on the leading
role of Count Danilo, and his inspiration for so doing had come
in the form of a calling he believed issued directly from God.

I witnessed those auditions, because Mother provided the
musical accompaniment, and I must say that Rickardt's calling
cannot possibly have come from above, but must have originated
with much darker forces who yearned for Rickardt's demise. His
audition that day continued to crop up in nightmares for a long
time afterwards.

So one should investigate one's callings down to the detail. I have no idea if Jakob ever did. All I want to do here is to cautiously point out that Jakob received his calling immediately after he and Tilte had become engaged with rings and spent a week alone together in a holiday cabin. And without mentioning Conny and me, I will say that although I am only fourteen years old, I have had plenty of opportunity to note how remarkably often people are beckoned away to something bigger and better, such as fame or promotion, or being called up for the first team or a life in the service of God, all because they find themselves confronted with the prospect of a long sprint in the company of their loved one.

And I would like at this point to quote our great-grandmother. She stood with her back to us in the kitchen brushing her teeth when Tilte told us of Jakob's calling. It was all new, the wound was still fresh, and Tilte was unable to look any one of us in the eye when she spoke. Great-Grandma finished brushing her teeth. She is proud of them and still retains several of her own, and besides that she boasts of being able to split open marrowbones with her gums, because her gums are as hard as horn.

When she was finished, she settled back down into her wheelchair and punted her way over to Tilte and looked her in the eye.

'What's wrong with most romantic relationships', she said, 'is that there isn't enough. Though sometimes there's too much.'

Many believed that Tilte would soon find herself a new boyfriend, but Basker and Great-Grandma and Hans and I knew she would not, because we knew how bad it was. And now more than a year has passed and Tilte is still alone.

When Jakob disappeared, showing people the door took on a new slant for Tilte. It became more missionary. I'm just telling you, that's all. Partly so that you can keep an eye on me. When someone wants to show you something, especially something they say is of great importance, and you can sense how excited they are about it, you must always be on your toes. Because that's when there's a risk of things going wrong.

Now I have told you about Tilte's grief, and you will have understood that Tilte and I are joined together by having lost the only one we will ever truly love. We speak of it only seldom, hardly ever. And yet it is always there, and I sense it whenever Tilte is present. Even when she looks like the carnival in Rio de Janeiro and is busy saving the world by showing everyone the way to find greater depths within themselves, there is always, at the same time and far within, a grief that serves to remind us that she too is a human being like any other.

18

TILTE AND I, THEN, ARE SEATED EACH ON OUR OWN SOFA IN
what we refer to as Father's study. From these separate vantage
points, and while I have informed you of how things stand with
Tilte, we have allowed our gaze to pass around the room. Without
having exchanged a single word on the matter, both of us know
that someone has already been here and searched through the
rectory. And we know that whoever it was has been careful to
tidy up after themselves. For we have noticed things only those
who have lived their whole lives here and been made to do the
housework twice a week, the small round on Mondays and the big
one including washing the floors on Thursdays, could possibly
ever notice. Mother's piano has made impressions on the rug.
This has been noticed by whoever was here, and the person in
question has moved the piano ever so carefully back to its original
position so that its wheels once again nestle in their impressions.
They have put the square of cloth back on the lid of the piano,
and on top of it Mother's two violins, in the exact way they
are always arranged. What they have failed to discover is that
the cloth covers a scratch in the varnish that was made one time
Mother and I were testing the remote controls of the Sopwith
Camel we had constructed for the Grand Kite and Glider Day a
few years ago. And now that tiny scratch twinkles at us in the
last rays of the setting sun.

They have returned the sharpened pencils to Father's desk.
There they lie ready for when he receives a revelation he can
include in his next sermon and needs to write it down, standing

motionless for a moment to make sure everyone has seen him, Father at work, Father brimming over with intelligence. But they have been laid out in the wrong order, because Father always has the hard leads foremost and the soft ones behind.

The housekeeping wallet is where it belongs on the low shelf. I open it and find a roll of notes of the same thickness Mother and Father would always leave when going on holiday and leaving us behind for a week. I put the money in my pocket. Something tells me it'll come in handy.

'Photographs,' says Tilte. 'They took photographs. Then they pulled everything apart and used the photographs to put it all back again. But when?'

Because the garden adjoins the churchyard to the north, one can easily get the feeling that the rectory is like a little house in the woods. Only it isn't, because other houses surround it. There's the old bellringer's cottage from which Bermuda Seagull runs her funeral home and midwifery clinic, and the tourist office, and the Fisher's House from which Leonora Ticklepalate runs her coaching business, and the Finø Local History Museum, and then the domicile of Finø Curtains and Drapes, which is the nursery of Karl Marauder Lander. Indeed, Finø Town is a veritable anthill, and poking a stick in one place means we all come running out at once.

'In the night,' I say. And I say so with all the weight that comes of a murky past prowling around in innocent people's gardens. 'They did it all in one night.'

19

MY MOTHER'S AND FATHER'S STUDIES ARE ADJOINING, AND the door between them is always open, except when Father is in solemn discussion with his parishioners. Until the point when our parents disappeared for the first time, the sound from these two rooms in a way kept the rectory on an even keel while Hans and Tilte and I were blowing through it like tornadoes. From Father's study came the sound of his pencil moving across paper as he composed his Sunday sermon, or the sound of the computer keyboard when he typed his final draft, and from Mother's study came the sound of nippers clipping at electric wiring, or the faint hiss that issues from tin solder when it melts, or her singing to herself whenever she was working on her speech recognition programme.

The first room one enters from the kitchen is Father's study, and from it there is a full view into Mother's. As always, they have tidied up and put things away before leaving, and their orderliness has been replicated by the forensic officers after they turned the place upside down, and theirs is the orderliness upon which we now gaze.

There's not much to see, because Father's study contains only a large desk, his computer, and a tall bookcase containing the books he consults in his work as pastor, more than a thousand volumes, but nothing compared to what he has in the living room. So we look at none of it. Neither do we consider the pictures on the walls, which Tilte says are reproductions from the Uffizi Gallery in Florence, and which portray holy men and women struck by revelations, or naked women coming out of cockleshells. Regarding the latter, Tilte once told Father that to have such matter on display was unacceptable, because how did he think the young confirmation candidates would feel when they were invited into the rectory. When Father still did not remove them Tilte went upstairs into the attic and found some underclothes from a Barbie doll and affixed them to one of the pictures in question, so that now it portrays the sea-born Venus in bra and knickers. Father left the underclothes where they were, and whenever people ask he says with solemnity: 'My daughter Tilte has positioned these garments in order that nudity may be suppressed.'

He says this especially when Tilte is within earshot, and it's one of those little jokes that are a part of any family idyll.

Concealed behind the picture is the rectory's built-in safe in which the church records are kept, and as we lift the picture, everything at first seems normal. But it isn't normal, because when we turn the handle the safe opens. The church records are in their usual place, but where the lock should be, and the microphone and the electronics that open the door, there is nothing, because someone has removed the entire mechanism.

We hang the picture back up without speaking and then turn towards the great closet at the far end of the room.

In that closet are some of my father's clothes.

One should never underestimate my father. Although, unlike Tilte and my mother, he does not require a separate goods carriage to contain his wardrobe just because he is going away for a week to the Theological Education Institute of the Evangelical Lutheran Church of Denmark, he always knows exactly what he is wearing down to the minutest detail. My personal view is that what they ought to have put to the ecclesiastical court, and what certainly would have provided grounds for disciplinary measures, are the minuscule swimming trunks he wears in summer when parading along the beach at Sønderstrand with his arm around my mother, trying at one and the same time to look like a family man who happens to be a pastor of the Evangelical Lutheran

Church of Denmark, married for nineteen years, and a beach bum on the lookout for some action.

So my father isn't just fussy about his clothes, he looks after them like they were religious relics, and for that reason a look inside his wardrobe will reveal to Tilte's and my own inquisitive gaze at least something about what he's up to.

At first it seems he is up to nothing at all, because all his clothes are there. Inside the vast closet, foremost and to the right, are the three dress forms on which hang his cassock, his dinner jacket and his dress suit. Behind them, his lounge suit and his overcoat. To the left are shelves housing the ruffs that go with his cassock. The whole interior reeks of a cologne called Knize No. 9, which he orders from Vienna, and I feel like closing the door again immediately, because my personal opinion is that if the ecclesiastical court couldn't nail him for those swimming trunks, they could surely have built a case on male perfume instead.

But Tilte won't let me close the door.

'Something's not right,' she says.

She pulls me inside. We proceed past several dress forms, through rows of shirts on hangers with loose mother-of-pearl cufflinks in little pouches, and then we are at the back of my father's wardrobe, standing in front of two more dress forms these ones bare.

'What are these for?' Tilte asks.

I activate my sense of order and my excellent memory for detail, and the answer comes to me. Not that I am accustomed to rummaging around at the back of my parents' wardrobes. But twice a year, everything is hung out to air in the sun and wind, and my mother says that doing so means never having to use mothballs, because the moths perish if they ever see the sun.

My own view is that if the vermin can survive the stench of Knize No. 9 and the sight of my father's silk shirts, then it will surely take more than a little sunshine and a sea breeze to kill them off, but the division of labour in our house deems Mother to be the expert on technical matters, so out everything comes twice a year, and that's how I know.

'His spare cassock,' I say. 'And an old dinner jacket. They were on the dress forms.'

We embark upon the journey that will lead us out of the closet once more. On the way, we pass by the first of the dress forms at the front. I allow my hand to pass over the black woollen garment.

'This is Father's old cassock,' I say. 'He's taken the new one with him.'

Any pastor in Denmark would be thrilled to own a cassock like Father's old one, which is fortunate because the garment comes from the Ballenkop Uniform Tailors on the island of Samsø, who make cassocks for the entire Danish clergy. With the exception, that is, of the pastor of Finø. Father's cassock is of cashmere and tailored to order by Knize of Vienna at a price we are compelled to ensure remains a family secret in order to avert the risk of popular uprising.

Tilte and I look at each other. We are thinking the same thing, which Tilte now utters. Bodil must be right.

'They're not in La Gomera at all.'

Our father will go to great lengths in order to attract attention to himself, and this is no less true at times when he is in the Canary Islands. But those lengths do not include appearing poolside in full vestments.

20

WE STEP INTO MOTHER'S STUDY. TILTE WHISTLES THE FIRST
bars of Mignon's 'Let Me Shine' from Schubert's Goethe-Lieder
and the room is immediately illuminated. All electrical functions in the house have switches, but may also be activated by
various excerpts from the songs of Schubert. The music system
is activated by the beginning of Mignon's 'Teach me not to
speak, but make me silent'. The toaster is turned on and off
by 'The gaze of your eyes in mine', and the guest toilet in the
hall flushes on 'Only he who knoweth longing can know how
much I suffer'.

Mother's study is not so much a study as a workshop, and in
fact it is not one but four workshops, because in each corner is
a different work station. Beneath the window are the computers,
facing the living room is a corner devoted to radio electronics,
diagonally opposite a long table with vices and a small lathe for
precision mechanics, and on the other side of the door a carpenter's bench.

Above each work station, appropriate tools hang with their
outlines on plywood boards, meaning that we can see at a glance
if everything is in place.

We stand in the middle of the room and look around. How
should we be able to find something the police's own crack
housework unit have missed?

I open the door of the broom cupboard and take out the vacuum
cleaner. If you vacuum a house containing women, very often
irreplaceable items of value such as earrings or necklaces or Tilte's

hair extensions will be sucked up into the dustbag. So I am rather practised in the investigation of dustbags, and my experience has taught me that they can be a mine of information.

Unfortunately, there is much to indicate that the police are equally practised in the field, because the dustbag is gone, replaced by one that is new and utterly empty.

Yet now, standing here with the vacuum cleaner in my hand, I upend the extension and notice that caught in the brushes of the floor tool is a wood shaving. I pick it up.

On its own, there is little that may be considered remarkable about a wood shaving, especially in a room containing a carpenter's bench and three planes plus one electric.

'It's three months since Mother last worked with wood,' I say.

I turn the shaving in my hand. The life of a wood shaving is brief, albeit replete with beauty. When fresh, they are as elastic as corkscrew curls, fragrant and almost transparent. But within a week they dry out and may break and become sawdust. The specimen I hold in my hand is still fresh. On its way towards old age, as indeed we all of us are, but fresh nonetheless.

Tilte and I think the same thought: we cannot rule out the possibility that the flying squad took the opportunity of indulging in handicrafts, that they perhaps spent time at the carpenter's bench, working with the fretsaw and the smoothing-plane. Perhaps they wanted to take a present home with them for the children. It's not impossible. But then again, it's not exactly likely, either. What is likely is that Mother used the plane on something just before she left. And that the police overlooked that little shaving in the floor tool of the vacuum cleaner.

The wood from which the shaving originates is dark brown with white markings. No one can ever inhabit a rectory that contains a wood-burning stove and a mother who dabbles in furniture making without becoming familiar with wood. This is a hardwood. Tropical. Without being mahogany or teak.

We remember at once. And again, there is no need to speak. It's like with me and Jakob Aquinas Bordurio Madsen: from kick-off to final whistle, Jakob and I were in telepathic contact with each other. Tilte and I head straight for the kitchen, and Tilte lifts her voice and sings: 'Alas, his kiss!'

The excerpt is from 'Gretel at the Spinning-wheel' and is a choice we children have learned to live with, because family life is all about compromise. The reward in this case is that no one could do anything but marvel at what now occurs before our eyes. The trapdoor of the larder is raised, the ladder unfolds, and from out of the floor appears a guard rail for the safety of small children and dogs who might otherwise fall into the depths. And then the light goes on.

What we call the larder consists of two rooms, one of which is the boiler room containing the boiler, a washing machine and a tumble dryer. And then there's the actual larder itself, which is where we are going.

It is a large room, which is just as well considering Father's love of food.

None of us knows exactly where he found his role models, though his primary source, as mentioned, would seem not to be his mother, and neither can it possibly be Our Lord and Saviour Jesus Christ, because he made do, as everyone knows, with five loaves and two fishes, or possibly vice versa, and then all that stuff about 'Look at the birds of the air, for they neither sow nor reap nor labour over duck rillettes, yet your heavenly Father feeds them'. My Father's style is quite another and is more about liaising with delicatessens and selected butcher's shops on the mainland, as well as endless hours spent in our kitchen in a mood of delirious exaltation. It is also about what is now in front of us, which is to say a very considerable collection of chutneys and relishes and compotes and syrups and jams of the seasonal fruits.

So we are standing in a room whose wall space is utilised to the full. But not a room in which things may be hidden. There is but the bare floor, a wine rack taking up an entire wall, and then metre upon metre of shelves crammed with bottles and jars.

The shelves are of meerbau and Mother made the last of them to use up the final bare wall space six months ago. That's what Tilte and I have recalled.

And that's the wall we're looking at now.

It's entirely in keeping with Mother's spirit and style to go on improving upon something she made six months ago. Or seven years ago. But it is not Mother's style to spend time planing shelves two hours before leaving for La Gomera, or wherever it was she happened to be going.

Tilte and I do not speak, but inside our minds we do the same thing. What we are looking for, and whose specific characteristics as yet are unrevealed to us, cannot be found by thought alone. Thoughts always move according to familiar patterns, and what we are looking for is outside the box. We consider the area of wall that is host to Mother's most recent shelves. We consider the rows of jars, the raspberries, the rose hip and plums, the blackcurrant syrup, the lemons from Amalfi and the tamarind chutney. We consider the brown wood of the shelves. The brackets. The whiteness of the wall.

And at the same time we reach inwards towards the beholder, towards the place inside the self where we interpret the messages of perception, and there we try to let go of each and every preconceived notion in our minds, so that we may make room for what we see and cannot yet imagine. This is what all mystics recommend.

We see it at once. Not one thing, but a pattern. The topmost and bottommost shelves and the row of brackets between them form a closed rectangle. Like a door.

Tilte runs her fingers along the joins. They are seamless. Mother loves joins. She will never drive a screw into a piece of wood without plugging the hole afterwards. I once sat with a centre bit and made fifteen hundred plugs for her when she laid the floorboards of Douglas fir in Father's study. So naturally the joins are seamless, and the join of the trapdoor leading down to the larder in which we are standing can only be discerned in bright light.

'There could be a door,' says Tilte.

We tap on the walls, but they don't sound hollow. And there is no handle.

'It would be controlled by a voice,' I say. 'And it would only react to their own voices. The code would be something they shared.'

We gaze at each other and call to mind our mother and father. We try to sense the presence of their beings. It sounds strange, but it can be done. And not only in the case of one's parents. It is as though we hold the imprints of all other people inside ourselves.

We realise together. A light goes on in Tilte's eyes. And she sees a light go on in mine. Neither of us needs to say a word.

It's one thing for two people in unison to form an idea of which both are certain. But what happens now surpasses that. It is as though our two consciousnesses are the same for a stretch. As on those three monumental occasions in the season when Jakob Aquinas and I found each other amid a defence as compact and impenetrable as a black, moonless night shrouded in fog, and Jakob delivered the ball to my left foot as when Basker delivers the Finø Gazette to Mother's and Father's pillow, and I sent the ball soaring into the top-left corner of the goal with the same meticulous composure as when returning a stamp to its place in the album. Until Jakob received his calling.

In the living room I dismantle the music system and carry the CD player into the cellar. Tilte carries the speakers. We both lift the amplifier, which is heavy, as if one of the forensic officers climbed inside and fell asleep and the others forgot him. Tilte finds the CD in the rack. And then comes the big moment.

The CD we insert into the player came out last year in support of Finø FC and may be purchased in all leading record shops and department stores, and it contains such musical highlights as Finø FC's official song, with the chorus 'Only a fool never fears Finø FC', which was a significant success for our family, because Tilte wrote the lyrics, Mother composed the melody, and Father, Hans, Tilte and I sing the chorus, and if you listen carefully enough you can hear Basker grizzling along in the background.

For this reason I feel able to concede, without risk of betraying any person or animal, that the record also contains boundless musical disasters, from which the hapless listener may never completely recover, and which, as Tilte would say, that unfortunate person most likely will carry with them to their deathbed, at which time they might even hasten the process of expiry. To give you an impression of how cautious you must be if this CD should ever fall into your hands, I will draw attention to the fact that it contains a song in which Rickardt Three Lions seeks to pay homage to the women and appetising young men of Finø. Regrettably one happens to be aware that he has in mind one's sister and older brother, and perhaps even one's mother and father, too. Moreover, it includes a track on which Einar Flogginfellow performs excerpts from the *Elder Edda* set to his own compositions and on which he is accompanied by Asa-Thor's giant sacrificial drum, the recording being made only a short time after his dismissal as headmaster, and as far as I recall the title is 'Yearning for Vehement Debate'. And as a final, shocking extremity, the disc features a recording of my brother Hans reciting one of his own poems beginning 'Here stands my darling rose and grows'.

So it is a record that spans the most vile and horrendous, but also the occasional blessing, and the track we select and turn up the volume on now is probably somewhere in between, because the singer is our mother, and if there is one thing any boy or girl of sound mind over the age of five will do anything to avoid hearing, it is the sound of their own mother singing. But at the same time one has to admit, if pressed, that there are singers worse than my mother, and on the track in question she accompanies herself on the piano and what she sings is, of course, 'Monday in the Rain on Lonely Avenue'.

To the best of my knowledge, I have never personally been down Lonely Avenue, and for that reason I would surely fail to recognise it. But the lower section of Mother's new shelving in the larder does. Two bars into the music, the lower part of the wall slides ten centimetres back, taking two hundred bottles and jam jars with it, and is raised up to reveal a dark opening.

Tilte whistles and the light in the cellar goes out. The opening in front of us is no longer dark. Now we can see that it opens out into a room where a faint light glows.

We duck through the opening and step inside. The space is small and whitewashed, and the light is the light of the moon. At first we think it comes from a window, but now we can see it comes from a mirror. At the base of the exterior wall in the west end of the rectory are small, arched windows covered with wire mesh. We have always thought them to be ventilation openings leading into a crawlspace. Now we see there must have been a proper cellar once. The walls of the room are of natural stone, the light comes from one of the openings in the base and has been drawn inside by means of three angled mirrors and in that way cannot be seen from above.

Inside the room is a desk with a lamp and a chair, and nothing else. I switch on the lamp, and the room is bare. Not a cupboard, not a shelf, and nothing on the table. And yet we remain standing for some time. There is something rather disconcerting about having lived all your life in one place like the rectory, thinking you know it inside out, only to discover a new room.

And though there is little point, we run our fingers over the wall in search of entrances to further rooms, but there are none. The only thing we find is a cork board put up at the opening into the larder. It has been used as a noticeboard and its surface is perforated with hundreds of tiny pinholes. My mother, especially, is fond of noticeboards, and above her own work stations are always diagrams and instructions for use and rough designs. But the board here has been cleared.

We return to the larder and remain for a moment admiring the technical aspects of Mother's arrangement. Then I run my finger across the place where the shelves on the movable part of the wall will return flush with those that were already there. It is here that my mother produced one final wood shaving with her plane before leaving, in order to safeguard herself completely against discovery.

We play the music. Mother's voice begins to sing, 'Monday in the Rain on Lonely Avenue', the wall descends and slides back into place, and nothing can be seen. The joins in the walls of white-painted plywood are hidden from sight behind shelves and brackets, and we are filled with devout respect.

But still something bothers me, what in finer circles is referred to as intuition. Intuition is an inkling that comes from without. Investigations have prompted Tilte and I to consider that it comes through the crack when the big door stands slightly ajar. Our experience tells us that most instances of intuition unfortunately must be regarded as rubbish, and the way you can tell if there's any substance to your intuition is to test it against reality.

So I switch on the CD again, the rain drums and Mother croons, and the door slides open without even the slightest hiss from the hydraulics.

The idea that has come to me from outer space is that tidying up so not a single piece of evidence remained is beyond the scope of what my mother and father could ever manage.

When on Thursdays I have completed my round of housework in the rectory kitchen, a team of laboratory technicians with a fine-tooth comb would be hard pressed to find as much as a grain of rice. Even Tilte, who is not generous with her encouragement, has been heard to comment that when eventually they let me out on parole I'll always be able to find work as a cleaner.

But in the case of Mother and Father there would be results. Not a barrowload, but something would have turned up. Proper cleaning is a skill mastered only by a select few. And Mother and Father are not among that happy band.

I'm back inside the room.

'Close the door,' I say.

Tilte's not with me, but does as I tell her. The wall slides into place, and I am alone in the moonlight.

No further search is necessary, because I see it immediately. And I know how it happened. They were in a hurry. They brought out the luggage they had left packed and ready in here. They cleared the noticeboard and cleaned up after themselves. And all the while they had the door open into the larder. Eventually, they took a final look to make sure everything had been removed, and then they went out and closed the door behind them. Missing one thing. They missed the oblong of noticeboard that is covered by the moving wall when the wall is raised in the upright position.

That oblong is in front of me now, silver in the light of the reflected moon. And on it is a piece of paper.

21

WE'RE SEATED AT THE KITCHEN TABLE WITH THE SHEET OF paper in front of us.

It seems to have been torn off a company notepad, because the words *Voice Security* are printed in blue lettering at the top. Beneath are three lines of writing, the first two in pencil in my mother's hand, and the last in biro in handwriting we are as yet unable to identify.

The first note says: *Pay P. Pig*.

P. Pig is without doubt Polly Pigonia, a friend of the family who heads the Hindu community out on Finø Point and moreover runs the main branch of Finø Bank in Nordhavn.

The next line consists of one word only, which is *Dion*, followed by eight digits that could be a mobile phone number, and the abbreviation *A. W.*

The note in biro is an email address: *pallasathene.abak@mail.dk*.

Tilte gets her phone out. She turns towards me. On the display is the name *A. Winehappy* and the phone number Bodil called when she and Katinka and Lars picked us up and we were driven off to suffer incarceration and torture and execution at Big Hill. The number on Tilte's display and the number on the sheet of paper in front of us are identical.

'A. Winehappy,' says Tilte, 'is a name we must remember.'

We are on our way out and remain standing in the hall for a moment to say goodbye to our house. My gaze picks out the board on which we hang our keys.

I point to the key of the letter box on its red tag. Tilte doesn't get me.

'It's shiny,' I say. 'Brand new.'

Now Tilte can see it, too. The key of a letter box is used almost every day, and ours was yellow and worn. Now it has been replaced by a new one.

We open the letter box, the key fits, but all we find is a card reminding us to read the water meter. We take it inside with us and sit down again at the table we have just left and at which we have always consumed our childhood's daily bread and duck rillettes.

'The police,' I say. 'They copied the key and put the wrong one back on the board. Most likely they copied others, too.'

'What for?'

'Lars and Katinka probably empty the letter box every day and read what's inside. To see if there's anything about Mother and Father.'

'Why don't they just collect it at the post office? You can do anything when you're in the police.'

'That would require a warrant issued by the court,' I explain. 'Perhaps they don't have one. And then the rumour would spread. You know what Paprika's like.'

Paprika Postmistress is a sprinkler. A steady flow of information on every resident of Finø passes into the post office each day to be disseminated onto the thirsty fields by Paprika.

Tilte nods.

'That explains why the letter box is empty. There ought to have been a whole week's mail.'

I pick up the letter that has been pushed under the door. It's from Finø Bank and it's unfranked. I tear it open. The envelope is the bank's, but inside is a card showing a god with an elephant's trunk seated upon a throne of rose petals, and the message is handwritten and says thanks for a lovely evening. The lemon soufflé will live on immortally in the recollection of the sender, who moreover has to say that the bank has more than a hundred on the waiting list now, for which reason they'll be needing a reply soon, and lots of love is from Polly P.

We would love to know what Polly was wanting a reply to, but we have no way of investigating the matter, because it's the Easter weekend, Finø Bank is closed, and when it opens on Tuesday we will either be long gone or else back in chains and behind locked doors in the charge of the social services.

Then Tilte returns to the first note and puts her finger to the email address. The handwriting is of the kind that with some benevolence might be described as individual, though more exactly as almost illegible.

'It looks like Danish written in Chinese,' she says. 'It's Leonora's.'

22

I WOULD LIKE TO CAUTIOUSLY APPROACH SOME OF THE EVENTS leading up to my mother and father's first disappearance, which occurred two years ago. But to begin with I ought to outline their outward characteristics in order that you may recognise them and hide away in a stairwell or in some other way remove yourself from their vicinity should you happen to bump into them in the street.

Both are of advanced years, my father being forty and my mother approaching the same figure, though with a year or perhaps two to go. My mother has blonde hair and is so tanned in summer that whenever she has cause to bring Hans or Tilte or me to accident and emergency, and some summers we've been there more than twelve times in all, the locum doctors of Finø Hospital feel prompted to ask if she speaks Danish.

Although in Tilte's words my mother may be halfway to the grave in terms of age, she nevertheless retains the appearance of a young girl, and since this is a place in which we strive to be honest, I am compelled to say that on several occasions I have sensed that some of my friends, even those I would have sworn to be mentally stable, are rather in love with my mother.

And as if that were not enough, as if it did not give rise to the feeling of being stricken by some curse of the kind that rains down on unfortunate souls in the Old Testament, the same or even worse applies to my father, only the other way round.

As their courses progress, it becomes clear that a great many of the young girls who attend confirmation classes at the rectory, except of course such utterly supreme and equable individuals as

Conny, begin to look upon my father in the same way Belladonna eyed her rabbits before we passed her on to the Tropical Zoo at Randers. And in the gaze of many a young bride in the process of being joined in holy matrimony in Finø Town Church, I have noted hesitation when my father says, for instance: 'Do you, Feodora Hollowhead, take Frigast Gooseherd to be your lawful wedded husband?' And regrettably it seems clear that such hesitation comes of Feodora standing so close to my father as to suddenly form the idea that by marrying Frigast she may be missing a golden opportunity, and therefore the two little words *I do* remain momentarily in her throat before being expelled as though by the aid of a stomach pump.

Leonora Ticklepalate, she among us who almost certainly possesses most knowledge about men, and probably women, too, says it has to do with my father and mother sharing a sorrowful expression around the eyes, as though they have lost something but cannot discover what, and it is this expression that prompts innocent men and women, and even children and youngsters, to feel that they must go up and touch them and help them to search for whatever it is they have lost.

The evening Hans and Tilte and I discovered what lay behind that sorrow was the evening our mother and father, instead of keeping their usual erratic course, began to steer more directly towards the abyss.

In case you haven't been to church for a long time, or took a funny turn or were absent that day in religious studies at school, allow me to discreetly remind you that almost everything that goes on inside a church is holy, but the holiest of all in the Danish Church are the sacraments, when you go up to the altar for Communion during the Eucharist, or to be baptised and blessed, and when my father recites the Lord's Prayer on everyone's behalf. That evening in the kitchen Tilte asked Father if God was present in the sacraments, and her asking seemed so innocuous, because Tilte will occasionally speak to Father about religious matters, in many cases without mishap.

This particular evening was of a kind I hope you will recognise from your own life, an evening on which one resolves to give the family a chance, because for some reason it feels like it may have a future after all, at least for the next fifteen minutes or so. Mother was centring axles in a watch she was making, and Father was preparing a veal stock, which is a kind of gravy he concocts from meat and bones and herbs that makes the whole rectory smell like a mortuary, and then it reduces down and congeals until it becomes so stiff you could stuff cushions with it if that were not such a marvellously messy thing to do. And because Father is at his stove, and the stock has congealed and spirits are high, he reaches out and plucks Tilte's question from the air as if it were a child's balloon and tells her that God is everywhere, like a kind of clear broth made from the Holy Spirit, but in the sacraments He is present as veal stock in its thickest and most aromatic form.

After he tells her this, he radiates self-satisfaction as thick as his stock, and it's plain to see that he believes he has explained things in a manner that is at once pedagogical and theologically profound. But then Tilte comes back at him.

'How do you know?' she asks.

'Primarily from the New Testament,' says Father.

'But, Father,' Tilte persists, 'what about baptism? Nowhere in the Bible does it mention Jesus baptising children. He baptises adults, so where does the christening of infants come in, if it's not from the Bible?'

Now the mood in the kitchen shifts. Basker's breathing becomes more troubled, and Mother looks up from her watchmaking. All of us are aware that Tilte is building up to what I would call a Genghis Khan in reverse. It's an expression that comes from thinking about the major villains in world history, the ones who really messed things up, like Hitler and Genghis Khan and Læsø FC's sweeper, who broke Hans' leg in a tackle from behind. When you think about them, you wish Tilte had been there at the same time, because she can repel anyone and force them back into the Siberian swamps whence they came, and that is exactly what she is building up to with Father now.

'Infant baptism,' Father begins, 'arose in the Middle Ages, when many children died at a very young age. It was to save their souls.'

Tilte is on her feet and crossing the room to where Father is standing.

'But if it isn't mentioned in the Bible,' she says, 'how can you be so sure the Holy Spirit is present? How can you be sure? On what authority do you have it?'

'I sense it,' Father says.

And shouldn't have. But he is retreating into the swamp, and in such a situation one will resort to every possible means to avoid being sucked down.

The problem is that we three children and Basker can tell that Father isn't being completely honest with us here.

In his sermons, Father has specialised in evoking the general mood in Palestine at the time of Jesus. He and Mother have twice been on trips to Israel with the Theological Education Institute, and from those trips Father has found much inspiration for his description of the sky and the sun and the throngs of people and donkeys, and let me assure you that my father can deliver a sermon that will almost make you feel the dust of Palestine crunch between your teeth and give you a case of sunstroke even on a cloudy Advent Sunday inside Finø Town Church.

But when he departs from that mood and ventures towards what actually happened, what took place when God in the Transfiguration appeared before Jesus in a cloud, and when he tries to explain what Jesus meant when he said 'My Kingdom is not of this world', and whether he seriously walked on water, and what the resurrection of the flesh is actually all about – that stuff about getting your body back in Paradise after you're dead, which would be quite a good thing, especially for the calf that has contributed itself to Father's stock – when he seeks to explain all these things, he stops sounding like himself and begins to sound like a person rattling off something he has learned by heart because deep down he doesn't understand a word of it.

If there's one thing Tilte and Hans and Basker and I cannot

abide, it's when our parents stop sounding like themselves and begin to sound like someone else instead, and that's the reason Tilte now follows Father out into the swamp to pursue the matter further.

'How exactly do you sense it, Father?'

She isn't malicious in her asking, merely insistent, but then something surprising occurs. What occurs is that Father looks at Tilte, and then at the rest of us, and says: 'I don't know.'

And then tears well in his eyes.

It's not like we have never seen my father cry before. When you're married to someone like my mother, who very often forgets everything around her, including her husband and her children and her dog, because she has become obsessed by the idea of making her own mechanical wristwatch and works twenty-four hours in one stretch to centre the axles of the wheels while we children and our father go hungry – when you're married to a woman like that you will need to weep on the shoulders of close friends at least once a fortnight, which Father almost certainly has done in the company of Finn Flatfoot or John the Saviour.

But he has never done it at home. On such occasions as we have seen Father weep, it has always been in church and on account of him saying something especially beautiful that makes him cry because he is moved and grateful for the Lord having provided Finø with such a magnificent pastor as himself. Or else he cries at a funeral in sympathy with the bereaved, and one must reluctantly admit that Father's sympathy is almost as great as his satisfaction at putting it on display.

But though his complacency and sympathy both may be great, they have never been so great as what we now witness in the kitchen of our rectory home. What we see is something that has always been contained inside our father, but which is released only now, and to begin with we have no words for it. Father leaves the kitchen and Mother goes after him, and Tilte and Hans and Basker and I remain behind and look at each other. We sit for a moment in silence, and then Tilte suddenly says: 'They're elephant keepers. That's Mother's and Father's problem. They're elephant keepers without knowing it.'

We all know what she means. She means that Mother and Father have something inside them that is much bigger than themselves and over which they have no control, and for the first time we children are able to see what it is: they want to know what God really is; they want to meet God, and that is why it is so important to be sure that He is in the sacraments. And it's not only Father, it's Mother as well. This is what they live for above all else, and it is this yearning that has given them that sorrowful look around the eyes, and it is a yearning as big as an elephant, and we can see that it will never properly be fulfilled.

Naturally, we leave Mother and Father alone for the rest of the evening, because we are neither sadists nor murderers. But we have seen something we shall never forget. We have seen their private elephants in actual size.

Most likely Mother and Father have always had their elephants inside them. Perhaps they were born with them. But until this evening in the kitchen of the rectory there was always a lid on top. Somehow, Father's and Tilte's little exchange made the lid fall off. It means that what we and the world see happen in the coming weeks and months is that the elephants break through their cocoons and unfold their wings and begin to flap about, if you can understand an image not wholly in accordance with any biology textbook, but which nevertheless is fairly appropriate in respect of what actually happens.

But since this element of my past is painful to me and fraught with details both agonising and sensational, I should like to let it rest for a moment and return to the here and now in which Tilte and I have left the rectory and gone to see Leonora Ticklepalate.

23

LEONORA TICKLEPALATE IS SEATED ON THE FLOOR WITH HER legs crossed, and though she must be able to see the Finø Old People's Home looming up on the horizon – Leonora is at least fifty – even I, who am otherwise known for my reticence when it comes to passing comment on women's appearances, even I must say that she is a feast for the eye. And the reason for this is partly what she is wearing, which is a red Tibetan nun's habit, and partly the fact that she is tanned and bald and looks like Sigourney Weaver in *Alien 3*. She is on the telephone and beckons us in, and Tilte and I sit down while she finishes her call.

'You are passing through the Court of the Lions at Alhambra,' Leonora says into the phone. 'You are stark naked. And your bottom is naughty and pink.'

The receiver is on the table with the loudspeaker switched on, and the voice of the woman at the other end is irritable and rather inflamed.

'I haven't got a naughty bottom. I've an arse as big as a spare tyre.'

'Size is unimportant,' says Leonora. 'What matters is the expression. I have clients whose backsides are like the rear wheels of a tractor. And yet men fall for them in their hordes. In that respect, the rear wheel of a tractor may be a potent weapon indeed.'

We are seated in a room that looks like it was conceived in Tibet sometime in the Middle Ages, yet the house was designed by an architect and built less than a year ago at a cost of five million kroner for the building alone, which is equipped with a jacuzzi and a Finnish sauna and situated on top of the highest dune at Østerbjerg with an unspoiled view across the Sea of Opportunity. This modest dwelling is Leonora's private cloister, and alongside everything else she might be, Leonora is the head nun of Finø's Buddhist community, which this year has surpassed eleven members, and at present she is in retreat for three years. Which is to say that she has made a vow to remain within her little shack here and not leave Østerbjerg, and to exist on rice and vegetables and otherwise to meditate and not commune with another living soul.

Tilte and I have driven here in Thorkild Thorlacius' Mercedes, a matter some would refer to as theft, though Tilte and I would not be among them. We believe it should rather be called borrowing, because what need would Thorkild have of his car now that he is locked up in the new detention centre? And besides, it's no good for a car to stand idle too long without the engine and the battery being taken for a run.

Now Tilte places the torn-off paper from the pad in front of Leonora and points to the note that is written in biro.

'That's your handwriting, Leonora.'

Leonora's expression changes. A shadow falls upon her face and blots out the innocent pleasure of our visit.

'Not me,' she says. 'That's not my writing at all.'

Leonora Ticklepalate is a computer scientist and an expert in information technology, and the rectory is so crammed with computers and mp3 players and docking stations and mobile phones that we live in a constant state of electronic breakdown, which we survive only because Leonora is a friend of the family and our own IT guru. She has done programming for just about everyone on Finø, and when she developed risk-evaluation programs for Finø Bank's investment department, which operates on the islands of Læsø, Anholt and Samsø, the rest of the country discovered her too. Many have since tried to headhunt her, but she has always turned them down so that she might devote herself to the concept she has developed with Tilte, which she calls *Sexual–Cultural Coaching*.

It started quietly enough with her providing phone sex and working as a gardener to help pay for her studies. Leonora has always maintained that one must specialise in order to find professional challenges, and as a gardener she specialised in churchyards. At one point she was in charge of the maintenance of all three of Finø's churchyards, and in the field of phone sex she specialised in people who need to be surrounded by culture in order to feel comfortable. That was when she began asking Tilte and me for advice, because she's not from what you could call a cultivated family such as ours, so whenever she had a customer who, for instance, wanted to imagine doing it beneath Brunelleschi's Dome, she would pay Tilte and I a symbolic sum to go to the library or search the Internet and find out where in the world that dome was situated, and we would provide her with pictures and help her describe what the space looked like.

As our collaboration developed and Leonora's clientele expanded, Tilte had an idea. She had been wondering why the men never wanted their wives to be part of the stories Leonora told them over the phone. Often they wanted a host of individuals involved, both men and women, and pigs and cows and hens, and it all had to take place in the Whispering Gallery of St Paul's Cathedral or in the Uffizi Gallery, but their wives were never in on it, and when we asked Leonora why, she said because that was too dull. So Tilte proposed that Leonora sneak their wives into the story by saying things like, 'We're on St Mark's Square and I'm smacking your bottom with my riding crop, and now I'm handing it to your wife and she's giving you six of the best with your pants down.'

After some protest, Leonora began to follow her advice, and once certain teething troubles had been overcome the venture was an enormous success and Tilte was ready for the next stage.

The next stage was that she asked Leonora how come the men never got their wives to give them phone sex, and Leonora immediately forgot all about her meditative inner balance and went through the roof. She was halfway through her first three-year retreat at the time, and I was present, and she yelled at Tilte and asked her what she thought she was playing at and couldn't she see it would destroy her business if all the wives began performing her own professional services. But Tilte said the wives would never be able to do it without Leonora's help, and that it would be Leonora's job to get the men to persuade their wives to call her so that she might teach them how to say naughty things on the phone. Again, there were some teething troubles, and again it was an unparalleled success. Now Leonora feels eternally grateful to us, especially to Tilte, and she says that Tilte helped her solve an age-old problem, which is how monks and nuns in the great religions may earn their daily bread. In the olden days they received money from benefactors or else went about begging, but on Finø no one would ever be likely to cough up for Leonora or Anders from Randers to enter into a three-year retreat.

So for that reason a light always goes on in Leonora's eyes whenever she sees Tilte and me, and therefore we must be wary of the shadow that falls upon the proceedings at the moment Leonora sees her own handwriting on the paper in front of her.

'That's not my writing at all,' she says again.

We say nothing.

'What do you want to know for?'

'Mother and Father have disappeared,' says Tilte.

Leonora once told Tilte and me something Buddha is supposed to have said, which is that if you're trapped inside the reality of ordinary life and have yet to find the door and escape, then it matters not one bit how comfortable you might find that life, because troubles are just around the corner, and Leonora is at this moment a fine example. When we arrived, she was in the pink with her rice and beans, and her mantras and her view out over the Sea of Opportunity, and now she looks like something the cat dragged in.

I sit down beside her and stroke her arm. People who live for three years on a diet of rice and beans can easily long for another person to touch them, even if they are able to derive some gratification from their vows and the jacuzzi. And again, it's to do with the division of labour, because where Tilte reaches for the big bottle-washer, I go with the feather duster.

'I helped them gain access to a site,' says Leonora.

'What site is that?'

Leonora says nothing. It's a very delicate situation. Leonora is what I would not hesitate to describe as a friend of the family. And yet she resists. But there is no time for resistance. We must assume Katinka and Lars are on our heels, and neither Tilte nor I will allow ourselves to be taken in by their romance, no matter how deep it may be, and no matter that it may already be directing them towards real love and a police wedding. Their love will not prevent them from doing their duty, which is to return Tilte and me to indefinite detention with blue bands attached to our wrists. In this situation we are compelled, regardless of how much it hurts, to reach for some heavier tools.

'Leonora,' I begin. 'We consider you to be a friend of the family. So for your protection, I must warn you against Tilte. You know her from her nice side. The side of her that is imaginative and helpful. But as her brother I know that Tilte has another side. It appears when she is under pressure. And she is under pressure now. We must find our parents. Tilte is thinking especially of me in this respect. I'm only fourteen, Leonora. How can a boy of fourteen get by without his mother?'

Leonora sends me a feverish look, and I believe I know what she's thinking. She's thinking about whether to ask Tilte and me if we've considered the possibility that with parents as deranged as ours we might be better off as orphans.

It would be deceptive of me not to admit that the thought had indeed struck me, now, as well as on numerous occasions in the past. But this just doesn't feel like the right moment to enter into that discussion.

'Somewhere belonging to Bellerad Shipping,' says Leonora.

'And what would they be wanting there?' I ask.

Leonora says nothing.

'I'm afraid Tilte may soon be so far gone as to report you,

Leonora,' I go on, 'for computer hacking on behalf of our parents. She may even stoop so low as to propose that the inland revenue cast an eye over your bookkeeping procedures. And to be honest, Leonora, I would hate to see Finn Flatfoot come and remove you from your retreat. My father meets the pastor of Grenå Prison once a year on the Theological Education Institute's winetasting trip to the monastery kitchens of Tuscany. From what he's told Father, there's so much noise inside a prison you can hardly hear your own prayers. What prospects would there be for meditation, Leonora?'

'They didn't tell me.'

I stroke her arm patiently.

'Leonora,' I persist, 'you mustn't lie to children.'

'They were looking for correspondence. I had to get by two passwords. And the documents were encrypted. *Triple DES*, a complex system of encryption of the kind used by the banks. It took me two days to discover the algorithm. I had to use the Finø Bank's server, it's the only one on the island that's powerful enough.'

Tilte has been standing at the window with her back to us. Now she turns.

'What was it about?'

'There were several people involved, all signing themselves with initials, apart from one. Poul Bellerad. There was an abbreviation, too. I looked up the name and the abbreviation. Poul Bellerad is a ship owner with two pages to his name in *Who's Who* for all the decorations he's been given abroad, and all the boards of directors he's on. The abbreviation was for a kind of explosive. Perhaps your parents are planning to landscape the rectory garden. Finø's situated on bedrock, so maybe they've been thinking about a new well.'

'Maybe,' I say.

'There was something about guns as well. Perhaps your mother's doing some work for the armed forces. Helping them out with some technical improvements.'

'It's not unlikely,' I say.

Silence descends upon the little temple. All four of us are now reflective, and what we are contemplating is the feeling that if there were anything one would never wish to see in the hands of two such people as my mother and father, it would be guns and explosives.

Leonora points a finger at her note in biro.

'That email address was a document all on its own,' she says. 'Along with the word *Brahmacharya*. It's Sanskrit, meaning "abstention", particularly in the sense of "sexual abstention". I wonder what it was doing among a ship owner's correspondence?'

'Abstention is something all of us can benefit from,' says Tilte. 'Including ship owners.'

We gaze out across the sea. The last remnants of sunset can still be perceived, though not as colour, more as the last light of day. I imagine the scene. Leonora sitting beside Mother and Father in the rectory, in front of the computer. Tilte once said that the main reason Leonora rejected wealth and fame when all those companies tried to headhunt her was that she is so interested in what goes on deep inside human beings. Sex and the encryption of digital information are two paths that lead into those depths.

24

HOW SIBLINGS WHO HAVE BEEN BROUGHT UP IN EXACTLY THE same way can turn out so different is one of the great mysteries of life. Take me and Tilte and Basker, for instance.

Many fond acquaintances on Finø say of me that the pastor's son Peter is such a polite and respectful young man, and if he should fail to play for Aston Villa, he will undoubtedly end up opening a school of etiquette.

One of the rules to which I always adhere is that looking through people's private things is not done, and that includes Leonora's temple in the dunes. But Tilte and Basker have never heard of that rule. They poke their noses in, wherever they go. When you're visiting strangers and Tilte and Basker are with you, Tilte wanders about while conversing, and she opens their drawers and looks in their diaries and address books and asks them what they're doing later on in the day and who that person is whose number is written there. And people put up with it, they sit and watch as Tilte turns their lives inside out and has a look to see what clothes they like to wear, perhaps because they sense there is no malice in it and that it's simply a sign of a curiosity so overwhelming they haven't the strength to confront it.

And so it is now. As we speak with Leonora, Tilte wanders about opening drawers and taking things out and looking at them and putting them back again, and then she draws a curtain aside and behind the curtain is a suitcase packed and ready to go.

'I didn't think you were allowed to leave a retreat,' says Tilte.

'His Holiness the Dalai Lama is coming to Copenhagen tomorrow,' Leonora explains. 'Every Buddhist in Denmark will be there.'

'What might His Holiness be doing in Copenhagen?' asks Tilte.

'There's a big conference on. A meeting of all the major world religions. The first of its kind. Ever. It's about religious experience. For scientists and religious leaders and ordinary believers. They call it The Grand Synod.'

Had we been in the rectory, I would have said that at that moment an angel walks through the room, meaning that we all fall silent at once. But Leonora is a Buddhist, and studies Tilte and I have conducted at the Finø Town Library and on the Internet have revealed to us that in Buddhism the heavenly beings are called *devas*, so technically it would be more correct to say that a *deva* walks through the room.

'How are you making the journey, I wonder?' says Tilte.

'Laksmi's picking me up,' Leonora replies. 'In the hearse. And then we're going on to collect Lama Svend-Holger, Polly Pigonia and Sinbad Al-Blablab.'

Laksmi is actually Bermuda Seagull Jansson, midwife and undertaker, and a member of the Hindu ashram on Finø Point, the same ashram led by Polly Pigonia, who bears the spiritual name Antamouna Ma, meaning Mother of Stillness. Polly and her husband inherited a pig farm on the outskirts of Finø Town, only for the council to close it down because even on Finø, whose inhabitants are hardy folk, there are limits to the kind of pong we're willing to put up with from the neighbours, and besides that there was a din from the farm like a lion's cage at feeding time, so perhaps that was why Polly was renamed something to do with silence. After the farm was closed, she took a sabbatical from the Finø Bank and went off to India for a couple of years, and when she returned it was with a new name and dressed in white robes with a little golden crown to go with them when she wasn't at work. And she began to teach yoga and meditation and attracted more and more pupils who also began to dress in white robes and be given new names. So a couple of years ago they bought Finø Point, and they're very nice people who are well-liked and respected in the local community if only you can get used to all those new names.

'There's no ferry until Wednesday,' says Tilte. 'How are you getting over to the mainland?'

'We're sailing,' says Leonora. 'All the way to Copenhagen. On the *White Lady of Finø.*'

I won't say what Tilte and Basker and I are thinking. When you're presented with a great opportunity, however complicated and fraught with danger, thinking will never get you anywhere. Instead, you must reach inside to the place from which great ideas come, and feel. This is what we do now, all three of us.

'Why the *White Lady*?' Tilte asks.

The *White Lady of Finø* is a ship not quite as tall as the Finø Ferry, but rather longer. She was built at the Grenå Shipyard for an Arab oil sheikh and his harem, and for this reason comprises forty-two separate cabins with gold fittings and a pool, and a gynaecological clinic at the bow end, and she is as white as whipped cream and crammed with more electronics than the rectory and twelve F16 jet fighters put together, and the reason Tilte and Basker and I are in possession of all this knowledge is that my mother has been summoned seven times to help the specialists from the shipyard sort out the stabilisers, and on two of those occasions we went with her.

'Svend Sewerman is a conference sponsor,' Leonora says.

Inside Tilte and Basker and me, a major decision has now been taken, simultaneously and without our exchanging so much as a glance. What we have decided is that the *White Lady* will now be sailing three more passengers. Firstly, it provides us with a unique opportunity to slip away to the mainland. But there's another thing, too. Although we have yet to secure incontrovertible evidence, it seems unlikely that our parents' disappearance should be unrelated to the conference in Copenhagen, and the combination of important persons of international standing who also wish to meet God and our mother and father and their private elephants signals to us a dire and explosive cocktail we must endeavour to disarm as quickly as possible.

And at this moment we hear the sound of an engine, we see lights in the night, and a vehicle that looks like it was built to take care of funerals on the moon pulls up in front of the temple.

25

TECHNICALLY, THE CAR NOW PARKED OUTSIDE LEONORA'S cloister is a hearse, which is to say that it is black and equipped with long windows at the rear and room for a coffin with wreaths on top, and it possesses just the right aura for Bermuda Seagull Jansson to pull slowly away and leave mourners with the feeling that the vehicle might just as easily ascend to the heavens.

The aura possessed by this particular hearse is more powerful than that of regular vehicles of the same nature, not just because the white number plates indicate that it is privately registered, but also due to it being four-wheel drive and half a metre taller and one and a half metres longer than its competitors. Besides space for the coffin, it contains seven extra seats on account of Bermuda occasionally filling in as school bus driver, as well as having to run her own four children around, and the extra traction allows her to get out to home births in distant corners of the island through snowdrifts the height of a man. So if you know what circumstances are like on Finø, you will never bat an eyelid at the sight of Bermuda in her hearse.

What does seem odd, though, is that at this moment there is a white coffin inside.

'It's Maria from Maribo,' says Bermuda. 'She's going to Copenhagen to receive a blessing. From Da Sweet Love Ananda.'

Basker sniffs at the casket with obvious scepticism.

'Hasn't she been dead for a while?' Tilte asks.

'Ten days. But she's refrigerated. There's a cooling element in the coffin.'

Da Sweet Love Ananda is Polly Pigonia's Indian guru. I send him a compassionate thought. For as long as we can remember, Maria from Maribo ran the ice-cream kiosk at the harbour, and in all that time she was renowned for fobbing the children off with hollow scoops so as to make her stocks last on particularly hot days with a risk of running out. May God have mercy upon her soul.

We pile into the car. So far, no one is asking why we're coming along. It wouldn't be too much to say that in many areas of Finø, Tilte and Basker and I are hailed almost in the way of mascots, and the general opinion is that wherever we turn up, projects succeed and pieces fall into place, and a hearty atmosphere always ensues.

Then the car pulls away from the drive, through the lyme grass and out onto the road. I squeeze Tilte's hand and give Basker a pat, and all three of us have the feeling that despite the gravity of the situation we are headed in the right direction.

In order to make use of our peaceful transport in this four-wheel drive as it forges its way across Finø's Great Heath, which covers the eastern part of the island and extends all the way to the woods, I must furnish you with some details as to what my father and mother set in motion following that evening in the kitchen when Tilte asked about the sacraments.

The following Sunday, which is the sixth Sunday after Epiphany, my father is delivering a sermon in Finø Town Church on the subject of the Transfiguration.

As I have explained to you, it is a text my father finds rather slippery. As long as he is describing the journey of Christ up the mountain in the company of the disciples, he remains on firm ground. On that stretch of the course he sounds like a cross between an Alpine guide and a Boy Scout pack leader, but as soon as he reaches the part where the cloud descends upon the expedition and God speaks from within it, he begins to lose his grip and to rattle things off from memory. One understands him only too well, because that is the point at which a veritable flood of questions begins to manifest itself, such as: if God can speak to Jesus and to the disciples, is He then a kind of man, and what, in such case, does that man look like, and what can you do if you wish to hear the voice of God address you personally, and how does the Saviour converse with deceased prophets? And to all these questions Father possesses so few answers that he hasn't the courage even to pose them. He is keenly aware of this, and afraid to admit it, and at the same time he is upset that he should be so afraid, all of which contrives to make him sound, at this juncture in the proceedings, like his mouth is full of porridge, and we three children sit with Basker and curl our toes and feel sorry for him and have absolutely no idea what we might do.

Then a small disaster occurs. Finø Town Church is abruptly engulfed by fog, and this happens at the very moment Father recites the passage in which Jesus disappears into a cloud.

It is by no means uncommon for the church, and all of Finø Town for that matter, to find itself enshrouded in this manner, the reason being that we are in the middle of the Sea of Opportunity, as well as something about warm and cold airstreams that my brother Hans would be able to explain in great detail and to the point of tedium. So the phenomenon is nothing less or more than natural. When Father begins to recite the verse, the sky is blue and the sun is shining, as though Finø were the pearl of the Mediterranean, and as he comes to the end a fog has descended and the church has been wrapped up in wadding. We've seen it before, we'll see it again, and that's all there is to it. But the moment Father reaches the part where the voice issues from the cloud, the great bell in the church tower strikes.

This, too, has its own perfectly natural explanation, as Tilte and Mother and I discover after the service when we ascend the tower and find one of the owls that lives there has flown directly into the bell. We think it's dead, until Mother picks it up and strokes its forehead, whereupon it opens its eyes and stares at her as though it were in love, and at this point I begin to perspire, but thankfully common sense prevails and the owl recalls that it is not the juvenile lead in some old-fashioned film and flaps its wings with a screech before disappearing further up into the tower.

However, this is not until afterwards. There in the church, no one is thinking of natural explanations, because it is so astonishing and so completely unnerving for the bell to strike right at that very moment.

Perhaps the situation could have been normalised at this point, and perhaps afterwards we might have been able to pull Mother and Father back down to earth where the rest of us are. But now things really go wrong.

Far be it from me to exclude the possibility that weather might be determined by something other than natural forces, but if on this particular Sunday morning something more is at play than mere meteorology, whatever it is must surely be dark and demonic, because as Father is about to conclude his sermon something happens to the fog that until now has been snuggled around the church like cotton wool in a children's nativity scene. All at once, a hole appears in it, and through that hole a Mediterranean sun shines down in just such a way as to send a shaft of light in through the upper section of the church window to illuminate the altarpiece.

The altarpiece of Finø Town Church dates from prehistoric times and is as famous as a film star. Volumes have been written about it, coachloads of tourists come to see it, and it features in a full-colour double spread in the tourist brochure.

As far as I can see, it must have been painted by one of the forefathers of the nitwits who wrote those patriotic songs about Finø being a baby in the blue carry-cot of the Kattegat, and constitutes clear evidence that being completely round the bend isn't something that's over and done with in one generation. Just because the descendant is a poet with no grasp whatsoever on reality doesn't mean the ancestor can't have been a painter whose brain fate injected with air.

The altarpiece of course depicts a maritime scene with fishing boats, and the sea looks like Slush Ice from the fair at Århus, while the fishing boats resemble floating bathtubs. But what fills the picture is the Saviour, who is seated in the company of some poor soul whose demons he has exorcised, and the demons have been put into pigs that look like grizzly bears. The Saviour himself doesn't look like anyone who could be bothered even getting started on any of the things he is supposed to have achieved in only three years. In fact, he looks like the kind of person any one of the depicted pigs could do away with in one swoop.

And yet something remarkable happens within the congregation when the sunlight touches the Saviour's face. It would not be any exaggeration to say that the churchgoers this Sunday morning are spellbound, not simply on account of that sudden burst of light, but because of the expression on my father's face. I would refer to it as a telling expression, and what it tells is that this occurrence, far from being accidental, is in some way under his control.

We children gaze up at him and try to attract his attention. But Father is not looking. Instead, he prepares to descend from the pulpit, and then the worst happens, the worst being that a sudden gust of wind causes the door of the porch, and then the door of the church itself, to burst open.

The explanation of course has to do with the fact that the doors don't shut properly, and sudden gusts of wind are not a matter to which we people of Finø pay much attention at all until they become violent enough to send thatched roofs sailing towards the heavens and mobile sausage stands hurtling into the harbour, but this particular gust wasn't even close. What puts it into a class of its own, however, is its timing, and this is what my father cannot resist the temptation to exploit, so when Finn Flatfoot and John the Saviour rise to their feet to close the doors, Father holds up his hands and says: 'Halt! Let them remain open. We have received a visitor.'

And while he omits to mention the specific identity of this visitor, explanation is superfluous because everyone inside the church knows that the visitor is the Holy Spirit, and the audience is completely in Father's hands.

When the service is over and we shuffle through the porch, where Father stands to shake the hands of his congregation, Hans and Tilte and I see a new and hitherto wholly unfamiliar expression on his face, and we know where it is from, because he has copied it from the depiction of the Saviour on the altarpiece.

And when our turn comes to shake our father's hand, Tilte stops.

'It was all coincidence,' she says.

Father smiles at her. To the rest of the congregation standing in line behind us and spilling out in front of us, Father's smile may seem benevolent, but to us it looks like someone injected air into his brain.

'In coincidence lies Providence,' says Father.

We gaze at him, and all three of us are aware of what is happening. Father's private elephant is swelling inside him like a balloon being filled with helium.

'Father,' says Tilte, 'you are a despicable conman!'

Sadly, this will prove to be the last occasion in a very long time on which a rational being comes close to reaching my father, and in fact Tilte doesn't even get close, because Father's smile simply grows wider and all the more forgiving.

'Dearest Tilte,' he says. 'Thou knowest not what thou sayest.'

26

I WOULD LIKE TO ASK FOR YOUR UNDERSTANDING SO THAT I might return for a moment to Bermuda Seagull Jansson's moon-mobile, because at this moment she suddenly pulls over, stops the engine and switches off the lights, and I can tell you one thing: it's dark out there.

Finø is one of the last places in Denmark in which the night can be truly dark. Finø Town is far behind us, and Nordhavn lies as yet concealed beyond the great woods ahead. The houses in between the two towns are few and scattered, and the moon has hidden itself away, which on this night is perhaps the best policy of all.

Around us we can sense the sheer space that is so peculiar to Finø. No one location on the island is less than fifty kilometres from the closest mainland, which is Sweden, which again is wilderness. Tilte and I have a theory that Finø provides special advantages for us as regards our search for the door, because thoughts are a hindrance that prolongs your captivity inside the prison, and here all thought is effectively sucked out of your head and expelled into the firmament, which, of course, must be rather a strain on persons such as Alexander Flounderblood and Karl Marauder Lander, who to begin with contain only small dashes of thought, all of poor quality. But for persons such as Tilte and I, whose minds are so replete with powerful ideas that we must live in constant fear of cranial fracture from within, for us the emptiness and open space of Finø is salubrious, as the hymnmakers put it, and as I myself wrote in the tourist brochure. I am the author of the passage entitled 'Finø by Night' on account of Tilte and Dorada Rasmussen firmly believing that I am more experienced than most when it comes to being up and about at all hours.

'Is something the matter?' Bermuda asks.

You can't be an undertaker and a midwife without a remarkable talent for interpreting the moods of others, and both Tilte and I carry heavy burdens upon our shoulders.

'Mother and Father have gone missing,' I say.

Bermuda maintains what I would call a straightforward, no-nonsense outlook on life, and this is something that presumably comes of continually helping new children into the world and putting the dead away into the ground. So we are unused to seeing her struggle to come to terms with a matter as she so clearly does now.

'Einar was going to fly them,' she says.

Bermuda is married to Einar Flogginfellow, who got his pilot's licence so as to be able to fly himself to Norway and Sweden and Iceland, there to tighten bonds with other Nordic branches of Asa-Thor. And in order to accumulate flying hours, Einar shuttles Finø residents back and forth to the mainland if only they pay for the fuel. He has flown our parents on many occasions, and they are also the best of friends.

'They were supposed to go to Billund,' says Bermuda. 'But all of a sudden they wanted to go the day before. Einar couldn't take them because of football practice. But he spoke subsequently to the man who did. They put down at Jonstrup.'

Occasionally, air passengers coming from Finø are indeed flown to the disused airstrip outside Jonstrup. But that's not the way to La Gomera. If you want to go from Finø to the Canary Islands, you fly to Billund Airport in Jutland and get off there.

'I thought I ought to tell you,' says Bermuda. 'Under the circumstances.'

Tilte pats her on the arm. She and Bermuda are close. Little can bring people closer together than helping each other put dead bodies in coffins.

Bermuda turns to face the front and starts the engine. We drive off into Finø's moonless night, as will be familiar from my tourist brochure description.

It is not pleasant, but we must endure what must be endured. All the great men and women of wisdom have said that spiritual progress can never be made without unrelenting honesty, and so I must return to Mother and Father and to the next step on their decline, a step that is taken during Father's sermon the following Sunday, which is to say only a week after the meteorological disasters, and though at first it may seem of little consequence, I can assure you that it is a very big step indeed.

The Lesson is from the Acts and at the very moment Father relates the story of the Resurrection, a white dove comes flapping down from above, circles the model of the tea clipper *Spray Dolphin of Finø* that hangs suspended beneath the vaulted ceiling and which was constructed by our own mother, and then decends towards the organ and Mother herself. At this moment I feel a chill run down my spine at the thought that the bird will now perch on her shoulder and rub its beak against her nose and begin to coo affectionately, but this does not happen, and though it indeed appears to swoop down towards the place where Mother is seated, it suddenly disappears into thin air and is gone.

It is but poor consolation that the dove would seem to be rather more intelligent than the owl in the tower, as well as several of my classmates, for now come further depressing details. The first of these is that the churchgoers, who on this day are perched on the very edges of their pews in anticipation of ascertaining whether what happened the previous Sunday was coincidental or the harbinger of a new era, almost shoot up into the air.

My father follows the dove with his gaze, though appears not to be the slightest bit surprised. Rather, he looks upon it as though it were in its rightful place, and then he continues, and the effect of this is that the air inside the church almost quivers with tension and the congregation is astonished. Without batting an eyelid,

Father concludes his sermon and Mother plays the organ, and hymns are sung, and the churchgoers file out of the church in a state of shock; except we children are not in shock, we are in a state of depression and we proceed through the door of the church and past Father in the porch without even glancing at him, apart from Tilte, who sends him the kind of look that would normally put a person into intensive care and then most likely in his or her grave, but Father is immune.

That day, we gather in Tilte's room, and Hans as always tries to figure out how the situation can be saved.

'In a way, it's beautiful,' he says. 'Perhaps it might strengthen people's faith.'

'Hansel,' says Tilte, 'telling people every Sunday that God exists and that life is meaningful is bad enough in itself if you're not one hundred per cent certain, and Father isn't, he's even admitted it. But he and Mother producing white doves and passing it off as a miracle is meddling with people's trust in God, and whoever is guilty of that digs his own grave.'

We don't waste time considering where the dove came from. Any speculation is unnecessary, because twice a year we are made to polish the brass chandelier inside the church, and the mechanism by which it is hoisted up and lowered is based on speech recognition and is situated above the vaulted ceiling. There is a beam across which you can crawl to get to the mechanism and the light fittings, and on that beam is plenty of room to position a birdcage, which my mother could have made as easy as pie, with a trapdoor in the bottom that could be activated by means of a remote control, so one minute the dove would have been sitting peacefully on its perch listening to Father's sermon and the next it would have found itself to its great astonishment in a freefall into the church.

Where the dove might originate from is likewise a matter upon which we have no need to speculate, our family having for some years enjoyed close business relations with the Grenå Pet Shop, whose proprietors put us in touch with the kennel from which Basker I, II and III all were purchased, these stylish suppliers furthermore having provided us with live animals to feed to Belladonna and Martin Luther, as well as fresh fish for the sand tiger sharks.

Hans makes a final valiant attempt to come to our parents' defence.

'What about your extensions?' he says.

Whenever we venture to help Tilte towards an improved state of financial security by drawing attention to her shocking expenditure on having hair extensions done in Århus, this money being earned working for Bermuda Seagull at Finø Undertaking and advising Leonora Ticklepalate's *Sexual–Cultural Coaching*, Tilte always ripostes that the reason for her doing so is purely spiritual and that she is helping God by improving such small details as He never got round to finishing during the Creation. So what Hans means is that helping God by jazzing up the service might be acceptable in the same way.

But now Tilte shifts into another gear, now she becomes menacing in a way that might prompt weaker individuals such as Hans and myself to take cover.

'The question of whether God exists is the most crucial in any person's life. Whether we believe, whether we know, or whether we remain in doubt, each one of us seeks to bring to light the meaning of our own existence. Each one of us strives to discover whether there is something outside the prison, something that made the world come into existence and to assume the form it has assumed. All of us want to know what happens when we die, and whether we were anywhere else before we were born, and for that reason no one should ever meddle with that place inside us all.'

After this rigmarole, all avenues are closed. So we sit around without speaking, though by no means in total agreement, and that's one of the interesting things about us siblings, because we can disagree so much as to be on the point of committing manslaughter, but while it's going on there's always something there which I would not hesitate to call mutual respect and appreciation.

Eventually, Tilte says something.

'They're digging their own grave,' she says. 'Not with a shovel, but with an excavator.'

And for then, no more was said.

27

WE HAVE NOW PULLED UP OUTSIDE A PRESENTABLE FORMER farmhouse that is the seat of Finø's largest firm of solicitors and home to the island's own Buddhist Sangha, and into the car climbs Lama Svend-Holger, who looks like a heavyweight boxer, which is exactly what he was before he began to read law and went to Tibet and became a lama, and he is, as mentioned, a friend of the family and moreover Mother's and Father's solicitor, and yet he fails to acknowledge us, the reason obviously being that Bermuda's presence weighs upon him, and in a moment it will be clear to you why.

We are now in the vicinity of populated areas, and as we turn towards Finø Point we can just see the lights of Nordhavn in the distance. We draw to a halt in front of Pigslurry Farm, now Finø Puri Ashram, and out comes Polly Pigonia and two of her female pupils, all three of them dressed in white.

Polly nods in the direction of Tilte and me, though not to Lama Svend-Holger, whereupon she and her friends pile inside and we drive off into the dark of night, through the outskirts and into Nordhavn, where we stop outside Bullybluff House, which is a block in the centre of town and home to the Islamic mosque, and out comes the Grand Mufti Sinbad Al-Blablab.

Sinbad isn't actually a grand mufti at all, he is only an imam. But the look in his eye and the full beard he sports were sufficient to win him the part of Long John Silver in the Finø Amateur Dramatic Society's production of *Treasure Island*, and his perform-ance in that role won him many friends and admirers among Finø's inhabitants.

His popularity was further enhanced when he entered into marriage with Ingeborg Bluebuttock of Bluebuttock Farm, who now has converted to Islam and wears the burka, and who talked her friend, Anne Sofie Mikkelsen, into doing likewise, all of which many consider to be a major improvement for the island. My own personal view is that the burka may be rather becoming, and I would encourage others to take it up, for instance Karl Marauder Lander, though in his case there need be no slit for the eyes.

But while Sinbad is a jovial sort, something occurs inside him at the moment he sees Svend-Holger and Polly Pigonia. He doesn't so much as deign to look at them, and neither does he acknowledge Tilte and me, despite our somehow being charged, along with Bermuda, with lugging his suitcases, which are so numerous we have to pile them around the coffin on the assumption that Maria from Maribo doesn't mind. Though she may not have been willing to put up with much in her lifetime, as things stand now we are expecting few protests.

Tilte and I have this spiritual exercise we sometimes perform and which we found in our studies of *Advaita Vedanta* at the Finø Town Library. *Advaita Vedanta* is about as supreme as you can get in Hinduism, its first eleven and the equivalent of Finø FC's AllStars, if you get what I mean. The exercise involves asking yourself who exactly you are. And when you get an answer out of yourself, for instance that I am Peter Finø, one metre and fifty-five centimetres tall, forty-seven kilograms in weight, and size thirty-nine in football boots, you must consider your answer and ask yourself if it embraces your inner being, and if it does not, then you must delve further inside, gradually dispensing with words and simply listening, and doing so without expectation of what you might encounter once you are all the way in, and the whole time prepared for the worst.

It is a game Tilte and I often play when we have a job to do together. It begins by silent agreement, and no one can tell by looking at us, not even now. But as we pile Sinbad's suitcases impassively into the hearse, we are asking ourselves who exactly are these two persons doing the piling, and when we have finished we pause, this being a vital part of the exercise highly recommended by Ramana Maharshi, whom general opinion on Finø holds to be a spiritual superheavyweight, and the reason one should pause is because the moment you are standing there getting your breath back and resting on your laurels, normal reality is said to be very thin and the door is supposed to be close by.

So Tilte and I are standing there with perspiration on our brows and our backs to Bermuda's spacecraft, and we are reaching inwards and at the same time looking out over Nordhavn Town Square. On the other side of the square we see that major player on the global financial markets, the Finø Bank.

The idea occurs to us at once. As I have already said, it is quite normal for people embarking upon the great spiritual journey inwards to encounter an idea. Preferably, one is supposed to release the idea and investigate where it came from. But this particular idea is so good and our situation so tight that I stick my head inside the car.

'Polly,' I say, 'we promised Mother and Father to pay a debt of theirs.'

'That'll be the fee for the box,' says Polly. 'Their safe-deposit box. But it's Easter weekend.'

Polly is a rather determined woman. When you think that she runs Finø Bank and an ashram, and is married and has three sons on the first team of Finø FC's handball section, all of whom play and behave like they were Neanderthals, then it might not seem at all adequate to call her determined. In that case, I would say that Polly is a woman who at such time as the present, when she refuses to move an inch on account of it being the Easter weekend, can only be budged by means of a crane.

The crane appears now, in the form of Tilte.

'Polly,' my sister says, 'there are two things in the world I thought would always be there when a person needed them. One is cosmic empathy. And the other is the Finø Bank.'

145

28

THE DOOR OF THE BANK REQUIRES TWO KEYS TO OPEN IT, and moreover Polly must turn off the alarm, because the bank is, of course, hooked up to Finø Security, which is reassuring. In the case of robbery, customers and staff may breathe easily in the knowledge that John the Saviour will be there within forty-five minutes in his neon-coloured safety boots accompanied by Count Dracula.

The safe-deposit boxes are located in a special vault the size of a hospital lift, and its door opens silently as though on a cushion of air. Polly has not switched on the lights, perhaps so as not to alarm the neighbours. The residents of Nordhavn, unlike those of Finø Town, have the reputation of scaring easily, but the street lamps outside are sufficient to light up the interior of the bank.

Safe-deposit boxes, it seems, come in a variety of sizes. Some would be big enough to conceal your mother-in-law, whereas others have just enough room for a pair of engagement rings in a matchbox. The one Polly now opens is the size of an illustrated Bible. I reach inside and my hand encounters something oblong and hard, wrapped up in a plastic bag with an elastic band around it.

Outside, fellow humans await our return. And yet Polly makes no motions to leave. There is something she wants to say.

'Are your parents enjoying La Gomera?'

'They're having a wonderful time,' I tell her. 'Plenty of sunshine, refreshing margaritas and toes wiggling in the sand.'

'How lovely for them. To get away. We all have so much to attend to, your parents included.'

We have known Polly Pigonia all our lives, but we have never seen her like this before. The moment is quiet and unobtrusive. But unobtrusiveness should never be underestimated.

'What with the bank, and the ashram, and a family to look after.' She sighs. 'It's no easy life.'

Polly Pigonia's three sons score goals like they breathe in the air. But yellow cards and two-minute suspensions rain down on them like confetti. They play handball as though it were armed conflict, and I have never understood why, because all three have been brought up on yoga and bowel irrigation and images of gods with elephant trunks. But at this moment, as we stand here in the bank, something I have never seen before is emerging: the elephant that lives inside Polly. I get the feeling that perhaps elephant keepers are able to recognise one another, and that Polly perhaps has seen something in Mother and Father that she finds familiar.

She wants to say more, but something stops her. She closes the box.

We drive south, out of Nordhavn and across the Northern Sands, which is a huge expanse of overgrown dunes with such steep drops to the sea that you would hardly believe you were in Denmark at all, and in a way we are not, because this is Finø.

I don't know if you have ever been in a car with leaders belonging to different religions. It's such an unlikely state of affairs that I feel sure you have not, because normally such luminaries would go a long way to avoid one another, and I can assure you the experience is not something you would care to write home about. Sinbad and Polly Pigonia and Svend-Holger and their various entourages have yet to exchange a single word between them, and each one of them carries an expression that says the others do not exist, and this does nothing to improve the mood inside Bermuda's car.

But then Tilte has an idea to relieve this rather cheerless atmosphere. At the place where the road hugs the coastline, and where there is an almost vertical fifty-metre drop to our right with waves washing onto the beach far below us, Tilte leans towards Bermuda and wrenches the steering wheel to the right, causing the hearse to career towards the crash barrier and beyond it the open air.

The crash barrier is so low it looks like it's only there for a laugh, and we graze it just as Tilte jerks the wheel again and the car is returned to the tarmac.

In the course of our comparative theological studies at Finø Town Library and on the Internet, Tilte and I have derived pleasure from the extent to which the great spiritual figures agree on the idea that the individual's deeper awareness of his or her own mortality is highly beneficial to his or her *joie de vivre* and general outlook on life.

This is clearly demonstrated now, because following Tilte's little prank, the mood is no longer as before.

Bermuda pulls into the side and turns off the engine, and the faces inside the car are so pale they glow oddly in the dark.

I don't know if you're familiar with the expression *silent as the grave*, but Tilte and I know the phenomenon it describes only too well from a time when she borrowed a coffin from Bermuda Seagull Jansson. Bermuda buys them wholesale from Anholt Coffinmakers, who can supply twelve different models, all spray-lacquered and exquisitely finished, and Tilte borrowed a white one, which Hans and I on account of its tremendous weight were required to help her lug up the stairs to her room. We put it inside what she calls her walk-in wardrobe, which is to say the rear of her room, where she has erected clothes racks made to specification by our mother. Tilte's plan, which she then proceeded to carry out, was that whenever her friends were visiting and they had finished trying on clothes and giving each other face masks and drinking tea on Tilte's balcony and watching episodes of *Sex and the City*, she would encourage them to lie down in the coffin and try to gain an idea of what it must feel like to be dead, and when they did so she closed the lid.

Tilte was extremely satisfied with the project and maintained that her relationships with her friends were the more profound for it. By *profound* she was referring to what occurred when her friends had lain in the coffin and listened to the silence of the grave, and Tilte then walked them home and talked to them about the fact that even though they were only fourteen or fifteen years old they would soon, in the greater scheme of things, be dead. After their little talk, and once Tilte delivered them safely to their garden gates, their relationship had often become profound.

Unfortunately, Tilte was forced to return the coffin after only a short time, because after their relationships with Tilte had become profound, so many of her friends – girls and boys alike – had been unable to sleep except in their parents' beds, and they refused to go to school for a week afterwards, all of which prompted their parents to have words with ours, and Father was obliged to have one of those talks with Tilte from which he always emerges with great patches of perspiration underneath his arms and a look on his face that would make you think Tilte had put him in the coffin, and moreover there occurred one final and decisive episode concerning Karl Marauder Lander to which I shall presently return, and after that Tilte was required to give the coffin back to Bermuda.

But before she did, Hans and I tried it out for size. Hans was too tall and his legs stuck out of the end, but I had the lid put on and lay in the dark and followed Tilte's instructions as she explained that I was to imagine I was dead and that worms were eating me, and she had learned from the Internet that such worms were actually larder beetles, and she described to me what they looked like. I can tell you that silence was inside the coffin, and that as I lay there I understood that expression, and that is why it comes back to me as that phenomenon now occurs inside Bermuda's armoured wagon.

Then Tilte speaks.

'Peter is only fourteen,' she begins, 'and yet he already has a history of substance abuse and lack of proper parental care. His personality is brittle and will break at the wrong word. And right now he feels the mood among us to be weighing him down. Therefore, he and I would like to ask if you might not at least say hello to each another, because if you do there might just be a chance that Peter will avoid succumbing to psychosis on the journey, and any hopes we may have of reaching our destination in one piece will be considerably heightened.'

Our fellow passengers have not yet come round, but now they exchange glances at least, and mumble words that with the aid of electric amplification and some benevolence on the part of the listener might be interpreted as greetings.

This is not to be confused with what one might call spontaneous, heartfelt compliance, but rather an expression of their being so afraid of Tilte as to be rendered almost incontinent. But it's a start.

Tilte has made an effort and delivered the goods, and this is beyond dispute, so now I allow her to drift back into midfield and pick up the ball myself.

'There's another thing,' I say. 'Our Mother and Father have disappeared and are wanted by the police. We should like to find them first, and to that end we need to sail on the *White Lady* to Copenhagen. We need your support. You all know Svend Sewerman. No one who might risk costing him as much as five kroner will be allowed on board before their business and identity have been checked back through three generations. Would there be any chance of our being able to say we were with you?'

The faces surrounding me are closed. After a moment, Svend-Holger speaks.

'If your parents are wanted by the police and you've done a bunk, then our helping you would be a criminal offence,' he says.

Silence descends again, and the only sounds are of the waves against the shore. Then Sinbad says something.

'I made note of you,' he says, 'when we played *Treasure Island* and my wife found a grass snake in her wig, on stage and in front of four hunded people. I recall that you, Peter, once entered the Mr Finø contest. And I thought about you when the Association of Danish Insurance Companies sent two private investigators and an appraiser over here on account of so many windows being broken and so many dried dab being stolen from people's gardens.'

Silence again. And then I speak. Not to appeal for their help, because I've given up on that. But in order to explain.

'It's not for our sake,' I tell them. 'We will get by. It's worst for Mother and Father.'

I scramble for words that might adequately describe our parents. Are they lost souls, or more like children? Have they mistakenly wandered off the path, or are they on course but going about it the wrong way? The language resists.

'It's not because we need them to come home and take care of us,' I continue. 'Tilte and I will be fine. We are inspired by mendicant monks and barefooted Carmelites. We can borrow orange robes from Leonora and strike out onto the roads of Finø with our begging bowls.'

Whether I am able to subscribe completely to this declaration, and whether Tilte and Basker are wholly in agreement as to the part about the begging bowls, I am rather unsure. But sometimes you must head for goal, even if your teammates aren't there to help you out.

'The fact is – and this may perhaps surprise those of you who know Mother and Father well – the fact is that we love them. And this is all about love.'

And now something changes in the faces around me. Sympathy is a strong word, not least in an assembly such as the one in question. But it would not be too much to say that a softening has taken place.

'There is a verse of the Koran,' says Sinbad. 'It says that small devils are often the worst. And yet they require the greatest mercy.'

151

29

NOW THAT THE MOOD IS TAINTED WITH AT LEAST SOME understanding of Tilte's and Basker's and my own situation, and Bermuda's hearse ploughs on through the fateful Finø night, as I referred to it in our tourist brochure, I should like to conclude my report of events surrounding Mother's and Father's first disappearance.

In the following months, my parents proceed with caution. There may be, for instance, a slight rush of wind at the very moment in Father's sermon when he speaks of the angels on the cusp of blowing their trumpets somewhere in Revelation, though outside the church there is not a breath of wind at all. Or else a pair of organ pipes begin to whisper just as Father quotes: 'What is whispered in your ear, shout from the rooftops', though Mother is seated not at the instrument but among the congregation. Or on the occasion of a funeral, when Father concludes the graveside ceremony with the words *from earth thou shalt again arise*, a little puff of white steam may be expelled from the grave, just a mite, like the finest plume of smoke, and disappear as quickly as it materialised, though almost causing the mourners to fall to their knees. And no one suspects the slightest thing, all of it being executed with such elegance, without joins, and one senses so clearly Mother's love of her smoothing-plane.

The occasion on which we come closest to catching them in the act is when Finø Town Church is given a new roof in May. A small team of plumbers is casting the lead outside the church, and for that purpose they are equipped with a tray of sand which they hold at an angle, and onto it they pour the molten lead, which hardens immediately. At one point, we notice Mother speak to them and when she sees us she sends us a look that is utterly devoid of the unconditional love with which a mother always looks upon her children, and though we turn our backs and pretend not to have noticed, we have seen that she has given the plumbers something whose use she now explains to them. So when two Sundays later Father once more has ascended into the pulpit and again taken up Revelation, and this time it has something to do with a city tumbling to the ground, at which point a section of lead releases itself from the roof with an almighty clatter, and when the same thing happens a minute later, Tilte and Hans and I resolve not to speak to our parents again for an indefinite period of time.

Unfortunately, Mother and Father fail to notice that we have ceased communication, and our resolve is therefore to no avail. As May progresses, Sunday services are packed, though to begin with this gives rise to little concern insofar as my mother and father have always been know to attract an audience. But later, as the month wanes, we find that parishioners now queue out into the churchyard, and people begin to flock in droves from Anholt and Læsø, and then even from Grenå.

People from the mainland, particularly those from the capital, have always wanted to get married on Finø. Perhaps it has to do with the inherent difficulty of standing on Blågårds Plads or in Virum and vowing to remain together for ever when all you can see around you is evidence to the effect that one should be lucky indeed if all the things people promise each other last until Wednesday. But it is so much easier on Finø, surrounded by half-timbered cottages from the eighteenth century, and the medieval Finø Monastery and hordes of faithful storks, and where the tourist brochure will tell you that Finø's primeval landscape remains untouched with its mulberry trees and polar bears, and Hans in local costume, and Dorada Rasmussen's colourful parrot. And for this reason the parish council has long since drawn up a waiting list in order to avoid the burden of four weddings a week. But now the list begins to swell ominously, and letters of application arrive from throughout the land, from soon-to-be parents and the parents of the newborn who want their infants to be christened in the church, and from the families of people who have died, who would like to know if the deceased might be buried in the earth of Finø, even though the person in question never set foot on the island in the time they were alive. And an elegant letter arrives from an elderly lady, which we children read, because at that point we have become so concerned that we on occasion permit ourselves to open our parents' mail. The lady asks if she might be cremated on Finø and then have her ashes rolled into treat balls, to be blessed by Father and thereupon delivered to the Finø parrots of whose presence in abundance on the island she has heard tell, and in this way she is sure to be evacuated all over the natural beauty of the island, on which she has learned that the Holy Spirit has now taken up residence.

That letter would have signalled to most people that besides addressing the everyday credulous, Mother and Father were now beginning to attract proper weirdos, and yet my parents remain oblivious and inhabit a rather tiny section of reality.

At the beginning of June, calls are sent out to them from the mainland. The callers are to begin with the various communities of the Free Church, who are always in the market for new clergy who can speak in tongues, or endure ordeal by fire, or walk on water, or who in some other way possess that extra panache which the Evangelical Lutheran Church of Denmark is so lacking. But soon, the business community, too, would like to hear about Christianity and ethics and money, and preferably in the form of a talk and a service of the kind in which they have heard that Father excels, so when July comes round Mother and Father depart on their first tour, and you could say that whereas until this point they have been paddling at the water's edge, now they are about to take the plunge with all their clothes on.

No one on the parish council or outside it declares in as many words that they believe the Holy Spirit to have descended and taken up residence in Mother and Father and in Finø Town

Church. But that certainly seems to be in the air. Therefore, arrangements are made without dissent for a locum tenens from Århus and a substitute organist from Viborg to be dispatched to Finø, and for Great-Grandma to come and look after us while Mother and Father travel the country on a month-long tour in the middle of Finø's main tourist season.

Despite its unprecedented nature, this occurs seamlessly and without friction, and an airy, elevated mood descends upon Finø's ecclestiastical circles at the thought of how in this unprecedented way the island is confirming its natural position on the map of the world.

Father and Mother are, of course, also touched by this mood as they pack their luggage into their new estate car, a purchase that may be construed as the first, though by no means final, indication that whatever all this is about it is also, regrettably, about money. And then before we know it, Mother and Father have waved goodbye, the ferry has sailed, and they are gone.

The airy and elevated mood that prevails across the island does not encroach upon their children, nor upon Basker and Great-Grandma. On the contrary, we are weighed down by bleak and brooding premonitions.

These become more oppressive as the weeks pass and rumour and newspaper articles reach back to Finø, telling of audiences and Free Church congregations and major business figures all tumbling down like bowling pins on account of the quite extra-ordinary mood that arises when Father begins to preach. Indeed, rumour has it that God now appears as a tangible vibration during the Eucharist, and when we hear of this we look up at each other in concern.

Though the door leading into Mother's and Father's studies remains closed for a month prior to their departure, we are nonetheless able to secure an occasional glimpse of the portable altarpiece Mother has been constructing. We recall immediately how some years ago she made a little platform incorporating a metal plate on which we would stand whenever we had been skating on Finø Leech Pond. It sent vibrations all the way through the body in a pleasant manner to which we all looked forward without ever realising that the contraption would later become a building block in a confidence trick.

At least once a week, Mother and Father send us a postcard with a message that is always a variation on the theme *They love us!* And in the envelope is a cheque and the suggestion that we treat ourselves to a six-course dinner at The Nincompoop's gourmet restaurant. Each time, we read the card and put the cheque away in the housekeeping wallet, and the only one who says anything is Tilte, and this she does only once, waving the cheque in her hand and exclaiming: 'Blood money!'

When Mother and Father return home, they are delirious and hand out presents we refuse to accept: football boots, hair extensions made with real hair, and a camera that can be attached to an astronomer's telescope, and two weeks later they take off again, the locum tenens and the substitute organist are kept on, and Great-Grandma returns.

This time they leave not in the estate car but in a nine-seater minibus with tinted windows into which they load their luggage one night after Mother has worked for seven days in a row without emerging from her study, and when they have gone we all of us fear the worst.

We are given an inkling that our fears may be justified when our attention is captured by an advert in the *Finø Gazette*, which it turns out Mother and Father have placed in all the major newspapers and by which they offer their services in the field of financial advice, forcing us to conclude that our parents, who have never been able to make their own money stretch, are now going about telling people what to do with their savings.

The mood plummets to a depressive low when the *Finø Gazette* quotes a feature from Denmark's great business newspaper *Børsen* reporting on a combined religious service and talk on the subject of Christianity and money, followed by one-on-one financial advising, which Mother and Father have given to the Association of Danish Banks. It is an event that has taken place at a manor house near Fakse, and the journalist reports that during the service wild animals gathered outside the house, deer and badgers and hedgehogs, and great flocks of birds, and during the financial advisory session shifting patterns of light and fog appeared mysteriously in the room.

How Mother and Father technically were able to pull off the wild animals stunt is a matter of some conjecture, but one must bear in mind that from the time of Belladonna our family is not without experience in the field of zoology, and the rectory garden has been home variously to bird-eating spiders, sharks, hens and, for feeding purposes, rabbits. But what is obvious to us is that Mother and Father are beyond the pale and have now ventured out into the field of miracles.

They come home the following week, but not in the minibus in which they left, because they have hired a driver to return that to us the following week. Instead they drive a Maserati, and when they roll ashore from the ferry, rumour of it has preceded them and Finø residents line the road all the way from the harbour to the town square.

I don't know if you have ever seen a Maserati, so in case you haven't I can tell you that it is a car designed for people who are exhibitionists by nature but who nevertheless wish to demonstrate that they are modest enough to not simply open their raincoats and flash their wares. It is a motor vehicle under permanent threat of exploding from the pressure of having to remain unexhibited. When it pulls up in the driveway of the rectory and Mother climbs out, the assembled masses, which unfortunately also number Hans and Tilte and Basker and myself, are presented with the sight of her in a mink coat that reaches all the way down to the ground and which makes everyone, apart from the eight hundred mink that have sacrificed themselves for the garment, catch their breath.

During the two weeks that follow we consider whether some compassionate, Christian way exists by which to return Mother and Father to the real world. Must we really knock them unconscious in order to get them to the psychiatric wing of the Finø Hospital and plead that they be placed in straitjackets?

Sadly, we find no solution before they strike out into the world once again, and we heave a sigh of relief because with their departure the pressure finally subsides from those of our friends who keep hoping either for a ride in the Maserati at 200 kilometres an hour on the bends and 260 on the straight down to the landing strip, or a glimpse of my mother nude underneath her mink coat.

The hammer comes down a week later when Tilte and I return home from school to find our brother Hans, who is supposed to be away boarding and bent over his maths homework at Grenå High School, seated on the sofa next to Bodil Hippopotamus and flanked by three individuals of foreboding countenance, who turn out to be Professor Thorkild Thorlacius-Claptrap with spouse, and the Bishop of Grenå, Anaflabia Borderrud.

I have already made mention of the fact that in my early youth, which is to say the period spanning from five years of age to twelve, I may on occasion have been pressurised into taking part in the theft of fruit and perhaps a fish or two from the odd drying rack, but that such activity is now firmly a thing of the past. Be that as it may, for much of my life I have often found myself to be the victim of unfair accusation, for which reason we at the rectory have on occasion received individuals demanding not merely swift justice but prompt execution.

And yet I am bound to say that the mood issuing from Bodil and her hit squad is much more ominous.

'Your parents will not be returning home for some time,' she announces. 'We have found room for you at the Grenå Children's Home, and there you shall stay during the coming weeks.'

Tilte and I have always taken the view that what you need in a tight spot is some good karma.

To our surprise, this is now delivered to us in the shape of our great-grandmother, who suddenly appears in the doorway, and when she addresses Bodil she does so in a tone I have never heard her use before, hushed and ingratiating, just as one might imagine a nun would address an abbess during Mass to ask if there was any chance of borrowing fifty kroner until next Friday, and this humility blindsides Bodil.

'To what do we owe the honour?' Great-Grandma asks.

'It's an emergency,' says Bodil. 'The pastor and his wife have been remanded in custody. While their case remains pending the children will be placed in care at an institution in Grenå. Starting this evening.'

'They'd be better off here with me,' Great-Grandma says.

'We've spoken to the school,' Bodil goes on. 'The headmaster believes the children will benefit from more definite boundaries, and indeed from monitoring the state of their mental health.'

'The thing that worries me,' Great-Grandma says, 'is the media.'

This is a twist that takes all of us by surprise. We were unaware that Great-Grandma even knew the media existed. She does not watch television, neither does she read the papers, and she has never so much as glanced at our computers or mobile phones, as though in her own childhood information circulated on runic stones and she has no reason to believe that things might have changed.

'Imagine if the *Finø Gazette* were to catch wind of this,' she says. '*Minors forcibly removed from their home and put away with the dregs of society.*'

It's hard to imagine that Great-Grandma would really go to the papers. But what becomes clear is that the path she treads is not the narrow path of truth, the one Father talks about when instructing his confirmation candidates, but rather a military thoroughfare used to bring armoured troops quickly into position.

This is clearly what Anaflabia and Thorkild and Bodil are beginning to sense too, because at first they looked at Great-Grandma like she was something colourful and exotic out of the tourist brochure, and now their expressions are changing.

'Of course, none of us in this family would ever let anything leak on purpose,' says Great-Grandma. 'But I'm over ninety years old and people my age can have difficulty holding their water. Not that I've ever been afflicted myself. I've never had trouble staying tight.'

Great-Grandma snips the air like she were cutting a hedge with a pair of shears.

'Oh, I can shut off the flow all right. Would the Bishop be able to do as well, I wonder?'

She fixes her gaze on Anaflabia Borderrud, whose face has now taken on a distinct pallor.

'But words,' Great-Grandma goes on, 'words run away with me. It may be Alzheimer's. An early stage, perhaps. Some days I can't remember half of what I've said or to whom. Imagine if I had one of those days and let it all come out. About children being taken away and miracles in the church. Imagine if a journalist from the *Finø Gazette* happened to be there.'

And so it is that good karma turns the situation our way. Thorkild and Bodil and Anaflabia beat a hasty retreat, and Great-Grandma follows them all the way to the door with a stream of advice about pelvic exercises designed to lead to that pinnacle of success whereby flow from the bladder may be terminated so effectively one would think it had been severed by a razor.

It is left to Finn Flatfoot to fill us in on the details in the days that follow. What happened is that Mother and Father were giving a service for the Association of Danish Investment Companies, on which occasion they were intending to perform a miracle. They were going to burn money, which would then appear again from out of the ashes. The burning part was a success. But the twenty-six million kroner of various denominations had yet to materialise.

The thing that puzzles us is not that Mother and Father should have been playing with fire, because they have done that so many times before. It is well known on Finø that Mother is highly skilled in the field of pyrotechnics, and in recent years she has been in charge of much of the firework display for Finø Town's New Year celebrations. And when Finø Heath is burned off every other year on account of it being a designated preservation area, Mother, aided by John the Saviour and Finn Flatfoot, is the mainstay in keeping the heath in its scorched state of natural beauty.

So none of us is surprised by the actual burning, even if currency does burn rather poorly, a fact we know because Tilte once burned a hundred-krone note that Maria from Maribo owed her in wages after Tilte substituted for her in the kiosk during the summer holiday. When eventually Maria coughed up after two months of trying to consign the matter to oblivion, Tilte declared that it was merely a matter of principle and now she was going to show Maria what she really thought about money, for which purpose she then held the hundred-krone note against the flame of the candle on the counter that was supposed to make buying ice cream such a cosy experience, and the money burned so very slowly, though was eventually consumed. So there is absolutely no doubt in our minds that Mother could send twenty-six million kroner up in smoke. What puzzles us is that she and Father should have been unable to bring it all back again.

An explanation, however, transpires. It is not pleasant, and it does not arrive until six months later. To begin with, we learn from Finn Flatfoot that Mother and Father have been charged with fraud, and then that charges have been dropped due to lack of evidence. There follow proceedings in the ecclesiastical court and mental examination by forensic psychiatrists, and when these authorities declare Mother and Father to be of sound mind and innocent of any matter demanding disciplinary measures, they return to Finø.

Perhaps you know the feeling from your own family that the only thing in the world to be happy about is that your parents have been released from jail on account of the prosecutor being unable to find sufficient evidence to bring charges, and that their latest escapade has not yet reached the front page of the national newspapers because the people who were the victims of their fraud have been keeping it secret due to fear of ridicule?

In case you don't know what that feels like, I can tell you that it means you proceed with caution and speak in a hushed voice so that the crystal in the cabinet doesn't suddenly shatter, and it is a time in which you sit pale and silent at the dinner table and prod at your food, even if it happens to be Father's fish rissoles.

No one on Finø or at Finø Town School knows anything for

certain, but many have an inkling, even though Tilte's lips and mine are sealed. Most are too polite to say a word, and those who are not hold their lives too dear, so all this time we are hemmed in by a wall of unasked questions.

But time is the healer of all wounds, as indeed is the conclusion of forensic psychiatry to the effect that Mother and Father are normal, though at the time of their crime presumably of unsound mind due to pressures of work.

When Father again takes his place in the pulpit, and Mother hers behind the organ, everything seems to level out, and though both are paler and thinner than before, and sometimes have the same look in their eyes as the pigs in the altarpiece, they remain more or less composed.

And before long, the everyday disasters and triumphs of ordinary life have consigned Mother's and Father's misdemeanours to the background, and it's at this point that Hans enters the Mr Finø competition and wins, whereas I am duped by Karl Marauder Lander into climbing onto the stage in the belief that I am to receive Finø FC's Player of the Year award, after which I lay my hands on an iron bar and begin to hunt down Karl, who flees into the great woods, there to live as an outlaw and only to return three days and nights later, by which time charity hath melted the cold ice of wrath, as the hymnmakers might once have put it, and against all this I'm sure you understand how the general public of Finø might quickly relegate Mother's and Father's sins to oblivion.

Their children, however, do not. We hardly speak to our parents at all, weighed down as we are by their misdeeds, and eventually it becomes unbearable to them.

Father is tampering with his ice machine in the kitchen, the only tangible remnant in economic terms of their recent adventure, the Maserati and the mink coat having been swallowed up in the court settlement, and Mother is working on a new device for voice recognition that looks like a cuckoo clock.

Father clears his throat.

'What happened,' he says, 'was that the miracle your mother

and I were channelling somehow became displaced in time. Meaning that the money disappeared like it was supposed to, but failed to turn up again. It caused much ado, but the investment companies and the authorities are settling things between them. I have been able to draw matters to a close to everyone's satisfaction and we are all in agreement that the case will be pursued no further. The funny thing was that the money suddenly appeared again a week later. From a theological perspective, your mother and I consider that this may be explained in terms of the miracle possessing temporal duration, rather than being of the more usual instantaneous kind. But before we had the chance to take stock of this new state of affairs we were regrettably contacted by the police, who in every conceivable way proved to lack the spiritual depth required to grasp the full significance of the situation.'

'Where did the police contact you?' Hans asks.

'At the counter of a firm called Danish Diamond and Precious Metal Investment, and they came at the very moment we were investing the money in gold and platinum in order that your futures might be secured.'

The kitchen descends into silence. If you think this silence is filled with sorrow over our parents turning out to be swindlers, and with respect for their having managed against all odds to convince investment companies, the Ministry of Church Affairs, the Danish police and an investigative committee of forensic psychiatrists that we are all best served by the matter being held so close to our chests that no one else will ever be able to see it, then you will have hit the nail firmly on the head.

But something else is in the silence, too, and the nature of it is so much harder to explain, because in a way Father actually believes that the reason he and Mother got away with it is because they were helped by the Almighty, and that what they did was done to sweeten our childhoods and our futures with gold and platinum bars, so what this tells us is that we must be prepared, because love can sometimes appear in such disguise that one might hardly recognise it at all.

At that moment, Mother and Father have our forgiveness. Nothing more is said, and the matter is dismissed, perhaps only to return in our parents' deserved nightmares. But at the same time, Tilte and Basker and Hans and I realise that if ever you should hold ambitions of being indulgent towards others, then you must also be able to forgive their elephants.

THE SEA OF OPPORTUNITY

30

WHEN YOU'VE PLANTED A FOUR-KILOMETRE AVENUE OF LIME trees leading to the place in which you live, and have made that avenue half as wide again as the main road, you have inevitably raised the expectations of anyone who cares to pay you a visit. Few buildings can live up to such expectation, but the manor house called Finøholm is one of them, and tonight it does so twice over.

Finøholm is by the shore, which means that the approach to the main house slopes gently from more elevated ground. After the final bend, the visitor pulls up between two circular glass pavilions housing tropical trees and ponds full of water lilies, each with room to accommodate shooting parties of up to eighty people at a time. And on top of these are the gilded figures of three seals balancing on three wild boar, a detail that may give the general impression of a circus act, but which in actual fact is taken from the coat of arms Svend Sewerman commissioned for himself when he became Finøholm's owner.

Svend Sewerman went to school with our father at Finø Town School until moving to Frederikshavn on the mainland, where he became a building contractor and made a billion kroner, which is one thousand million, by digging holes and renovating most of the sewers of mid-Jutland, after which he was voted into Denmark's parliament, the *Folketing*. My father has told us of how, even when they were at school together, Svend dreamed of becoming an estate owner and would always try to instigate games in which the other children were to be peasants and serfs, while he would be lord of the manor and bailiff and be carried around in a sedan chair. So when he returned from Frederikshavn, he bought Finøholm from the Count of Finø, who was advanced in age and so impoverished he could only afford to heat up one room at a time and that was the staff kitchen. And it was at this time he changed his name from Svend Sewerman to Charles de Finø and rebuilt the manor and took on twelve woodsmen and two gamekeepers and two cooks and twenty labourers and two estate managers and maids and cleaners and a man who specialises in how things are done in the great manor houses of the mainland, and uniforms were made for the staff so that whenever Svend Sewerman hosts a shooting party followed by dinner they can flit about and look like footmen in the Tivoli Boys Guard. Another thing Svend bought was the *White Lady of Finø* when she was still called something in Arabic meaning the *Will of Allah*, but Svend changed that.

The manor house itself is arranged over three floors. It has a tower, and wide steps leading up to the main door, and behind the house is the pathway to the quay where the *White Lady of Finø* lies decorated with flags for the occasion. The whole scene is brightly illuminated, and Svend Sewerman's staff are in uniform, and from a distance they look like a period piece put on by the Finø Amateur Dramatic Society.

Tilte has had much to say during the drive, so it falls to me to voice what Lama Svend-Holger and Sinbad Al-Blablab and Polly and the rest of us are thinking.

'Why would Svend Sewerman sponsor a religious meeting in Copenhagen?'

It is an obvious question in light of Svend Sewerman having demonstrated on countless public occasions that as far as miserliness goes he compares more than favourably with Scrooge McDuck, one example being that Finø FC received not a penny from his hand when in desperate need of sponsorship, and when Tilte and I tried to sell tickets for the club's annual lottery and forced our way past his staff and all the way in to Svend Sewerman himself, he told us he had just run out of change, but instead we could take these two delicious pears from the garden, they were worth their weight in gold, and then he sent us packing.

And yet no one is prepared to answer my question, a fact that might seem rather peculiar when you think of how much wisdom and knowledge of local affairs happens to be gathered together at this moment in Bermuda's hearse. So Tilte provides the answer.

'He wants to be a minister in the government,' she says. 'He wants to start with the Ministry of Church Affairs and go on from there.'

We pull into the parking area, which is covered with the finest gravel and is half the size of a football pitch. Then Lama Svend-Holger clears his throat.

'As a solicitor, I am of course bound to professional secrecy,' he says.

Tilte and I nod earnestly. We all understand the importance of professional secrecy.

'Three weeks ago I dined with your parents at the rectory. I have not seen them since. They asked that I bring along with me Karnov's *Compendium of Danish Law*.'

We remember the evening well. Father had prepared whole roasted turbot. The turbot that are caught in the waters around Finø are extremely difficult to roast whole on account of their being as fat as bricks and boasting a diameter comparable to that of a manhole cover. Indeed, stories abound even in distant lands of my father's talent for roasting them whole, and on this particular evening he once more demonstrated their legitimacy, a matter that gave cause for celebration in the usual manner, whereby he and Lama Svend-Holger polished off a crate of Finø Brewery's Special Brew and thereupon sought to bring order to a number of theological quibbles such as the questions of whether God exists and what part of us exactly is reincarnated if, as the Buddhists claim, we possess no individual soul, then proceeding on to such weighty issues as why have we run out of beer and can't we send some children up to the petrol station to get some more.

And we remember Karnov's *Compendium of Danish Law*, and that it was yellow and heavy as a baptismal font.

'I recall that it was late in the evening. I went out to the lavatory and opened the wrong door by mistake, a rather regrettable effect, I'm sure, of intense meditational practice during the course of the meal. At first I was bewildered, but soon realised I had stumbled into your father's study. On his desk was a little copy machine still switched on, and next to it a volume of the *Compendium* with a bookmark inserted into it. Purely from habit, I cast a glance at the entry and was rather puzzled to find that the section in question concerned somewhat obscure statutory instruments relating to the police. Then my gaze fell upon the pile of copies that had been run off, and I saw that they were from the Lost Property Act. Not merely section 15 and Circular no. 76, but the entire legislation and all the judgment examples to boot. More than fifty pages. When subsequently I returned to the kitchen, my intention was to ask what on earth they wanted with it all. Unfortunately, my attention became distracted by matters of my practice. And the fish. The *beurre blanc*. The new potatoes. So I'm afraid I never got round to it. But now that your parents have gone missing, I begin to wonder if they might have lost something.'

During the last twenty-four hours, Tilte and I have come into possession of several items of baffling information concerning our parents, which we have found difficult to digest. This is another.

'If they have,' says Tilte, 'it can't have been worth much. The only thing of value our parents own is us.'

31

THE MAIN DOOR OF FINØHOLM OPENS INTO A HALL BIG enough for four large families to inhabit for many years without ever having anything to do with each other. At the door is a man in a blue coat and a powdered wig whose job it is to receive guests warmly and make sure gatecrashers are given short shrift.

Tilte takes Sinbad Al-Blablab by the hand, I curl mine into Polly's great fist and at once we are past security and have entered the hall.

For the occasion, a cloakroom has been set up attended by servants who take one's coat while perspiring beneath wigs and who all seem to be kicking themselves for not having read the small print when they signed their contracts of employment as woodsmen.

From the entry hall, a stairway wide enough to appear in the film of a Broadway musical leads to the first floor and the banqueting hall, which instead of suits of armour contains marble statues of naked women and men upon which Leonora Ticklepalate pensively dwells. Spread out in front of the statues is a buffet which serves as a reminder that the days when you could feed your guests on three loaves and five fishes, or vice versa, are long since gone, because this looks like something from a Roman orgy. Moreover, a notice says that all meat is halal. And in front of the buffet stands Svend Sewerman.

Anyone who has never seen Svend Sewerman might conjure up all sorts of interesting images as to the appearance of a man who voluntarily took on the name of Charles de Finø, but I can assure you that all of them would be inappropriate, because Svend Sewerman looks exactly like what he is: a man who runs a large and lucrative business. The only notable thing about him is the hunger that may be detected in his eyes. I have seen it before and it reminds me of something I am at present unable to place, but it must surely be that same hunger that prompted him to change his name and buy a manor house, and commission someone to design him a coat of arms. Perhaps it is also the reason he looks so ravenously upon his interlocutor, as though he believes him to be a man who knows the score on everything. Because his interlocutor is none other than Count Rickardt Three Lions, resplendent in a dinner jacket of silver lamé, a cummerbund of rose-red silk around his waist, and a pair of pointed patent leather shoes that are so long and shiny as to consign the dinner jacket and the cummerbund to shadow.

Surrounding these two men of the gentry is a swelling sea of Finø society, among them the island's doctors and its two postmasters, solicitors and the manager of the cooperative supermarket, directors of the boatyards and the brickworks and the fish factory, and the editor-in-chief of the *Finø Gazette*, and then all the delegations who will be sailing away this evening to the Grand Synod.

It is a colourful sea of evening dresses and dinner jackets, of Svend Sewerman's staff in livery, Polly Pigonia and her congregation in Hindu whites, Sinbad Al-Blablab in his turban, Ingeborg Bluebuttock in her burka, the Buddhists in purple and the three members of the Jewish community in black hats, and in the middle of this great palette I catch sight of Dorada Rasmussen in local costume.

And all of it is a spectacle into which one might immerse oneself and swim around were it not for the fact that we stand before what seems like an insurmountable problem, which is how to secure tickets and access to the *White Lady of Finø*, and this is a question we as yet have found no time to address.

At this moment, I sense something is about to happen to Tilte. To say she now receives divine inspiration directly through the open door would perhaps be to exaggerate matters, and after what has happened to our parents and to Jakob Aquinas, and after Rickardt Three Lions' attempt to secure the leading part in *The Merry Widow*, we are rather wary of addressing the question of where big ideas come from. Nonetheless, I'm willing to say that what I now sense surging through Tilte's organism is at the very least a monumental vision.

'Polly,' says Tilte, 'you must back us up.'

Polly has no time to reply. Tilte takes hold of her free hand and the three of us part the waves of Finø society until we are standing in front of Count Rickardt and Svend Sewerman.

Tilte lets go of Polly and extends a hand towards the evening's host, Svend Sewerman, aka Charles de Finø.

'Allow me to present myself, Mr de Finø. My name is Tilte,' she says. 'Tilte de Ahlefeldt-Laurvig Finø. And this is my brother, Count Peter de Ahlefeldt-Laurvig Finø.'

My brain has shut down. As far as I can see, what Tilte is doing now is tantamount to suicide. We are standing before Count Rickardt, an intimate friend, and Svend Sewerman, who may only have seen us once, but less than six months ago, and at that point in time we were sellers of lottery tickets for Finø FC and of rather less than noble birth.

It would therefore be reasonable to assume that in a moment we shall be recognised and sent away into the night without a chance of leaving Finø before the ferry sails on Wednesday, by which time it will all be too late.

And for that reason, what now happens before our eyes most immediately resembles a miracle, not one of Mother's and Father's, but a real one as featured in the New Testament and the Vedas and certain passages of the Buddhist Canon, which is somewhat shorter on miracles than other religions.

What happens is that Svend Sewerman kisses Tilte's hand.

Of course, part of the reason for this is that Tilte has extended her hand in the first place, as though expecting it to be kissed. And when Tilte extends something in that way, even if it should be a cowpat on a pizza base, people tend to oblige.

'*The* Ahlefeldt-Laurvigs?' says Charles de Finø.

'*The* Ahlefeldt-Laurvigs,' says Tilte.

I look into Svend Sewerman's eyes and find there a variety of emotions: humility, joy and awe. But no recognition. And I begin now to sense the genius of Tilte's plan. Because if only one appeals to the deepest desires inside a person, then common sense will short-circuit, and the deepest desire inside Svend Sewerman is the desire to mingle with nobility.

How Tilte envisages moving on from here is a question that certainly becomes salient, but whose answer is postponed by Count Rickardt Three Lions suddenly coming to life. Since the moment he caught sight of me and Tilte, he has remained stock still in the way of people whose nervous systems have been struck by some debilitating affliction. But now the power of speech returns to him.

'Well, I never diddle!'

My first thought is that he is about to blurt out everything and give us away. But then I trace his gaze and can see that his outburst is aimed at other parties altogether. For in the doorway of the banqueting hall stands Thorkild Thorlacius. And behind him the Bishop of Grenå, Anaflabia Borderrud.

How such suspect types managed to get themselves released so promptly is unclear. And neither do we have time to dwell on the issue, because Svend Sewerman now lights up even more.

'And there we have the Professor!' he exclaims. 'And my dear Bishop! Both will be in attendance at the Synod. As representatives of the Evangelical Lutheran Church of Denmark and the natural sciences, respectively.'

Tilte and I act as one. As I have already told you, we are a family that gels when it matters, we play as a team and know each other's game. What's important is to have an overview that spans the length and breadth of the pitch, and this is something I possess and which allows me to see that there is only one exit by which we can possibly escape in time.

In time means before Thorkild and Anaflabia catch sight of us. And not only them. Because behind them come Lars and Katinka, and although they may be holding hands and their eyes sparkle from their new-found love, which has progressed significantly since Tilte and I helped them discover each other beneath the acacia tree only a few short hours ago, their vigilance remains unaltered, their eagle eyes scan the hall, and I for one would wager that they are looking for us.

It is a situation that might have gone terribly wrong. But through one innocuous movement, Lama Svend-Holger and Sinbad Al-Blablab demonstrate unique compassion and a sense of occasion by simultaneously blocking further entry into the hall and preventing Katinka, Lars, Thorkild Thorlacius and Anaflabia from seeing inside.

Tilte and I duck away into the human sea, emerging from beneath the surface only when we have passed through the door.

32

THE ROOM WE NOW ENTER IS DIMLY LIT AND COOL, THE AIR
inside it thick with the smell of food. From out of the darkness
loom the outlines of tables laden with supplies for the buffet,
crates of beer and soft drinks, batteries of wine bottles. On an
adjoining table, cloth napkins have been placed in neat piles, and
on another is a different kind of material altogether. I pick it up
and unroll a length. It's not regular fabric, but the sort from
which Finøholm's curtains are made and which already is draped
before one of the room's two windows. It feels like something in
between tent canvas and stage curtains.

The curtains that hang before the windows of Finøholm are
embellished with gilded flag halyards and golden tassels as big
as paint brushes. But seemingly, the curtainer was unable to finish
his work before the evening's revels kicked off, and for that reason
he has left a roll of material behind on the table here. One explanation would be that the curtainer is none other than Herman
Marauder Lander of Finø Curtains and Drapes, our neighbour
and father of Karl, which in itself would be reason enough for
the man, alarmed as to whether his house might still be standing,
to drop everything and hurry home to see.

I'm aware that we must act quickly, and that my presence is
required in the role of initiator, because Tilte is still completely
immersed in her own inspiration.

I venture to suggest that Cinderella was afforded no better
treatment by the small animals in preparation for her encounter
with the prince with whom she would live happily ever after,

than the treatment I now bestow upon Tilte. I make her a turban, and a kind of Roman toga, and I'm able to do so because Mr Lander of Finø Curtains and Drapes has been kind enough or sufficiently distracted to leave behind his scissors and a large number of safety pins. Then I wind a second turban and cut a long robe for myself, and finally, from the lining material that is like a cross between medical gauze and fishnet, I make a veil for Tilte.

Now we are transformed, and all in less than five minutes. And then the door opens and in front of us stands our host, building contractor and honourable member of the Danish parliament, Charles de Finø.

The situation is prickly, but Tilte is clearly still surfing on the crest of invention.

'We were hoping you would come,' she says.

Svend Sewerman's eyes have yet to adjust to the dim light, but he instantly recognises Tilte's thin voice.

'Miss Ahlefeldt-Laurvig!'

Then he notices our costumes and some systemic confusion becomes apparent.

'We represent the Advaita Vedanta Society of Anholt,' Tilte explains. 'And thereby one of the world's most supreme forms of non-dogmatic meditation.'

Advaita Vedanta is, of course, well known on Finø as well as on the mainland, not least on account of the efforts of Ramana Maharshi, whose smiling mug adorns the wall of many a teenage bedroom in Denmark, and for this reason alone much ought now to be explained. Svend Sewerman relaxes noticeably.

'We wish to speak to you concerning a matter of the utmost importance,' says Tilte. 'A rather urgent matter, I'm afraid, and perhaps our most significant reason for being here this evening. However, we must insist on your complete confidence.'

Svend Sewerman nods his head. His eyes are what I would call vacant, a sure sign that he is now being sucked into Tilte's troposphere.

'At home at Anholt Manor,' Tilte continues, 'my brother and

I, and indeed our parents, too, are highly taken up with a phenomenon with which few in Denmark are as yet familiar. We call it
hidden aristocracy. The idea is that in all the great noble families,
children have been born outside of wedlock, and that these children have the inherent right to bear a title. The families involved
have naturally always done their best to conceal this fact with a
view to maintaining control of their vast fortunes. We believe the
time has come for transparency. To this end we have begun
searching for those children and their descendants. And we have
discovered that there are two things in particular that characterise
such persons of the aristocracy who are unaware of their own
standing. Firstly, there is what we call *inner nobility*, a sense of
natural belonging in respect of noble circles. And the second thing
is *physiognomical similarity*.'

I cannot profess to having followed Tilte in all that she has
said. But I'm in no doubt that she has now ventured beyond the
point at which solid ground begins to crumble underfoot.

And yet it immediately becomes clear that I can relax. Svend
Sewerman's breathing quickens, his eyes become milky white, and
anyone who didn't know better might think he was on the verge
of breakdown. But Svend Sewerman was born a navvy and
possesses the strength of a carthorse.

'Peter and I have grown up surrounded by hundreds of family
portraits,' says Tilte. 'And when we set eyes on you, a chill went
down our spines. It really is striking how much you, Charles,
resemble a true Ahlefeldt-Laurvig Finø.'

Once again, Tilte and I stand before a man who shows how
speaking directly to the deepest desires of a person will be sufficient to trigger the complete shutdown of all cognitive systems.
Svend Sewerman is at this moment putty in our hands, and the
path forward onto the *White Lady of Finø* would seem to be
opening out before us.

So imagine my dismay when a voice from the dimmest part
of the room says: 'Would that be on account of his protruding
ears?'

We turn and see a woman seated at the back of the room. Her

hair is yellow as corn, and piled up like a haystack with a perm. Her arms are like the sides of beef on the buffet table, and at her feet is a bottle of cold beer. Tilte and I both know straight away who she is: Svend Sewerman's wife, Bullimilla Madsen, whom we recall having seen drive past once in a horse-drawn carriage with Svend, and of whom we have heard tell that she is a sandwich maid by profession and that she refused to change her surname to de Finø. And we know, too, that this is a woman more generous by nature than her husband, because the day after Tilte and I had been sent packing from Finøholm without having sold a single lottery ticket, our brother Hans made his own attempt and was greeted at the door by Bullimilla, and she bought the whole lot.

So our overall impression is of a human being whose personality comprises many qualities.

Charles de Finø clearly feels that presentation is now called for.

'Tilte and Peter Ahlefeldt-Laurvig,' he announces. 'In the ceremonial robes of the Supreme Veranda.'

Bullimilla takes a swig of her beer.

'Looks more like our curtains, if you ask me, Svend.'

This is an astute comment that passes Svend Sewerman by. Svend has more important matters on his agenda.

'How do we proceed?' he asks. 'As to this possible – or likely – kinship?'

'Genealogy,' says Tilte. 'We shall be needing your family tree. And then we must go to Copenhagen, to the State Archives. Unfortunately, the ferry doesn't leave until Wednesday, so we shall have to wait.'

'The *White Lady* sails tonight,' says Svend Sewerman. 'We'll provide you with a cabin. And that tree you'll be needing.'

His head disappears into a drawer. Bullimilla pensively pours the last half of her beer down her throat and plucks a new bottle from the crate.

'How fitting that you should belong to nobility, Svend,' she says. 'Coming from that fine family of yours. Four generations of toilet cleaners in Finø Town. And before them a haze of shepherds and half-wits wandering about on the heath.'

Her tone is not without warmth, though it is mostly weary. I find myself wondering if she lives with an elephant keeper.

'Tonight,' she says, only partly to herself, 'I have seen more nutters than in all the years I managed the canteen at Kolding Town Hall. And the night's still young.'

As so often before, Tilte elects to proceed along the direct path.

'Mrs Madsen,' she says, 'what would you say if it should turn out that you were a countess?'

'I'd pay money not to be,' says Bullimilla, 'if it meant not having to be lumbered with nutters like the ones here tonight.'

Svend Sewerman hands us a memory stick and a book bound in golden leather, presumably his family tree and such like. Time is short and we must be off.

'I don't suppose there'd be any chance of getting those curtains back from the supreme whatever-it-was?'

The question comes from Bullimilla.

'Most certainly,' says Tilte. 'And when they return they will have been blessed and sprinkled with holy water by leading religious figures.'

Svend Sewerman holds the door and we dive back into the human sea. The last thing we hear is Bullimilla's voice.

'Nutters, Svend. Like all your other friends. And these were only children.'

33

WE PASS THROUGH THE CROWD ONCE MORE, BUT THIS TIME
our passage is smoother for our being hidden behind Svend
Sewerman. We catch glimpses of Thorkild Thorlacius and
Anaflabia, and of Lars and Katinka, but remain unnoticed by
them all, and the only unpleasant surprise along the way is that
I happen to eyeball Alexander Flounderblood, whose presence I
hasten to explain away by him being the ministerial envoy and
thereby a natural member of Finø's intelligentsia, and by that
time we have reached the door at the other end, and thereby our
finishing line. There, however, we come to a halt.

Our standstill is down to Tilte, who has stopped dead in front
of a person whose skin is slightly too olive-coloured to be ghostly
white, but which nevertheless is palid in the extreme. In his right
hand, the person in question holds a rosary, but at the sight of
Tilte all prayer is arrested.

'Allow me,' says Svend, 'to present my wife's nephew and my
own very dear friend, Jakob Aquinas Bordurio Madsen. Jakob is
reading theology in Copenhagen and has set his sights on
becoming a Catholic priest. He will be sailing with us to the
capital tonight. Jakob, may I present Tilte and Peter Ahlefeldt-
Laurvig of the Supreme Placenta at Anholt.'

Tilte slowly draws her veil aside. Jakob has, of course, recognised her despite the disguise, so the old adage that love is blind
is not true, because love clearly is sighted. But now at least she is
able to look him directly in the eye.

She indicates our costumes.

'In case you should be wondering about this, Jakob,' she says, 'I can tell you that I have received a calling.'

And with that we are out of the door. It closes behind us.

We emerge onto a lofty terrace, beneath which lies a rose garden. At the bottom of the garden, three carriages are waiting. All three make our own from Blågårds Plads look like a farmer's cart, and each is drawn by six horses of the Finø Full Blood race that make the fiery steeds of Blågårds Plads look like something the vet has agreed to put down.

'Passengers will be driven to the ship,' Svend explains. 'To the accompaniment of fireworks. In ten minutes. You're in the first carriage.'

He bows and kisses Tilte's hand, presses his own into mine and pats Basker on the head, as though Basker, too, were an Ahlefeldt-Laurvig, and then we stride off through the roses.

When finally we are on our own, I succumb to the feeling of offence that has weighed heavily upon my heart for the last five minutes.

'Tilte,' I say, 'all the great world religions have much to say in recommendation of truth. What is anyone supposed to think about the whopper you just told Svend Sewerman?'

I can sense Tilte begin to writhe inside, a sure sign that she is far from content.

'There's a story in the Buddhists' Pali Canon in which Buddha kills fifty pirates so as to prevent them from committing murder. As long as your intentions are sound, you can cut yourself some considerable slack.'

'But you're not Buddha,' I say. 'And Svend Sewerman isn't a pirate. He's going to be very disappointed.'

Tilte stops. She has an answer brewing. It is no easy answer, because what she happens to be facing is a classic problem of theology, which concerns how hard you can twist someone's arm while claiming to serve some higher purpose.

But her answer fails to transpire. A familiar figure opens the door of the carriage for us.

'Noble friends!' says Count Rickardt. 'Three minutes until departure. Fifteen until she sails!'

I would say that the carriage ride down to the *White Lady of Finø* to the accompaniment of ten minutes of uninterrupted Japanese fireworks is something Tilte and Basker and I under normal circumstances would allow ourselves to enjoy. Unfortunately, we encounter some minor difficulties, and the first of these now stands before us in the shape of Count Rickardt Three Lions.

'My word, how scrumptious you look!' says the Count. 'Oriental and Nordic all at once.'

'You, too,' says Tilte. 'Supremely withdrawn and yet ready to pounce like a simple flasher.'

Rickardt smiles with joy.

'We've adjoining cabins,' he says.

Tilte and I brace against the door.

'You mean, you're coming, too?' Tilte's voice quivers slightly with the hope that we misheard as the fireworks started.

'I'm even one of the hosts,' Rickardt replies. 'Filthøj Castle is my childhood home and a real treat! We run an organic farm there. On the full moon, the air is thick with elementals.'

Neither Tilte nor I have the energy to ask what elementals are. It's all we can do to get over the shock.

It's not that we aren't fond of Rickardt. As already mentioned, we consider him to be a member of the family, though we have long since conceded that he is the kind of family member one must accept will always be a menace to public order and security.

'Besides, it's a conference about religious experience,' says the Count. 'My own turf!'

There is nothing we can do but heave a sigh of relief that he seems not to be taking his archlute with him.

The horses are impatient. We step into our carriage.

And here we find another point for our agenda.

Seated in the corner is an elderly lady with her hat pulled firmly down to the rim of her dark glasses, asleep and with her mouth wide open. None of which presents us with the slightest problem. But seated next to her is Thorkild Thorlacius, next to him his wife, and next to her Anaflabia Borderrud.

I conceal Basker immediately underneath my curtain. Tilte and I are masked. But Basker is undraped.

We take our seats. The Count helps another person inside, that person being Vera the Secretary, after which he sits down himself. The driver cracks the whip, and the horses lunge forward, not quite in the same way as they would have done had my brother Hans been at the reins, but then not like a team of snails either.

The Count beams.

'One final word, people,' he says. 'To all you merry sailors: let's jolly well go for it!'

Twitches begin to animate the faces of Thorkild and the Bishop, and what they indicate is that of all the suffering they have endured during the last twelve hours, their encounter with Rickardt Three Lions may top the lot.

I concede that neither I nor Tilte is able to concentrate fully on the fireworks, for we must now contend with the double risk, firstly of Count Rickardt opening his big mouth and inadvertently giving the game away, and secondly of Thorkild or Anaflabia recognising us.

And now I sense the Professor's gaze fall upon my turban and then on Tilte's veil.

'Have we not met before?' he asks.

'We're from the Vedantist Sangha on the island of Anholt,' I reply. 'Perhaps you've been there?'

Thorkild shakes his head. His eyes have narrowed.

'Are you not accompanied by an adult?' he asks ponderingly.

I nod towards the sleeping lady in the corner.

'Only the Abbess,' I say.

Irresistible forces now mobilise inside the minds of Thorkild and Anaflabia all the shrewdness, the powers of deduction and the psychological insight needed to become a bishop and a world-famous neural scientist. And it is abundantly clear that in a very short time Tilte and I are going to have to run for our lives.

But at this strategic moment, the old lady lays her head comfortably on Thorkild's shoulder.

I would say that my personal view of miracles is the same as of people's tales of how brilliant they are at football: I want to see the ball in the net first. On the other hand, though, I can only admit that the jolt of the carriage at just that moment is sufficient for the old lady's head, and her hat and dark glasses with it, to loll and then come to rest on Thorkild Thorlacius' shoulder. And the fact that this occurs at all can only give rise to the feeling that the door must be open and that on the outside something lush is being done for Tilte and Basker and me.

But if anyone should think that we now merely lean back in our seats and savour this helping hand offered by Providence, if that's the right word for it, then they would be wrong indeed. And even if we actually feel like leaning back in our seats, we're given no opportunity to do so, because as the old lady's head lolls over and comes to rest, her hat is pushed up and reveals her to be none other than Maria from Maribo.

More naïve souls than Tilte and I would perhaps be inclined to believe that all doubt as to the existence of miracles must surely now be dispelled, because Maria has risen from her casket and put on her hat and dark glasses and climbed into the carriage to take her seat, all of it ten days into the process initiated by death. But Tilte and I are buying none of it. Both of us sense Rickardt's immediate alarm, and it tells us that in one way or another he is behind Maria suddenly being among us again.

A man of Thorkild Thorlacius' scientific standing ought by rights to be able to tell that something is not quite as it should be with Maria's appearance. But he is so embroiled in his suspicion as to our persons, that his eagle eye is temporarily blinded. And now he places his hand on Maria's arm.

'Madam,' he says, 'are you familiar with these young people?'
And then he pulls it back sharply.

'Jesus Christ!'

The Bishop gives a start, accustomed to her presence deterring invective. But one understands the Professor only too well. Maria has been immersed in dry ice. And yet he gathers himself remarkably quickly, and on that count one senses his Finnish *sisu* and professional overview.

'Madam,' he says to Maria, 'if you would permit me? A medical appraisal. You are suffering from hypothermia.'

Now, the situation that for such a brief moment appeared to brighten is once again becoming critical and requires prompt intervention.

'It's her training,' I say. 'Her meditative training. She fully absorbs herself when under transport. Body temperature plummets, and breathing all but ceases.'

Thorkild turns to face me, and at the same moment Basker stirs beneath my ceremonial robes. I sense all eyes switch immediately from Maria to my midriff.

'Tummy rolls,' I say. 'Exercise of the deep stomach muscles. A technique of yoga.'

At this point, another of those events occurs that to be frank feels like a friendly pat on the behind from the hand of Our Lord. The carriage comes to a standstill and a livery-clad serf opens the door and invites us to board ship.

Anaflabia and Vera and Thorkild and his wife follow on the heels of the powdered wig. I sense they would rather remain behind and investigate their suspicions further, but the funny thing is that a great many grown-ups, even born generals and field marshals like Thorkild Thorlacius and Anaflabia Borderrud, lose some of their powers of judgement when addressed by a person in uniform, so within a moment they are gone and only Maria remains, together with Basker, the Count, Tilte and me, and now we form a circle around Rickardt Three Lions and he is painfully aware that unless he delivers an explanation, he will be lucky to get away with severe corporal damage.

'It was my archlute,' he says. 'Forces of darkness took it away from me. All of a sudden it was gone. But I need it with me, I've promised to play at the conference, and music is the path to religious experience. I was in a pickle, but then the little blue men came to my aid. They showed me where it was locked up, and where the key was. But how was I to bring it on board? I needed to think quickly. And that was when the little men told me about the coffin. I opened it, though it was a challenge. I'm not good with my hands, as you know. The lute fitted perfectly, and the coffin was even upholstered.'

'So you put Maria in the carriage?'

'I'm afraid I didn't know the lady at the time. But I followed the instructions of the little men. She's as cold as a cold turkey. I had to wear gloves. And she, of course, needed a hat and a pair of sunglasses.'

'Rickardt,' says Tilte, her tone ominous, 'did the little men also tell you how to get her on board the ship?'

The Count shakes his head.

'That's sometimes the problem. They only give you the initial inspiration, if you know what I mean.'

It would be a stretch to say that Maria from Maribo was loved by one and all when she was alive. A closer approximation of the facts would be to admit that most people took it for granted that on a full moon she transformed into a werewolf. So her posthumous reputation would be unlikely to cause Tilte and me to break down and weep at the thought of leaving her behind on the quay. On the other hand, Bermuda Seagull Jansson and all the great world religions do stress the importance of treating the dead with respect and consideration, and moreover both Tilte and I realise that once it was discovered Maria was missing, a search would be initiated, and if there's one thing you don't need when travelling under a false identity, it's a maritime inquiry and subsequent cabin search.

'Rickardt,' I say, 'how did you get her from the hearse down to the carriage?'

The Count opens the luggage box at the rear of the carriage and takes from within it a folding wheelchair. Tilte and I gaze at each other, in telepathic agreement as to the nature of our next move.

34

THE SHIP IS BOARDED BY MEANS OF A GANGWAY, AND AT THE gangway stands the ship's captain in white uniform and gold-braided cap together with Svend Sewerman in order that he may wish us all a safe and pleasant journey. Svend lights up in a big smile when he sees us, and then his gaze falls upon Maria in her wheelchair.

For a moment I fear that Tilte will present Maria from Maribo as yet another member of the Ahlefeldt-Laurvig family, but fortunately even she appears to think it would be pushing our luck.

'The Leader of the Vedantist Sangha,' she says.

Svend moves forward with the clear intention of kissing the hand of Maria from Maribo. It is an intention that must be thwarted.

'I'm sorry,' I whisper to Svend. 'Chastity vows. I'm sure you understand. No man must ever touch the Abbess.'

Svend steps respectfully aside, an aluminium ramp is produced, and muscular seamen roll Maria on board and show us to our cabin. I am struck by a slight sadness at the fact that Maria was unable to be a part of all this when she was alive. Being manhandled by several muscular young men all at once would most certainly have given her far more pleasure than even her hollow scoops of ice cream. As we pass through the ship, we notice the restaurant and the galley, and at once Tilte and I exchange knowing looks, because where there's a restaurant there's a kitchen, and where there's a kitchen there's a cold store, and if there's one thing a person is looking out for when lumbered with a dead body, it's a cold store.

Anyone who thinks that ship's cabins are always cramped broom cupboards with bunk beds and a porthole would do well to take a trip on the *White Lady of Finø*. Our cabin is as big as a ballroom and looks like something out of the *Arabian Nights*. The bed is in the shape of a heart and draped with red velvet. There's a three-piece suite and a marble bathroom complete with dressing gowns and Persian slippers, and in any other circumstances Tilte and I would have permitted ourselves to enjoy such luxury to the full. But as soon as the seamen have gone, we roll Maria from Maribo back out into the corridor, through the empty restaurant, and into the deserted galley, at the rear of which we find the cold store we have been hoping for.

It is a cold store that sets out to make an impression on the world, as big inside as a caravan and packed from floor to ceiling with all manner of quadrupeds hanging from hooks, skinned and slaughtered in accordance with the prescriptions of Islamic law. And there at the very back of the store, from where she may enjoy the passage undisturbed until we manage to locate her coffin and put her back inside it, we park Maria and cover her up with some white bin liners. That done, we return to our cabin, sit down on the sofa and place the parcel from Mother's and Father's safe-deposit box on the table in front of us.

Inside the wrapping is the kind of black cardboard box in which Father stores his sermons. It contains several bundles of paper held together with elastic bands. We begin with a bundle of newspaper clippings.

They are about the Grand Synod, and there are hundreds of them. At first, we have no understanding of how Mother and Father could have laid hands on them, because they are from all sorts of different papers, and the only one to which we subscribe in the rectory is that well-known international journal the *Finø Gazette*. But the explanation is that they are all printouts from the Internet that have been cut to size. They go back three years, the first of them mentioning the conference as though it were still a flight of fancy, but they become increasingly definite and sensational, and the most recent are fully confident of the event being realised. These latter articles even contain pictures of important delegates who have already agreed to come, and the papers report that they will be arriving from all over the world to represent Christianity, Islam, Hinduism, Buddhism and Judaism, as well as various forms of nature worship and schools of the occult.

There is a large photo of the Dalai Lama with what I would call a penetratingly kind look in his eyes that makes you think that, styled and with a white beard and red hood, he would make a marvellous Santa in the Christmas grotto at Finø Town's community hall. Next to him is the Pope wearing a smile that in no way poses any danger to the Dalai Lama's candidacy in that respect, but which nevertheless might conceivably qualify him to look after the smallest children during the Christmas revue. There are pictures of the Metropolitan of Constantinople, and of other metropolitans, too, and one can only give Tilte her due and say that Finn Flatfoot could double for any of them at a religious service if only he kept his mouth shut and left Titmouse at home. There are a number of Grand Muftis as well, and while I have said that I am rather uncertain as to what that title actually covers, I can confess to not having seen a more awesome outfit than theirs since the Finø Amateur Dramatic Society put on *Son of Ali Baba* last year. And there are pictures of monks from Mount Athos, besides, and Mongolian shamans and Spanish Carmelite nuns, and the papers write that the Grand Synod will be the largest ever gathering of representatives of the world religions, and that moreover it will be the first time in history that the subject of religious experience will be discussed on such a huge scale. And then the journalist writing that particular piece goes completely over the top, because not only is this true, but the whole event is to take place in Denmark, at historical Filthøj

Castle in northern Sjælland, which is absolutely fantastic because it once more goes to show that even though we consider ourselves to be a small nation, in the broader scheme of things we are actually the most tolerant and welcoming, and one gets the feeling from his writing that the greatest and most widespread religion of all is and always will be self-satisfaction.

And now Tilte and I have read this far, we stumble upon the bombshell. Because the next clipping in the pile focuses not on the conference itself, but on something else altogether. At the top of the article is a picture of a black, pointed hat that looks like it might belong to some great wizard, and another showing some small, dark statuettes that could be from the bargain bin of a jumble sale. Next to these are pictures of jewel-studded tiaras, the kind you buy from toy shops off the Internet and which Tilte used to wear until she reached the age of five. A final picture shows what could be creme eggs and stones from the beach all mixed up together, but then follows the caption:

The Grand Synod is accompanied by an ambitious series of major concerts presenting world religious music. The largest exhibition of religious treasures ever shown at one time will run simultaneously. From the Tibetan refugee community, the Karmapa Trust will display relics from the Rumtek monastery in India, among them the Black Crown of the Karmapas. From the Islamic world, visitors may look forward to tapestries never before exhibited outside Mecca. Japan provides highlights from the Tokyo National Museum's collection of kimonos, and swords from the hands of Zen masters, so precious as never to have been put on sale. Indian Hinduism will be represented by gold statues belonging to the Tantra Museum at Lahore, while the Vatican has lent out unique relics of Christ and of the Saints, as well as a collection of jewel-encrusted crucifixes from the Renaissance. These alone are insured for the sum of one billion kroner, making the exhibition, to run in twelve countries during the next three years, the most expensive touring exhibition ever.

Tilte and I exchange looks. The ship rolls beneath us.

It goes without saying that we do not shun the opportunity to reach inside and ask ourselves who at this moment is experiencing such total paralysis.

But after we have done so, we must make room for indignation.

It's not that one can't take pleasure in seeing others make progress in life, especially when it's your parents. But making progress isn't enough on its own, one also has to consider in what direction such progress is progressing. And right now, as we sit here in front of all these newspaper clippings, Tilte and I share the thought that our mother and father seem to be progressing in giant evolutionary leaps towards at least eight years in prison.

The next pile of papers contains invoices, and at first they make no sense. Everything they itemise has been puchased within the last three months, from perhaps twenty different firms, some of which are located abroad. We flick through them at random and pick out bills for equipment bought from Grenå Electrical Supplies, fittings from Møll & Madame in Anholt Town, overalls of waterproof Beaver Nylon from Rugger & Rammen of Læsø. There are bills for two mobile phones and SIM cards, for something called *closed-cell foam leg protectors*, and two from the Grenå Pump Factory specifying *syringe pumps*. There are bills for stopwatches, for neon propylene rope, and an inexplicable invoice for something called an *18-foot wavebreaker* to the tune of fifty thousand kroner, to which has been added a 40 h.p. outboard motor for another fifty thousand. And this is all the more inexplicable because we know that Mother and Father have never voluntarily boarded any vessel less stable than the Finø Ferry. Then come a number of invoices in languages we cannot read, and a slip of paper upon which we gaze rather more pensively, which is a receipt for five two-hundred-litre containers of soft soap from Samsø Sanitation Ltd.

We look at each other.

'It's all the gear they need to pull off the heist,' I say.

We open the last parcel and find that it contains a flash drive and nothing else.

'We must pay Leonora a visit,' says Tilte, 'and appeal to Buddhist compassion.'

We permit ourselves to enter without knocking. Leonora's on the phone. She blows us a kiss.

'Listen carefully, dear,' she says to the woman on the other end. 'I'm on my way out to sea where there's no mobile coverage, so in a minute our connection will be lost. What you must do is to tighten the noose, give him six of the best with his fishing rod, look him in the eye and tell him: *This is what love feels like, Fatty.*'

The desperate housewife on the other end protests.

'Of course you can do it,' says Leonora patiently. 'But love without a filter is too much to begin with. That's why we need to start off with the thumbscrews and the dildo and the guillotine. They're like sunglasses to stop you being dazzled by the light. You have to get him used to it gradually. When autumn comes, spanking can be replaced by playful love bites. And by the end of the year, he can make do with the fetters and the sjambok.'

The connection is lost. Leonora mumbles a mantra to get her annoyance under control. Tilte places the flash drive in front of her.

We are gathered around the laptop, because Leonora, of course, has her computer with her, and the *White Lady of Finø* is naturally equipped with high-speed Internet. The drive whirs, Leonora glances up at the screen, and this time a mantra is not enough, this time she swears.

'Protected by password. Nothing I can do about it.'

'Break the code,' says Tilte.

'It'll take three days. We'll be there in nine hours.'

Tilte shakes her head.

'Apart from speech recognition, Mother and Father haven't a clue when it comes to computers. It's all they can do to get onto the school's website to see when there's a parents' meeting. The code will be as easy as pie.'

'Even standard codes may be labyrinths,' Leonora replies.

Tilte and Basker and I say nothing. But our silence is a mild exertion of pressure.

On many occasions, whenever she has grown tired of all her vegetarian food, Leonora has cut off her retreat to come sneaking down to the rectory, where Father has served *Veal Cordon Bleu* and pork brawn and duck rillettes and a couple of the big 75 cl bottles of Finø Brewery's Special Brew.

So there's no getting around us, and Leonora knows it. And besides her capitulation in the face of the inevitable, something appears in her gaze that you often see in adults who've known you for a long time, perhaps some kind of astonishment at their standing still while the rest of us are racing ahead at full speed.

'When you were little,' Leonora says, 'you were both so mild and gentle.'

She opens the cabin's minibar and produces a bottle of chilled white wine.

'This is my *tsok*,' she says. 'A Tibetan way of paying gratitude for all that one has gained from being in retreat. And *tsok* may be accompanied by alcohol.'

Tilte and I allow this to pass without comment. There is only one thing more far-fetched than the grounds given for religious rules, and that's the grounds given for breaking them again.

'We are still mild and gentle,' says Tilte. 'Only now more insistently so.'

35

WE ARE STANDING ON THE QUARTERDECK WATCHING FINØ
sink into the sea. You need a breath of fresh air when you've just
found out your parents have got their minds set on nicking
crucifixes to the tune of two hundred million dollars, plus whatever else they can lay their hands on in the process. The moon
has ventured out, and the island is a dark, elongated ridge, dotted
here and there with lights and with the beam of the Northern
Lighthouse sweeping out across the sea at intervals, and there on
the deck I suddenly become aware that Tilte and I will never
return, and that this has something to do with our being almost
grown up.

Now you'll most likely say, oh, do me a favour, the boy's only
fourteen and his sister sixteen, and does he think he's going to
live on the streets or something? But allow me to explain: a great
many people never get to say goodbye to their childhood homes.
A great many of those born on Finø move back there again sooner
or later, or else they join a branch of the Society of Finømen in
Grenå or Århus or Copenhagen, and go to meetings every
Thursday in local costume and dance to the tunes of the Finø
Fiddlers in wooden shoes lined with straw. And it's not only Finø.
Wherever you go, there are people who yearn for the place in
which they were born, and in fact it might not be the actual place
they yearn for at all, because it's said that over the past two
hundred years of history even people born in Amager have longed
to go back there.

I suspect my feeling has to do with something else entirely, which is Mother and Father. The Danish family has a reverse side, and the reverse side is sticky. This becomes especially evident when playing football. I've often seen first-team players eighteen or nineteen years old whose mums and dads have stood on the sidelines yelling out their encouragement while their little Frigast runs around like a headless chicken and you find yourself thinking: *Do his parents go to the toilet with him, too?*

The interesting thing for me and Tilte as we stand here on the quarterdeck is that we sense freedom. It comes of us in a way having lost our parents, and seen from one point of view that's a terrible thing. Just imagine, a fourteen-year-old boy left on his own. It's like someone pulled the rug from under us. But the interesting aspect, seldom mentioned, is that once the rug is gone you have the chance of finding out what it feels like to stand on the bare soil, and actually it feels rather nice, apart from the fact that we are obviously not standing on soil at all, but on the deck of the *White Lady of Finø*.

This feels like a golden moment in our unceasing spiritual training, because all of a sudden we're no longer someone's son or daughter or little dog, but are drifting alone upon the Sea of Opportunity, and I can tell you it's a terrifying experience, but rather intoxicating, too.

Unfortunately, there are two quarterdecks on the ship, and as we look down on the other, we catch a glimpse of Alexander Flounderblood, who has also stepped out into the air to look back on Finø and most likely forward to the day he sails away never to return, so at this moment we pensively retreat with the question of what on earth Alexander Flounderblood might be doing on board the *White Lady of Finø*.

In order to explain Tilte's unease and mine towards our headmaster, I must now say that regrettably there is much to indicate that Alexander Flounderblood has gained a rather poor impression of my family, and even of me personally.

The afternoon on which he had his first run-in with Tilte about the full meaning of the proper noun Kattegat, Basker and I were on our way to visit some friends who previously had coerced me into taking part in the theft of dried dab, and the purpose of my visiting them now was to inform them that I wished to embark upon a new, decriminalised life.

On our way, Basker and I bump into Alexander Flounderblood, who was out walking Baroness, and when Basker and Baroness discover each other's presence they feel an immediate desire to express their emotions, if you understand what I mean. This state of affairs so angered Alexander Flounderblood that he began to hit out at Basker, at which point I attempted to calm him down by saying that we might look forward to beautiful puppies. Indeed, if Basker's speed and intelligence and fine heart were combined with Baroness's long legs we might even establish a whole new Finø breed, which in time could become further refined and have its picture in the tourist brochure, and perhaps we ought even to fetch a stool for Basker on account of Baroness being a metre and a half tall and Basker having difficulty reaching.

Counter to my expectations, this failed to calm Alexander at all, and instead he put Baroness in her harness and marched off with her. I felt it important at this point to try to re-establish the good mood between us, because for spiritual searchers like myself, paying heed to the heart is of crucial importance. So I went after him and said that I understood him completely, because what he was afraid of was most likely that the puppies should inherit the looks and intelligence of Baroness and the coat of Basker, in which case we might just as well feed them to Belladonna. Unfortunately, this, too, failed to make the correct impression, and Alexander began to lash out at me with the reins of Baroness's harness, and these lashes were dealt with the utmost precision. Perhaps the reason he was awarded his doctorate in education was on account of his thrashing children with the reins of dog harnesses, but in any case Basker and I were forced to beat a hasty retreat.

Now destiny dictated, for better or worse, that the friends I was visiting – I shall hesitate to refer to them as the Finø mafia, because both the Sicilian and the East European mafias, should they ever wish to settle on Finø, would find themselves to be little more than a girls' choir alongside our local capacities – somehow managed to talk me into stealing dried dab one very last time. And the garden in which I would later find myself atop a rack of drying dab in the light of the full moon happened to belong to the old lighthouse keeper's cottage owned by the Ministry and in which they had installed Alexander Flounderblood and Baroness. The builders had only just finished doing the place up the day before, so we had no way at all of knowing that the house was now occupied. And as bad luck would have it, Alexander and Baroness stepped outside to take in the moon and immediately became aware of my presence. Thus it transpired that the only thing Alexander likes about Finø at all is dried dab, and only on account of Basker and Baroness going at it again and my performing a Fosbury flop to clear the garden wall was I fortunate enough to escape.

All this might have been redeemed, I think, by my keenness and diligence at school and by my general awareness of the importance of making a good impression, had it not been for the fact that only a few days subsequent to these fateful events, I was to fall foul of a sudden twist of fate. I was busy honing my skills in bending a free kick with the outside of my left foot, a detail which already then imparted terror into the opponents of the Finø AllStars at any set-piece and which I more generally perform to such perfection that the people of Finø no longer refer to it as a banana kick but prefer instead to speak of Peter's Horseshoe, and this wholly without exaggeration and mentioned here only in all modesty.

I'm sure you know how much practice it takes to get such a thing off pat, and one essential element of training in this respect is a suitable wall. As it happens, our situation is so unfortunate that the most suitable wall in Finø Town, which as you know is littered with half-timbered homes from the eighteenth century and medieval brickwork all as squint as an accident, is the monumental and completely windowless gable end of the chemist's shop adjoining the old lighthouse keeper's cottage. And at this point in my continued prowess, by my striking the ball so cleanly that it curved like a billiard ball around the wall of the chemist's shop, my free kick dropped sharply and directly against the great panorama window of the lighthouse keeper's cottage, behind which Alexander Flounderblood and Baroness were enjoying their afternoon tea.

And since then, even though compensation has long since been paid, and despite my writing a letter of apology and including, just to make it clear what I meant that day, drawings of the puppies I believed Baroness in the most fortunate circumstances might produce in liaison with Basker, since then the mood between us has never been entirely peaceable. And this is at least part of the reason for Tilte's unease and mine at the sight of Alexander Flounderblood and Baroness on the quarterdeck of the *White Lady of Finø*.

I would like to add one final point before Tilte and I return below deck. At the risk of sounding deranged, I would like to say that at this moment in time I nourish warmer feelings for Mother and Father than ever before. Perhaps on account of their being such foolish appendices to their private elephants, and perhaps because it's easier to be fond of people once you've managed to dilute the sticky stuff on the reverse side and slacken the line somewhat between you and them.

We enter Leonora's cabin. She turns to face us, and two things are immediately clear. One is that the white wine is almost finished, and the other is that we stand facing a woman who feels she has reason to be pleased with herself.

'In Buddhism we speak of the Five Poisons,' says Leonora. 'Five harmful psychological states of mind. One of them is Pride. Therefore, you will not hear me say that I am proud. But what I will say is that I'm in.'

We pull up chairs and sit down next to her.

'There are seven files,' she says. 'Sound and image files, one for each day of the week, and they're labelled from the seventh to the fourteenth of April.'

The speakers of the laptop hiss and an image appears on the screen. A dark grey square with a black circle inside.

Leonora's fingers flutter at the keys, the contrast changes and now we get the feeling of a room. But only the feeling. The camera must be positioned quite high up and must be equipped with a curved lens, giving the observer a distorted panoramic view of the whole room from halfway up the wall.

'CCTV,' I say.

I need say no more. These women trust me. In an age where increasing numbers of homes are equipped with private alarm systems, one cannot enjoy the reputation of being Finø's most foolhardy fruit thief without also being able to identify a security camera.

The room on the screen is empty apart from a dark, circular mat on the floor by the far wall. The walls are bare, yet the room must be very large, because it counts no fewer than six windows on each side.

'Can we run through it?' asks Tilte.

Leonora's fingers dance. We jump twelve hours ahead, and now the image is just a grey surface.

'Eleven p.m.,' I say. 'No daylight. Try speeding it up.'

'Two hundred times normal speed,' Leonora says. 'An hour is less than seventeen seconds.'

We stare at the screen. Daybreak, and the room appears, suddenly filled with people who are then gone, only to return again. Leonora freezes the image.

The people are men in white work clothes. They could be painters and decorators, but it looks like they're assembling furniture. One of them has his back to the camera. Tilte picks him out.

'Can we zoom in?'

Leonora obliges and the man's back fills the screen. On his white jacket is a large V with something resembling a little treble clef.

We resume on fast-forward and the white men jump like fleas, the light dims and then it's night. Leonora selects another file, the room fills with light, the men are little sparks. Tilte lifts her hand for Leonora to stop the film.

Something, which at first seems to be a mirror, has been placed on the dark mat on the floor.

'It's a round table,' says Leonora.

'It's an exhibition case,' says Tilte, 'which stands on the mat.'

'It's not a mat,' I say. 'It's a hole in the floor.'

Leonora's fingers dance the jitterbug and then we're eighteen hours back in time and all of us can see that what we took to be a mat is, in fact, a circular hole in the floor. It's even roped off with a cord on thin poles. We hadn't noticed.

'Fast-forward,' says Tilte.

Leonora obliges again, and a new team of workers are busy with what looks like a big sewage pipe.

'Is it a lift shaft?' Leonora wonders.

Tilte and I say nothing. We get to our feet.

'What's it all about?' says Leonora. 'Where was all this taken?'

'Is it not the case,' Tilte replies, 'that in Buddhism the individual strives to achieve neutral balance in life, and that regardless of what should come in the way, one must always let it pass with an unworried smile?'

'In Finø Buddhism,' Leonora says, 'the individual has surplus to worry about her madcap friends. And their lunatic children.'

This is a new outlook for Leonora, who has always addressed us with a measure of deference. I know that at this moment Tilte is thinking the same thing as me, namely that the risk in helping people towards enhanced self-esteem and improved finances is that one day they will rise up and turn against you.

'Leonora,' I say, 'the less you know, the fewer lies you'll need to tell in court.'

We close the door behind us. The last thing I see is the reproachful look on Leonora's paling face.

36

WE ARE BACK IN OUR CABIN, WISER THAN WHEN WE LEFT IT, but with fewer hopes of our childhood being blessed with a happy ending.

'There'll be exhibition cases in the other rooms as well,' says Tilte. 'But the real jewels will be in the round one. It's like when we went on that school trip to London and saw the Crown Jewels in the Tower, and it's the same at Rosenborg Castle in Copenhagen. The most valuable treasures are all in the same place, and if the alarm goes off, the whole case automatically descends into the hole.'

We think about that for a while, all three of us. And I don't consider myself to be overstepping the bounds of our usual modesty when I say that when Tilte and Basker and I put our heads together not a stone will remain unturned.

'Why did they want the footage?' Tilte asks. 'And where did they get it from?'

I allow her second question to hang in the air. So as to afford the first my undivided care and attention.

'They'll have wanted to make sure no one discovered them.'

'Then their plan, whatever it might be, involves an installation visible to workers, security guards and anyone else,' says Tilte.

'They must have been there themselves,' I venture. 'Mother was away for one night. Do you remember? They got Bermuda to do the flowers in the church.'

A recollection brushes by, and from my pocket I produce the folded piece of paper with the scribbled notes in pencil. I unfold it and turn it over. The blue heading says *Voice Security*. The V is emphasised. And inside the V is a little swirl of a treble clef.

Tilte and Basker and I exchange glances.

'She must have been doing some work for them,' Tilte ventures. 'For *Voice Security*. That must be it. She'll have been there as a security consultant.'

We know nothing about a company called *Voice Security*. But our hearts go out to them, whoever they are. They'll have wanted to make such a good impression. And yet they brought a wolf into the hen house. Or rather: an elephant.

We peruse the newspaper clippings again. And I can tell you they're given our rigorous attention.

The most recent is from last Monday, the day before Mother and Father disappeared. It concerns some sort of sneak preview of the exhibition whereby journalists and invited guests were allowed in to see the treasures. It's clearly an invitation they've taken seriously, because all of them are done up to the nines so you'd think it was the end-of-term dance for the pupils of Ifigenia Bruhn's Dancing School.

There's about a kilometre of exhibition cases, and gold and jewels glitter and sparkle behind the glass. It's hard to make out anything in detail, but one gets the clear impression that if only you could get your long fingers inside just a single one of those exhibition cases and secure a long-term agreement with your conscience, then all liquidity problems would be solved once and for all and your cashflow ensured for the next three or four centuries.

One of the photos is from the room where the seven days of footage was taken. The exhibition case now contains items on display, though it's impossible to see what's in it, only that it shines in a way that is at once intense and fluid, like a neon tube submerged in water. People are standing around it, their faces illuminated because of the light reflected from all the precious stones, and for that reason their features are unclear. But one face is darker than the rest. A dark, pensive face beneath a green turban.

'If we had a feather, you could knock me down with it,' says Tilte. 'That's Ashanti, from Blågårds Plads!'

And indeed it is, and behind her stand two men. Both are in suits and their faces are hidden, but not enough to disguise the two bodyguards with the BMW and the impressive sprinting abilities.

We sink back into the sofa. The pieces of the puzzle seem to be falling into place. Only the most important remains. Basker growls quietly.

'Basker wants to say something,' says Tilte. 'He wants to point out that a lot may certainly be said about Mother and Father. They have their weaknesses, their soft spots and their holes in the head. But they have also demonstrated cunning and guile. It would be unlike them to lay a plan that would put everything they own in jeopardy: their liberty, their children, their dog, their jobs, their good names and reputations. Only then to leave a big fat clue in a safe-deposit box they forget to pay for.

'And then go off like this,' I add, 'in a rush.'

We think about that for a while, all three of us. The room quivers.

'It was spur of the moment,' says Tilte.

'There was something they realised,' I say. 'Something they hadn't thought of.'

Now Tilte and I are playing together.

'It must have been something important,' says Tilte.

I repeat her words slowly, partly because Basker is a dog and on occasion rather slow-witted compared to us, and partly because it all sounds so odd it needs to be said again.

'Mother and Father plan a heist from the exhibition that's being put on alongside the Grand Synod. Everything's ready. And then they realise something. Whatever it is, it's something they realise only at the last minute. It means they have to leave right away. And it's so important they forget to cover their tracks, or else they couldn't care less.'

37

THERE ARE THOSE WHO MIGHT CONSIDER THAT AFTER ALL THE work Tilte and I have done this past hour we might deserve a break. We ourselves would, certainly. But there's nothing quite as dangerous as leaning back into a comfy chair after a gruelling first half, with a second half ahead that's going to be even tougher, because before you know it you're out of steam and there's nothing left in reserve, and Tilte and Basker and I know this only too well.

'There are two things we need to do,' says Tilte. 'We need to get Maria back in the coffin. And we need to speak to Rickardt.'

At that moment we rise from our chairs as though a miracle suddenly were happening in front of our eyes, the name of the miracle being bilocation, which is known in all religions and which means that certain highly developed individuals allegedly are able to manifest themselves out of thin air, thereby to impart the joy of their presence in two different places all at once. And the reason we rise up like this is that beside us we hear a voice that belongs to Svend Sewerman's wife, Bullimilla Madsen.

'Ladies and gentlemen,' she says. 'It is my pleasure to announce that dinner will now be served in the aftermost saloon.'

With all due respect for Bullimilla Madsen, she is by no means the first person one might suspect to be capable of bilocation, but it becomes immediately clear to us that her voice in this instance issues from a public address system of such quality you would think that she had put her lips to your ear.

Tilte and Basker and I are on our feet. Not only on account

of our stomachs being empty and our throats parched, but because the aftermost saloon is the one through which we passed earlier, at which time it was deserted, and in the cold store of its galley we have parked Maria from Maribo.

We're there in seconds, initially to heave a sigh of relief. We're the first, apart from Bullimilla herself and a waitress who stand ready to serve mountains of what looks like cold *smørrebrød*, which allows us the hope that the galley might be empty and that we'll be able to sneak in and bring Maria out. And sure enough, there's no one there, and no one has seen us either, because we peeped ever so cautiously from our hiding place behind the door, and now we're down on all fours, crawling under cover of tables and chairs, and round the back of the high serving counter that separates the galley from the saloon, and now we are out of sight.

What we envisage is a commando raid into the cold store to snatch Maria, then to await an unguarded moment for our getaway, and for Tilte and me this would be much like plucking ripe fruit in the gardens of Finø Town. But now a series of events occurs that makes us understand why Eckhart and the Zen patriarchs and the Vedic prophets and the Sufi sheikhs would seem to be in such complete agreement about one thing at least, that when asked to describe the world in one word, they all say: *unstable*.

The first thing that happens is that Count Rickardt Three Lions suddenly enters the saloon. He is carrying his archlute, and gives Bullimilla such a start that a suspicion of mine is confirmed, which is that she is the one responsible for trying to conceal the instrument from Rickardt, almost certainly for fear that he might begin to perform during dinner.

'Ladies,' says the Count, 'I have been encouraged into providing diners with some musical accompaniment. The piece is from *The Merry Widow*.'

Bullimilla's protest is surprisingly lame: 'We're having canapés. They're not suited to music.'

We hear the Count's spurs jingle across the floor. He considers the buffet.

'Little piles like that need to be digested with music,' he says.

At this point, Tilte pops her head out from our hiding place and beckons Rickardt towards us, putting a finger to her lips before ducking back behind the counter. The Count changes tack.

'Allow me to test the acoustics,' he says to Bullimilla.

And then he's round the other side of the counter to where we're hiding, and we drag him through the galley and out into the cold store and remove the bin liners from Maria.

'We need to put her back,' says Tilte. 'Before it's too late. Where's the coffin?'

Rickardt is not over the moon about seeing Maria again.

'In my cabin,' he says.

At this moment, the door of the cold store opens. We cover Maria up again and the three of us dive behind her wheelchair.

The person who now enters the cold store is arguably the person we least would have expected: Alexander Flounderblood. He stands motionless for a moment to allow his eyes to adjust to the dim light. Then he comes straight towards the wheelchair.

He stops half a metre away. Had he taken one more step, he would have seen us, and a situation would then have ensued from which we would have had more than a little difficulty extricating ourselves.

But he doesn't notice. All his attention is focused on a shelf containing a number of what look like, and indeed probably are, vacuum-packed sheep's brains, most likely of the highly praised Finø breed, and next to them stand two bottles of champagne. Flounderblood picks these up and investigates their touch. Then, less than satisfied, he puts them back, turns and is gone.

We heave a sigh of relief, and when you heave a sigh of relief in a cold store your breath is white steam in the air. We open the door, and the galley is empty. The Count wheels Maria out while Tilte and Basker and I lie prone at the corner of the counter, peeping to see if the coast is clear.

Unfortunately it isn't. The table closest to the kitchen is now occupied by Vera the Secretary, Professor Thorkild Thorlacius and his wife, and Anaflabia Borderrud, and this intense little group has been joined by Alexander Flounderblood and our two officers of the Police Intelligence Service, Lars and Katinka.

Tilte and I have no need to resort to verbal communication, because we each know what the other is thinking. What does the ministerial envoy to Finø have to do with Anaflabia and Thorkild?

The answer soon transpires.

'Five minutes more,' says Alexander Flounderblood with proud authority. 'Champagne must never be served above ten degrees Celsius. Certainly not on an occasion such as the present. And here comes our delightful hostess with the crystal!'

Bullimilla places the glasses on the table. When she has gone, Anaflabia leans forward. She speaks softly, which means that every word would be audible from the foredeck.

'I've just received an email. From Bodil Fisker, municipal director of Grenå Kommune. They've received the Professor's appraisal of the situation following our inspection of the rectory and interviews with the children. The verdict would seem to be *severe endogenous depression*. The local authority is backing us completely. Tomorrow, the Ministry of Church Affairs and the parish council will be issuing a joint statement to the effect that Konstantin Finø has been released from all clerical duties and Clara Finø likewise from her services as organist. The statement will not include mention of their psychological habitus. However, we shall let it be known to selected members of the press that expert opinion initially indicates that both are suffering from severe depression. Bodil has ensured us that the social services will remove the children from the home, and that they are to be separated as soon as they are found. We on our side have voiced concern that the girl in particular exerts a bad influence upon her younger brother. He will be placed in the children's home at Grenå, she to begin with in a youth detention centre on the island of Læsø. The press will not be informed of their intended whereabouts. This means that regardless of what the parents are up to we shall be able to put a lid on the matter, or at the very least say that whatever crimes have been committed were done by persons no longer in the service of the Church and from which we can only distance ourselves. Alexander Flounderblood has provided us with the entire inventory of the children's misdemeanours during the past two years, which in itself cries out for intervention from the authorities, and from which it furthermore transpires that the boy suffers from water on the brain. So, dear friends: an extremely prickly situation would seem to be resolved. To be frank, we are well deserving of champagne!'

38

AT THIS POINT, BEFORE CONTINUING MY REPORT OF EVENTS, I must clear myself of any suspicion and explain that bit about water on the brain.

It all takes place two years ago while Mother and Father are away on the second of their three tours leading to their remand in custody and the ecclesiastical court, and at that time Conny and I have known each other since we were little, just like everyone else who goes to Finø Town School. But since that time in the barrel, which was six years earlier, and which in a way was a shock to me, even if I was asking for it myself, since then there has never been any real contact, and I'll be quite frank and say that the way I feel about her, even at a distance, there's no way I would ever be able to gather courage enough to initiate any again.

I don't know if you have friends who are always messing about with their hair, but Conny does that. Let her out of sight for ten minutes and she's changed her hairstyle, and it means that her neck, when you're sitting behind her in class, always shows itself in new and surprising ways.

In this particular situation I am about to relate, Alexander Flounderblood has just begun in the capacity of headmaster and has taken on a small number of lessons himself so as to gain evidence of our miserable academic state, and at this moment he's giving us a History lesson, sketching out some memorable details of Hannibal's journey across the Alps when my attention falls on Conny's neck, which today presents itself in hitherto unseen perspective. Her hair has a hint of red, perhaps like the first blush of morning in the chestnut trees when you've been out collecting gulls' eggs and are on your way home to the rectory at four in the morning, if you understand what I mean. Below her hair is an area of fine down that gradually becomes more golden until eventually it wanes away, and from there her skin is white, but deeply so, like mother of pearl in the voluminous oyster shells found by the Northern Lighthouse, as though one might almost see through it. With my study this far comes the thought of the aroma that might be found in that place, and what it would feel like if one were to come close enough to touch it, and at that moment Hannibal's journey across the Alps has slipped rather unnoticeably into the background, and suddenly Alexander Flounderblood is standing in front of me exuding military anger of the kind one might easily imagine Hannibal to have plagued his surroundings with.

Flounderblood takes hold of my arm, and one has to give him his due and say that his grip is like a vice.

'Get out and stand in the corridor,' he says, 'and remain there until the lesson is over. Afterwards, you and I will pay a visit to Boleslaw and have a little chat about your stance on the pursuit of academic knowledge.'

Boleslaw Daddyboy is deputy head of Finø Town School and Alexander has brought him with him from the mainland. Rumour has it that he gave up a promising career in the army in order to purge Finø Town School of unwanted elements. Meeting him is never a pleasant experience, but having to do so in the company of Alexander Flounderblood is a serious turn for the worse.

At this point, something wells inside me. My own view is that it's because of my spiritual training, because at this time Tilte has long since discovered the door and we have embarked upon what in the field of mysticism is referred to as a deeper process. What happens is that I sense myself rise up to the full height of my twelve-year-old frame and look straight into Alexander's eyes, which at this moment look like the mouths of the cannon on the Frigate Jutland, which lies permanently docked in Ebeltoft harbour and is the destination of Finø Town School's annual trip every year on the first Sunday of September.

'I would gladly,' I then hear myself say, 'exchange all academic knowledge in the world but for a glimpse of Conny's neck!'

An indeterminate span of the aforementioned silence of the grave now descends.

And then Alexander Flounderblood picks me up and carries me out of the classroom, thereby demonstrating that he is in possession of more raw muscle than his slim and well-groomed exterior might otherwise suggest, and on our way down the corridor to Boleslaw Daddyboy's office I find solace in their evident need to manage my execution in tandem.

But then Alexander comes to a halt, and he does so because Tilte has blocked his way.

'Alexander,' she says, 'I should like to exchange a few words with you in private.'

By now it'll be as apparent to you as it is to me that Tilte could bring a hurtling goods train to a halt if that was what she wanted, so of course Alexander Flounderblood stops in his tracks as though frozen by a death ray from some alien, and then he lets go of me and follows Tilte into the book depository with an empty and rather glazed look in his eyes.

Tilte closes the door behind them, and on the other side they exchange words that would forever be sealed for posterity by their discretion and professional confidentiality had it not been for my accidentally putting my ear to the keyhole and thereby overhearing their brief conversation.

'Alexander,' Tilte says, 'I don't know if you realise that my younger brother, Peter, suffers from minor cerebral damage on account of his having water on the brain, the regrettable result of an accident at birth.'

Alexander says he had no idea, and he speaks in the lacklustre, rather mechanical way of many men who find themselves in a one-on-one with my sister Tilte.

'That's the first reason,' she continues, 'for my now suggesting that you refrain from taking him with you to the office. The second, and most important reason, is that your so doing would serve only to tarnish your own teaching practice, which in every other way is known to spellbind the pupils of this school.'

Alexander makes an attempt at a counterattack, stammering something along the lines of me still polluting the learning environment. But Tilte thwarts his effort even before he reaches midfield.

'Peter will soon undergo surgery,' she says. 'A tap will be inserted so that the fluid may be drained each morning before he goes to school.'

This information is apparently sufficient for Alexander to back down. I dart away from the door just before he appears and looks at me with something resembling compassion, and I realise immediately that his encounter here with Tilte has been profound, even if he hasn't been put in her famous coffin. We return to the classroom, and everyone stares at me as if I were a zombie that quite plainly is animate, but cannot possibly be alive.

Further into the lesson, I manage to heave my gaze from the floor and venture to cast my eye on Conny. She is enshrouded in a haze of pensive thought.

And the next afternoon, Conny sends Sonja to ask if I want to be her boyfriend.

You need to know all this in order to understand what happens in the saloon of the *White Lady of Finø*. It should now be clear why Alexander Flounderblood thinks I have water on the brain and that Tilte's deed was indeed heroic. At the same time, it's an example of how karma actually works, because what started life as a little white lie now returns to slam us in the back of the neck.

Peeping under the counter from our hiding place, we can see Lars and Katinka holding hands underneath the table.

'We accompanied the children from Copenhagen,' says Katinka. 'They didn't seem like obvious criminals to me.'

The air freezes around her.

'I've been observing them for two years,' says Alexander

Flounderblood presently. 'Not to mention their dog, which attempted, not once, but on several occasions, to mate with Baroness, my Afghan hound. And not in the manner of any normal dog. This inclined more towards rape.'

Though Lars and Katinka have their backs to Tilte and me, we nonetheless sense their mild surprise.

'I quite agree,' says Thorkild. 'In my professional capacity of physician and psychiatrist. One only has to consider the manner in which the boy pretended he was a reptile. I suspect they may even be on board this ship. As representatives of a religious sect.'

Lars' and Katinka's surprise increases, Tilte and I both sense it, and their confidence in Alexander and Thorkild seems at once to be waning.

Now Alexander Flounderblood rises.

'Champagne!' he announces. 'And as soon as the children are taken into care, I shall personally destroy the hound.'

It's probably meant as a joke, but Lars and Katinka don't appear to get it. Their gaze follows Alexander as he goes off to fetch the champagne.

We give Rickardt a sign. He backs out into the cold store and lets the door close behind him. Tilte and I duck behind the piles of napkins and tablecloths.

A moment passes and Alexander emerges. He has the champagne in his hands. But now his face is the same colour as the vacuum-packed sheep's brains.

He walks round the counter and up to the table, where he remains standing.

'There's a carcass in the cold store,' he says.

His voice is loud and firm. The hymnmakers would call it sepulchral.

Bullimilla has heard, and now she approaches the table with a look that makes you relieved for Alexander Flounderblood's sake that she hasn't got one of those big meat cleavers in her hand.

'I should hope so, too,' she says. 'There's over three tons of the finest organic meat in there.'

'Human meat,' says Alexander.

214

The rather peculiar silence of before now builds. Tilte and I sense Katinka and Lars thinking that Alexander perhaps might not be the kind of person who ought to be walking around freely. And Bullimilla glares at him as though considering whether human meat in the cold store might not be a good idea for the future, starting with Alexander Flounderblood.

'It may be the woman from the carriage,' says Thorkild all of a sudden. 'An elderly woman was sitting beside me. She was at death's door. Professional viewpoint.'

'And then,' Katinka says in a kind voice, 'she went into the cold store to lie down and expire?'

'To *sit* down, actually,' says Alexander. 'The woman is seated in a wheelchair.'

Katinka rises slowly.

'Let's go and have a look, shall we?' she says.

She nods at Alexander.

'You, me and our hostess.'

At once, Tilte and I pounce to the door of the cold store like a pair of cats. And before the others are even on their feet, we've waved the Count and Maria out, wheeled the chair behind the table with all the napkins on it, pulled a tablecloth over the two of them and ducked back into hiding again.

Alexander, Katinka and Bullimilla enter the cold store. The door closes behind them. A minute passes. The door opens and they emerge. Now Alexander resembles the meat that's hanging from the hooks and waiting to be made into meals. They return to the table without so much as a glance in our direction.

'It was a mistake,' says Katinka. 'Perhaps Mr Flounderblood was hallucinating.'

The mood for champagne has passed. The bottles and crystal glasses stand untouched and abandoned. The party breaks up. Only Katinka and Lars remain seated.

People have begun to enter the saloon. But Lars and Katinka pay them no heed. It's obvious they're shaken. Lars opens a bottle and pours two glasses of champagne.

'We should have listened to that policeman on the island,' he says. 'The one with the dog that looks like a rug. This lot shouldn't have been let out again. Not even the Bishop. This is a job for forensic psychiatry, not us.'

'He's a brain specialist,' says Katinka. 'The bald one with the killer look in his eyes.'

They sigh.

'We could apply to the fraud squad instead,' says Lars. 'It'd be cushy. Cardboard boxes full of documents, instead of these lunatics. People who deceive others are often quite charming. But those who deceive themselves . . .'

They stare into each other's eyes and raise their glasses.

'The children,' says Lars. 'You'd hardly wish they were your own kids, but they're not exactly criminals, are they? In a way, you could say they brought us together. Is the phone tap still not turning anything up?'

If like Tilte and I you happen to have delved deep into religious mysteries in the course of your studies on the Internet and at the Finø Town Library, you may be aware that a majority of the true greats, and allow me merely to name Jesus, Muhammad and Buddha, have stated that one has no need to change one's personality at all, and that a person can easily attain the highest levels of insight even when equipped with a temper as fiery as Einar Flogginfellow's.

This is an aspect of mysticism I personally appreciate. For although many members of Finø FC believe that the Pastor's Peter has come on a ton with his personality, some pockets of what could be termed rage do still linger, and this is what now flares up behind the stacks of cloth napkins when I hear that the Police Intelligence Service has tapped our phones.

At this moment, my gaze falls upon Katinka's handbag, a slim, elegant thing of shiny black leather deposited at her feet. Many women would have preferred to hang it over the back of the chair. But Katinka is a detective constable attached to police intelligence, so hers is under the table where it cannot be seen unless one happens to have concealed oneself at floor level, and where she is able to maintain contact with it by means of her foot, thereby to ensure that none of its contents are stolen.

Under normal circumstances it would be rather difficult to get one's hands on that bag. But at this moment I am positioned favourably, less than an arm's length away from it. And Katinka is absorbed by Lars' presence. She has removed her foot from the bag in order to wrap her leg around Lars' under cover of the tablecloth.

So I reach out, open the bag and investigate its contents with my hand. I find keys, something that could be a notebook or a diary, and in a separate pocket what must be cosmetics, a mirror, a nail file. And then my fingers encounter something cold, a rather pleasant grip surface, only then I feel the hair rise on the nape of my neck, because it is most surely the butt of a pistol. I move on and discover two mobile phones, a hairbrush and a flat piece of plastic.

Katinka's foot is returning. I go for one of the phones. Admittedly, it's all very Old Testament: a phone for a phone. But the thing is we are no better than we are, and as the great spiritual figures have pointed out, there's no reason for any of us to change.

Tilte gives a sign to say we can wait no longer. Two romantic police officers can dwell over two bottles of champagne for a very long time indeed, and the saloon is filling up. We pull three black tablecloths over Maria, snatch a handful of canapés that we wrap up in a napkin, wait until Bullimilla is distracted at the other end of the room, and then push the covered wheelchair away through the restaurant.

We are followed by the enquiring gaze of Lars and Katinka, and so penetrating is that gaze that it may even have been capable of revealing Maria underneath her tablecloths. But to Tilte's surprise and mine, Rickardt smooths out the wrinkles.

'I'm going to be singing,' he explains to the officers. 'An accompaniment to dinner. This is my little portable stage.'

We're across the room and at the exit when a person steps into the saloon and must give way to our little procession, and that person turns out to be Jakob Aquinas Bordurio Madsen. He says nothing. But to give you a sense of what might be happening inside him at this moment, a crisp clatter of beads is heard as he drops his rosary on the floor.

The last thing I hear as we edge the wheelchair out into the corridor is a loud whisper from Katinka.

'Lars,' she says, 'we could try a different profession altogether. Gardening, perhaps.'

We're out and away before I can hear his reply.

39

WHEN IT COMES TO CERTAIN ISSUES, TILTE AND I HAVE BEEN prompted to say to the major world religions that we encounter difficulty providing our support, and one such issue is the question of whether justice exists.

We rush back to Rickardt's cabin, and as we turn the corner of the corridor his door opens from inside and out come Lama Svend-Holger, Polly Pigonia and Sinbad Al-Blablab.

Obviously, it should please anyone to see Polly and Sinbad and Svend-Holger ambling together through life, shoulder to shoulder in the manner of best friends, indicating that the good mood Tilte and I established during our drive in Bermuda's hearse prevails and that there is every reason to hope that the personal goodwill we have worked hard to attain still holds. However, the fate of such goodwill is in question, because in a moment they're going to discover us to be little more than body snatchers.

Count Rickardt is stricken by fearful paralysis, and one senses that Tilte has yet to fully recover from her latest chance encounter with Jakob Bordurio. So all responsibility now rests upon my shoulders, and this is where one might come to doubt the notion of cosmic justice, because we have entered choppy waters and the wind is beginning to howl.

One of the secrets of playing on the wing is to lurk on the edge of offside like a cat reclining in the sun, and then be away after a quick, deep pass almost before the ball has left the grass, and this is exactly what happens now. Before Svend-Holger and Polly and Sinbad close the door behind them and discover our presence,

I pull Tilte and Rickardt and Maria back round the corner and tumble through the nearest door.

It's important when relating such ill-starred events as these not to awaken suspicion of wishing merely to entertain, and it is for this reason I have taken every opportunity to refer to the research Tilte and I have conducted in the source texts of high mysticism. Now, such opportunity arises again. The room in which we stand is pitch dark, and to begin with I can't find the light switch. It is a situation that cannot fail to remind me of the fact that a majority of spiritual heavyweights whose lifetimes have spanned the invention of electric light have said that truly escaping the prison feels like having a personal light switch installed. Whereas before one fumbled around in the dark, one can now turn on the light and have a whale of a time.

I have been frank about the fact that Tilte and I have yet to arrive at that place. Nevertheless, we feel we are on our way, and this is confirmed to us now as I find the switch and turn on the light, because after that everything is suddenly so much clearer in so many different ways.

We are standing in the gynaecological clinic, which as I have mentioned was formerly an appurtenance of the harem belonging to the *White Lady*'s previous owner. Before us are two couches of the kind seen in doctors' surgeries. There are stainless-steel tables with sinks, the walls are white-tiled, and on the ceiling is a large surgical lamp. In glass-fronted cupboards, shiny instruments are secured with black elastic straps so as to remain in place on the seas, and on a hanger is a white coat.

The Count and Tilte are still not quite in the game, and outside the door I hear footsteps approach. A person more certain of heavenly justice would perhaps remain standing and take in the atmosphere, but not I. I pull the white doctor's coat from the hanger, noting with relief that it's one of those that opens at the back. I put Maria in it, throwing her hat into a pedal bin and pushing her hair up under a little white cap that was also on the hanger. Then I snatch a surgical mask from a box and place it over Maria's mouth. The finishing touch is the stethoscope I hang around her neck.

The overall result is not bad at all, though of course you wouldn't be interested in Maria wielding the knife during your scrotal hernia surgery, but at a glance she can pass.

And a glance is in fact just what she receives, because now there's a knock at the door. It opens, and Svend-Holger, Polly and Sinbad enter.

All three are intelligent individuals with deep personalities. Nonetheless, one can quite understand their surprise. It's clear that none of them have met Count Rickardt Three Lions before, and the sight alone of his silver lamé dinner jacket and cummerbund could prompt anyone to doubt their own soundness of mind and powers of judgement. Moreover, it is clear that none of them recognises Tilte and me in our disguises, although it seems equally obvious that they have the strange feeling of having seen us before.

In this precarious situation, it seems only reasonable that they should now address the natural authority among those present.

'Doctor,' says Polly to Maria, 'I don't suppose you would know who has the cabin around the corner?'

Now Count Rickardt awakens.

'It's mine,' he says.

Polly and Svend-Holger and Sinbad stare blankly at the Count. Questions dance on the tips of their tongues. Polly asks the most obvious one.

'What's the coffin doing there?'

Tilte has been catching her breath on the substitutes' bench, and now she returns to the field.

'On the advice of the ship's doctor, Rickardt here has been playing *ragas* for the deceased. To provide her with solace in her post-mortal state.'

'Doctor,' Polly then says, 'we are most grateful for your care, and I should like to take this opportunity to discuss with you the issue of life after death.'

Tilte straightens her shoulders. She opens the door into the corridor.

'The doctor is collecting herself to perform difficult surgery,' she says.

Difficult surgery clears the deck. Sinbad and Sven-Holger turn and leave. Polly, however, is reluctant.

'This, I assure you, is a unique opportunity to continue the dialogue between spirituality and the natural sciences. You are an unprejudiced person, Doctor. By no means uncritical, but driven by an open mind. I sense it so clearly.'

Tilte bundles Polly through the door.

'Later, perhaps,' she says. 'The doctor won't be going anywhere. And she's always one for a good natter.'

40

TILTE, BASKER AND I HAVE COLLAPSED ON THE HEART-SHAPED harem bed in our cabin. We've agreed that we're too tired to manhandle Maria back into place tonight and that Rickardt will sing for her in the clinic instead. We've said goodnight to Rickardt and polished off the canapés, and to say we're tired is hardly the word, because the truth is we're near-fatally exhausted and ready for the last rites.

But thought persists. That's the problem. All research, mine and Tilte's included, reveals that the great mystics have pointed out that we are each of us thought factories whose machinery never idles, and in all the noise you can never hear whether silence might contain even the bare beginnings of an answer to weightier questions such as why we are here in the world and why we must leave it again, and why someone is now knocking on our door.

The door opens and in walks Count Rickardt Three Lions with his archlute.

'I don't like it on my own,' he says. 'It's as though she's watching me. A message came in from my inner advisory level and told me I should sleep with you.'

Basker is lying flat out between Tilte and me. We would never dream of having animals in our bed, but Basker's not an animal, he's a sort of person, and now we shove him aside to make room for the Count.

'I was doing my best,' Rickardt says. 'A pot-pourri of Milarepa, Byzantine highlights from Mount Athos and Ramana Maharshi's odes to Arunachala, but she just wasn't swinging.'

At that moment, Rickardt notices the newspaper clipping with the photo of the circular exhibition case and Ashanti and the two bodyguards.

'That's where I'm to sing,' he says. 'In the old chapel of the castle. The acoustics are magnificent.'

Tilte and I don't sit up. But we do fall very silent indeed.

'It's one of Filthøj's most stylish rooms,' Rickardt says. 'A most beautiful setting for the Grand Synod.'

A moment passes during which we are mute. Tilte is the first to regain the power of speech.

'Rickardt,' she says, 'what's under the floor in that room?'

'Historical casemates,' says Rickardt. 'And the ancient sewers, later rebuilt as vaults. Very atmospheric. The Earl of Bluffwell is buried there. He was on a visit to Denmark sometime in the eighteenth century when he died of alcohol poisoning. It's a magnificent space. We used to dry our pot down there when I was a boy. Not to mention playing doctor with the little sons and daughters of the kitchen staff. The chambers are well ventilated, the humidity keeps stable and the temperature's actually rather pleasant.'

'Rickardt,' says Tilte, 'did you tell Mother about these vaults?'

'I showed her them. They were looking for a safe place to put all the treasures in case of burglary or fire. So I said to her, we've got just the place you need. And the openings are there in the floor already, where there used to be stairs. I even told her how they could do it. Your mother was very impressed by how clever I could be. It reminded me of when I was a boy and my own mother used to say: "Rickardt, it won't be easy for you to find a place in the world big enough for that brain of yours."'

'When did you actually show the vaults to Mother?' I ask.

'We were over there together. On three occasions. Such a pleasure it was, too, to travel with your mother. A very attractive woman, if you don't mind me saying. If I hadn't chosen you two first, there's no telling what might have happened. Then again, perhaps it needn't be a hindrance at all. Just imagine, mother and daughter and two sons in one go. What a kinky little harem that would be! Just the ticket for a ravenous sexuality such as mine. And ships do encourage that sort of thing, don't they?'

'Rickardt,' says Tilte. 'Is there a way out of the vaults?'

Rickardt lowers his voice and winks.

'Don't tell anyone now, will you, my little fancies. Officially, there's no way out. But we discovered the tunnel when we were children. It leads due east. A secret passage, if you like. Actually just an old sewer, bricked up but with a concealed door. Probably dating back to the Dano-Swedish Wars. We used it when our parents kept us in and we wanted to go dancing at Vedbæk Marina. It comes out at the shore, you see, inside the castle's boathouse, right on the Sound. We kept a little rubber dinghy there with a great big outboard motor, and glad rags in water-proof bags. We'd be through the tunnel in no time on our skate-boards, with lamps on our heads like miners. It slopes away, you see. But all this is strictly confidential, of course. It leads straight to the underground security box now. Not that I suppose it would matter if anyone got that far. It's all reinforced steel and armoured concrete. The box, that is. Burglarproof. Fireproof. The works. And two tons in weight. They had to winch it in from the courtyard with a crane.'

'Rickardt,' I say, 'did you by any chance happen to show Mother this tunnel?'

Rickardt's expression becomes pensive.

'I may have done. It's a very romantic place, the tunnel. Tiles on the floor. A whirl of astral activity all around. Wonderful place to smoke a joint. I may have fantasised a little about stealing a kiss. It's not often one gets the chance to be alone with your mother. Don't tell anyone, though. Anyway, she turned me down, didn't she? Not that I've given up on that account. Some women need to be besieged.'

Rickardt makes himself comfy.

'I shall have a sleepless night, I fear,' he says. 'In bed with three delicious plums.'

It's an utterance one can only take as a compliment, though it can hardly be sincere, because a moment later Rickardt is sound asleep with his arms around his lute.

We lie awake in the dark. Despite our exhaustion, there's something that won't go away.

'Petrus,' says Tilte, 'would you say Mother and Father were robbers by nature?'

'No,' I reply.

'Would you say they were obsessed by money?'

I have to think a moment about that one, because it's a question any child would prefer to answer in the negative. They were delirious, of course, when they came home with the Maserati and the mink coat, back when the riches flowed. But if you put their joy under a microscope it seemed mostly to be about my father being able to give my classmates a ride and touch 260 kilometres an hour, or maybe even 280, on the straight out to the landing strip. And in Mother's case it was as if as a child she'd seen films with naked ladies parading about in mink coats in front of roaring fires in manor houses, and now she wanted to see what it felt like herself.

'The Maserati,' I say. 'And the mink. I think they were mostly about giving others some kind of religious experience. That's what they live for. The money was just a means, though rather unfortunate.'

'So, Petrus, if Mother and Father are not naturally jewel thieves and are by no means avaricious, are we then to believe that they would sacrifice their work, their home, their children and their reasonable names and reputations to enter a life of crime, wanted by Interpol in fifty countries, and all for a couple of aquariums full of shiny stones they'd probably never be able to sell on anyway?'

We look at each other. Until now, we've been so caught up in events that we've been unable to see things from above. But now we're beginning to do just that.

'And yet they've planned a robbery,' says Tilte. 'So they must have been intending something else than to do a runner with the swag.'

Our fatigue is gone. My hair rises.

'The Lost Property Act,' I say. 'There must be something in it about rewards.'

We both sit up.

'They could make it look like someone else had stolen the stuff,' Tilte says. 'And then give it back. And cash in the reward.'

'They wouldn't even have to open the box,' I say. 'All they'd need to do was make it disappear.'

'But it weighs two tons,' says Tilte.

'Mother will have worked something out,' I say.

'They'd get ten per cent,' says Tilte. 'Rewards are usually ten per cent. The crucifixes alone are valued at one billion. Ten per cent of that's a hundred million. I think they could make do with that.'

We lie down again. It's rumoured that the great mystics no longer sleep once they've attained a certain level. Their eyes may be shut, but they register everything.

It's not a claim I personally have ever been able to verify, but if I should get the chance, if some great mystic should ever settle on Finø, for example, then I should certainly want to investigate the matter further before believing – for instance, by sneaking in at night and quietly removing the false teeth from the glass on the bedside table and waiting to see if the saintly individual in question could identify me as the perpetrator the next morning.

Until that happens, I shall consider it merely to be a nice story and a sign that Tilte and I have yet to become fully enlightened, because when we sleep we sleep so heavily that whoever is standing outside hammering on the door of our cabin has most likely been standing there for some time before we realise what's going on and open up to see who it is.

It's Leonora Ticklepalate. In her nightdress, with her laptop under her arm and her eyes wide open.

'Part of the file's been deleted,' she says.

At first, we have no idea what she's talking about. It always takes a few minutes for Tilte and me to reach full intellectual capacity when woken after midnight.

Leonora puts the computer down in front of us and opens one of the files. From within our mental haze we identify what we now know to be the old chapel of Filthøj Castle. The time in the corner says it's seven in the morning, and there's not a soul in sight. The image brightens as daylight comes, workers enter and leave. Evening falls, then night, and in the corner time races away. Leonora slows the film. Now the seconds pass tardily, the time is 02.50 in the morning, 02.58, 02.59 – and then a sudden leap forward to 04.00.

'There's an hour missing,' says Leonora.

'A power cut?' Tilte suggests.

'Power cuts don't happen on the stroke of the hour,' I say. 'And alarm systems always have back-ups.'

We look at each other.

'They've deleted an hour,' says Leonora. 'Your parents have deleted an hour.'

'Leonora,' says Tilte, 'didn't you once say that in principle anything that's ever been deleted from a computer can be retrieved?'

'In principle,' says Leonora. 'But not at half past twelve at night. And besides, I've got the jitters about this. Knowing your parents like I do. They're nice people, but risky. Nothing personal. I'm just worried about what they might be up to. And it's not nice to lie in bed on your own, tossing and turning and wondering what's going to happen. I was thinking I might sleep with you?'

In this overpopulated bed, I fold my hands together. Tonight, my prayers are all about being spared further visitors in need of nocturnal comfort.

THE CITY OF GODS

41

'COPENHAGEN IS A GLOBAL SPIRITUAL CENTRE,' SAYS COUNT
Rickardt Three Lions. 'She's the City of Gods, and I can smell it.'

The *White Lady* is on her way into the Port of Copenhagen.
We are standing on the foredeck with the Count and a handful
of other passengers who've managed to haul themselves out of
bed and through the after-effects of the buffet at Finøholm and
Bullimilla's canapés and champagne.

It's a crisp, clear morning, the sun is shining, the sky and the
water are blue, and all of it is dotted with white seagulls.

'It all begins up north,' says the Count. 'With the wellness
centres of northern Sjælland, macrobiotics, yoga, Dr Bach's flower
remedies and Balinese massage. Towards the city, it picks up speed
with the centres of Tibetan Buddhism, the Sufi Academy and the
private Catholic schools at Hellerup. The Swedenborg Institute
and the Martinus Institute, and the theosophists of Frederiksberg.
The centre is a vibrant, ecstatic thrum: Copenhagen Cathedral,
the Faculty of Theology, the Catholic Church in Bredgade, the
Russian Orthodox Church, the yoga schools of the old city, the
mosques, the synagogues. In the southern districts, it all veers off
into occultism: the Occult School of Christiania, the Satanic
Consortium on Amager Strandvej, the astrological institutes on
Gammel Køge Landevej. And then the majestic finale with
Asa-Thor and the great sacrificial site of Amager Fælled.'

The Count snatches his breath.

'I can smell it. The incense. The aroma of *sattvic* cuisine. The
unleavened bread. The halal butchers of Nansensgade. The votive

candles for the Virgin Mary. The sacrificial smoke rising from the fields of Kløvermarken. And I hear it, too. The sound of colonic irrigation, the glugging of the neti pots. The church mode, and the bells. The prayers delivered to Mecca. I've even composed a song about it.'

We've already taken cover when the archlute appears above the railing.

The morning has otherwise been pleasant. We've slept like logs and have woken early, refreshed and feeling almost new. We've showered, and this has been nothing at all like at home in the rectory, where time and again one must pause to wonder whether heredity or environment is to blame for female showering never taking less than an hour and always emptying the hot-water tank, because the *White Lady* has endless amounts of hot water, and our cabin has two shower rooms, one for Tilte and one for Basker and me, as well as stacks of white towels, and two hairdryers, both of which I use at once on Basker, who seems to have resolved the great theological issue of where Paradise is to be found, if it exists at all. In Basker's opinion Paradise is right there, positioned between two hairdryers turned up on full.

After showering we put on our ceremonial robes and trip along to the clinic to wish Maria good morning. She's still nice and cold. We wheel her along to Rickardt's cabin and get her back into her coffin, and once the lid's been secured we heave a sigh of relief and make our way to the ship's restaurant.

Many of the great religions take the view that if only one leans back in one's seat everything will be all right. This is a school of thought for which Tilte and I share a large measure of sympathy, and on this particular morning a great many things indeed seem to fall into place on their own. On our way to the restaurant Tilte checks her text messages and is able to announce that one of her acquantainces is letting us borrow her flat so we won't have to sleep in cardboard boxes on the city streets, and when we enter the restaurant we find ourselves standing before a breakfast buffet of the kind that makes you wish you were wearing a hat in order that you might kneel down and remove it.

Indeed, it is because of this breakfast that our attention fails. As we lift our gaze from the fruit salad and the butter croissants and the crisp pancakes with maple syrup and whipped cream, and the coffee whose aroma is like the spice markets of all Arabia and for that reason may have been left behind by the *White Lady*'s previous owner, we notice that the restaurant has quietly filled up and that in front of us is the nape of Anaflabia Borderrud's neck.

Not that there's anything wrong with Anaflabia's neck. On the contrary, both it and her hair, which is swept up, would be an encouraging sight indeed, though in contrast to Conny's not one for which I would be prepared to risk my life. The problem is that next to Anaflabia sits Vera, and next to Vera sits Thorkild's wife, and next to her Thorkild himself, and at the very moment I happen to look up our eyes meet and his gaze is fixed directly upon us, and not only that but Tilte has lifted her veil to shovel pancakes into her mouth unencumbered.

'Ah ha,' says Thorkild. And then rather louder: 'Ah ha!'

Had he been allowed a third *Ah ha*, I'm sure he would have attracted the attention of those around us. But at that moment something unexpected occurs.

Alexander Flounderblood comes staggering across the room like a drunk, knocking over chairs and overturning tables and finally slumping down next to Thorkild.

'A crime has been committed,' he announces.

Alexander Flounderblood is a person capable at any time of commanding the full attention of others. In addition to this natural gift comes the fact that on this occasion his eyes are as wide as plates, his hair is sticking up as though he just removed his fingers from an electric socket, and he has Baroness with him, and Baroness's coat is sticking up too, making her look like a porcupine.

233

So now he has the full attention of the entire saloon, including Lars and Katinka, because the two detective constables of the Police Intelligence Service are seated at the adjoining table.

'Early this morning I visited the clinic,' he says. 'For treatment.'

Katinka takes time to swallow the last of a cinnamon whirl.

'Sounds like a good idea to me,' she says.

To Tilte and I it seems obvious that regardless of their having fallen in love with each other, and despite the coffee and the cinnamon whirls, Katinka and Lars are rapidly tiring of the company on board, and perhaps especially of Alexander Flounderblood.

'It was five o'clock,' Alexander says. 'I awoke in peristaltic distress. Stomach cramps. My first thought is: The canapés! My second is to waken you, Professor! But I've no idea which cabin is yours.'

At this point it would seem that Thorkild's relief at not having been woken at five in the morning to attend to Alexander Flounderblood's digestion has caused him to forget all about Tilte and me, if only for a moment.

'So there I am staggering down the corridor. And then all of a sudden, I find myself outside the ship's hospital and literally fall through the door. Imagine my relief to see the female physician in front of me. I explain to her my predicament and ask to be examined. I remove my trousers and lie down on the couch. She seems oddly unconcerned by my pain. I fall down before her and reach for her hand. Only to discover that the woman is as cold as ice. I feel for her pulse and there is none. She's dead!'

Bullimilla has now approached and is standing behind Alexander, and one can tell that the insinuation that her canapés may have been the cause of a bad turn has given rise to disapproval.

'The woman from the carriage,' says Thorkild. 'She must be the ship's doctor. I warned her. "You are dying, Madam", is what I told her.'

But Alexander Flounderblood hasn't finished yet.

'I stumble through the ship. Racked with pain. Meeting not a living soul until finding a man on the bridge. An officer of the ship. He refuses to believe a word, but I persuade him to come back with me to the clinic. We open the door. The room is empty. The corpse is gone.'

Tilte and I exchange glances. Our timing was apparently such that Flounderblood was away when we collected Maria and reinstalled her in her coffin. It's the kind of coincidence that can make a person reconsider the concept of cosmic justice.

'I demand an investigation. People are making me out to be a fool. Casting aspersions concerning alcohol consumption. So now I have come here. To report a death. Perhaps even a crime. The body has been removed.'

The *White Lady* rocks slightly. We have now docked at the Langelinie quayside. A rumbling vibration from the hull indicates that the gangway is being positioned.

Katinka rises slowly to her feet.

'If I may sum up,' she says. 'The ship's doctor, who is dying, is driven by horse-drawn carriage to the ship. Once on board, she retires to the restaurant cold store for a little rest. I'm sure we all recall looking for her there last night. From the cold store she at some point removes to the ship's clinic, there to carry out her duties as ship's doctor. Only she dies instead, and is subsequently whisked away some time early this morning.'

'Indeed,' says Thorkild. 'Such must be the chain of events.'

'There's just the minor detail of where the body is,' Katinka adds.

'Indeed,' says Thorkild. 'The only uncertainty.'

From my position opposite him I sense that Thorkild is impressed by Katinka's ability to draw together the facts, though rather less aware of the sarcasm that oozes from her recapitulation.

'Yesterday,' Katinka goes on, 'when Lars and I released you from custody, a decision we now realise to have been a severe mistake, you, sir,' – and at this juncture she indicates Thorkild – 'presented yourself as a neural scientist. I suggest now that you and your companions remove yourselves from Langelinie to a place where you all can have your brains examined. What's more, I think you should take that gentleman with the sticky-up hair with you.'

This she says with a nod in the direction of Alexander Flounderblood.

And with that she removes her gaze from Thorkild.

One should always be careful about removing one's gaze from Thorkild. Recent events have opened Tilte's eyes and mine to the fact that the Professor is equipped with the temper of an Italian donna, and this fate of nature has been reinforced by the blows that have been dealt him of late. Added to which is the man's long-standing membership of the Academical Boxing Club.

And sure enough, Thorkild now springs to his feet like a jack-in-the-box and launches a fierce upper-cut towards Katinka's abdomen.

It is a blow invested with his full body weight. Had its delivery been completed, Katinka would most certainly have had a struggle on her hands. But the punch falls short. Or rather: a hand as heavy as a meat cleaver is brought down on the Professor's arm to foil his attack. And the hand belongs to Bullimilla.

'What was that I heard about my canapés?' she says.

By rights, Thorkild is not the one to ask, but he readily provides Bullimilla with a reply, which takes the form of a left hook aimed at her temple.

This punch, too, is thwarted as Katinka comes in from behind, grabs the Professor's hand, and twists until he is forced down onto the table. In the same seamless movement she produces a pair of handcuffs, and for the second time in less than twenty-four hours the Professor finds himself with both hands cuffed behind his back.

Tilte and I have read with interest about how patterns of the opposite sex always form around the great mystics, like, for instance, the female attendants of Jesus and Buddha and Einar Flogginfellow, who never goes anywhere unless accompanied by his mother and his daughters and at least two top-flight players from the women's team. Tilte and I have discussed whether some system kicks in every time a major personality unfolds, and this is a theory that is nourished empirically here at this breakfast table, where it becomes clear that the women surrounding Thorkild Thorlacius have not the slightest intention of retreating to their Danish pastries while their alpha male is led away.

One minute his wife is sipping her herbal tea and nibbling her crispbread without butter, the next she's spitting flames and smoke is coming out of her nostrils as she hurls herself at Katinka and Bullimilla.

Tilte and I choose this strategic moment to sneak away. As we depart, I see Lars place a hand on the arm of Vera the Secretary, presumably to prevent her from putting her oar in.

'I can't stand to be touched,' says Vera.

She says this in a voice that would have prompted Lars to let go if only he had heard it. But he is fully entangled in the catfight that is now ensuing and which soon will be out of control.

'Release her!' Anaflabia orders. 'She's my secretary!'

'I don't care if she's your make-up artist or your personal shopper,' says Lars. 'You two are coming down to the station where you can explain everything in a statement.'

At this moment, Vera reveals the truth of her claim that she cannot stand to be touched, and she does so by planting her knee firmly in Lars' abdomen.

And this is the last thing Tilte and I and Basker see before we escape down the gangway.

42

AWAITING US ON THE QUAYSIDE IS NOT ONLY A WELCOMING committee but also a crowd perhaps a hundred strong, including journalists and photographers and people with television cameras, which again goes to show the importance of Finø in the greater scheme of things.

Tilte and I are looking to disappear into the throng, because now that we've got this far without being recognised by Lars and Katinka it would be tragic indeed if that were to happen at this point, so we're the first to hit the quayside.

But we forgot to take account of the journalists, and it now transpires that this is a section of the population that can organise a defensive wall worthy of any set-piece involving Tilte and I on the edge of the penalty area, and they are upon us like hawks, sticking their microphones under our noses and wanting to know what confession we belong to and what our expectations are as to the conference, and I have to admit they catch us unawares.

In this kind of situation, in which all your plans fall apart, the great systems of spiritual guidance will tend to rub their hands together in glee and say that it is at this point exactly that the world becomes fresh and open in all its shocking unexpectedness, and the Zen Buddhists would say that one should concentrate on one's breathing, and the Vedantic Hindus would say that one must ask oneself who exactly is experiencing this outlandish breakdown, and the nuns of St Teresa of Ávila's convent somewhere in Andalucia would say that one must recite the Lord's

Prayer, and in a way all of this is what Tilte and I attempt to do at one and the same time.

But this is also the point at which forgetfulness and distraction enter, and I forget to keep hold of Basker, who has tired of being kept underneath Svend Sewerman's curtains and instead wants out and in on the action, and so he wriggles himself free and runs back up the gangway to gain a view of what's going on.

And at this very moment, the worst possible of all, Alexander and Thorkild and the three women appear, all of them handcuffed, and behind them come Lars and Katinka.

Lars is sporting a black eye that is already so swollen that one ought to have a word and recommend he and Katinka putting off the wedding for at least five or six months until the swelling goes down. But his injury does not prevent him from spotting Basker, and now Katinka sees him, too. And not only do Lars and Katinka both see Basker, they also recognise him and draw the reasonable conclusion that Tilte and I cannot be far away. Their searching gaze falls upon us, at which point their common thought process grinds to a halt, foiled by our disguises. But then logic steps in to sweep all doubt aside, and now they realise that they have found the individuals they were supposed to have been guarding, but who nevertheless managed to escape from their watchful eyes.

Until this point, Lars has been keeping hold of Alexander and Thorkild, but now he lets go of them both and starts to run towards us.

In a way, it's rather touching for Tilte and I to witness how eager a detective constable can be to carry out his duty, even in such a tight spot as this. It's the kind of diligence that means we all may sleep soundly in our beds at night.

Unfortunately, it now undermines his cool, detached thinking. Personally, I would never leave two such individuals as Alexander Flounderblood and Thorkild Thorlacius unattended at any time, certainly not in their current state of mind. Because all it takes is just such a moment's inattention for everything to go to pot.

I turn to the journalists in front of us. It seems they've noticed very little of all this, and what they have noticed they lack the deductive premises to comprehend. So they're still standing waiting to find out who Tilte and I are.

'We're singers, that's all,' I tell them. 'We accompany the two trance dancers, Alexander and Thorkild. That's them up there on the gangway.'

'They're handcuffed,' says one of the journalists.

'Indeed, but only to make sure they don't hurt themselves when they're in a trance,' I tell them.

'Which is when they make contact with the dead,' Tilte adds.

Tilte and I have no real notion of how journalists prioritise their time, but it becomes clear that trance dancing and contacting the dead are right up there at the top of the list, because now the defensive wall moves as one organism up the gangway, pinning Lars against the railing in the process.

Here, however, his superior physical shape prevails. Half a dozen journalists are swept aside as though they were bowling pins, and for a brief and rather threatening moment Lars has a clear view.

But then he is engulfed. And what engulfs him is Lama Svend-Holger, Polly Pigonia, Sinbad Al-Blablab and their respective entourages, and the whole process looks rather haphazard, as though they merely want to get a look at what's happening, but Tilte and I can see the gleam in their eyes, and in it we see the noble compassion that is the hallmark of all the great religions.

We are about to turn and vanish into the crowd when the first journalist claws his way forward to Thorkild Thorlacius and in a clear voice asks him if he believes trance dancing will be a big thing at the conference and if he would mind showing the viewers a couple of steps.

We're spellbound, and thereby also able to hear the second question, which is put to Alexander Flounderblood, and which concerns whether he might have been in contact with any dead person recently.

It is a question that is followed by a scream, from which it is apparent that Alexander, whose hands are cuffed, has delivered a kick to the groin of the inquisitive journalist. And after that, all hell breaks loose and the gangway dissolves into what most often would be referred to as a scuffle. By this time, Tilte and Basker and I have already made ourselves scarce.

43

WE WEAVE OUR WAY THROUGH THE CROWD AND PAST THE waiting cars. If like us you've been cooped up with a shipload of lunatics and then suddenly discover the whole wide world lies open at your feet, you will no doubt feel an urge to expel a whoop of joy, and this is indeed what we are about to do when the claw of a crane grips us tight and lifts us into the air.

Many people in this situation would incline towards throwing in the towel, but not me. I've scored heaps of goals from positions such as this, hemmed in by four defenders who could have made a name for themselves in Hollywood as stand-ins for King Kong without even having to wear a mask. I have only a hundredth of a millimetre in which to manouevre. But for the strong of faith, a hundredth of a millimetre is enough, so I whirl around and put the boot into the bloke behind us.

It feels like kicking a fully inflated tractor tyre, which is to say that it gives slightly, though without moving, and makes no sound. I know only one person with that kind of resilience, so I tip my head back to look straight into the blue doll's eyes of our brother Hans.

'Nice try, brother,' he says softly, and I can tell from his voice that I at least managed to disturb his breathing.

Then he opens the door of the car beside which we are standing, bundles us into the back seat, slips behind the wheel and whisks us away.

*　*　*

Although we have only glimpsed Hans' face, it's obvious that something about it has changed, and the resolute manner in which he is now acting seems only to confirm the impression. Part of the explanation is immediately apparent, because sitting beside us on the back seat is a person wearing a familiar sweater and running shoes, and that person is the gorgeous singer of Blågårds Plads.

'You've met Ashanti, of course,' says Hans.

I'll be frank and say that the moment he utters those words I feel a sudden jolt in my heart. Though there ought to be plenty of other things to think about as we move along Langelinie quayside, and a great many questions need to be addressed, for a brief moment something else becomes salient. Because when Hans utters her name, Ashanti, he speaks it in the same way that Conny, who now is gone with the wind, spoke my own name, and it is a way of speaking a name that cannot be emulated and may only occur when a person is genuinely in love with another.

For that reason, it's as sure as fate that in the short time that has passed, something has taken place between the singer and our brother, which has completely rearranged his furniture and pulled a major part of him down from the stars and back to earth, and which moreover has turned him into a person who is deliriously in love. And though this is exactly what Tilte and I have always wanted for him, the realisation that it has now happened feels almost devastating. Because now I realise that I never really thought it would happen at all. Deep down, I always thought Hans would be there to look after me right to the very end, and now the end is suddenly nigh, now everything hurts and there's a knot in the pit of my stomach.

The car in which we are seated is a Mercedes, a make Tilte and I are beginning to take for granted. We turn towards the Langelinie bridge, but then Hans crosses the cycle lane, pulls up on the grass verge and turns off the engine. Tilte and I cower in the depths of the car, peeping cautiously out of the windows. We see taxis passing by, and behind them the limousines that have picked up Polly, Lama Svend-Holger and Sinbad Al-Blablab, a

243

hearse containing Maria's coffin, two police cars and a black van with bars across the windows, and inside we catch a glimpse of Alexander Flounderblood staring straight ahead with a look that suggests he might be thinking of biting his way through the steel plating and throwing himself upon innocent passers-by.

'We need to go to Toldbodgade, Hansel,' says Tilte. 'If that's part of any galaxy you can find without the aid of astronomical navigation?'

This is but good-natured banter, most people would say. Yet beneath the seeming innocence of it I hear something else, and what I hear is that Tilte feels the same way as I do about Hans and the Gorgeous One. We want so much for him to be happy. And I hear, too, that we now have another job to do if that happy childhood is ever to be brought back home to take its place alongside all those other trophies.

44

WE DRIVE ON ALONG ESPLANADEN. TILTE MAKES A SIGN. WE
stop and she gets out, goes into a kiosk and comes back with a
SIM card. This is an action replete with timeless wisdom, because
although Katinka has already had a full morning, a mind such
as hers is bound to discover that she's lost her phone and then
have it blocked.

Tilte gets back into the car. As Hans prepares to pull away
from the kerb, she and I catch sight of something that prompts
us to say: 'Wait!'

Esplanaden is a very fine boulevard and an obvious choice for
excursions and walks organised by the Society for the Improvement
of the Capital. On such occasions the Society's members most likely
dwell upon the building that is now diagonally behind us and which
exudes such character as to make even us, who are so familiar with
architectural distinction from our rectory home, feel like the Little
Match Girl, despite our being seated inside a Mercedes.

The main entrance of the building is a glass door as wide as
a carriageway, and on the wall next to the door is a marble
plaque, and this is what has attracted Tilte's attention and mine,
because engraved on the plaque are the words *Bellerad Shipping*.

It's hard to fully explain why Tilte and I now leap into action
like two members of a synchronised swimming team, and all I
can say is that we are driven by a sense of being at one with a
higher purpose and with our own extensive experience at elbowing
our way into even the most inaccessible places in order to shift
lottery tickets for the benefit of Finø FC.

'Reverse back three metres,' Tilte says to Hans. 'Then get out and hold the door for Peter and me. Salute us when we get out. And then open the glass door for us.'

As noted, everything indicates that Hans has been through a remarkable phase in his development. But he has yet to reach that advanced stage at which one might venture to contradict Tilte. So he reverses, gets out of the car, opens the door and salutes. And then he holds the glass entrance door open for us.

We enter a large reception area. Behind a desk sits a middle-aged woman in her early thirties, one of the kind familiar from the great religions, who guard something valuable with a Gurkha knife or a flaming sword.

But right now, her guard is down, and the reason for this is the Mercedes, Hans standing to attention and saluting, and Svend Sewerman's curtains draped in the manner of the Supreme Vedanta.

In situations such as this, Tilte and I divide our labour. I break through the defence, while Tilte lurks to pick up the rebounds.

I look around me for inspiration. The walls are adorned with photographs of the company's ships. The first thing one notes is that these are not Optimist dinghies but container ships and supertankers from upwards of 100,000 gross register tons. The next thing to catch one's attention is the names. The ships have names like *Aunt Lalandia Bellerad*, *Cousin Intrepid Bellerad* and *Uncle Umbrage Bellerad*.

On the basis of this information I deduce two things: the vessels of Bellerad Shipping sail not with coconuts and tourists on Jutland's Gudenå, but with fuel oil and heavy cargo in the Persian Gulf; and Bellerad is a man who is proud and extremely fond of his family.

I lean forward towards the guardian of the threshold.

'I'm from the Saudi embassy,' I tell her. 'With me I have Her Royal Highness Princess Til-te Aziz. We are here to inform Mr Bellerad that he has been awarded the Order of King Abdul Aziz.'

Next to the woman stand three men, who have been studying

a map of the world on the wall. Now they turn slowly towards Tilte and me.

Two of the men are bald and thickset, and equipped with the kind of aura that for a moment makes me think that perhaps Tilte and I ought not to have acted on that higher impulse at all but remained outside in the car.

But it's the man in the middle who now commands most of our attention. We know that this is Mr Bellerad himself, and if you ask me how we could possibly know I would only be able to say that if one day you should find yourself standing in front of Hannibal or Anaflabia Borderrud or Napoleon, which is to say any of the great generals of history, then you wouldn't be in any doubt either.

The good thing about the situation is that we have the initiative. Bellerad and the two baldies and the woman with the flaming sword are quite nonplussed. So Tilte and I have the chance to digest these first, bare impressions of the ship owner's psychology.

There are three things we notice. The first is that Bellerad is a man who resembles most others insofar as he starts to quiver inside when he hears that an award is being bestowed upon him, a medal he will be able to show Aunt Lalandia, Cousin Intrepid and Uncle Umbrage.

The second is that he is a man whose life has taught him that when a person bestows something upon another, it's because the bestower is aware that everything will be returned to him twice over, and now the immediate question is what might be engraved upon the reverse side of this particular medal.

The third piece of information Tilte and I tap directly from our bare impressions is that Bellerad is a man who has something to hide. Not your usual, medium-sized secret of the kind all of us have lying around somewhere. Bellerad's secret is big and angry. Tilte and I feel like we're standing in front of an old male elephant excluded from the herd on account of bad behaviour and now feigning repentance while he awaits a chance to strike back.

'The medal will be awarded during the Grand Synod,' I say.

'By His Majesty the King himself. And Her Royal Highness the Princess.'

Tilte and I retreat towards the glass entrance door. Bellerad and his two henchmen are not the kind one cares to turn one's back on. Hans opens the glass door for us, then the car door. He salutes, climbs behind the wheel and pulls away into the flow of traffic.

I venture to glance back over my shoulder. All four have spilled out onto the pavement, where they now stand gaping in our direction.

We continue on past office buildings and more destinations for excursions of the Society for the Improvement of the Capital. Tilte points and we take a left. We are silent and pensive, and what we're thinking about is that we hope Bellerad hasn't discovered that Mother and Father have hacked their way into his private correspondence, because he doesn't look like a man who would let that sort of thing pass. In fact, he looks rather like someone who would have a bazooka at the ready on his hat shelf for just such an occasion.

We catch a glimpse of what might once have been a warehouse, but which now has been given a loving hand and two hundred million kroner to become a place most people only see from the outside and from a distance, unless they happen to have won the pools. The Mercedes descends into an underground car park and comes to a halt in front of an iron gate equipped with a push-button panel. Tilte enters a code from Katinka's mobile and the gate opens into a basement of such calibre that the parking spaces could be rented out as hotel rooms if you put up a few partition walls and installed beds. We leave the car and ascend in a lift made of mirrors and tropical wood. It projects us upwards like a bullet and stops as gently as if in the down of a seagull. We step out onto a landing decorated with orchids in bowls of marble. Tilte produces a key from one of them and we step into the two-room apartment she has borrowed from an acquaintance.

It's true that the place has two rooms. But what Tilte has neglected to tell us is that each of them measures a hundred square metres. And if one should still feel one's style to be cramped, there's a balcony outside running the entire length of the place and looking out onto the blue waters of the harbour.

The furniture is of the kind you'd expect the designer to have signed personally and only yesterday, because everything is brand new, and there aren't even any pictures on the walls yet.

At first I feel like asking Tilte who might own such a place, but a thought descends like a sudden blanket of cloud: what if Tilte has an admirer? If she has, then having an admirer with such impeccable taste might indicate this to be a serious matter indeed. It would mean that in a year's time Tilte would be all engaged and married and gone from home. Which is to say that the only thing we'd need then would be for Basker to find some cute little bitch to run away with and I would be all on my own, mother and father gone, siblings well on their way, and all forlorn in the vacuum would be me, myself and I, Peter Finø, solo.

We all sit down in the designer chairs. But then Ashanti stands up ever so slowly and walks through the flat to the far end where the lounge becomes an open kitchen. Although she says nothing, I sense why she has removed herself, and it's because she wants to allow the three of us to be alone, and it's such a fine gesture that one can only feel warmth for her, even if she is on the verge of kidnapping one's older brother.

And yet I can't help feeling a sadness inside. None of us says anything, and the feeling becomes all the more intense. In fact, it would be no exaggeration to call it grief, and the cause of it now begins to emerge. For some reason it becomes apparent that Tilte and Hans and I will not be together for ever. Ashanti and Hans have sparked it off, but in a way it's not only the fact that they're now a couple. What I sense all of a sudden is that eventually we will arrive at the end of our days, whereupon one of us will be the first to die, to be followed inevitably by the others.

At this point you might say so what, everyone knows they're

249

going to die, and this would indeed be true. But normally it's something we know only in our minds. Knowing you're going to die is never here and now, but something far away in the future, so distant you can hardly even see it, and for that reason alone it need never be taken seriously.

But at this moment it suddenly becomes here and now.

I know you're familiar with that feeling, because it's something all of us have experienced at some time. I don't know where it comes from. But looking at Hans' hand as it rests there on the back of the chair, his large, square hand, which is always tanned, I suddenly understand that a day will come when that hand will no longer be there to take hold of me and lift me up to see the world from above.

I glance at Tilte. Her face is tanned, even though it's still only April. It's a thing she's inherited from our mother. In Tilte's face, age is fleeting. When you look at her you often find yourself unable to tell if she's seven or sixteen or sixteen hundred years old, because her eyes seem always to look out across great spans of time. And besides that, there's a kind of inquisitiveness about Tilte, she always wants to know everything there is to know about people, and there's a kindness, too, and even if it's pointed and sharp, it's a kindness so immense that only Great-Grandma is ahead of her, and she's had ninety-three years of practice.

One day I shall look into these kind, venerable eyes for the last time, and this is what has become clear to me now. And my sadness is compounded, as though that time had already come.

But then something happens that is so quiet and unobtrusive that no one would ever notice. And what happens is that I remain seated, and refrain from removing myself from my grief and anxiety.

Normally it cannot be endured. Knowing in your mind that you're going to die can be bad enough in itself, but feeling it in your heart, feeling the reality of it, is a thing humans generally find themselves unable to cope with. I am no exception. I'm no braver than you. But when you've got a sister with whom you've been able to start investigating the path that leads to the door, and the two of you have been able to complement each other in thorough-going theological studies on the Internet and at the Finø Town Library, there comes a time when you can no longer stand to close your eyes and blot everything out, and for me that time would seem to have come now.

What I do in a way is to give the feeling space. That means allowing images of death to come to the fore, and for some reason I see myself being the first to die. I see it vividly: I'm lying in a bed, saying goodbye to Hans and Tilte.

I don't know where such images come from, because when you're fourteen it's hard to see yourself dying of anything in particular, but perhaps my own death as I picture it is the result of accumulated injuries sustained at football practice. Playing at such a high level as the first team of Finø FC is not without its drawbacks.

Actually, this might not be true, because the injuries I've had have never been the kind you could present to the intensive care unit of the Finø Hospital and receive credit for, seeing as how I've always been able to float above the sliding tackles like a fairy would float above lilies of the valley, and the worst I've ever had is a slight hint of a pulled muscle. So where the image of my own decline comes from I have no idea, but nonetheless I see myself saying goodbye to Tilte and Hans, embracing them and thanking them for allowing me to have known them, and I look at Hans' square hands one final time, and into Tilte's kind eyes, and then I reach inside into the feeling of death itself.

By doing so, it all becomes that much more real. Indeed, it feels almost as though it were happening now, in this luxury apartment facing Copenhagen's harbour on a brand-new day of sunshine.

I try to refrain from seeking solace in the thought of some miraculous reprieve. I refrain from seeking comfort in the thought that most likely a light will simply go out, or that Jesus will be waiting for me, or Buddha, or whoever else you might imagine stepping forth with a broad smile and an aspirin to say it won't be anywhere near as bad as you think. I refrain from imagining anything at all. The only thing I can do is to feel the weight of the farewell none of us can ever avoid.

At the very moment I sense that everything will be lost, and hence nothing is worth holding onto, something happens. It has happened before, and in a way it's such a little thing, so innocuous as to be barely noticeable, which is why really you need someone to show it to you. Tilte showed it to me, and now I'm telling you. What happens is that a little gleam of happiness and freedom appears. Nothing else changes: you're still sitting where you were when it came, and no one has come to your aid, no seraphim or angels or houris or holy virgins or heavenly support of any kind. You're sitting there, and you see that you're going to die, and sense how much you love those you will lose, and then it happens: for a very brief moment it's as though time stops. Or rather: it doesn't exist. As though Langelinie and Copenhagen and Sjælland are a room inside a shell, and for a very brief moment the shell disappears. That's all that happens. The feeling of anxiety and incarceration is gone, and what you feel instead is freedom. You sense that there is a way of being present in the world that will never expire and which means that you are not afraid, because the feeling of freedom is something that will never go away. Hans and Tilte and this delicate footballing frame of mine will, of course, die. But there's something else beyond, a thing for which there are no words, but of which one is a part and which never comes to an end, and that's what the feeling is.

I know that at this moment I am standing at the door. And to be exact, it's not a door at all, because a door is in one place, but this is everywhere. It belongs to no religion, it does not say that you must believe or worship or stick to rules. It says only three things. The first is that you should reach inside your heart. The second is that for a moment you should be willing to accept it all, even the unreasonable detail of having to die. And the third is that you should remain standing quite still for just a second to watch the ball cross the goal-line.

This is what I experience now, in this two-room apartment on the fifth floor.

And I can tell by looking at Tilte that something very similar is going on inside her, too. I'm more uncertain about Hans, because his faculties are rather curtailed at the moment and I'm not sure if he has room for revelation, because everything would seem to indicate that his beautiful singer has taken up all his available space.

It takes a moment, and like I said it's all very quiet and subdued, nothing to write home about, no flags or decorations. All there is is the realisation that if you look straight into the feeling of having to die, you will find freedom and relief.

It's there, and then it's gone. Ashanti is standing by the table. She places a sandwich in front of each of us.

'Enjoy,' she says. 'Or as we say at home in Haiti: *Bon appétit.*'

45

I'M SORRY TO SAY THAT THE WELFARE SYSTEM IN DENMARK is unevenly distributed and in certain areas completely absent. Wherever I happen to be, for instance, death by starvation is ever lurking.

I don't know why that should be, whether it has to do with my age or my level of training, or perhaps I simply carry an unknown parasite around with me in my colon. Whatever the reason, I'm forever hungry. That's the way it's always been. When I was a little boy, I would often imagine Jesus making me a sandwich, and with his natural talent for catering I could only look forward to the feasts he would almost certainly be able to conjure up for me.

This is exactly the kind of sandwich Ashanti now puts in front of each of us. She must have been out shopping for the ingredients and spent some considerable time preparing them. A mood of solemnity descends upon the table.

The bread is freshly leavened, and I must offer my apologies because I am compelled, in the midst of this meal, to note that the aroma is the same as I recall from Conny's scalp. Moreover, the crust is as crisp as glass, the crumb resilient and elastic, and pocketed with air.

Picking through the contents of one's sandwich is normally considered to be bad manners, but in this case I just can't stop myself. I lift the lid, the uppermost piece of bread, and gaze down upon all that is sacred to me. First, there are slices of butter cut with the thick edge of the cheese slicer. Then comes a spreading of mayonnaise with an aroma of garlic and lemon and a tropical spice she must have brought with her from the feverish jungles of Haiti. This is followed by small leaves of a variety of salads: purple, bitter, curly and crisp, then chunks of North Sea tuna of the kind caught off Finø, lightly grilled and ever so slightly pink and fleshy inside. On top of the tuna are wafer-thin rings of red onion and a sprinkling of large capers, and blow me down if they haven't been in pickle together with fish eggs that pop one by one inside your mouth, leaving you with the very taste of the Sea of Opportunity.

Many a cook and sandwich maid would have stopped here, because the creation has at this point already topped ten centimetres in height, but our singing antelope has been holding back to put in the final flourish. On the underside of the uppermost piece of bread is once again a thick spreading of Caribbean mayonnaise, and into it Ashanti has mixed small pieces of olive and red and green peppers.

It all has the kind of artistic touch that makes you bow your head in acknowledgement, because even if there are enough calories here to propel the Finø AllStars to the top of the Danish *Superliga*, they are presented with such delicacy that all five sandwiches look like they're about to float out of the window and do a lap of honour with the seagulls over the harbour.

Ashanti places a tall glass next to each of our plates, which she fills with sparkling mineral water from the Finø Brewery, and looks briefly into the eyes of the person whose glass she has just filled.

I am the last to receive, and as she looks into my eyes she notices something of which I only become aware at that same moment: that I am the youngest. And though I have peered into the depths of existence and have lost my parents on two occasions and play for a selected team and have seen true love rise and set like the sun that shines on Finø, I am still only fourteen years old. And if there's one thing you need in a situation such as this, it's for a woman like Ashanti to understand and make you a sandwich that postpones death by starvation indefinitely, and to look upon you with what I will venture to call solicitude.

Then she sits down beside us, and we have reached a point at which some of the great questions find an answer.

46

'I SUPPOSE YOU REMEMBER I GAVE ASHANTI MY NUMBER,' says Hans. 'Before we went our separate ways.'

Tilte and Basker and I stare emptily at him. We're too polite to remind him of how she actually received his number.

'She called me an hour later when I was in Klampenborg unhitching the horses. I went and picked her up straight away. We've not been separated since.'

'He read his poems for me,' says Ashanti. 'On the jetty at Skovshoved.'

It is a testimony to Tilte's self-control and mine that we remain collected. Following exposure to Hans' poetry, many women would have dived into the sea to escape the threat of more. But not this one. It tells us something about the depth of feeling that exists between these two individuals and which is now unfolding before us.

'She's a priestess,' says Hans.

His voice is thick, partly because of mayonnaise, partly with admiration.

'The Yoruba religion. She grew up in Haiti, but attends the university here. She's going to be dancing at the conference . . .'

'A sacred Santeria dance,' says Ashanti.

'A dance in preparation for the journey from the body,' says Hans.

Tilte and I look at Ashanti again. Just the way she eats would bring tears of joy to the eyes of Ifigenia Bruhn, proprietor of Ifigenia Bruhn's Dancing School. And though we have yet to see her dance, we have seen her walk, most recently through the room in which we are seated, and her gait is such that no one would ever be surprised if she made a little detour up the walls and across the ceiling. So personally I wouldn't be in such a hurry to leave my body, if only hers were mine. But then again, all of us are searching for the door in our own way, and one shouldn't meddle too much in the affairs of others.

'Where's the car from?' Tilte asks.

'I borrowed it,' says Hans. 'From my employer. He's away and won't be missing it. And what he doesn't know will never hurt him.'

Tilte and I aren't sure. Hans has probably heard about infringements of the law, but little would seem to indicate that he believes them to exist. No one from Finø has ever known him even to cross the street against a light, and not only because Finø has no traffic lights or pedestrian crossings. And now he's stolen a Mercedes.

An hour has passed, and Tilte and I have briefly, yet conscientiously, related everything we've been through. We've put the newspaper clippings out on the table, and the invoices from the safe-deposit box, and as we run through events Hans begins to mull things over and eventually he gets to his feet as though intending to break something, perhaps a load-bearing wall or two. Once again this side of him emerges that is familiar to us only from those few occasions on which misguided tourists have made the mistake of picking on him and his female companions. Apart from that, meek is the word that most obviously springs to mind to describe my brother's psychology.

But now something has happened. So when he hears all this about our parents he gets to his feet.

'They're planning a robbery,' he says. 'They're planning to steal religious treasures that mean a great deal to a great many people.'

'But something made them change their plans,' Tilte adds.

'They want more,' says Hans. 'If they changed their plans, it's because they thought of something that would increase their yield. So I'm against our helping them. We should let things pan out. Even if it's into the toilet.'

Now Ashanti says something, and we have to concentrate on what she is saying in order not to become wholly absorbed by the sound of her voice.

'I've never met your parents,' she says, 'but I sense how very fond of them you are. That clinches matters. If you love someone, it will never go away.'

Now that she has spoken, her being a high priestess makes perfect sense, because it's plain to anyone how easily she might hold a congregation spellbound.

Hans certainly is spellbound. He sits down.

Then Tilte's phone, which by rights is Katinka's, but which now has a new SIM card inside it, rings.

Tilte answers the call and listens for a moment, and then her expression becomes grave. A minute passes, perhaps. The call ends and she puts down the phone.

'That was Leonora,' she says. 'She's worried. She wants us to meet her in fifteen minutes.'

47

THE INSTITUTE OF BUDDHIST STUDIES IS LOCATED BEHIND THE church on the square called Nikolaj Plads. It's a quiet, idyllic place. People sit at small café tables in the square, enjoying that particularly Danish combination of second-degree burns and frostbite, because the temperature is twenty-seven degrees Celsius in the sun and minus something in the shade. Viewed from the outside, the institute looks like a place full of Danish history. There's a gateway whose door resembles that of a church, and the gold lettering on a plaque says this is where the illustrious Danish poet Sigurd Skullsmacker lived until his rather untimely death in 1779.

Inside, it's a different story altogether. We're received by a small monk in red robes who ushers us in. The house opens out onto a courtyard around which runs a covered cloister, and in the middle is a fountain and at each corner a guard. In the car, Tilte has shared with us what Leonora has told her about the place being a kind of monastery and university all at once, and this is where the Dalai Lama and the 17th Karmapa will be staying for the duration of the conference. Already, security people are milling about. The Danes among them, colleagues of Lars and Katinka from the Police Intelligence Service, wear sunglasses and earpieces, while the Tibetans are as tall as American basketball players and as broad as football goals.

And yet there's something about the place that makes you want to become a monk. In fact, this is an urge I have always felt, and since Conny left me it's a feeling that's grown stronger. If I could find a monastery with a strong first team I'd seriously consider doing something about it, though there would have to be close bonds with a nearby nunnery, because even though no one will ever take the place of Conny, and I am destined always to be alone, one wouldn't want to be entirely devoid of female company.

We're led up some stairs and along corridors into a small room with a view over the roof of St Nicholas, and at the table sits Leonora in front of her laptop, looking nothing like the happy, smiling coaching expert we know so well.

She casts a glance at Ashanti, but Tilte and I nod approvingly. We sit down around the laptop.

'When you delete things from a computer,' Leonora says, 'you don't actually delete at all. What you delete are *file pointers*, or electronic addresses. The information itself remains behind in other directories. Your parents didn't know. So the hour they thought they deleted lived on, hidden but intact.'

The image of the exhibition room appears on the screen. It's daytime, and workers are busying themselves at exhibition cases and with a raised platform at the rear of the room. Leonora runs the footage at normal speed. We can see the company names on the overalls of the workers and sense how different the atmosphere is here compared to a normal place of work. Everyone wears white gloves, they work quietly and meticulously like lab technicians. We watch them clear away when they're done, and their cleaning would be a match even for me: after vacuuming, they wipe everything down with microfibre cloths and afterwards there's no sitting down for a beer at the end of the day, all they drink is mineral water, spilling not a drop and taking their rubbish away with them when they go, and after that the room is empty, apart from the sunlight of early evening.

Leonora fast-forwards and the light fades.

'It's night,' she says. 'Shortly after three o'clock.'

There's a faint light in the room, perhaps from the moon, perhaps from the lamps in front of the castle building. Not enough for a normal camera to pick up, but for *Voice Security* only the best equipment is good enough.

We feel almost devout. We are watching the hour our mother and father have deleted.

I don't notice the figures until they're inside the room. They have entered without a sound, the first sign of their presence being a faint, white light passing over one of the black squares that mark the shafts above which the exhibition cases will be positioned. Then a voice comes out of the darkness.

'Henrik, I think there's a mouse!'

The voice belongs to a woman, and she sounds out of breath.

'Impossible, my dear. What you sense are rats. And mice and rats hardly ever—'

Because the face is hidden and only white hair visible, our attention is focused on the voice, which is full in a way that would allow its owner to slip easily into the high tenor row of the Finø Church Choir. In which case, he wouldn't need to be up at three in the morning. But now he's cut short before finishing his sentence, because the woman emits a squeal, presumably at the mention of rats.

Then two more figures appear.

'Ibrahim, is it in place?'

It's Henrik asking. Ibrahim chuckles.

'All set and ready. A little explosion first makes the cases descend into the box. Then comes the big bang inside. There'll hardly be a sound on the outside. But the job will be done.'

'Why can't we keep some of it, Henrik?'

Now it's the woman asking. And one can understand her. Especially with all those rats.

'It's the principle of it, Blizilda. Divinity requires one to set aside one's own needs. If one destroys for one's own benefit, only Hell awaits. My mother once said—'

'I want new shoes, at least. Look at these heels . . .'

Blizilda again. One feels only sympathy for Henrik. It's clear that he is rarely allowed to finish a sentence. And yet it's obvious, even in the dark, that his patience is being tested.

'I'd prefer to say that anyone stupid enough to wear high heels on a mission such as this would be—'

'Did I hear the word stupid, Henrik? Because if I did . . .'

A movement in the darkness indicates the intervention of a fourth party, who now addresses the still-chuckling Ibrahim.

'Aren't diamonds hard? How can we be sure they won't be left undamaged and sit there taunting us?'

The voice is clear, and the accent foreign, though the man's Danish is so fluent and correct that even Alexander Flounderblood would have been pleased.

Ibrahim giggles.

'Diamonds are very hard indeed. But the temperature in the sealed box during the explosion will be very, very high. Maybe ten thousand degrees. The diamonds will be gone, vaporised. The technical term is pyrolysis. There'll be nothing left inside the box. A little glitter, that's all, or a smudge of black powder. You could hoover it up.'

Silence. The mood is restored. And now again something white in the darkness. A handkerchief. Henrik dries his eyes.

'I'm sorry,' he says. 'It's all so very emotional. I used to play here as a child . . .'.

He's about to say more, probably something about his mother, but then he pulls himself together.

'Let us pray.'

The prayer is a disharmonious mumble, the four individuals praying separately rather than together. It takes maybe thirty seconds, and then all is quiet again.

And with that they are gone. Just as I failed to see them enter, I miss their departure, and the room is at once empty, as though they had never been there at all.

We sit quietly for some time. But then Hans says what all of us are thinking. It's a new role for him, but my brother's personal development is obviously accelerating.

'They're going to blow the treasures to smithereens. They're terrorists!'

He looks across at Ashanti. And then he realises that the scene

263

of this intended terrorist attack is in close proximity to where she is scheduled to perform.

They may well have amazing trance dancing in Haiti. But we're not bad ourselves on Finø, as Hans now demonstrates. He leaps to his feet, his blue eyes glazed over, and his trance is of the more uncontrolled variety. His hands open and close as though reaching out to squeeze the juice from a pair of boulders.

And then he is stopped in his tracks. The arm that stops him is only slender, but it belongs to Ashanti and it breaks his trance and ushers Hans back into the real world with its view of Nikolaj Plads.

'That's what Mother and Father discovered,' says Tilte. 'They wanted to make certain no one had spotted their little installation underneath the floor, whatever it might be. So they went through the footage. And found this. It made them change their plans.'

We sit still, paralysed and mute before the empty screen. Eventually, Hans speaks: 'This means it's out of our hands. It's no longer a family matter now. What we're going to do is to put this computer under our arm and go quietly along to the police station on Store Kongensgade where other people will be able to take care of this, and then the five of us are going to drive into the country and rent a holiday cabin with a bombproof cellar and stick our heads into the bush until—'

Hans comes to an abrupt halt. Tilte has raised her arm.

'Can we see that last bit again? The part where they're praying.'

Leonora presses rewind and we hear Henrik's distinguished voice repeat the words: 'Let us pray.'

We listen to the voices as they mumble.

'Listen to each voice in turn,' says Tilte.

I'm able to identify Henrik, nearest the camera and the microphone. He's reciting the Lord's Prayer. The other voices merge together.

'Again,' says Tilte. 'Run it again. Concentrate on one voice at a time.'

Now I hear the clear voice with the accent. It seems to be

chanting. The words are inaudible, but as the child of a pastor I would say that the rhythm is foreign to Danish liturgy and might at a push be an Eastern raga.

I pick out the woman's voice, deep and introvert, almost plaintive and accompanied by the jangling sound of prayer beads, a rosary or a *mala*.

'They're not just from different countries,' Tilte says pensively. 'They're from different religions, too.'

Hans is on his feet again. 'That can't be right. They're terrorists. And terrorists always belong to the same religion when they act together. Besides, we needn't pay it any more attention. This is a matter for the police, the intelligence services and Interpol.'

Tilte remains seated. 'It's now twelve o'clock,' she says. 'We have eight hours until the conference kicks off. Seven until people start to arrive.'

Hans begins to twitch. He knows where Tilte is headed.

'If we hand this over to the police,' Tilte says, 'they're going to ask us how we know. Which means we'll have to snitch on Mother and Father. And they'll discover that we're on the run. The wheels will all be set in motion, I'll be sent to Læsø, and Peter will be put away in the children's home at Grenå.'

Hans has ground to a halt. I'm at the window, yet to find my point of view. On the square below, where we have parked the Mercedes belonging to Hans' employer, a black van is waiting. It might be the darkened Finø glass of its windows that makes me aware of it and causes my famous memory to kick in, the one that has secured me many a stupendous victory when playing games involving the recognition of number plates on family camping trips. The registration of this black van is T for Tilte and H for Hans, and the first figures are 50 17, the seventeenth of May, which is the date on which Finø FC gained promotion to the DMISL, the Danish Minor Islands' Super League.

'Two hours,' says Tilte. 'We're so close. Let's give ourselves two hours.'

'To do what?'

The question is Leonora's.

'The man with the white hair,' I say. 'Henrik. He said he played at the castle when he was a child. We could show the footage to Rickardt.'

48

FOR A BATON, COUNT RICKARDT THREE LIONS USES A HAVANA
cigar as long as a headmaster's cane, and now he gestures sweep-
ingly with it in the direction of the panorama window.

'All the *deepest* cities have a square as their spiritual centrepoint.
Think of St Peter's in Rome. St Mark's Square. The Church Square
of Finø Town. The square in front of the cathedral in Århus.
Think of Chartres, or the Blue Mosque in Istanbul. In Copenhagen
that place is Kongens Nytorv.'

We're seated on the terrace of the Hotel d'Angleterre. On
the other side of the glass windbreak, life goes on as ever.
Tourists puzzle over how Copenhagen in April can be full of
sunshine and spring and yet conceal a freezing northerly wind
in its top hat, so no one knows whether to go about in bikinis
or ski suits. At the edge of the elliptical parterre known as
Krinsen in the middle of Kongens Nytorv, a red double-decker
sightseeing bus stands waiting for its passengers, and on the
table in front of the Count at the hotel overlooking the square
is a plate of *smørrebrød* heaped high with delicacies, and a tall
glass of frothy beer.

'The Seaman's Mission of Nyhavn,' the Count goes on,
'the Christian foundations of the Royal Theatre, Heiberg's
Elverhøj, the ballets of Bournonville. Profound works indeed,
and evangelical. One feels the vibrations from the Church of
Holmen.'

With his knife the Count separates the layers of one of
his open sandwiches. From a small metal box he picks a pinch

of something resembling curry powder. He winks at Tilte and me.

'Magic mushroom. Plucked only yesterday from the green lawns of the northern suburbs. Dried and brought to me by the little blue men this morning. Where was I? Ah, yes. Kongens Nytorv. Can't you just feel how close we are to the Palace Chapel and the Marble Church? The Institute of Buddhist Studies. St Ansgar's and the Catholic Institute. What a magnificent force field.'

And then he realises that not one of us is sharing his enthusiasm.

Tilte puts Leonora's laptop down on the table in front of him.

'Rickardt,' she says, 'there's something we want to show you.'

We've been here for five minutes. Ashanti captured Rickardt's attention even as we approached his table. Her presence prompts him to put down his cigar.

'A pleasure indeed to meet you,' he says. 'Enchanted, I'm sure.'

Then he sees the rest of us and nods, only to turn his attention back to Ashanti.

'You're a foreigner, I see? Perhaps I might show you the city? I have a Bentley waiting. A convertible, of course.'

'I'd love to,' says Ashanti. 'Would there be room for my partner?'

Count Rickardt looks up at Hans, then back at Ashanti, at Hans, then Ashanti. He licks his lips, and Tilte and I can tell that a variety of scenarios are passing through his mind, none of which I would care to outline here, seeing as how this is meant for families.

But then he pulls himself together and shows a glimpse of the spirit that comes of six hundred years of nobility.

'I have a better idea,' he says. 'You and Hans take the car. A drive north along the Strandvej, two young lovers in an open Bentley. A truly religious experience.'

And at this moment the *smørrebrød* and the beer are served, whereupon Rickardt proceeds to extoll the virtues of Kongens Nytorv, only to be curtailed by Tilte putting Leonora's laptop on the table in front of him.

A moment passes before Rickardt identifies the room.

'The old chapel,' he says. 'Where I shall soon be singing.'

Tilte speeds up the film. It becomes night. The four figures enter.

'People,' says the Count. 'What are they doing there at night?'

'Listen to the voices,' says Tilte.

She turns up the volume.

'I think there's a mouse!' says the woman's breathless voice.

Rickardt shakes his head. He's blank.

Tilte runs the sequence from the beginning again. Now that I've seen it several times, I'm able to make out the figures as they enter.

'Impossible, my dear. What you sense are rats.'

Something has caught Rickardt's attention. The film continues.

'It's all so very emotional. I used to play here as a child . . .'

Rickardt makes a sign. Tilte freezes the image. Rickardt turns the laptop to view the screen in shadow.

'Well, I never diddle!' he says. 'If it isn't Black Henrik. What's he doing in the chapel?'

Tilte places her hand on his arm.

'Rickardt,' she says, 'why do you call him *Black* Henrik when his hair's so white?'

Rickardt's eyes glaze over.

'Because of the gloves,' he says. 'They were black.'

We've huddled closer together at the table. Rickardt is trying to collect his thoughts. The mushrooms brought to him by the little blue men aren't helping. I gaze out onto Kongens Nytorv. The red double-decker is still waiting on its own, which is a fate many of us must learn to deal with. The yellow city buses, on the other hand, are everyone's darlings. In between the parked cars is a black van with tinted windows. The first letters of the registration plate are TH, followed by the digits 50 17.

It may, of course, be coincidence. It's a free country. Before, it was parked on Nikolaj Plads, now it's parked here. Nonetheless, it's one of those coincidences that can't help but make you wonder.

'It must be more than twenty years ago now,' says Count Rickardt. 'There were a bunch of us breezy boys and girls around Filthøj. I was the natural midpoint. It was the golden age of childhood. But the years pass, and all of a sudden everyone is spread to the wind, married or else in the care of the Prison Service. Henrik was a lark among us. We called him *Holy Henrik* back then, on account of his parents being so devout. Ten years pass during which time I never see him. Then one Christmas I'm home for the holiday and the whole castle's been invaded by rats. The exterminators are summoned, and who should be standing there at the door but Henrik. A warm reunion, indeed. There he was with his own firm and an army of employees. But because the castle was his playground as a child he wants to do the job himself. For nostalgic reasons. So I pull a chair out into the courtyard between the farm buildings and light a cigar so as to enjoy the sight of a former playmate at work. Henrik paces slowly around the yard, which is a big space, fifty metres by fifty, and with him he has a suitcase with rubber bungs of different sizes, like the ones they use in laboratories. Every time he finds a hole he plugs it with one of his bungs. I suppose he finds about fifty or more. It takes him the best part of an hour, but he only goes round once, and I know he's found them all. But one hole he leaves open and in it he puts a gas cylinder of the kind we used to gas moles before it wasn't allowed any more. A piece of legislation I can only applaud, I might add. We should all be kind to the animals.

'Anyway, he lights the cylinder, crosses the yard and kneels down at another hole. Then he puts on gloves. Thin, black latex ones, to get a better grip. And then he takes the bung out of the hole. A minute passes, perhaps, before the first rat appears. Henrik grabs it. A gentle, seamless movement, but quick. And then he breaks its neck. The same with the next one, and the one after that. He puts all the dead ones in a pile next to him, and the pile gets bigger and bigger. To begin with, the rats come at intervals, but gradually they appear one after another in quick succession, but he doesn't miss a single one. And not one of them is quick enough to bite him. By the time he's finished, there are a hundred and twenty-eight rats in the pile. We have the staff count them before they're burned. Then Henrik gets to his feet, takes off his gloves and says a short prayer. It's a sight that's stuck in my mind. His white hair and his folded hands. The prayer. And the pile of dead rats next to him.'

Count Rickardt has journeyed back to his happy childhood. But now he returns to the Hotel d'Angleterre.

'I've seen him only once since then. At the premises of one of my regular suppliers. He must have got behind on his payments, the supplier that is. Because Henrik was there. I hid under the sofa so he wouldn't see me. He'd become a debt collector. Working the whole Copenhagen area for the biker gangs and the immigrants, the Polish mafia, some Danish firms. Very generous and broad-minded. My supplier coughed up immediately. Though I must say he was very pale afterwards.'

Rickardt puts his finger to the frozen image on the screen.

'That's him. That fine voice of his. He could have been a singer. A decent profession. Who knows, he could have made a name for himself doing backing vocals for me. But what's he doing in the old chapel? Bit of a surprise, I'd say, for him to be part of the conference.'

'Our view entirely, dear Rickardt,' says Tilte.

We get up to leave. My eyes dwell on the Count's cigar. He traces my gaze.

'Peter,' he says, 'you know what I've promised you if you never begin to smoke. A guided Ketamine trip and a regal blowjob on your eighteenth birthday.'

'The band,' I say. 'Can I have it?'

Everyone looks at me. Carefully, I draw the red and golden band from around the cigar. I sense a degree of bewilderment at the table. They're wondering if the pressure's got to me.

If little Peter has been whacked back in his development by what the mystics call astral regression, which is to say that you become a child again and at the age of fourteen start collecting things that glitter.

I leave them in the dark about that. All they get from me is a mysterious look, veiled by my long, curved eyelashes.

49

WE'RE ON OUR WAY OUT AND I STOP AT RECEPTION. ON THE wall are signed photographs of all the celebrities who have stayed at the hotel. I notice Cruyff, Pelé, Maradona. And Conny. Smiling from a large photo, in the bottom corner of which she has written: *With thanks to all the staff for two marvellous weeks.*

All good photographs make their subjects come alive. The way this happens in Conny's case is now what's making her famous. So besides all my other sorrows and concerns, I'm standing here in the reception of the Hotel d'Angleterre with my already broken heart in ribbons, if I may put it that way.

The feeling of Conny suddenly coming alive in front of me is so real I almost miss the bike messenger who now places a bolt cutter, a hacksaw and two metal files on the counter and says: 'For the Ministry of Education. Attention of Alexander Flounderblood.'

This is obviously a situation demanding further investigation, even if the blood of one's heart is ebbing away, and now a young waiter appears from nowhere, pushing a serving trolley containing brunch for five. And then the receptionist puts the bolt cutter, the hacksaw and the metal files onto the trolley.

'Fourth floor,' she says. 'They called down concerning a call to be put straight through from an A. Winehappy. Tell them the switchboard's aglow at the moment, but we'll put it through as soon as it arrives. We haven't forgotten them.'

I'm sure you know the feeling when your opponent's on the attack but all of a sudden your defence has robbed them of the ball, and then comes a pass from your own penalty area, and there you are, a hair's breadth from offside, and you see yourself dart forward without a thought in your head.

Well, the same thing happens now. The young waiter wheels his trolley away, I make a sign to the others, grab Ashanti's sunglasses and am off on the heels of brunch for five, through reception and into the lift.

He's a couple of years older than me, and some of the hotel's superiority has rubbed off on him. And yet I can tell he's a footballer. It's hard to say what it is. Einar Fakir says football is addictive to the character. My own take is that football is a spiritual pathway promoting the development of a shared consciousness with one's teammates, enhanced concentration, *one-pointed* presence and a purity of heart all directed towards one single goal, which is to put the ball in the back of the net, and some of all this is what I sense to be present in the boy in front of me.

'Brøndby or FC Copenhagen?' I ask.

'Copenhagen.'

I chant: '*When you hear the NOISE of the Copenhagen boys . . .*'

This goes down well in the confines of the lift. For anyone born on Finø, only Finø FC exists, but politeness may often dictate demonstrating one's knowledge of inferior local teams.

All his airs have vanished now, and standing in front of me are the bare bones of a friend.

'Flounderblood,' I say. 'The one you're taking brunch to. He's my favourite uncle and it's his birthday. We're playing a practical joke on him, hence the tools. He's always game for a laugh. And what would really make this day unforgettable for him would be if you lent me your jacket and gave me four minutes to serve him his food.'

I take the housekeeping wallet out of my pocket and produce from it a five-hundred-krone note, holding it in the light to give him the full benefit.

'He's fifty today,' I tell him. 'Lovely man.'

He takes off his jacket. I put it on, then Ashanti's sunglasses.

The mirrors in the lift reveal that even my own mother would have to look twice in order to recognise me.

The boy extends his hand.

'My name's Max,' he says. 'I play for AB. They call me *Max-attax*.'

'I'm Peter,' I say. 'It means rock in Latin. On Finø they say I'm the rock on which the Finø AllStars are built.'

And then I knock, open the door and wheel in the trolley.

50

THE ROOM I ENTER MUST BE A BRIDAL SUITE. EVEN IF IT ISN'T,
I for one certainly wouldn't mind spending my wedding night
here if it weren't for the fact that my life is devoted to a mere
memory.

The suite has two large rooms facing Kongens Nytorv and the
standard of comfort is a match even for the *White Lady of Finø*.

At a table sit Anaflabia Borderrud and the wife of Thorkild
Thorlacius, and behind them stands the great scientist himself.

None of them condescends to look at me, part of the reason
being that the staff of such exclusive establishments as the
Hotel d'Angleterre merge into the wallpaper, and another part
being that they are mesmerised by the food, and understand-
ably so. Most likely they haven't had a bite all day, because
in the ship's restaurant this morning they became embroiled
in scuffles and were then put in chains. And now, still handcuffed, they have escaped, and the effort must have cost them
no end of calories.

It's clear that they're not merely hungry. They're ravenous.

But they are also in distress. All three of them endeavour to
keep their handcuffs hidden, and again one understands them
only too well. Indeed, the fact that they have escaped Lars and
Katinka to seek refuge in the Hotel d'Angleterre without being
apprehended commands respect and is testimony to the combined
powers of science and religion.

Just as I begin to serve, the telephone rings. Thorkild Thorlacius
answers it, which is no easy matter, seeing as how his hands are

restrained behind his back, and his wife must hold the receiver to his mouth. I hear the voice of the receptionist announcing Albert Winehappy.

You can learn a lot about a person by observing what they can effectuate over a telephone. Thus, when Thorkild hears the voice on the other end, he straightens his shoulders immediately as though caught in the act of stealing dried dab.

'I see,' he says. 'Indeed. My pleasure. We're at the Angleterre. Yes, I realise there may be a warrant out for our arrest. But once again the whole regrettable matter is down to police incompetence. Even as I speak, we are preparing our complaint in the expectation that two detective constables will be suspended pending charges of wrongful arrest and unwarranted use of force.'

On the street below, a couple of patrol cars pass by with sirens blaring. The noise, and perhaps the first germ of paranoia as regards officers of the law, stuns Thorkild Thorlacius into immediate silence. I become aware of the extent of the police presence at Kongens Nytorv. And now I sense the pride and tension that prevails over Copenhagen on account of the impending conference. It feels as if the whole city is trembling.

At the same time, I sense, or rather hear, something quite different indeed, something that is at once banal and so surprising that to begin with I am unable to comprehend its significance. The calamity of police sirens that bursts into the bridal suite from without, and which has compelled Thorkild Thorlacius to pause in his lament, issues simultaneously from the receiver of the telephone in his wife's hand.

The sound dies away and Thorkild returns to the now.

'Then there's the matter of the children,' he says. 'The fugitives. We have reason to believe that they are now in Copenhagen. We almost certainly identified them on board the ship. In disguise, of course. It is my considered opinion – as a psychiatrist – that they pose a serious threat to their surroundings.'

Words are uttered at the other end. Words that compel Thorkild Thorlacius to sit down.

'I see,' he says.

He fumbles for paper and pen, which again is no easy matter with your hands cuffed behind your back.

'Why a code?' he asks. 'My name is usually more than sufficient. I am known by the public. From television.'

More words are uttered at the other end, and it's plain that they anger Thorkild Thorlacius, because when Albert Winehappy terminates his call, Thorkild attempts to headbutt the receiver.

'Disrespectful,' he splutters. 'He told me to put a sock in it. To mind my own business. Even had the audacity to suggest I find myself another hobby instead of assaulting policemen. He proposed *lap dancing*. Whatever that might be.'

'That's his Jesuit nature,' says Anaflabia Borderrud. 'Rumour has it he was a Catholic priest before joining the police.'

'In the corridors of government they call him the Cardinal.'

The voice is Alexander Flounderblood's, and it comes from inside the adjoining room, which is why I haven't been aware of him until now.

'He's come all the way up the ladder,' Alexander goes on. 'Now has one of the top jobs in Interpol. Called home to oversee security for the conference.'

His voice is full of awe. One can only conclude that top jobs abroad are a permanent fixture of Alexander Flounderblood's most intimate dreams.

'He went on about a code,' says Thorkild. 'A code by which we are to identify ourselves when entering the conference. I have never before needed to identify myself on any official occasion. I shall speak to my dear friend the Minister of the Interior on the matter.'

I remove the lid from the dish of hot scrambled eggs and small cocktail sausages. The aroma draws Thorkild Thorlacius out of his chair.

This allows me to filch the piece of paper with the access code and stick it in my pocket. And to peer into the adjoining room. Alexander Flounderblood is lying outstretched on the couch, and Vera the Secretary is massaging his scalp.

This is a sight that fills me with immediate and deepfelt joy.

It speaks volumes of the transformational power that resides in the relationship between a man and a woman. Less than four hours ago, there had been little cause to doubt Vera when she stated to the police that she did not care for physical contact. And until this moment, I and most others on Finø have been convinced that with the possible exception of Baroness it would be impossible to dig up another living soul who would voluntarily caress Alexander Flounderblood.

Both prejudices have now been put to shame.

This fact elevates me, yet the sudden lift in spirits causes a small measure of my rock-solid composure to crumble. What happens is that I briefly remove my sunglasses so as to send Alexander Flounderblood a wink of congratulation.

Instantly, I realise that I may have been pushing my luck and hasten to whisk the trolley out into the corridor where I return the jacket to Max, shove Ashanti's sunglasses into place on his nose, stick five hundred kroner into his breast pocket and whisper: 'See you at the match.' And then I push the button to summon the lift.

Behind me comes a gargling sound, a rattle of handcuffs and then a thud as something heavy falls to the floor. From which I deduce that Alexander Flounderblood has attempted to leap to his feet straight from prone position.

'The waiter! The boy! It's him! Peter Finø! The little devil!'

I hear Anaflabia and Thorlacius trying to hold him back.

'Calm down, man!' Thorlacius commands. 'We're all under duress. Studies show that in situations such as the present, hallucinations are commonplace . . .'

The lift arrives and I step inside. Alexander is now in the corridor, and once again one has to admire the meticulousness of the Ministry of Education in selecting their staff, because despite being bound like a hog the man moves with the speed of a bullet. He pins Max to the wall with his chest. Anaflabia and Thorkild Thorlacius are right on his heels.

Max removes Ashanti's sunglasses. Alexander stares at the face in front of him.

'But that's impossible,' he groans.

The doors of the lift close. The last thing I hear is the sound of Max's voice.

'This is assault. I'm calling the police. From the look of things, I'd say they know you already. Though for five hundred kroner I could start to consider putting it all behind me.'

51

HANS AND TILTE AND ASHANTI AND BASKER AND I ARE SITTING
in the car looking out on Kongens Nytorv. The future seems
mixed. In a moment, Hans will start the engine and drive us to
the Store Kongensgade Police Station. Four individuals will thereby
be prevented from vandalising religious treasures to the tune of
a billion kroner, if I've understood things correctly, and that's the
positive aspect. But then comes the search for Mother and Father,
and the proceedings against them, the prison sentences they will
receive, and long spells in a children's home for me and a youth
detention centre for Tilte, not to mention a rather bleak outlook,
at best a kennel, for Basker.

We've done all we could. We couldn't have done any better.

Between what we've done and what we're about to do comes
this brief half-time interlude. The studies Tilte and I have
conducted have revealed that all the great mystics have pointed
to the half-time interval and said that in it resides the very
particular chance to sense that worry is of our own making, and
that only one place exists in which one may be relieved of it, and
that place is what they call the here and now.

The next moment, the flow of thought has carried you away
with it, you're taken by the splendour of Kongens Nytorv,
by the red double-decker bus, by all the tourists, the pigeons
and the black van whose registration number begins with the
letters TH.

But then the chance comes round once more to haul yourself
ashore into the present, into the car, and to look upon your own

brother and sister and sense the pleasure of being present in the here and now.

And at that moment, Ashanti begins to sing. She does so quietly, and the listener has no hope of picking out the words, but my assumption is that it's some kind of voodoo song, hopefully not a hymn in praise of Haiti in which that island is portrayed as a baby cooing on the changing table of the Caribbean, but at any rate Ashanti's voice now fills the car like some enchanting liquid.

We try to join in on the chorus. The verses are many and we allow the final note to die away. A lot may be said about us, but we go to the gallows with a song on our lips.

Hans grips the wheel. The future is now.

And then Tilte leans forward.

'We still have an hour left,' she says. 'We agreed on two hours.'

None of the rest of us recalls having entered into any agreement. What we recall is Tilte saying 'two hours'. But then, the forces of nature may only seldom be resisted.

'There's something I need to do,' Tilte says. 'We'll meet back in the apartment on Toldbodgade. In an hour. Then the police can take over.'

This sends the rest of us into a state of slight shock. But once again we manage to haul ourselves ashore and back into the present, where it is said there should be no worries. The first of us to crawl ashore is Hans.

'Ashanti and I,' he says, 'will spend that time putting her family in the picture. They've arrived now with the delegation from Haiti.'

One senses the wisdom of the project. Mummy and Daddy from Port-au-Prince have doubtless envisaged marrying their little girl off to a man of good prospects, and then here she comes with a two-metre-tall stargazer as poor as a church mouse.

Tilte is about to open the door. I cough discreetly.

Everyone looks up at me. It's like in the fairy tales: the youngest son's a nobody. No one imagines anything other than that little Peter is going back to Toldbodgade to pass away the time and keep out of the way while Hans chats up the in-laws.

But out of my pocket I now produce the coloured band from Rickardt's cigar.

It's a flash of gold, with a red line-drawing of a woman in profile. On her head she wears an antique Greek helmet. Underneath are the words: *Pallas Athene. Abakosh.* And a phone number. And an address on Gammel Strand. I take out the sheet of paper from the concealed room at the rectory. I hold it up for the others to see what is written at the bottom in biro: *pallasathene.abak@mail.dk.*

I extend my hand to Tilte.

'Katinka's phone,' I say.

I dial the number from the cigar band and switch on the speaker.

It's hard to say exactly what's going on inside me. But if you play football, I'm sure you recall that there comes a time when you find the guts to go for goal all by yourself. For my own part, this occurred some time during my first season on the first team. It was one of those magical moments I've told you about. There was a long pass from behind, the midfield had pulled back into defence, there was no one with me, and yet I knew immediately I had to run forward to receive. It wasn't a logical feeling, and there was no time to think about it. The only thing I felt was that the door was opening. I took the ball down like it was a little bird settling on my foot, then passed two defenders who had me marked as though they could swat me like a fly, rounded the keeper and followed the ball all the way into the back of the net. Not until I was standing there did I truly understand that I had gone through the door. Not the real door, the one that leads out into freedom, but one that takes you into the hall, an anteroom of true emancipation.

This is the kind of moment that now occurs inside the car. I sense that this is a thing I must do on my own.

'Abakosh.'

The voice is a woman's and it spans at least two things: the first is a secret, and the second is a project that entices others to see what the secret might be.

'This is Peter,' I say. 'I need to speak to Pallas Athene.'

'Have you got a password, dear?'

I look down at Mother's and Father's note.

'*Brahmacharya*,' I say.

Silence. Then the voice appears again.

'I'm very sorry, but Pallas Athene is busy at the moment. How about one of the other goddesses?'

I'm dribbling the ball in the dark. But I feel I'm on the right track.

'It has to be her,' I say. 'I've got an appointment.'

Silence again. But I hear her fingers on a keyboard.

'Can you be here in fifteen minutes?'

'I can be there in a jiffy.'

'She's only got twenty minutes, though.'

'Twenty minutes with a goddess,' I say. 'That's as good as an eternity with a mere mortal, wouldn't you say?'

That gets me in and deflates her professional demeanour. She giggles.

'I should say,' she says. 'Would you like us to send a car?'

'My driver's just parked the Merc here on Kongens Nytorv.'

'Should I open a bottle of bubbly?'

The others in the car are agog. I can see the wonder in their eyes. And I'm sure they see the wonder in mine.

'Of course,' I say. 'But I'm strictly non-alcoholic myself. The outdoor season's already underway, and I need to be at my peak in two weeks. And to stay there. I'm a monk at the moment.'

'Looking forward to seeing you,' she says.

We say our goodbyes. I open the car door.

'We're going with you,' says Hans.

I shake my head.

'You're going to talk to your in-laws, Hansel. That should be enough for anyone.'

'But you're only fourteen,' Hans says.

I straighten my shoulders.

'There comes a time,' I say, 'when a man must find his own way.'

52

I'VE NEVER UNDERSTOOD THE SYSTEM BEHIND COPENHAGEN street names. Where is the blue courtyard on the square called Blågårds Plads, if that's what *blå gård* means? Where is the king of Kongens Nytorv, the *King's New Square*, which isn't even new? And if *strand* means beach, then what's Gammel Strand all about? *Gammel*, as anyone knows, means old, and maybe the houses there were old once, but they've certainly been given a facelift since then, and not only have their faces been lifted, they've also had their insides and all their vital parts replaced, so anyone would think they were built only yesterday and the owners had just been handed the keys.

Those keys are most likely made of gold, for the brass plates next to the doors bear the names of stockbrokers and high-flying lawyers, and the gateways are all equipped with wrought-iron gates and security cameras. Where I now stand there are two closed-circuit television cameras looking at me.

The nameplate says *Abakosh*, and twirled around the name are engraved vines, but there's no button to press on the intercom. Instead, I position myself in front of the cameras, and as I wait I'm forced to concede that I may have bitten off more than I can chew.

It's a rare feeling. Ask anyone on Finø and they'll tell you that Peter Finø never exceeds the bounds of his natural reticence.

If anyone should mention the time I joined the Mr Finø contest on the harbour promenade, I would once again stress that this was due to malicious conspiracy, and let me now sweep rumour

285

aside once and for all and share with you the exact circumstances of this unfortunate event. It came about because Tilte invited Karl Marauder Lander, who is in the same class as her, into her walk-in wardrobe with the aim of letting him try out the coffin, and her doing so can only be explained with reference to her wish to help people improve their characters, a wish that occasionally blurs her vision when it comes to some of the more hopeless individuals in our midst.

Nevertheless, in order to help Tilte out and to enhance Karl Marauder's chances of learning to search his conscience – if indeed he possesses such a thing – I had recorded a few sequences from *The Tibetan Book of the Dead* and transferred them onto an mp3 player at two-thirds normal speed and then concealed the device inside the lining of the coffin, later to play back the recording by means of a remote control when Karl Marauder had made himself comfy and the lid had been closed on top of him.

It was a very expressive recording. And at two-thirds normal speed, my voice sounded like the Prince of Darkness suddenly coming right at you. I was certain it would have the desired effect.

And indeed it seemed to do the job. Karl Marauder came out of the coffin like a rocket on New Year's Eve, bathed in a cold sweat. But rather than exploiting the situation to delve into his soul and enquire of himself as to the source of his anxiety, this being the recommended procedure in all spiritual traditions, he instead ran back across the road and snitched to his parents, who turned up in unison at the rectory fifteen minutes later, which was to be the decisive factor in Tilte being instructed to return the coffin to Bermuda Jansson.

Instead of recognising my good intentions, Tilte was angry with me, so angry, in fact, that she entered into an alliance with Karl Marauder, and this must surely rank alongside the great treacheries of world history.

Their spiteful conspiracy involved Karl enticing me onto the football field, promising to stand in goal while I practised bending free-kicks with the outside of my right foot, just as the Mr Finø finals commenced. All of a sudden, Tilte comes running to say that Einar Flogginfellow is looking for me on account of my being awarded the Finø FC Player of the Year trophy, and in order that I might receive the full honour I so deserve, Einar is planning to hand me the trophy on stage, for which reason he wants me in football shorts, football boots and preferably topless so as to provide a visualisation of what such an award costs a player in terms of perspiration.

I believe in the good of all people, and in that innocent belief I entered the stage completely unaware that the crowd of more than a thousand locals and tourists had just been entertained by Norwegian swimmers and Danish rowing champions weighing in at two hundred kilos, posing and flexing with olive oil rubbed into their glistening bodies.

So basically that time doesn't count. Normally, I feel my way along with my fingertips.

'We don't accept newspapers or door drops.'

The woman's voice from the telephone crackles on the intercom. The loudspeaker must be in the nameplate.

'You're in luck, then,' I tell her. 'Because if there's two things I haven't got, it's newspapers and door drops. But I do have an appointment with Pallas Athene. So I think you should let me in.'

The gate opens. But I sensed hesitation.

53

I DON'T KNOW IF THE HOUSES OF GAMMEL STRAND HAVE always been half-timbered with sash-windows on the outside and Greek temples on the inside, but that's what this particular house looks like now.

The stairway is as wide as a road and flanked by pillars, everything in marble. It leads up to a reception area with more marble. Behind a desk sits a woman with blonde hair, clad in Greek sandals and a toga whose neckline is so plunging that it's difficult to say whether she is naked or clothed.

The walls are adorned with murals, though their style is quite different from those of Finø Town Church, because these depict naked men and women drinking wine from what look like soup bowls, or else having their bottoms birched, or just sitting around on benches and chairs with mournful expressions, perhaps because they think it ought to be their turn to drink wine or have their bottoms birched, or simply because they don't know who has taken their clothes away from them.

'You look young.'

There's a school of philosophy that has established itself on Finø and elsewhere in Denmark that believes blondes with plunging necklines to be warm-hearted, though empty-headed. The woman in front of me dispels that theory at once. She's as cool as a refrigerator and her aura suggests she is continually processing information at high speed.

'Most of those who said that,' I tell her, 'are now pushing up daisies.'

She giggles and yet is obviously in a dilemma, the specifics of which remain unclear to me, so I'm still dribbling the ball in the dark.

'Andrik will show you in,' she says.

The man behind me has appeared so silently I failed to hear him approach. He too is wearing a toga, and his hair is done in the way of Greek statues. I'm not sure which of the deities he's supposed to be, as I was absent the day we did Greek mythology in school, but the god of murderers would certainly be a decent guess if there is one. He has the build of a decathlete and baby-blue eyes, and reminds me of the most lethal individuals you can encounter on the football field, people with no end of fine talents, all of which they've placed at the disposal of malice.

He opens a door for me and we enter a room that erases all hopes of the house bearing any relation to historical Copenhagen. It's a space of some two hundred square metres with a glass ceiling through which one may observe the blue sky, and all around are enough green plants to fill up the great greenhouses of the botanical gardens at Århus.

But apart from that, all resemblance to those gardens is purely coincidental, because the plants here are arranged so as to form enclosures, each of which contains a marble bath in which men lie outstretched while being washed behind the ears by women who could be, but most probably are not, twin sisters of the woman in reception. In the middle of the room is a table on which bottles of champagne have been placed in coolers. There's no time to find out which one might be non-alcoholic, and anyway I'm not thirsty. There's also a thing that looks like a refrigerator, only with lamps and a humidity gauge and a glass door, behind which can be seen boxes of Havana cigars, and I bet that if you could see the bands around them they'd be the same as the one on Count Rickardt's cigar.

Andrik opens another door, this one leading into a changing room done out in marble.

'Take off your clothes here,' he says. 'Then go straight through.'

On a bench is a white bath towel the size and thickness of a polar bear skin. As soon as Andrik has gone, I drape it around my shoulders and go through into the next room.

This is where the marble stops. Instead, everything's golden and red, and there are two raised areas. On one is a double bed, on the other a bidet.

On a small table, someone has placed a steaming cup of coffee, and next to it are a pair of reading glasses and an address book bound in brown leather.

I sidle over to the table. From an adjoining room I hear the sound of a person brushing their hair. I flick through the address book to H for *Home*. Everybody's got a mobile phone now, and none of us can remember our landline numbers any more, at least we can't at the rectory.

And neither, it seems, can Pallas Athene. Under *Home* are eight digits that I enter into my mobile in the hope that police intelligence haven't accessed my list of contacts. There's no address. I close the book. I don't know what motivated me, but maybe it was to see if goddesses, too, have private addresses.

I sit down on a chair, nervously on the edge.

Pallas Athene enters.

I'd make her about one metre eighty-eight in her stockinged feet. Which means that if she's any good with a ball she could step right in as a guard on Finø FC's women's basketball team.

But she's not in her stockinged feet, she's in red stilettos that add about fifteen centimetres to her height. And besides that, she's wearing a red wig, and on top of the wig is the kind of Greek helmet now familiar to me from the house's own Havana cigars.

But apart from that, all she's wearing is a pair of skimpy red panties, a liberal quantity of lipstick and a broad smile that turns out to be of only limited durability, because as soon as she sets eyes on me it disappears completely.

I should like to draw attention to the fact that I would never normally describe a naked woman in any detail to anyone, not even to myself. The reason I now endeavour to do so is purely pedagogical, the intention being to enlighten you as to the exact nature of what I am faced with.

I shall therefore mention to you that the woman's breasts are not merely large, they are the size of basketballs and so well inflated one could put them on a string and sell them as helium balloons to the kids at a theme park.

She towers above me, picks up a kimono from the bed and puts it on. And then she sits down, removes her helmet and places it on the table.

Her expression tells me we're no longer frolicking in the Mediterranean sun, but have relocated north of the Arctic Circle.

'At your age,' she says, 'we need a signature from your parents.'

'That'll be a tall order,' I tell her. 'They've gone missing, you see. That's why I'm here. They left the name of this place behind them.'

I hand her the piece of paper with my mother's note on it. She picks the reading glasses up off the table and puts them on, casts a glance at what's written and hands it back to me.

'What are your parents' names?'

I tell her. She shakes her head, her gaze not releasing me for a moment.

'Never heard of them. Where did you get the address?'

Not wishing to give the Count away, I say nothing.

'And then there's the password,' she muses. 'Where's that from?'

I can't answer her without telling her about Mother's and Father's misdemeanours. So I remain silent.

'It's very important to us, that password,' she says.

There's something menacing about her voice that would make anyone forget all about the outfit and the red lips. Now one senses oneself to be sitting in front of a person who not only possesses a great deal of willpower, but also knows how to use it.

She must have pressed a button somewhere, because all of a sudden the murderer is standing beside me, and once again I failed to hear him approach.

'Andrik,' she says, 'the boy has a password that doesn't belong to him. He won't tell me where he got it from.'

Andrik nods and looks concerned, which means I am now faced with two individuals, both of whom wear the same expression.

'I could ask him about it in the steam baths,' says Andrik.

One can only hazard a guess as to Andrik's techniques of enquiry. But it seems unlikely that he would coax the answers out of me with mint humbugs and little words of encouragement. He probably wants to coax them out of me by holding my head under a jet of steam and then slamming it against the tiled floor.

'I'm a dishwasher,' I tell him. 'One of the guests in the restaurant left the band of a cigar behind and on it were an address and a phone number. The password was written on the inside.'

They stare at me. Then the woman nods.

'Sounds plausible, I suppose,' she says. 'Andrik, would you be kind enough to see the young gentleman out? By the back stairs.'

The man doesn't touch me. He doesn't need to. All he does is take a step closer and that's enough for me to leap out of the chair. The woman opens a door at the other end of the room.

The so-called back stairs are classy enough for most people to dream of having them at their main entrance. As we step out onto the landing, the woman clears her throat.

'How long have your parents been missing?'

'A few days.'

Andrik and I begin our descent. She clears her throat again.

'Andrik, he's just a child.'

The man nods. I sense some disappointment.

We cross a courtyard with palms in great pots and a red vintage Jaguar parked at one side. Andrik must have a remote, because now a double gate opens and then we're standing in a narrow street. Andrik looks both ways. The street is deserted. He puts his hand around my upper arm and squeezes tight.

'Cry baby, are you?' he says.

On this point, however, he is mistaken. If I shed a tiny tear it is only at the thought of the revenge I will take for him squeezing so hard.

'I think this should be the first and last time we enjoy the pleasure of the young gentleman's company,' he says. 'Do you know what I mean?'

'I do,' I say. 'But what about them?'

I peer into the darkness of the gateway we have just left.

It's the oldest trick in the book. But it's also one of the best. If correctly employed, it provides ample illustration of something Tilte and I have studied at length. Great mystics all agree: words make reality.

More than that, it's the very basis of what all Danish football and handball players will know as the dustman's trick: look one way, then go the other.

Andrik's fast, I'll give him that. He spins round on his heels and stares into the gloom of the gateway to see who got past. And he's alert, too, because as he does so he makes sure to keep a tight grip on my arm.

But it's too late. His grip on the situation is gone.

I extricate myself as I have done so often when penned in by three defenders who could find work as steamrollers any day of the week. I twirl round like a ballerina on my left foot. And then I boot him up the behind.

He's in good shape. I can tell, because his buttocks are like footballs, firm and elastic against my instep.

In case you are unfamiliar with the finer details of football, I can tell you that any great kick issues not from the leg, but from the deep muscles of the abdomen. The most exquisite execution involves a seamless sequence of acceleration, contact and follow-through, and this particular kick is indeed exquisitely executed. My whole body's behind it, and its force is so perfectly directed as to send Andrik careering onto his nose four metres into the gateway darkness whence he came.

I toss him the white towel that's still draped around my shoulders.

'Andrik,' I say, 'what would you say to both of us trying to bear in mind the notion of compassion, before this escalates any further?'

No answer is forthcoming, which hardly surprises me, because Andrik is already up and running in my direction.

He's a fairly decent sprinter. But his natural surroundings are marble bathtubs and expensive bottles of champagne, not the football fields of Finø, and his buttocks have not even begun to stop aching, so before I reach Højbro Plads he's lost me for good.

Even so, I keep running. Someone like Andrik might easily jump inside his great BMW and cruise the old city frothing at the mouth until he finds me again. So from instinct I run like a gazelle, because how else should one run in a strange city, through the narrow streets parallel to the pedestrian thoroughfare called Strøget until reaching Kongens Nytorv, where I slip between the cars that are parked to face the waterfront of Nyhavn?

Reaching the Krinsen parterre in the middle of the square, I pass the red double-decker bus and catch a fleeting glimpse of the driver.

He doesn't see me, because he's busy kissing a woman who is sitting on the seat diagonally behind him. And their kiss isn't just a peck on the cheek, but one of those kisses in which everything else ceases to exist, and the only things left are petals floating down from the sky, and butterflies, and violins weeping with joy.

Which means I've plenty of time to make absolutely sure. There's no doubt about it. The driver is Lars, detective constable of police intelligence. And the woman behind him is Katinka.

In a way, it's only natural. Lars and Katinka have carried out the intentions of changing profession that they voiced earlier on board the *White Lady*.

It's not hard to understand why. Anyone whose job involves the continuous risk of being assaulted by the likes of Alexander

Beastly Flounderblood, Anaflabia Borderrud and Thorkild Thorlacius-Claptrap would put in for reschooling as soon as humanly possible.

On the other hand, it's puzzling. A thought emerges, only to be denied the space it deserves, because the knowledge that a serial killer like Andrik is stalking me through the city compels me to concentrate on keeping my speed just above steady.

54

I CROSS THE SQUARE IN FRONT OF AMALIENBORG PALACE AND run down a narrow road, at the end of which I catch a glimpse of the harbour. I haven't seen anything of Andrik, but then life on Mount Olympus is filled with nectar and ambrosia and too little exercise. I've started to look forward to telling Tilte and Hans and Basker and Ashanti of the inroads I've made, even though they perhaps point us in no particular direction.

I take a left onto Toldbodgade, and at the same moment a black van comes up the ramp of the underground car park. It turns away from me and I catch sight of its number plate, T for Tilte and H for Hans, and the digits forming the date of Finø FC's promotion to the Danish Minor Islands' Super League.

I sprint like a man possessed, but it's already round the corner and gone. Soon, there'll be no breath left inside me, and yet I manage to tumble through the door and take the stairs six at a time.

The door is closed though unlocked, the apartment empty. It's ten minutes after the time we agreed on. Normally, ten minutes would be of no consequence to Tilte. She always says the great religions operate with two kinds of time: profane time, which is the one shown by clocks, and sacred time, which is the one on which she runs.

As far as I can see, the distinction is nothing but an excuse to turn up as she sees fit. But this is different. In this case, I know she ought to be here.

I'm worried now. I look for signs.

The apartment is still easy to survey. Once people move into a place, all its subtleties are lost in the mountain of clutter with which we all fill up our lives. That's what we're like in the rectory, at least. But no one's properly moved in here yet, so I see it right away.

Leaned against the wall by the bed are a number of framed pictures waiting to be hung on the walls, one in front of the other and their reverse sides facing outwards. Between the outermost picture and the next one in, someone has tucked a piece of thin card. It is small and rectangular, yet clearly visible, at least to a specialist such as me in the field of housework.

I squat down to pick it up, and from there I can see along the floor.

From this angle, the light reflects differently. And I see that something has been spilled in the kitchen area in the other room. Whatever it is has been wiped away, but the floor has not been washed afterwards, and a dry film remains.

I walk over and moisten a finger, draw it across the floor and taste. It's faintly sweet, faintly sour, and would seem to be juice.

I open the cupboard where a rubbish bag hangs from a holder. Uppermost in the bag is a dishcloth. I remove it, and underneath is a broken wine glass with a tall stem. I pick up a shard with the fleshy remnants of a yellow fruit stuck to it. Then I drop it back into the rubbish bag.

Ordinary people such as you and I drink our juice from ordinary tumblers. Tilte drinks hers from wine glasses. She says it's a sacred drink to be imbibed ritually.

Tilte has drunk from the glass in the rubbish bag. But Tilte very seldom drops a glass on the floor. And if she ever did, she would never toss the shards into the rubbish without first wrapping them up. If you live in a household of six that produces as many bags of rubbish a day, you are aware that they need changing and carrying out to the bin and that some other member of the family might risk having an artery severed if you weren't careful with broken glass.

So now I'm really scared.

My cognitive system stalls and I return to the bed to retrieve the little piece of card. To do so I must first tip the outermost picture, which is a photograph. I remove the card and allow the framed picture to fall back into place.

But then I turn it round to look at the photo properly. It's of a boy in football kit after what seems to have been a match played in rain, because it's obvious the subject has been through several mudbaths.

On his jersey are the words: *Finø AllStars.*

The boy is me.

I don't know who organised the cosmos. But sometimes one could have wished for rather more consideration. As if I didn't have enough on my plate already.

The picture was taken by my brother Hans after my first game for the Finø AllStars, in which I scored a goal that was so lucky I ought to have been embarrassed about it. But everything counts in football, even flukes.

There are only two copies of the photo. I have one. The other I gave to Conny.

I study the framed pictures one by one. There are film posters. Flyers for end-of-season dances at Ifigenia Bruhn's Dancing School on Finø Town Square. In one frame is a collage of photographs showing three children.

I know those children well. They are Smilla, Filla and Mandrilla, Conny's nieces.

I go over to the window so as to at least become mobile and get some of my concern circulating.

Some people in this situation would find sufficient reserves to recall the advice of the great mystics and reach inside towards the door. Perhaps you would find such reserves, but I can't. Instead, I feel dizzy. If one thing is certain in all this uncertainty, it's the fact that this is Conny's apartment.

I stare blindly into space. And yet, I can't be entirely blind, because now I see a car turn down the ramp of the underground car park.

A red vintage Jaguar.

Of course, it can't possibly be the one I saw only minutes ago in Pallas Athene's courtyard.

On the window sill in front of me is a telephone. I pick up the receiver.

55

I CALL DIRECTORY ENQUIRIES AND GIVE THE GIRL THE HOME
number from Pallas Athene's address book and ask for a location.

'You're calling from it,' says the girl.

But then she corrects herself.

'No, sorry. It's the floor below. This number's registered on the
fourth floor.'

I clutch at the window sill to steady my balance.

'Is there a name?'

'Maria. Maria and Josef Andrik Fiebelbitsel.'

'I don't suppose there's a Jesus Fiebelbitsel, by any chance?'

'Nothing here.'

I hang up.

Standing there alone in the doorway I know someone has
kidnapped Tilte. And that it has something to do with the visit
we paid to Bellerad Shipping. Someone must have followed us
when we left.

It's a thought that has a very particular effect on me, a something that until now has only ever presented itself a couple of
times a year, and only on the football field. I feel that my next
move will be decisive, that no one will be able to stop me. If a
block of flats should get in my way it'll be too bad, because all
that'll be left will be rubble and homeless tenants.

It doesn't feel like I'm the one pulling the strings. It comes
from without, from the sky above the harbour.

I don't wait around for Hans. I walk out of the door, go down a floor and ring the bell.

Andrik opens the door. In the short time that has elapsed since we parted company, he has taken a bath, and his hair is still wet. He has also picked up the kids from kindergarten, because they wedge themselves against him on both sides, two white-haired twins, perhaps three years old.

But he most certainly hasn't had time to recover from the boot I gave his behind. So much is plain from the rather strained manner in which he is standing and from the pained look in his eyes. It's a look that now makes way for another, for which dumbfounded astonishment would not be exactly the right expression, but which nonetheless falls short of shock and perhaps lies somewhere in between the two.

'I'd like to speak to Maria,' I tell him.

Pallas Athene now looms up above him, because even though she has discarded her stilettos and has put away her wig and helmet, she's still a head taller than Andrik.

The twins sense the situation is rather less than relaxed.

'Daddy,' the girl asks, 'is he dangerous?'

Andrik shakes his head. But has yet to find his voice.

I address Pallas Athene directly. Often, it saves time to skip the middleman and go straight to the top.

'Aren't you going to ask me in?'

She shakes her head.

'That's quite all right,' I say. 'I'll come back in ten minutes and let myself in. Together with six strapping policemen and a search warrant.'

They gape at me. And then they step aside. I walk in.

The apartment is a big sister to the one upstairs. The layout's the same, but this one's larger, the balcony more expansive and there are at least two more rooms. Pallas Athene ushers me into one of them and closes the door behind us.

It's a sort of conservatory. Beneath the glass ceiling are wicker chairs and a table, and vines with tiny grapes on them. There's a bowl made of granite, containing a naked cherub and a little fountain. And there's a view across the harbour to Holmen and further afield to Langelinie.

'We're staying in the apartment upstairs,' I tell her. 'I just got home to find someone kidnapped my sister, Tilte. Everything points to it. I'm one hundred per cent certain. You know something about the people whose password I used. I want to know what it is.'

'I'll need a smoke,' she says.

Her hand does not tremble as she picks out a cigarette. But that's only because she's concentrating.

'Every year, young people die in their droves, victims of passive smoking,' I say.

She lights up, slowly and meticulously, and blows the smoke away from me.

'You'll survive,' she says. 'I've got you sussed. You'd survive if you were run over by a tank. And the tank would come off worst. How old are you, anyway?'

'Twenty-one,' I tell her.

'That would make more sense. But you look more like you're fourteen.'

'I'm young at heart.'

'Is it true you kicked Andrik's backside?'

'He was squeezing my arm.'

I pull up my T-shirt and show her the marks.

'Tell me about it,' she says. 'Sometimes you have to hit back. I've got seven convictions for violence against men. At work I can control it. It flares up in traffic. Some jerk blowing his horn before the lights have even changed. Or else running into the back of me. I go mad. Can't control myself. Before I know it, I'm out of the car, pulling their door open and smashing them in the face. My dad was a boxer. There was a lot of slapping around in our house. It's in the system. But I've never touched the kids.'

She takes a drag. People relate differently to smoke. Most smokers go on automatic pilot once they put a cigarette to their lips. But Pallas Athene relishes each and every drag with her entire being.

'Do you know what Abakosh is?'

'It's a brothel,' I say.

'But top-flight. Andrik and I run five others. Abakosh is the flagship, though. It's themed on the Greek Mysteries. We give the clients brief instruction in meditation and inner peace as part of the package. And we receive all religions. We have a costume collection as big as a theatre wardrobe department. Monks, nuns, houris, angels, dakinis. The Virgin Mary, Kwannon Bosato, bishops' mitres, lamas' hats. There's something for everyone. It's all a roaring success, and the location couldn't be better. We've got Parliament, the Church of Holmen, the major bank head-quarters, Slotsholmen and the government ministries, all the solici-tors' offices and the newspapers. We're raking it in. What's more, we're making people happy at the same time. Andrik looks after the ladies. A third of our clients are women.'

She stubs out her cigarette deliberately, and in her movements I suddenly detect anger.

'The drawback is it gets you so narky sometimes. I love Andrik. But three months in the year I send him away to our holiday cottage at Tisvilde – just so I won't need to see a man outside working hours. He comes into town and sees the kids every other weekend.'

She meets my gaze, fixes her eyes on me, unbuttons her blouse and lifts her breasts from her bra.

'Do you have any idea how many hours of surgery there are here? Eighteen. Three operations, three implants in each. They'll last ten years, fifteen at most. And they're as sore as hell. No one's allowed to touch, not even Andrik. I cried my eyes out every time I fed the twins. That's how much they hurt. Have you been to a brothel before?'

I shake my head.

She's now on her feet. Something's going on inside her. I can't work it out, but we're touching on something, approaching it. I just don't know what it is.

'Listen to me. The deal is this: you can have everything. You can stick it in wherever you want. Blow job, handjob. You can bathe in ethereal oils, or have your backside spanked. But all of it's with a condom on. No kissing. And our hearts are outside in the cloakroom. No feelings involved. I have this ritual every time I get myself ready. I've a box in the dressing room with a photo of the twins in it. I pretend to take my heart out and put it inside the box. Do you understand me? It works. But three months a year I hate men.'

'I've got a sister,' I tell her.

'I don't do girls.'

'Neither does she. But she's got some interesting viewpoints on anger. Building on in-depth studies of the spiritual classics. She can help you.'

'No one can do a thing. The world's the way it is.'

On that point I believe she's wrong. The thought alone of what a person like Tilte could do with a place like Abakosh and a woman such as Pallas Athene is enough to make me dizzy. But I say nothing. There's a time for everything, as the Old Testament says, and product development of such nature will have to wait.

She pulls up a wicker chair and sits down close to me. Now we're getting there.

'I'll do up to four men at once. Men often come together. Especially before something important. It may be four actors before a premiere. Politicians in the middle of some major negotiation. Businessmen about to sign some big contract. That password you've got. Yesterday, four people came in with that password. Three men and a woman. It's personal. Assigned to one person only. The Dane. All I know is his name's Henrik. The other three are foreigners, though they speak the language. Henrik's a regular. Always on his own. But yesterday he had three others with him.'

She lights up another cigarette.

'I had a funny feeling. Something wasn't quite right. So afterwards I sat and thought about it, trying to figure out what it was. And do you know what? It was fear. They scared me. I've been in the business fifteen years. But this was the first time. Do you know why I'm telling you this?'

'Anger, partly,' I say.

'True.'

Her sense of unease makes her rise from her chair again.

'I'm thirty years old. I've three years left at the most. We've got our savings, of course, and the holiday cottage, and the apartment here, and a studio outside Barcelona. But I've given this all I've got. Yesterday was no exception. The one called Henrik rang me up, wanting me to go to them. I said no. I had this feeling about it. I did myself up, got into the part. Henrik always wants me to play his mother. Scold him, feed him, change his nappy. And the two others wanted the same. All three wanted to sit in high chairs and be fed. And they each had their own religion. Never done that before. I had to change clothes eight times in two hours. And read from the holy scriptures while they played with their food. It was like the chimps' tea party at the zoo. And then they wanted a pillow fight. With bare backsides and baby-food all over the place. The woman wanted Andrik to be her father and give her a ride. But when Henrik wanted to take a dump on the floor I put my foot down. We've all got our limits, wouldn't you say? Would you have allowed it?'

'Probably not,' I say.

'So then they have this last wish. They want me to tell them, one at a time, that *Mummy's proud of you, Mummy's very proud of what you're doing*. I ask them for more details, so it'll be easier for me to play the role. But they close up on me. All they want is for me to pat them on the head and tell them Mummy's proud as punch and wishes them good luck. And then it's all over, and when they leave they're quiet and won't even say goodbye, and that's when I begin to sense something. I sense they're up to no good, and whatever it is it's big time and sinister. And in some way they've used me and Andrik so as to pluck up the courage. So I owe it to you to help. This is the first time in fifteen years I've told someone else about a client. You never do that, it's the most important rule there is in this business. But now I've done it. For the first time. Will you accept my help?'

'If it's all right with you, I'll jump at the offer.'

She gives me an expectant look.

'Can we leave the twins with Andrik for an hour or so?' I ask.

She straightens up. 'He's a wonderful father!'

'There's someone we need to meet,' I say. 'Someone who needs to hear all this.'

56

ONE MIGHT PERHAPS HAVE WISHED FOR A MORE INCONSPICUOUS mode of transport than the red Jaguar. Nevertheless, this is what takes us, Pallas Athene and I, from Toldbodgade to Kongens Nytorv.

We arrive without Pallas Athene having smashed in the faces of innocent male motorists, a fact for which I am grateful. Now I ask her to park as close behind the red double-decker bus as possible, and this she does in her own inimitable fashion, there being a free space reserved for the handicapped, and this is where she parks, producing from the glove compartment a blue badge bearing the wheelchair symbol, which she places on the dashboard with a comment about many of her customers being in the medical profession.

I borrow her mobile and instruct her to press the horn once when I give the sign. Then I dial Albert Winehappy's number.

The mood is devout and solemn. For the first time, I am about to establish contact with one of the individuals who is most likely behind the scheme that has turned me and Tilte and Basker grey-haired and added ten years to our age in just a couple of days.

'Yes?'

If like me you have a mother who's in love with Schubert, or an aunt or a female cousin, then you might have heard some of the Goethe-Lieder performed by Fischer-Dieskau. And if you've heard these recordings, then you'll have a good idea of what the voice at the other end of the phone sounds like.

It's a voice that knows things it has no intention of revealing. Perhaps the man to whom it belongs killed twelve people in a clan dispute one moonlit night. Perhaps he plundered the grave of a pharaoh. Or perhaps he was the lover of three government ministers all at once without any of them ever finding out about the others, and now it's over.

Whatever his secret, one thing is certain: this is the voice of an elephant keeper. And beneath the polished tone, one hears the elephant snort.

'Does the name Finø mean anything to you?' I ask.

At first is silence.

'Go on,' he says.

'I do hope it does. Because the island of that name is home to three neglected children who have lost a great deal indeed. And who believe that you ought to help them get some of it back.'

'Who the bleeding hell . . . ?' he begins.

I give Pallas Athene a sign and she sounds the horn. The Jaguar roars. Faintly, yet distinctly, I hear it in the receiver, too.

Then I hang up.

'See that bench over there?' I say to Pallas Athene. 'By the front end of the bus? Sit down there, light up a cigarette, lean back and watch what happens.'

I run across the square, slowing down to a trot as I reach the entrance of the Hotel d'Angleterre, slow enough as not to attract attention. I pass through reception and peer into the restaurant.

Inside the door, gateaux and cakes are housed in their own glass tower, one per storey. I glance around. The waiters have their backs turned. I swipe a whole layer cake.

Layer cake may be a poor description, because in actual fact it consists of one layer only, albeit fifteen centimetres thick, topped with whipped cream and crumbled nougat and raspberries, and with a crisp base that almost certainly would provide anyone with an unforgettable confectionery experience.

At home in the rectory we were taught to whip cream by

hand with a whisk. Should you come from a more unfortunate home in which cream was whipped by mechanical means, perhaps even with the aid of an electric appliance, all may not yet be lost.

An electric mixer infuses air all too quickly into the cream, whereby the bubbles take up too much space and the skimmed milk separates prematurely from the fat. Cream whipped by hand with a whisk takes on a completely different texture altogether.

This is a fact known to all in the kitchens of the Hotel d'Angleterre. The cake is firm and unperturbed by my ascent of the stairs, even though I take four steps at a time. So when I get to the bridal suite and knock on the door and step inside, it's only me who's out of breath and whose cheeks are flushed, the cake looks exactly like the confectioner just sent it off with a kiss.

Thorkild Thorlacius, Anaflabia, Thorlacius' wife, Vera the Secretary and Alexander Flounderblood have been taking their time. They've cut the chains of their handcuffs, and the pieces are on the floor together with the bolt cutter, the hacksaw and the metal files. What they haven't been able to remove are the actual cuffs around their wrists. So they have partaken of brunch with these still on, and they're only just finishing up now.

I approach the table and deliver the cake in a gentle arc into the face of Alexander Flounderblood.

'In time,' I say, 'you will all understand that this is for your own good.'

When you see people in films having custard pies pressed into their faces, the pies, I'm sorry to say, are invariably dummies or cheap tarts of dubious quality. But a high-class layer cake such as the present one produces a completely different visual effect altogether. In films, the victims will often be able to remove most of the custard pie with just a couple of swipes of the hand. But the eyes of Alexander Flounderblood have only just become visible after perhaps twenty seconds or more of vigorous and whole-hearted swiping.

And with that, his line of vision is now once more unhindered, whereby all his attention and his plans for the immediate future shift from the cake to me.

Thorkild Thorlacius and Anaflabia, too, rise from their chairs. But Alexander Flounderblood's movements are in a class of their own. He projects himself upwards onto his feet as fast as a pinball machine.

I've a clear, albeit tiny, head start. So when I unexpectedly pass Max on my way down the stairs, I've no time to stop. All I register is him gaping at me, and then he's far behind in my wake.

I'm out of the building and Alexander's after me. I've seen him out jogging with Baroness, but am nonetheless surprised to receive his company at such close quarters, so close I would venture that the base of the layer cake must have involved some kind of walnut meringue.

We cross the street in heavy traffic. Brakes are applied, horns blare. I'm nearly at the red bus now and cast a glance over my shoulder. Alexander's only a few strides behind. Fifty metres behind him, Thorkild Thorlacius and Anaflabia, too, have negotiated the traffic and are picking up speed.

I glance through the windscreen of the bus. Lars is still in the driver's seat. And so, for that matter, is Katinka, who appears now to have straddled him.

Some might consider this not to be the done thing in public. But then, isn't it exactly the kind of sight most tourists would come flocking to see? And is it not love's very nature, if I remember correctly from when love was still a part of my own life? Sometimes it builds a room around the lovers, inside which they are no longer aware of anyone else existing in the world but themselves.

Regrettably, I must now break down the walls of that room. I slap my palms hard against the windscreen, then duck down between the front wheels and slip beneath the bus.

From this point on I can see only as much as can be viewed from underneath a bus. But even this is encouraging. I see Alexander halt, and from the expression on his face it would seem that he has caught sight of Lars and Katinka and that they have caught sight of him and recognised him through the remains of the cake. Alexander turns on his heel, as indeed do Thorkild Thorlacius and Anaflabia somewhat further away.

It is testimony to the mental agility of these three individuals that in a split second they can switch their attention from a heartfelt desire to apprehend and mistreat me, to an entirely different one involving them making themselves scarce. In the manner of the true cons they are rapidly becoming, they split up and leg it in different directions, thereby forcing their pursuers to divide themselves. The last I see is the three of them at full pelt on their way over Kongens Nytorv, dispersing to various corners of the globe with Lars and Katinka hot on their heels.

I bow to Pallas Athene.

'All clear,' I say.

Her gaze follows the absconding trio and their pursuers.

'I've only known you for just over two hours,' she says. 'But I must say that if you keep this up you're going make yourself a lot of enemies.'

'At least I've no record of violence,' I tell her. 'Unlike some.'

'You're only twenty-one,' she says. 'Wait till you get to my age.'

57

WE STEP INSIDE THE BUS. THE DRIVER'S AREA IS SEPARATED from the rest of the bus by a partition wall, and when we open the door, it becomes clear that using this vehicle for a sightseeing business would be a total non-starter, because all the windows are blacked out and all the seats have been removed to make room for elecronic equipment comprising maybe fifty monitors, in front of which sit four people equipped with headphones and microphones, all four so absorbed in their work that not one of them turns to look up as we pass.

In the middle of this space, a small winding staircase leads us upwards into an almost identical room, once again containing four dedicated individuals immersed in whatever it is they're doing. This space is only half as big, constrained as it is by another partition wall with a wide door in it, which I now proceed to open without knocking.

The room we enter amply makes up for the blackout of the rest of the bus, because here there are windows from floor to ceiling, as well as in the roof. The glass must be polarised and tinted in a special way, because none of this is visible from the outside, though inside it is like a very comfortable aquarium.

The man seated comfortably here is Albert Winehappy. I know this immediately, and Anaflabia hit the nail on the head: the man is a cardinal, maybe even a pope, because cardinals presumably have someone higher ranking above them, but the man who reclines here in his chair does so in such a way as to suggest that he could lift off without ever banging his head against another living soul, if you understand what I mean.

The only problem he would encounter about lifting off would be of a quite different nature altogether, to do with the fact that he's as fat as a prize sow at the Finø Agricultural Fair, and there's absolutely no reason to believe that his superfluous weight has been an easy thing to achieve. Rather, it has obviously involved some considerable work, work that he is just as obviously willing to perform, because in front of him is the biggest packed lunch I've ever seen in my life, and as he considers us, he unwraps it to reveal at least twenty slices of rye bread, all generously heaped with delicacies.

He has cottoned on to my gaze.

'One hundred and sixty kilos,' he says. 'I'm aiming for one hundred and eighty.'

'I'm sure that won't be a problem,' I tell him.

'Some of it's comfort eating,' he says. 'On account of having run into your family.'

A more impolite individual would say that in that case he must have run into us generations ago, but I was brought up in a rectory.

I place the flash drive containing the footage from the old chapel in front of him and write down the registration number of the black van on a pad.

'My sister Tilte has been kidnapped,' I tell him. 'An hour ago, in a van with that registration. That's the first thing. The second is that there are four people, three men and a woman, intending to blow up the exhibition that's going on alongside the Grand Synod. On that flash drive are image and sound files that show them in dim light for a minute and a half.'

He must have pressed a button, because now a woman enters. She's thirty years younger than him, but in full possession of the aura of power needed to succeed him as Pope. She picks up my notes and the flash drive, and then leaves.

Pallas Athene and I have both taken a seat. Albert Winehappy considers us for a moment. Perhaps he abandons himself to the pleasure of the sight before him. Perhaps he is merely thinking. My guess is the latter.

'If you'll allow me to be frank,' I say, 'and speak freely to a civil servant of high rank and advanced years. We've never met before. But it seems to me that you have been personally responsible for warrants put out for the arrest of my parents and my older brother, and for my sister and I being taken into custody and banged up in a rehab centre for substance abusers. Moreover, it seems that you gave the go-ahead for us to be forcibly removed from our home by the authorities, that it is your doing that our same childhood home has been taken apart and gone over with a fine-tooth comb, and that a bishop, a neural scientist and a representative of the Ministry of Education have been let loose upon us. Not to mention your issuing the order that our dog, Basker, be put down.'

Albert Winehappy wears a beard, and this is an insightful move on his part, because his face would otherwise be devoid of contrast, rather in the manner of a full moon. Now he strokes that beard pensively. I sense his intelligence. It's as though just behind his frontal lobes is a buzzing hive of bees.

The female successor returns.

'The vehicle was stolen this morning,' she says. 'From a carport in Glostrup. The owner's away. We got hold of him on his mobile. It wouldn't have been missed for another week. We've had a look at the footage. It'll take a while to go through it all. But we've got a positive ID on the four floaters.'

Albert Winehappy fixes his gaze on Pallas Athene.

'I run a brothel,' she says. 'I did three men and a woman last night. We've got a card number for one of them. A Dane by the name of Henrik.'

She writes some digits on the pad that's lying on the desk as she consults her mobile. She must have investigated while I was serving cake to Alexander Flounderblood.

Albert Winehappy turns back to me.

'Do tell me what you've been up to since you gave us the slip.'

314

I give him the short version, though with all the relevant head-lines: our escape from Big Hill, the trip to Finøholm, the crossing on the *White Lady*, and our morning in Copenhagen. As I relate these events, I sense unease on the part of Pallas Athene. Perhaps it occurs to her that life may hold more severe fates than being bothered by men in traffic. But Albert Winehappy reveals no emotion, apart from profound satisfaction with his *smørrebrød*. By the time I reach the end of my tale, all twenty pieces have departed whence nothing ever returns.

'You're fourteen years old,' he says. 'Technically, a child.'

'But my soul has age. And I have reached deep into my being.'

These are words I'd be reticent about uttering in the dressing room of Finø FC. But it's imperative the man in front of me takes me seriously.

He stares at me. His eyes seem to widen. And then he chuckles.

He reaches a hand the size of a plum pudding under the table and produces what looks like a pirate's chest. And from it he takes out his real lunch, the twenty pieces of *smørrebrød* heaped with delicacies merely being an appetiser. He senses my gaze.

'I had a difficult childhood,' he says.

'You should come and see mine,' I tell him.

He lifts an open sandwich that seems to be little more than one great dollop of mayonnaise with the occasional shrimp peeping out coquettishly. He places it on his tongue and then closes his mouth, whereupon the whole thing disappears. From a folder on his desk he takes a sheet of paper on which are affixed four photographs of three men and a woman. Pallas Athene gives a start. One of the men has hair so white it looks like it's been dyed with peroxide. I assume him to be Black Henrik, enemy number one of rats and the indebted alike. It's hard to say anything about his appearance other than that this is a man of confidence who doesn't mind demonstrating that fact.

'You've heard of *fundamentalism*,' Albert Winehappy says. 'Well, religion didn't invent it. Most people are fundamentalists, and the world is a den of thieves.'

Behind him is a small cask of draught beer. With pleasure and pride I note that Finø Brewery's Special Brew seems to be winning market shares across the country. He fills a half-litre glass and pours the contents down his throat.

'Cheers,' he says.

I find myself thinking that if anyone should ever wish to discover Albert Winehappy's weakness, all they'd have to do would be to take away his packed lunches or his draught beer and they'd have a fundamentalist on their hands before they could say Jack Robinson.

'Globalisation is putting the squeeze on the great religions, and their response is to go fundamental. The whole fucking lot of them. Fundamentalists are everywhere. Christians, Hindus, Buddhists, Islamists, and whatever else they all choose to call themselves. There's only one safeguard, and that's the police and the armed forces.'

At this point, I'm very close to asking if we shouldn't also mention Asa-Thor, which on Finø has recently demonstrated clear fundamentalist tendencies. Its membership has plummeted from seven to five since word got out that Einar Flogginfellow is considering sacrificing his son, Knud, who's in the same class as Tilte, to Odin in order to compete with the Evangelical Lutheran Church of Denmark, not to mention Polly Pigonia and Sinbad Al-Blablab and Lama Svend-Holger, which consideration I warmly applaud seeing as how Knud is an habitual criminal second only to Karl Marauder Lander in despicability. But again my sense of timing tells me the moment would not be well chosen.

'Fundamentalism begets terror,' says Albert Winehappy. 'And most people harbour a terrorist inside them. It's only a matter of time before he appears, and for that reason people have to be kept on a short lead. Ninety-five per cent of the earth's population needs to be told how to behave. That's why terrorists work within organisations. Not one in a thousand ever works alone.'

His eyes pick out a piece of *smørrebrød*. One must assume the towering heap of delicacies to rest somewhere upon a slice of rye bread, but this is nowhere visible. What is visible is a hunk of liver pâté as thick as a loaf, on top of which lies the greater part of the country's annual yield of mushrooms, elegantly topped by rashers of crispy bacon from half a pig.

'Those who do work alone are the tricky ones. We call them *floaters*. No permanent fixpoints and always on the move. They're my area of expertise. And I'm going to tear their fucking heads off!'

He drums a finger on the sheet of paper in front of him.

'This lot here are floaters. We've known about them individually for more than ten years. What we've not seen until now – and what has never been seen before in history – is that they appear to have joined forces. And how the hell they can do that without murdering each other is something we've had more than a little trouble getting our heads round. So much so that we're almost off our food.'

I feel an urge to comfort him and tell him how confident I am that his appetite will survive, but at the same time I've no wish to distract him from the worthy successor to his liver pâté, which involves roast beef and would seem to require the aid of a forklift truck in order to successfully make the journey from plate to mouth.

'The world's a filthy place,' he says. 'And when people get together they do so only out of need. We think that what brought these four hooligans together is something they believe to be even more dangerous than each other. And that something is the Grand Synod.'

He now feels compelled to get to his feet and stand by the window. Propelling himself those few steps would seemingly equate to a marathon.

'All the great religions have two sides to them. And if you ask me, one's dafter than the other. There's a side that faces outwards. They call it *exoteric*, and it's what the vast majority of adherents relate to. Then there's the side that faces inwards. That's what they call *esoteric*, and it's reserved for the chosen few. The exoteric, outward-facing side is what's practised in the Evangelical Lutheran Church of Denmark, in the Catholic Church, in mosques, temples, synagogues and *gompas* all over the world. It's all about external rites and rituals comforting believers, telling them that while they might be going through a rough patch right now, everything will be all right once they're dead. The other side, the esoteric part, is for the loonies.'

From the window, he casts a long glance back at the ten open sandwiches that remain alluringly on his enormous plate.

'It's for those who can't make do with just a taste. The ones who can't wait until they die, but who want all the answers here and now.'

'You're like that, too!'

I blurt it out, with no idea why. But all of a sudden, I'm in no doubt that Albert Winehappy is an elephant keeper.

'What the hell are you talking about, lad? Are you completely mad? Of course I'm not. All that's in the past. I'm reformed. Religion is a disturbance of the brain.'

He pauses, clearly intent on continuing. But I've been close to stealing the ball.

'The Grand Synod is all to do with the innards of the great religions. It's the first attempt ever on such a scale to open up a dialogue among madmen and mystics about the possibility of their being something unifying behind those faiths. The lunatic idea they've taken into their heads is to investigate whether their various religious understandings might share some common foundation. And to that end they've brought in neural scientists and psychologists. What the floaters are afraid of is that the different religions should discover themselves to have more in common than they thought. And if they do, fundamentalism loses its legitimacy. No one's likely to feel threatened by a person who's basically as deranged as themselves. That's what's brought them together.'

He gulps a mouthful of air and returns to his chair to finish his lunch. He doesn't actually lick his plate, but my feeling is that's only because he's got company. From the larder underneath the desk he now produces a chocolate cake.

It's big enough to give pleasure to an entire parish council. Albert Winehappy considers it closely for a moment and decides there's enough for all three of us. He cuts me and Pallas Athene two wafer-thin slices.

'You're a sportsman,' he says to me. 'It's in your file. You need to watch your weight.'

'What about yourself?' says Pallas Athene.

I can tell from Albert Winehappy that he is suddenly placed under pressure. It's now glaringly obvious that the quickest way of freaking him out would be to go for the cake.

'With your profession,' he says, 'you need to keep yourself slim and attractive. And this, I'm afraid, is a calorie bomb.'

He stuffs the cake into his mouth and swills half a litre of coffee from a thermal mug, then delicately brushes away the crumbs from his beard with a serviette.

'What about my mother and father?' I ask him.

And then he says something that bowls me over.

'Your mother and father are upstanding citizens. They called and reported an explosive device. Concealed within the under-ground security box into which the jewels will descend in case of fire, vandalism or attempted theft. The bomb squad were deployed immediately and took care of it all. I met with your parents. Your mother has done a splendid job of security. Decent people, both of them. Keen. Polite. Law-abiding. How the hell they managed to produce children like you is a mystery. But then again, the brain can be affected during a pregnancy. Your headmaster even states as much in the report. Water on the brain, wasn't it?'

Cautiously, I endeavour to open and close my mouth. It works, though only just.

'So there's no warrant out on them at all?'

'Who? Your parents? Why the hell should there be? More likely they'll be given a medal. Either that or a hundred million for having saved the valuables. That should be enough for them to get you and your sister a babysitter. Maybe they should enquire about bringing the Hell's Angels in for the job. Cheers!'

He downs another half litre of frothy special brew.

'Why did they have to remove us from our home?' I ask. 'And how come Hans was to be arrested?'

'Request of your parents. So they'd know you were safe.'

Among the first team of Finø FC, the Pastor's Peter is renowned for his Oriental inscrutability. So you can't tell by looking at me. But inside, I'm combusting. And the reason is that Mother and Father most certainly did not have us banged up with blue wristbands on for our own safety, because our safety was never threatened by anyone but themselves. The reason was so we wouldn't be able to pick up their trail.

'And my sister?' I ask.

Albert Winehappy's expression turns grave.

'We've four thousand police officers on the streets. Civilian reinforcements from Sweden, Norway, Germany and the United States. Close on seven thousand in all. We've got surveillance helicopters and coastal patrols, and we're backed up by the civil defence and the fire brigade. As we speak, her picture has gone out and the search has been initiated. We're going to fucking find her!'

58

WE'RE SITTING IN THE JAGUAR OVERLOOKING THE SQUARE and the Nyhavn waterfront. We've called Hans and Ashanti, and it turns out they never got any further than a lovers' bench with a view of the harbour, and now they've met up with us here. We've told them everything. Pallas Athene starts the car and I realise she's now driving differently than before, as though somehow she's absent, which would be understandable considering how quickly she has been introduced into our family.

Personally, I feel so low as to be bordering on despair. My in-depth religious studies in the company of Tilte have time and again brought to our attention that all the great masters recommend viewing any suffering one might be fortunate enough to experience in terms of a godsent opportunity, and all of them stress the notion that one should savour the experience and make sure not a drop is spilt.

This is easier said than done, and even the smallest measure of success will render it impossible to retain control of anything else at the same time, one's limbs, for example, and now my hand appears from out of my pocket with a small, rectangular piece of card in it. This is what I found tucked between the framed pictures in Conny's modest abode, just before everything took off, so I never actually got the chance to examine it. I do so now, discovering it to be a business card with a crucifix embossed on it. Next to the crucifix are the words *Catholic University of Denmark*. The address alongside says *Bredgade*. And below it is that very Danish of names, Jakob Aquinas Bordurio Madsen.

What now happens inside me is difficult to explain and impossible to excuse. But a flash of madness zips through my brain. And the question that follows like a clap of thunder is this: what can the fact that this business card was found in Conny's apartment mean, if not that Jakob Bordurio, the puma of Ifigenia Bruhn's Dancing School, has set his sights on Conny and is now stalking his prey?

I know what you're going to say. Was I not dealing spiritually with my grief at Tilte being gone? And if that was the case, then how come I'm now spinning scenarios about Jakob and Conny all of a sudden? Of course, you'd be quite right, and the only thing I can say in my defence is that of all the demons depicted in the great religions, jealousy is and always will be captain of the team.

But the very next instant I relax. Because the business card must have been put there by Tilte. And Conny is fourteen, whereas Jakob is seventeen, and no historical precedent exists whereby Conny has chased an older man. So common sense prevails, and the question now is why Tilte would have left it behind. Because Tilte, as I have already mentioned, isn't one for dropping things, and everything would seem to indicate she left it for me to find.

We turn right and pass a long, narrow park. At the end of the street we can see the harbour. Basker grizzles. He's worried about Tilte, too. I turn the business card over in my hand, and on the back Tilte has written the figure '13' in biro.

Thirteen is Tilte's lucky number. She says it's a lot better than it's rumoured to be. She was born on the thirteenth and is very pleased with the rectory's address, which is Kirkevej 13, and Count Rickardt, who has conducted extensive research in numerology, has at length explained a great deal of matters whose details I am no longer able to recall, but which all have to do with how well Tilte is suited to the number.

But why that should prompt her to write it down on the back of Jakob's business card is a question to which I find no immediate answer.

'We need to make a detour,' I say. 'To Bredgade.'

And then a number of things happen in quick succession.

The first of these is that Pallas Athene wrenches the steering wheel, pulling the Jaguar up onto the pavement and slamming on the brakes. We come to an abrupt halt amid the sound of squealing tyres and the waft of burnt rubber.

'I've got it,' she says.

What she's got is something we're given no time to grasp, because now someone thumps a fist against the roof of the Jaguar, and not in the manner of a polite enquiry as to anyone being home, but rather in a way that would make anyone think we'd landed in a scrap yard and the Jaguar was now being squashed into a cube. And that sets everything off.

The face of a man inserts itself through Pallas Athene's open window.

The man is seated on what looks like a brand-new Raleigh. He's wearing a suit and a white shirt and tie, bicycle clips keep his trouser legs in place and his shoes are shiny. On the pannier is a leather case for a laptop, and in his hand a voluminous bunch of long-stalked roses wrapped in cellophane, and now he yells into Pallas Athene's face.

'What the hell do you think you're playing at, you stupid cow! Won your licence in a lottery, did you? Never heard of the Highway Code?'

I don't know the man personally. And yet I'd give ten to one he's a solicitor, that he's now on his way home from the office to his apartment in Charlottenlund, that his fiancée is waiting for him, and that they'll soon be married and have two, perhaps three children and a dog, and then live happily ever after until the end of their days.

It's a project I can only warmly support. Even if I myself am destined to remain alone for ever, I can still find pleasure in the happiness of others.

That's why I wish I'd had the time to tell the solicitor about how to keep one's anger in check, a strategy all the great religions recommend and on which they even provide guidance. Unfortunately there's no time at all, because now he's already yelled into Pallas Athene's face.

Hers is the wrong face into which to yell. Her eyes glaze over, and before we know it she's yanked the solicitor through the window by his lapels.

Then she hesitates. She is almost certainly pausing to choose between two equally excellent avenues down which to proceed: should she break the man's neck or simply begin to tear off his head?

This brief interlude is our chance. Hans, Ashanti and I grab her, just as it becomes apparent from the look of satisfaction on her face that she has made her decision.

For a moment, I don't think we can hold her back. But then Hans flexes his muscles, and when Hans flexes his muscles all natural movement is suppressed. Slowly, the glaze disappears from her eyes. She looks at the solicitor and returns him through the window onto the saddle of his modest mode of transport.

'On your bike, fat arse!' she says.

He kicks off from the kerb, accelerating away without looking back. As far as I can tell, he's unharmed. But I have to say, as many of the great masters have said before me: a solicitor who has looked death in the face is no longer the same solicitor.

Pallas Athene has returned to more or less the same reality as the rest of us. And now she turns to face us.

'Ship horns,' she says.

59

WE LISTEN. A SINGLE HORN CAN BE HEARD IN THE DISTANCE.
But it's not something one would ordinarily be inclined to
announce to the world. The thought strikes me that Pallas Athene
has just been prevented from terminating the life of a male
cyclist, and the experience may perhaps render it too hard for
such a sensitive system as hers to suppress its spontaneous
emotion.

'He rang me up yesterday. Henrik. Wanting me to go to them.
I turned him down. Hardly ever do it. Too dangerous. I like to
have Andrik around. So they made a booking for the next day.
But in the background was the same sound. I live on the harbour
myself. It was the sound of horns from the ships.'

'Did you get an address?' I ask.

She nods slowly.

'That's what was odd about it. Normally we know as little as
possible about the clients. But in this case he gave an address.
To tell me how close it was. An address in the Free Harbour
district. Pakhus was the street name, and then a number.'

We hold our breath while she thinks.

'It's gone, I can't remember,' she says, distraught.

Then another man approaches the open window. I put my hand
on Pallas Athene's arm. But this is a different scenario entirely.

'I'm sorry,' he says, 'only I was just on my way to see you. At
the address on Toldbodgade.'

Standing on the pavement with a rosary in his hand, sporting
a clerical collar and looking like a sheikh of the desert, is the

pin-up boy of Ifigenia Bruhn's Dancing School, my former team-mate on the first eleven of Finø FC, Jakob Aquinas Bordurio Madsen.

I pull Jakob into the car. It's no exaggeration to say the Jaguar is now at bursting point. One has to bear in mind that, strictly speaking, my brother Hans requires a car to himself. But this isn't the right time to complain about the conference facilities.

'I want to speak to Tilte,' Jakob says.

'Too late,' I tell him. 'She's been kidnapped.'

He withers in front of our eyes, and this indicates two things to me. First, that he knows something about what Tilte and the rest of us are up to. And second, that although he now has his own business card and has received a message from God, and even if his rosary may not have been idle for a moment since he left Finø, his heart still isn't done with Tilte.

I hold up the business card in front of him.

'She left this behind when they dragged her away,' I tell him. 'She must have spoken to you.'

His eyes wander.

'The police,' he says.

'The police have been informed. They're looking for her all over. They've called a search for the van that took her away. We want to find out how much you know.'

Tremendous forces are at work inside him. Their exact nature remains unrevealed to us. But one of them is definitely love. And love prevails.

'She was with us an hour and a half ago.'

'Who's us?'

'The Catholic University. She came to see me there. She told me everything. In brief, but leaving nothing out. About your mother and father. The attack that's being planned. I took her to see an officer.'

'An officer?'

'An officer of the Vatican. He's here for the conference. The

326

Vatican has its own intelligence service. Ten times the size of the Danish one.'

He tells us this with a trace of pride in his voice, as though comparing AC Milan to Finø FC.

'He knew all about it. And he knew the Danish police had removed the incendiary. But he knew nothing about your parents.'

I feel disappointed. He doesn't have anything new. One would have hoped there to be more to Jakob Aquinas than just an elegant ballroom waltz.

'Why would Tilte have left your card behind?' I ask him. 'What was she trying to say?'

He shakes his head emptily.

'What did you talk about?' I ask.

'Spadillo, the Vatican officer, told us how they think the four floaters have been financed.'

Now I sense it. Like in football. The goalkeeper has kicked the ball upfield. It's all been so clouded, but now the mud sinks to the bottom and the water begins to clear.

'I don't know a thing about politics,' says Jakob. 'But it had something to do with arms. There's a syndicate of major arms dealers. Officially, they only supply armed forces at the national level, sanctioned by the UN. Unofficially, they'll supply anyone. There's some sort of lobby. The Vatican and the Danish police believe they're footing the bill. I can hardly believe it. It would be so profoundly sinful. Despicable, don't you think?'

I place a hand on his shoulder.

'Beyond contempt,' I say. 'Were there any names, Jakob?'

He tries to think back. It's plain he would have preferred me to have asked him to do the foxtrot.

'A ship owner. He mentioned a ship owner.'

I point to the figure thirteen that Tilte has written on the back of the card.

'What about this, Jakob? Does this have to do with that ship owner? An address? A phone number?'

Jakob is distressed.

'I was away in my own thoughts. Tilte was present though.

The sun was shining in from the garden. Through the treetops. She looked like the Virgin Mary. All of a sudden I felt something. It was like a new calling, like a voice was speaking to me. It said: This girl is your future!'

'Jakob,' I say, 'try to think back. The great mystics, Catholics among them, say there's always a part of the self that forever remains awake. Even in the rosiest of daydreams. That part of you that remains awake, Jakob. What did it hear? What was the soundtrack in the background when you saw Tilte as the Virgin Mary?'

His gaze grows distant, only then to become alert.

'She asked about the ship owner. What his name was. Spadillo wouldn't say. She was insistent. You know what Tilte can be like.'

He's right about that. Several of us in the Jaguar know exactly what Tilte can be like.

'She must have got what she was after,' I say. 'A single Vatican officer against Tilte is about as much use as a snowball in hell.'

He shakes his head.

'Jakob,' I say, 'focus on the details. Like when we go through a match in the dressing room after the final whistle. Spadillo refuses to divulge the name. Tilte insists. He refuses again. Then what?'

'Tilte goes to the bathroom. Then she comes back. She says the door is stuck. We investigate. It's odd. Both doors are locked, but there's no one inside. Anyway, we manage to get it open.'

'You and the officer get the door open,' I say. 'Where was Tilte while you were doing this?'

He shakes his head.

'Did you leave the computer on in the living room?' I ask.

He stares at me. He grew up part of a secure little family in Denmark, and the only thing there was to remind him of the big, bad world outside was his name. He can't believe what I'm now suspecting.

'But Tilte would never . . .' he stutters. 'Tilte would never . . .'

I say nothing. If Jakob Bordurio knew how far Tilte is willing to go for a good cause, it's quite possible he'd be praying for another calling to send him back to the Catholic University and a long and peaceful life in celibacy.

Pallas Athene has been quiet. Perhaps she's been dealing with her grief at not having severed the jugular of the bicycling solicitor with her teeth. Now she leans over and takes the business card out of my hand.

'It was number thirteen,' she says. 'Pakhus 13! That's one of the reasons I said no. It's an unlucky number. Even if they were offering to pay double.'

60

I DON'T KNOW IF YOU'VE EVER NOTICED HOW ALL RELIGIONS agree on what Paradise looks like. If, like Tilte and me, you look it up in illustrated bibles and study mosaics and paintings and the brochures of the Jehovah's Witnesses, then you will know that according to all these reliable sources, Paradise looks exactly like the Finø Garden Centre. There's a big lawn and a babbling brook with plants all around, and trees a bit further back, and then some happy people, who believe the meaning of life involves spending Sundays caught up with hardy perennials and garden gnomes.

Without in any way wishing to belittle such notions, I should nevertheless like to say that Tilte and I consider this to be a serious delusion. Personally, I believe that if Paradise truly exists it must surely look more like Copenhagen's Free Harbour area, through which we are now driving. This is an area dotted with restaurants of the same high standard as The Nincompoop on Finø Town Harbour and shops that seem to suck you in and make you forget all about the fact that your sister has been kidnapped and that your parents would be sent down for twelve years if word of what they most likely have been up to ever got out. All over, warehouses have been renovated and converted into the kind of apartments one might look forward to being able to afford after turning professional in Italy, and there are jetties and moorings and cranes and containers and warehouses enough to disguise the fact that this is no longer a working harbour but one great big window display.

So under any other circumstances a drive through the Free Harbour would be a heavenly experience indeed, but this is far from the case now. The only thing on my mind is Tilte, so these surroundings are more reminiscent of a nightmare, which in turn indicates that our perception is mostly related to how we feel inside.

We pass by a dock, and Pallas Athene slows down. To our right is a long quayside bustling with idyllic waterfront activity in front of a row of converted warehouses. And then there's a sign saying *Pakhus Quay*, and another saying *Pakhus 1–24*. So now we're there.

In front of these warehouses, boats are moored. There are houseboats, a vintage sailing vessel, and an orange tugboat belonging to the Port authority, and if you don't mind a recollection from my childhood I can reveal that my father read *Tuggy the Tugboat* aloud to me when I was small, and Tuggy was married to just such an orange vessel as two men of the Port authority are now making ready, and after their marriage they lived happily ever after to the end of their days and begot a great many little tugboats. This was a book that got Tilte's back up, and I remember her on several occasions expressing an interest in offering its author a course of therapy, this being prior to the time she borrowed the coffin, so I wouldn't care to hazard a guess at the kind of therapy she might have had in mind.

The Pakhus buildings are warehouses, but because the Free Harbour is upmarket, warehouses here are swisher than the great majority of private homes. Number 13 is some fifty metres along, just at the place where the Port authority's boat is moored. There are no cars parked outside, the blinds are drawn, and all the doors are closed.

Pallas Athene pulls the Jag up to the kerb.

In so doing, she crosses the cycle lane.

I have previously had cause to mention the ferocity of emotion that may be awakened on Finø when tourists mistakenly drive onto the pedestrianised streets of Finø Town. I mention this again in order that no doubt may arise as to my likings for cyclists and pedestrians. Because at this particular moment I cannot help but note that Pallas Athene's manoeuvre causes us to nudge a cyclist, a mishap that naturally directs one's sympathy towards the unfortunate individual in question.

And yet that cyclist would seem to be overreacting considerably when he thumps his fist against the roof of the Jaguar, because the sound has obviously not been produced by a ladybird landing on the varnish, but might more likely be taken to be some precursor of World War III.

And then the man's head appears. His teeth are bared and his lungs filled with air, ready to expel his battle cry.

Pallas Athene and I stare at each other. The man is the solicitor we encountered ten minutes ago.

I actually understand him. He has cycled through the Free Harbour. The route is perhaps longer than if he had carried on along Strandboulevarden. But coming this way will have allowed him to recover from his encounter with Pallas Athene and to renew expectations as to meeting his fiancée, and perhaps she may even have promised to show him her new tattoo, so it would be of the essence for him to be at the top of his game.

So the man will have been absorbed in his own thoughts, and now he's been forced off the road again, his wound opens and he doesn't realise it's the same red Jaguar until it's too late and he's hammered his fist against the roof.

Pallas Athene opens the door and gets out.

'Are you following me?' she asks.

From where I'm sitting I'm unable to see her face. But it's clear from her tone that she's on her way towards her eighth conviction, and chances are this time it's going to be for manslaughter.

Once again, however, we are provided with a shining example of the transformational power of love and the influence the Gorgeous One has exerted upon my brother Hans. Because now, without his even pausing to consider the position of the planets, Hans physically intervenes and Pallas Athene is brought to a sudden halt.

This time, it's all he can do to keep her restrained. But his grip is firm. It allows me to get out of the car, calm and collected, and to walk round the other side and approach our solicitor friend.

'Do you realise we just saved your life?' I say. 'She's famous for chewing up razor blades and spitting out needles.'

The man nods, temporarily unable to speak. Meeting Pallas Athene in a foul mood twice in brief succession can mark a man for life.

'So if I might borrow your flowers,' I go on. 'We're paying a visit unannounced. And we need a peace offering.'

Pakhus 13 comprises a low office section adjoining four separate storage facilities, and we're in some doubt as to where to start.

We've left Pallas Athene and Ashanti behind in the car, this being one of those situations requiring women and children to be kept out of harm's way.

As we pass the office, a vehicle draws to a halt in front of the entrance. I hesitate to use the rather profane designation *car*, but no other word seems to exist that would be fitting.

The vehicle is a large Maserati, and out of it climbs a uniformed chauffeur. Three men leave the office building, and if for a moment one removes oneself from one's prejudices and considers the scene with what the spiritual systems refer to as *choiceless awareness*, one would have to concede that the sight is uplifting indeed.

The car is such that one can think only that if the great Prophets had been free to select the kind of fiery chariot on which they tend to be transported into the heavens, they would most certainly have chosen this one. And the suits the four men, including the chauffeur, are wearing could never be a cause of embarrassment, not even on Judgement Day in front of the Lord himself. Even here in Copenhagen's Free Harbour, they're a touch of class.

The two men taking up the rear may be bald and built like the kind of two-hundred-kilo blocks of concrete that are used to fortify coastlines, but the clothes make them float. And the man in front possesses an implicit authority that makes you think there really must be justice in the world, because this man looks like a person who deserves to be as rich as an oil sheikh and would seem to be just that.

The only blemish is that his self-esteem ran away with him when he purchased the car, because the number plate is personalised with his own name: *Bellerad*.

The ship owner and his two bodyguards have turned to face us and are momentarily paralysed by unexpectedly having run into us again.

And once more we find ourselves in one of those situations in which something from without takes hold of me. I know why it happens, and the reason is that I now sense Tilte's presence, and because we desperately need to know if the van that took her away is nearby.

So I walk straight up to Bellerad. His bodyguards refrain from intervening. It's happened before and is one of the advantages of being small: the defence is always going to underestimate you, and before you know it you're in front of goal.

'The men in the van,' I say. 'The one that came in here. They dropped a wallet. I want to return it.'

No matter how well prepared you might be, if you're taken sufficiently unawares reality always breaks down. And before Bellerad collects himself again, I trace his gaze as it points me towards the gate in front of the nearest storage facility.

I hand him the roses I'm carrying. He accepts them mechanically.

'These are from His Majesty King Aziz and the Grand Synod,' I say. 'In advance of your medal. With heartfelt greetings. Mind the thorns.'

Bellerad stares blankly at Hans, at Jakob and then at me. He looks towards the Jaguar. He tries to assess our relative strengths. And then he climbs into the Maserati, the two baldies follow him, and the car pulls away.

There's no doorbell to ring, only a sign that says *Bellerad Shipping*. I place my ear to the door and can hear what sounds like sobbing. I knock. The sound stops. The door opens just a crack.

'Pink Messengers,' I say.

The crack widens. The man who peers out at me has tears in his eyes.

'You don't look like a messenger,' he says.

'Well, I am,' I tell him. 'And the message I bring is a sorrowful one.'

And then Hans kicks the door in.

When Hans kicks a door in, standing behind it is not recommended. But that's exactly what the man is doing.

I don't know if you share my interest in the finer points of kicking techniques, but if you do I can tell you that from a technical angle Hans' kick involves the application of the same kind of force employed in football when delivering a long, flighted pass. This particular kick removes the hinges from the frame, propelling both the door and the man backwards into the room.

Hans and Jakob Bordurio and I follow them in. We enter a large storage space, which occupies most of the building. The van is parked on the bare concrete, otherwise the place is empty.

'The New Testament doesn't condone violence,' says Jakob Bordurio.

Numerous central defenders undoubtedly wish Jakob had taken that stance during his time on the first team, because they would have been spared many hours of surgery and Jakob could have avoided all his red cards and subsequent suspensions. But I'm too polite to remind him about it.

Our host is on his feet again and making straight for Hans.

It's plain he's been crying, his face is streaked with tears, and normally I would have encouraged him to tell us what was wrong, because as everyone on Finø knows, the Pastor's Peter is a patient listener who has provided solace to many people.

But he doesn't give me a chance. He's up and at us so adroitly and with such elegance he would surely have drawn attention to himself at Ifigenia Bruhn's Dancing School, and now he thrusts a kick at Hans' knee.

It's the kind of brutal tackle that would have necessitated plaster casts and crutches had it been carried through to completion.

But Hans is no longer standing in the same location.

What the man in front of us has no way of knowing is that my brother Hans is now in the grip of the forces I have told you about, which rear up inside him whenever he finds himself compelled to defend women from dragons. So when the studs-first assault reaches its full extension, Hans is no longer in front of the man but at his side, and now he places a hand over the man's face, lifts him into the air and slams him against the wall.

The wall is made of metal. Polly Pigonia once imported a gong from Bali for which my mother constructed a frame so that it might be used to call the residents of the ashram to yoga and meditation. Its deep resonance shimmers in the air.

The metal wall of the warehouse gives off a sound that reminds me of Polly's gong. The man's eyes glaze over, his legs give way and he slumps to the floor and becomes temporarily absent from the proceedings.

It takes a matter of seconds to check the van, the little office, the toilet and the kitchen, but the place is empty. Desperation begins to take hold. Now we must wait for the man on the floor to wake up so we can ask him about Tilte's whereabouts, and even then he's unlikely to reveal anything. He looks like a cold fish, despite his cheeks being moist with tears.

I peer through the blind and look out on the jetty where fairweather sailors dally, oblivious of how callous the real world can be.

In front of my eyes is the orange tugboat, about to raise anchor. A man in waterproofs the same colour as the boat has the last of the mooring warps in his hand, and in the wheelhouse a woman stands at the helm. It's like they're waiting for something.

What I then see has me almost completely flabbergasted. Both of them are crying. Perhaps not wailing their hearts out, but crying all the same.

It's not unknown for sailors to shed a tear when heading out to sea and leaving their loved ones behind. But for two employees of the Port authority to be crying ahead of a jaunt into the harbour on board Tuggy the Tugboat is rather more surprising. I turn round. The man on the floor is in orange waterproofs too. He may be from the Port authority. But then again he may not.

'The boat,' I say. 'Tilte must be on board.'

A roll-up door leads directly onto the quayside and it's unlocked. Hans presses a button and it goes up with a clatter. Now we're outside in the sun.

It goes without saying that three defenceless youngsters should never be foolhardy enough to assault grown men. But we're afraid for Tilte. And Hans is no longer under control. For my own part, I feel as if I've been propelled into motion and cannot come to rest until brought to a halt, dead or alive. Even Jakob Aquinas Bordurio Madsen seems driven by the kind of momentum I haven't seen since his first calling, but which I'd put my shirt on comes from what might only be referred to as *true love*.

And yet everything almost goes wrong.

When the man with the warps catches sight of us, he first takes a handkerchief from his pocket and dries away his tears, and then he makes another seemingly innocuous movement and produces a gun.

One can only admire his style. There's no messing about to unbutton his waterproofs, no threats uttered, and no needless fumbling around with a shoulder holster. In fact, one hardly notices the movement at all, and then all of a sudden he has something in his hand that may well have a short barrel, but is equipped with a long magazine and a retractable shoulder support of ergonomic design.

And then there's the expression on the man's face. I would imagine that if I were going to wave a sub-machine gun around in Copenhagen's Free Harbour in broad daylight at the busiest time of day, I would first glance around me rather sheepishly and give the situation a great deal of consideration, but this man has no such concerns: he casts a single glance in the direction of the other boats and has already made up his mind.

We never learn exactly what he has decided, because at that same moment someone on the tugboat calls out to him, and that person is Tilte.

Her cry prompts him to swivel round. It's a movement that never reaches its conclusion. Because now he catches sight of Basker.

Basker must have escaped from the car to come to our aid, and I must say he's worked fast.

It's well known that fox terriers are good with children. Most people will also be aware that they are intelligent animals. What may be rather less familiar is the fact that the primeval instincts of the fox terrier have never been bred away. Though Basker might look like a cuddly toy, in genetic terms he's a wolf weighing in at eight kilos. This becomes salient now. I see that his eyes are yellow, and it's very seldom indeed they are ever this colour, but when they are I can only advise people to lock their doors and windows and barricade themselves into their basements.

Unfortunately, there's no time to tell the man on the quayside any of this. Moreover, he is clearly not an animal lover, nor does he know the first thing about dogs. He aims a kick at Basker, which is the equivalent of trying to frighten a sabre-toothed tiger with a bottle of perfume.

Basker sets his teeth into the man's leg.

Basker possesses three kinds of bite: a snap, a nip and then something like a buzz saw and an angle grinder mounted on a bear trap. He employs the last of these, causing the man to emit an ear-splitting howl as his leg buckles beneath him.

If at this point the man had let go of his gun, what ensued might have been rather more gentle. Regrettably he does not. And therefore Ashanti and Pallas Athene now go for him. Or rather: the red Jaguar does.

This is a car with truly impressive acceleration. It's doing 90 kph by the time it reaches us, sideswiping the kneeling man and sweeping him along the quayside before veering off and hurtling directly towards the waters of the harbour.

The tug is basically on its way out, maybe a metre and a half from dry land. But its deck is lower than the quay. The Jag projects into the air, crumpling the railing and landing crosswise on the foredeck.

It's only a small boat, and the car is longer than the vessel is wide, so the sight is at once surprising and outlandish. I sense from the woman in the wheelhouse that she, too, is taken aback by the sudden presence of a Jaguar on deck.

Pallas Athene climbs out of the car, walks round it to the door of the wheelhouse, enters and delivers a punch to the woman's jaw.

There are many ways to deliver a punch to another person's jaw, but I venture to suggest that where Pallas Athene has made her mark, no roses shall ever grow. One minute the woman is standing proud at the helm in the salty breeze, the next she's something to step over and ignore, in a heap on the deck.

And then Tilte is in the doorway.

Research I have conducted with Tilte indicates that if there's one thing the great saints and travellers within the human mind have been in agreement on through the ages, it's the notion that people inhabit their own realities, and it's quite certain that Basker and Ashanti and Jakob Bordurio and Pallas Athene and Hans and I have all been looking forward to this reunion with very different expectations. But what we share is a feeling that together we have saved the princess, and that what is to follow will involve tears and embraces and eternal gratitude at the very least. But what happens is that Tilte assumes a stance in the doorway of the wheelhouse where she can be seen by us all, and then she fills her lungs with air and yells: 'Do you know what you are? Dim-wits!'

61

WE'RE SEATED AROUND THE TABLE IN THE BOAT'S SALOON, and you'd have to see the scene to believe it. Those who see it are Hans and Ashanti and Pallas Athene and Jakob Bordurio and Basker and me. And what we see is that the woman from the wheelhouse and the man from the storage facility and the man who was given a little nudge by the Jaguar are all seated with us at the table as free as the birds, because Tilte has forbidden me and Hans to tie them up. Moreover, she has ordered Hans to make coffee, which he has now done, and aside from offering refreshments to the three floaters, Tilte is now applying a dressing to the man Basker has bitten, all the while she comforts him and calls him *poor little Ibrahim*.

'Half an hour ago,' she tells us, 'Ibrahim said farewell to arms for ever. He only drew his gun because he feared he was being attacked. Isn't that right, Ibrahim?'

'It was self-defence,' Ibrahim says. 'And perhaps old habit, too.'

Basker considers him from his corner. Basker's eyes are still yellow, and his nose is smeared with blood. I can tell he's hoping that Ibrahim's old habit will prompt him to draw from the hip in self-defence one last time, so Basker can finish off his hors d'oeuvre and move on to his main-course massacre.

Little, however, would seem to indicate that this will be likely, because Ibrahim is crying again.

'Before you came barging in so violently,' Tilte explains, 'Ibrahim was telling us about his childhood, and we'd got to the part where his mother made him lie on wet sheets all night in punishment for having wet the bed.'

'I'd just like to say at this point,' says the woman from the wheelhouse, 'that compared to my own upbringing, which I shall tell you about presently, Ibrahim's was a bowl of cherries.'

We look across the table at her. The side of her face that came into contact with Pallas Athene is swollen enough to look like a case of the mumps. It makes her diction rather slurred, but nonetheless one gets the gist: she wants Ibrahim to conclude his confessions in order that she can take the stage herself.

Now the man who flew back with the door when we entered the warehouse speaks. His gaze is somewhat unsteady, indicating that he is suffering from concussion, and his face looks rather on the flat side following his encounter with the door.

'I'll hold back on my own story,' he says. 'Otherwise, you'll find it hard to go on.'

I can tell from looking at Ashanti and Pallas Athene and even Jakob that they are in shock. Which is only understandable. This isn't exactly what one would expect from the flower of international terrorism.

Hans and I are better prepared. We know Tilte, and we know the kind of effect she can have on people. All she needs to do is buy a packet of chewing gum and the lady in the kiosk begins dictating her memoirs and ends up inviting her home to save her marriage and train her disobedient dog and cure the kids of their picky habits.

And yet the situation is surprising even for Hans and me, and even Tilte recognises the need for an explanation.

'We had an hour,' she says. 'After they kidnapped me. While we were waiting for Bellerad to arrive. I spent that hour telling them about the door.'

The three floaters nod.

'It was very intense,' Tilte goes on. 'So I invited them into the coffin. Of course, I didn't have a real coffin on hand. But there was a wooden crate. It's not quite the same. But once we'd removed the sub-machine guns and the explosives, it was all right. Luckily, I had this with me.'

At first I'm unable to see what it is she's holding, but then I recognise my old mp3 player, the one with *The Tibetan Book of the Dead* at two-thirds the speed.

'It was a very profound encounter,' says Tilte. 'By the time Bellerad got here, everything had changed.'

The woman with mumps nods.

'When Balder – that's Bellerad – turned up, we turned the money down. And the passports, too. And then we suggested he have a go in the coffin. He didn't want to. But we'll ask him again.'

I look round the table at the three floaters. It's a satisfying sight. Surprising, but satisfying. Emotional, too. There are tears, and remorse. And even if Basker's bite looks severe, there's no reason to believe that Ibrahim won't be able to show off his legs on the beach again after some fairly straightforward plastic surgery.

One could be concerned as to the durability of such a swift conversion. But Tilte and I have often bumped into the concept of *instant enlightenment* in our studies at the Finø Town Library. So perhaps it may prove lasting. On the other hand, thinking about football and the family, it's hard not to muse upon the fact that all practical experience shows that life changes are gradual.

I'm too polite to share these learned considerations. But I do have another relevant question.

'Where's Henrik?'

This hits a soft spot. And provokes a flurry of confusion.

'He's the brains,' says the woman. 'It was his idea.'

'The rest of us were brainwashed,' says Ibrahim. 'And threatened. We're afraid of Henrik. And I'm more afraid than the others.'

I understand him immediately. It brings to mind the darker sides of my own childhood, episodes in which I was coerced into pinching apples and dried dab.

'We intend to come clean,' says the man from the warehouse.

'About Henrik. There are lots of examples to suggest that co-operating with the authorities results in shorter sentences.'

It's hard, in such a state of emotional exposure, to keep a cool head. But someone has to.

'And where did you say Henrik was?' I ask.

They gaze at me emptily. Even Tilte.

'He was on the phone,' Tilte says. 'Just after we came here. But then he disappeared.'

'He'll be apprehended,' says Hans. 'Everything's under control. The incendiary's been disarmed. There's an iron ring around the castle. We can take it easy now.'

'Perhaps he sought solitude in order to repent,' Ibrahim says.

I recall a pile of dead rats. One hundred and twenty-eight of them. It suggests to me that Henrik doesn't leave a job of work until it's done.

'The explosives you took out of that crate. What did you do with them?' I ask.

They stare at me. Hans and I exchange glances. And now Tilte's with us again.

'We need to get there fast,' says Hans. 'To Filthøj. The conference kicks off in an hour and a half. We can be there in one. We'll take the boat.'

'We'll need help sailing it,' I say.

We look at the three floaters, all of whom shake their heads.

'We're afraid of Henrik,' says Ibrahim.

'We're in the middle of a profound process of self-examination,' says the woman.

'What we need,' says the man with concussion, 'is to rest.'

Now Pallas Athene leans across the table.

'Did we have a nice time yesterday, or what?' she says.

Often, one may fail to recognise a person in unfamiliar surroundings. The three floaters are acquainted with Pallas Athene as an individual in skimpy underwear, stiletto heels and a red wig, occurring in a biotope of marble and Havana cigars. So they don't recognise her at all until now.

'Within me,' says Pallas Athene, 'are many dark emotions to

which I can never submit without running the risk of lifetime imprisonment. But now I sense an opportunity to release them upon you without fear of punishment.'

Silence. Then Ibrahim wipes away his tears.

'The first time I set eyes on you people here on the quayside,' he says, 'even though I could see there might be a few little hurdles, I felt right away that we were a team. The dog included.'

62

THERE'S NO NEED FOR ME TO DESCRIBE FILTHØJ CASTLE, it being known to everyone, even if they might not be aware of the fact. Filthøj, you see, is always pictured among the wonders of Denmark whenever they try to sell the country abroad: it's all Filthøj Castle, bacon, beer, Niels Bohr – and Finø in bright sunshine in the middle of a blue sea.

Filthøj is situated on a little green island in the middle of a blue lake, and when shots are angled from below it looks like Disneyland, with towers and cupolas and symmetric rosebeds and beech hedging that must take a whole football team of gardeners to look after.

But seen from the Sound whence we arrive, it looks more like a cross between a den of thieves and a medieval monastery, because the high walls and the boathouse at the shore are almost all that can be seen.

If your conception of a boathouse is a wooden shack at the water's edge, you would in this instance be mistaken. The building in front of us resembles a five-star beach hotel built partly on stilts and finished with a great arched door facing the sea, and this construction is what we now torpedo.

The expansive space in which we find ourselves contains only one thing besides boats, and that is a large armchair, and in it sits Count Rickardt Three Lions practising his archlute.

Some people would be put out to receive visitors in this manner, but Count Rickardt is not among them. He jumps to his feet as though we were the very thing he'd been waiting for.

'We who are profoundly joined in soul,' he says, 'can only but heal the ruptures of the cosmos.'

We go ashore. There's no time for the usual pleasantries.

'Rickardt,' says Tilte, 'where does the tunnel come out?'

Rickardt points. What he points at bears little resemblance to what might spring to mind when thinking of the mouth of a secret tunnel. A glass door stands open, and through it we can see the tunnel clearly, though it doesn't look like a tunnel at all, but more like a corridor of a luxury hotel done out in subdued colours with lamps on the walls.

'Has anyone been through it today?' Tilte asks.

'Not a soul,' says Rickardt. 'Apart from Henrik. You know, Black Henrik. He happened by. It turns out he's involved in security. But he was only here to check.'

We drive up to the main entrance in Rickardt's open Bentley, he himself at the wheel, and on the way I suddenly find myself asking Rickardt if he remembers Black Henrik's surname from when they played together as children, and Rickardt replies that he most certainly does, because Henrik bears that most Danish of surnames, which is Borderrud. He must be able to sense our reaction, because he says how important it is not to judge Henrik, that he was always such a lovely boy, but fortune has not always been on his side. In fact, Rickardt recalls some terrifying stories about Henrik's mother, and take today, for instance, when Henrik needed to check the tunnel, it was a wonder he stayed on his feet, and Henrik reckoned someone must have poured soft soap all over the floor.

At this point, Tilte asks him to pull over.

'Rickardt,' she says, 'did you say soft soap?'

Rickardt confirms this information, adding that while it would be highly unlikely for someone to fill a four-hundred-metre-long tunnel with soft soap, the story might be illustrative of Henrik's psychology, Henrik being a person easily led to believe that people are after him, and though Rickardt has never actually seen his horoscope, everything would seem to indicate that Henrik has Neptune on the Ascendant and the Moon in the Twelfth House.

Although we're in a hurry, Tilte and I get out of the car and stand beside each other in silence for a moment.

'That's how Mother and Father were going to get the box away,' says Tilte. 'They made a slide for it with soft soap.'

In order that you might gain a more complete understanding of the technical details involved here, I must reveal to you the nature of my family's research into the spiritual benefits of soft soap, and in so doing relate the story of Karl Marauder's conspiracy with Jakob Bordurio, an alliance for which I have found considerable difficulty forgiving Jakob, and even now I am uncertain as to whether such forgiveness actually has transpired. To this end, I must return to that Sunday afternoon over post-church coffee in the kitchen of the rectory, when Count Rickardt Three Lions confided to us about the first time he smoked heroin.

Normally, we in the rectory do not encourage Rickardt to relate events of his happy youth, the reason being that it so easily gets him going, and before you know it his eyes are alight with enthusiasm and there's no holding him back. But on this particular occasion we were unable to stop him before he had told us that the first time he smoked heroin was in the company of four good friends and pupils down at the harbour in Grenå, these four individuals to this day making up the core and the inner mandala of the Knights of the Blue Beam. Besides the heroin, they had equipped themselves with one hundred litres of diesel in fifteen-litre jerry-cans, a boombox and Bach's *Die Kunst der Fuge*, all of which had been described in detail to Rickardt in the form of a vision delivered to him by the little blue men, and then they found an empty ship's container and smoked their heroin outside in the sun, took off all their clothes, poured the diesel onto the floor of the container, put Bach on the boombox, and for the next four hours, Rickardt told us, they were in Paradise, hurling themselves around in their lubricated environment, and it felt like they were weightless.

At that point we stopped him, but his story had already made an impression on me, particularly the part about feeling weightless. As it happened, we were fortunate enough at the time to have had a new floor put down in the parish community centre, which as luck would have it was in the process of being treated with soap. So the following evening, I and my good friend Simon, whom Tilte calls Simon the Stylite, poured fifty litres of soft soap onto the new floorboards and took off all our clothes, and it turns out that a thick film of soap is just as good as diesel, offering no resistance at all if one takes a run-up and flings oneself onto the floor, this being easily sufficient to slide twenty metres as though upon a cushion of air, and we went on the whole night.

When we returned the next day, Karl Marauder and Jakob Bordurio had invited the pupils of Finø Town School's classes six to nine to witness our experiment, and unbeknown to us they had all taken up position in the gallery. We lit candles and removed our clothes, and I recall taking a run-up and hurling myself along the floor on my back as I cried out Conny's name, and Simon cried out Sonja's, and the idea was that we should slide weightlessly and reach inside to the place at which the door begins to open. But as we slid along on our backs we looked up and saw fifty faces peering down at us, among them Sonja's and Conny's.

This is the kind of experience that throughout history has prompted individuals to renounce all hope of higher justice and to take matters into their own hands, and I must concede that the first thing Simon and I did afterwards was to get our hands on a couple of lengths of lead piping and chase Jakob and Karl into the great woods, where they remained without daring to show themselves in any inhabited area for several days. Subsequently, however, kindness of heart prevailed, and Tilte spoke with me and gave me a go in the coffin, one of her alternative sessions whereby the lid stays off and she instead massages one's feet and speaks of the importance of forgiveness if one is ever to proceed in one's spiritual development.

Simon and I intended to go back and clean up after ourselves in the community centre, anticipating both a kangaroo court and a firing squad, but my mother and father said we needn't bother,

348

because there were technical details of the soap treatment of wooden floors they wished to investigate, and when late one night I saw lights on in the community centre and sneaked over there to take a look, I saw Mother and Father trying out the great soap slide, and they had brought with them two one-hundred-litre containers of soap, so their investigations must have been thorough indeed.

These recollections of past events, along with the fact that Mother's and Father's collected invoices included among them a bill for one ton of soft soap and a couple of pumps, are now collated by the shared perspicacity of Tilte and myself.

'Every night,' I say, 'the displayed valuables are run down into the box. So Mother and Father were planning on waiting until nightfall. All they needed to do then was to sail up to the boathouse in their new fibreglass vessel and savour the sunset, and Mother would have had the remote control with her from the Grand Kite and Glider Day, and she would have pressed a button, and in some clever way that would have been as easy as pie for her she would have disconnected the box from the lift shaft. And with a thick film of soft soap on the floor, the box would have begun to slide, and it would have gone through the brick wall if Mother hadn't also attached some device to the hidden door that made sure it opened like the one back home in the larder, and then the box would have come sliding all the way through the tunnel to the boathouse, where somehow they would have loaded it on board and sailed it away to some unknown destination where at some later stage they would have revealed it to the world along with a suitably concocted story and claimed their reward in accordance with section 15 of the Lost Property Act, Circular no. 76 of 24 June 2003.'

'And they would have gained themselves a great deal of attention,' says Tilte. 'It would have been just like a little miracle. It would have brought them into the big league.'

We walk a little, immersed in bleak musings as to how wrong it all could have gone.

'It makes sense,' I say. 'In its own frightening way. But there's still one question that needs an answer. How come the tunnel's full of soap now?'

Tilte stares at me with wide-open eyes. The answer appears to us at once.

'They're going ahead with the plan,' says Tilte. 'They think there's still a chance. They're the heroes now the floaters have been uncovered. They stand to pocket a huge reward. And no one has found out about their little idea. So they say to themselves: Why make do with a reward when we can double up? Why piddle around with a hundred million when we can have two? So tonight, when Filthøj Castle closes and the lights go out, they'll sail out in their gondola and press the button on the remote and pull off the job as first planned.'

Obviously, with parents such as ours, Tilte and I share a long history of episodes involving neglect. Nonetheless, this ranks right up there alongside the most shocking examples. In fact, the only other incident I am able to recall offhand that even comes close was when Tilte and I had been allowed to go to Århus on our own for the first time and we called home from a phone box on the main pedestrian street. The lady who was going to perform the piercings we had spontaneously decided we wanted said she would need the consent of our parents, and when Father answered the phone he told us he wasn't convinced it was a good idea, but that he would have a word with Mother. On that occasion, Tilte and I very nearly turned ourselves in to Bodil Hippopotamus at the Town Hall in Grenå with a request for the authorities to remove us from our home, but at the last minute Father called back and said it was fine by them. The sense of parental failure that time in Århus was immense, but this is worse. And no one's calling back this time. Climbing into the car, I'd say we were weighed down.

63

IT WOULD BE FEEBLE TO SAY THAT FILTHØJ CASTLE IS GUARDED. The palace of Sleeping Beauty in its heyday would have been an open invitation compared to this. The lake is buzzing with police motorboats, a wire fence has been erected along its length and the whole area is jumping with dogs, helicopters and armed police, as well as all those who are more inconspicuously clad. A security point has been set up on the causeway that leads across the lake and into the castle, and there's a Portakabin for the security guards.

'We'll never get in,' says Tilte.

But then I take a folded piece of paper from my pocket.

'These are identification numbers,' I say. 'I borrowed them from Anaflabia and Thorkild Thorlacius.'

They all stare at me.

'Petrus,' says Tilte, 'I have to say that you've come on no end these past couple of days, though exactly where you're heading is perhaps rather more unclear to me.'

We drive up to the barrier. Tilte quotes our ID numbers.

Documents are studied. And then a voice says: 'You don't look like your photos.'

Normally, it would be marvellous to hear such a friendly and familiar voice from back home. But under the present circumstances it's hard to feel pleased at all. The voice belongs to Finn Flatfoot.

The explanation is a simple one. Whenever the Danish police have a major task on hand, the finest officers in the land are summoned together. And who finer to head up the team guarding the main entrance to the Grand Synod than Finn Metro Poltrop and his police dog Titmouse, whose characteristic wheezing, like an electric fan blowing through a doormat, comes through loud and clear to me now.

'We're so fortunate, Finn,' says Tilte, 'as to become more beautiful by the day. The photographers can't keep up. No sooner is our picture taken than we look ten years younger.'

She's turned on the charm, which includes a smile they could broadcast in harsh winters to keep the shipping routes free of ice.

But Finn isn't thawing.

'Tilte,' he says. 'And Peter and Hans. What are you doing here?'

It's a question that could take a while to answer, and we haven't the time.

And then Rickardt surprisingly enters the field.

'I am Rickardt Three Lions,' he announces. 'Owner of this seat and co-host of this conference. These people are my guests!'

This is a side of Count Rickardt never before revealed to any resident of Finø. It is the part of him that was born with a servant at each finger and peasants to take care of the hard graft.

The hard graft in this instance is to raise the barrier, and Finn Flatfoot is about to, when all of a sudden he pauses.

'But I just let you in,' he says, 'with the Countess.'

Finn turns a monitor in our direction and indicates a camera above the gate.

'We take pictures in case we need to check.'

The man on the screen certainly has Rickardt's dark mane. But whereas Rickardt is slim to the point of emaciation, this man is more muscular. Moreover, he sports a moustache, a facial accoutrement worn only by a minority of Danes, but which to our considerable regret is all too familiar to me and Hans and Tilte. The long, blonde hair of the Countess at his side is plaited in the way of an Alpine dairy maid.

'Well, I never diddle,' says Count Rickardt. 'It's the Pastor from Finø! And his wife!'

352

And then he presents the ultimate proof of him being in complete command of his surroundings.

'It's your parents! They must have forgotten to return my ID card.'

Tilte takes hold of Rickardt and pulls him towards her.

'You mean you've seen Mother and Father?' she says in a quiet voice.

'They came down to the boathouse. To check the tunnel. Surely you know your mother's in charge of the alarm systems?'

We all fall silent. Our difficulties are mounting. Finn Flatfoot won't let us in. And Mother and Father have slipped past him, perhaps even Black Henrik, too.

By her own standards, Tilte was rather subdued on the boat trip to Filthøj. I sense that she is considering the future of Jakob Bordurio. But now she leans forward to the open window of the car.

'Finn,' she says, 'wouldn't you say that guarding the main entrance here was a job of utmost responsibility? And that if you fulfil that responsibility satisfactorily, they shall be obliged to honour you with a medal?'

Her voice is sweet as filled chocolates.

'I believe something like that has been mentioned, yes,' says Finn.

'The Order of Merit, for instance,' says Tilte. 'That would indeed look splendid on that suit of yours with the large check pattern. The one you wear in church. But do you know what, Finn? If they find out you let Mother and Father in with false IDs, you won't only be saying goodbye to the Order of Merit. Most likely you'll be given the sack or moved to Anholt. Perhaps even to Læsø.'

Silence once more.

'What you can do,' says Tilte, 'is to let us in so we can find Mother and Father and get them out again as quickly as possible. Before they're discovered.'

The barrier goes up.

64

AS WE DRIVE SLOWLY ACROSS THE CAUSEWAY I TURN MY HEAD
back, and what I see behind us both surprises and concerns me.

It's a taxi. Not in itself an alarming sight, but it's hurtling
along as though its passengers have forced the driver to
ignore all the rules of the road and put his licence on the line.
Now it screeches to a halt in front of the barrier and out of it
pile Anaflabia Borderrud, Thorkild Thorlacius, Alexander
Flounderblood and Bodil Hippopotamus.

They move in a way that from a distance looks like trance
dancing, but which most probably is an expression of rage, and
now they stand pointing in our direction.

By now, Tilte and I are convinced that the basis of all spiritual
training lies in the ability of the human heart to empathise and
understand the feelings of others. I can easily imagine how the
six individuals behind us are feeling – I say six, assuming that
Vera and Thorkild's wife, too, are about to emerge from the
vehicle – in view of the suffering they have endured during
the last twenty-four hours. And I would very much have liked
to tell them that one's chances of discovering that the door is
opening may be enhanced by training one's inner balance and
neutrality and one's ability to let go of such powerful emotions
as those that now compel them to dance about in front of the
barrier. But I am out of earshot, and I can see that they are now
surrounded by police, and it would seem, moreover, that the
officers in question are acting in full accordance with modern
security philosophy, which states that it's better to be a

conflict-solver than to come across as an officer of the law, and as such they are now attempting to talk things down and reach agreement. And yet Anaflabia knocks one of them to the ground with her umbrella, and I see another officer slump to his knees, possibly due to Thorkild Thorlacius having delivered a right hook to his abdomen. And then more widespread scuffling breaks out. The last thing I see before we cross the bridge and enter the courtyard is Alexander Flounderblood breaking loose in a magnificent escape attempt, throwing himself into the lake and proceeding to swim away.

And then we drive through a gateway into the courtyard.

It's always a moving experience to see the surroundings in which one's closest friends – in this instance Count Rickardt – spent their childhoods and smoked their first joints. And I must say that Filthøj is a proper castle of the kind fit for kings and queens. The courtyard is the size of a football pitch and the buildings as big as handball arenas, though with gilded elements, inscriptions and ornaments, and the steps into the main house would be wide enough for fifty guests to proceed to the main door with everyone holding hands.

On the steps is another security point, and we're happy and relieved to discover that it's manned by Lars and Katinka of the Police Intelligence Service.

The reason we feel happy is because their presence at this strategic point means that Black Henrik can't possibly have slipped by. For while it may be conceivable for him to have passed Titmouse and Finn Flatfoot without being noticed, it's quite unimaginable that he could ever pull the wool over the eyes of Lars and Katinka. At this moment, Polly and her white ladies are going through in the company of four police officers carrying the coffin of Maria from Maribo, and the way Lars and Katinka study their documents it's plain that nothing is left to chance.

The question now is how we ourselves are going to get in, it being fairly reasonable to assume that Lars and Katinka might feel that things have happened between us in the last twenty-four hours that require explanation.

Tilte and I exchange a glance. What we communicate is that we're now going to come clean and tell it like it is. I run a hand through my hair, moisten my lips and prepare to smooth the troubled waters with well-chosen words.

Because Tilte and I both have our eyes on the coffin, as though to bid Maria a final farewell, we notice immediately that the lid begins to tremble.

It's obvious the police officers carrying the coffin have noticed it too, and yet they wisely resolve to ignore the fact, a choice one can well understand, for do we not all of us shrink away when confronted with the inexplicable?

Again, Tilte and I send each other a look.

For a moment, the situation is uncertain. The natural reaction of those such as Tilte and I who are practised in matters spiritual is to seek to restore one's inner balance, and with this aim in mind I now proceed towards a peaceful bench against the outer wall of the main building.

A woman is seated on the bench. She is wearing what looks like a witch's garb, with the pointed hat pulled down over her eyes. One of the problems with all religions is that women are so poorly situated, so whenever one sees a woman of prominent office, one is invariably pleasantly surprised and will often wish to show one's respect, and this is what I endeavour to do now, regardless of my own personal distress, by bowing deeply.

By this movement, I am accorded a view of the woman's face underneath the brim of her hat, and it transpires that she is Maria from Maribo.

I take her hand and find it to be cold as a cube of ice. Tilte appears beside me and grasps the situation at a single glance.

'Henrik,' she says. 'He's put her in one of Rickardt's costumes. And taken her place in the coffin.'

Now it's imperative we win the hearts of Lars and Katinka.

At that moment, the taxi from before pulls up in front of the steps and out pile, once again, Anaflabia, Thorlacius, Vera the Secretary, Thorlacius' wife, Alexander Flounderblood and Bodil Fisker.

We never learn how they managed to get through the gate. Perhaps some people simply possess such an abundance of charisma and what is sometimes referred to as nobility of soul that they have no need of identity papers, their mere presence being sufficient to identify them and moreover allow them to proceed – as they do now across the courtyard of the castle – with a natural right to be present in their surroundings.

If this indeed is the correct explanation, it must be added that Lars and Katinka have a different understanding. In their defence, however, it should be recalled that Alexander Flounderblood has been out for a swim in the lake. How he returned to dry land is a matter of uncertainty. All we can say is that he has had no time to clean himself up in any way that might make him seem like the confidence-inspiring individual his appearance otherwise tends to indicate.

Few Danish lakes remain crystal clear all year round, those of Finø perhaps being the only exception. The average Danish lake has its ups and downs during the course of a year, and in bad periods may look mostly like a natural slurry tank, and the lake of Filthøj Castle is going through just such a period now. Alexander Flounderblood, therefore, resembles something that would frighten his own mother, and when Lars and Katinka catch sight of him and Thorlacius and Anaflabia, they're out of their blocks as though the starter's pistol had just been fired in an Olympic final.

Which leaves me and Tilte and Basker and Hans and Ashanti and Jakob Bordurio and Pallas Athene with a completely open goal leading straight into the heart of the Grand Synod.

65

THE ROOM WE NOW ENTER, THE SAME ROOM WE HAVE SEEN on our parents' video file and which has hardly been absent from our thoughts these past twelve hours or however many have passed, is larger and more splendid than we had envisaged. It is a room one could imagine a great many of Leonora Ticklepalate's clients might consider as a potential backdrop to their private coaching sessions. The ceiling is as high as a cathedral's, and the location commands a magnificent view of the evening sky above the Sound.

The exhibition case, too, is larger than we have been able to assess, and the light that shines from it is brighter.

Moreover, there is something rather overwhelming about standing face to face with eight hundred people who have gone to great pains with their appearance.

And yet, what strikes us most forcibly is something else entirely: the atmosphere.

Let me say right away that I do not believe that all eight hundred individuals contribute equally to this atmosphere. Most likely, some are here because they consider their religion to be their livelihood. These are people who might just as easily earn their daily bread doing something else entirely, and who perhaps ought to be doing so now, for their own sakes at least. But aside from such slackers as will be found on any team, regardless of how meticulous the selection procedure, I would say that gathered in this room are so many people who have passed through the right door, the one that leads to freedom, leaving it ajar behind them in such a way that one senses the stir, that it almost knocks us off our feet. If you imagine the kind of keenness possessed by Tilte, and an ability such as my great-grandmother's to take even the likes of Alexander Flounderblood and Karl Marauder into her heart, and if you multiply these two qualities by one hundred and fifty thousand, then you'll have at least some idea of the atmosphere in this room at Filthøj Castle immediately prior to the opening of the Grand Synod. It's the kind of atmosphere that could be cut into thick slices with a cake knife, if one only had such a thing about one's person.

The stage is some distance away, and yet I am in no doubt as to who now appears upon it, because that person is Conny.

My heart rate leaps to two or three hundred, so the details of what's said are lost to me on account of the blood rushing in my ears, but what I do catch is that she presents herself as one half of a host couple who will be providing the musical entertainment, and her partner is – and at this juncture she throws open her arms – Count Rickardt Three Lions.

You could have knocked me down with the fluff of a fledgling's feather. Fortunately, no one in the vicinity appears to have such a thing or seems even in the slightest bit interested in knocking me down, because I am invisible in the throng. What has affected my balance in such a way is not the fact that Conny is the evening's musical hostess, even if she is only fourteen, because it seems only reasonable that this should be so. Truth be told, from now until the end of our days I am expecting nothing but one long, uninterrupted demonstration on Conny's part of the immeasurable distance between her galaxy and mine. What makes such an impression on me is rather how on earth those responsible could ever have been duped into letting Rickardt in on the act.

Before I even have time to reflect on the matter, Rickardt takes the stage and has changed into a garment that could easily be Wee Willie Winkie's nightshirt, and on his feet are a pair of long-toed *poulaines*.

It's a sight from which no one under normal circumstances

would be able to wrench themselves away. But now something happens that commands my full and undivided attention.

The four police officers have placed Maria's coffin on three chairs, and a tall Indian gentlemen wearing a robe of much the same cut as Count Rickardt's is leaning over it. Tilte and I know straight away that this must be Polly's American-Indian guru, Da Sweet Love Ananda, now preparing to bless Maria and help her onward on her journey into the afterlife.

We leap into action immediately. But too late. Polly removes the lid of the coffin, Da Sweet Love Ananda places his hand on the forehead of the deceased and begins to whisper some words.

Then he removes his hand, this being a movement rather less dignified than the first, because he does so as though he just came into contact with an electric fence.

At which point Black Henrik sits up in the coffin.

He's pale, his skin having almost the same colour as his hair, and the reason for this is obvious, because the cooler in the coffin is designed to keep anyone who happens to be inside at a temperature just above freezing.

A number of the journalists present are quick to discover what's going on. Flashbulbs go off. A TV camera is turned towards him.

Henrik climbs out of the coffin. With by no means the same elegance he might otherwise tend to demonstrate in such a situation, but still fast enough for him to be over the hills and far away by the time we reach the scene.

Given my size, I'm now able to duck down and spot Henrik between the legs of the assembled delegates, whereupon I set off in pursuit. He's headed for a doorway, beyond which a flight of stairs leads upwards. I'm on his heels and catch up with him on the floor above.

We come out onto a kind of gallery, which affords us a full view of the old chapel below, meaning this would be the former organ loft, and indeed the organ is here still.

Henrik turns to face me. I shy behind the keyboard. Henrik flexes his fingers to wake them up after his layover in the coffin. I find myself thinking about a hundred and twenty-eight rats.

'Henrik,' I say, 'don't do anything you might regret.'

It's not the kind of comment that clears the table and compels the mighty to fall to their knees, unlike my famous statement about the nape of Conny's neck. But it does cause Henrik to pause and scrutinise me for a moment.

'Do we know each other?' he asks.

'Not yet,' I tell him. 'But one of the beautiful things about life is the new friendships that lie ahead.'

It's cutting no ice. Instead, he begins to move towards me.

But then a shadow falls upon him. It's the shadow of my brother Hans. At once, Hans has his arms around Henrik and has locked him in a tight embrace.

Although, as I've said, a clear majority of the population consider Hans to be distinctly princely, it's an undeniable fact that when it comes to defending the weak and innocent from the misdeeds of others, Hans is able to take on a demeanour more reminiscent of Frankenstein's monster, prompting one to think that by the time he's finished with his opponent there'll be little left but hair and fingernails and a sprinkling of bonemeal. And that's exactly what he looks like now.

Henrik is clearly aware of it, for which reason he chooses to remain calm.

'If you don't mind,' I say.

I frisk him, finding only a small, flat camera.

What I was hoping to find was a remote control. For one cannot help but think that if a man such as Henrik has been on a jaunt through the secret tunnel while in the possession of plastic explosives, the purpose of his expedition will most likely not have been to experiment in peace and quiet with new methods of rat catching.

'Henrik,' I say, 'could we ask you to tell us where you've hidden the explosives?'

He smiles at me. But it's a smile devoid of the warmth and understanding one always hopes to elicit in grown-ups.

'You'll know soon enough,' he says.

This is a tricky situation. I look down on the room below. The delegates have turned towards the stage and taken their seats. Rickardt Three Lions has everyone's attention.

'I would like to remind you of Goethe's final words,' Rickardt says.

This is a thing he has learned from Tilte, who has drawn up a lengthy list of famous last words, from which she often quotes, asking people to think about what their own last words should be. Right at this moment I could have done with something rather more upbeat, but no one asked me.

'More light!' says Rickardt.

At once, the lights are turned up. Rickardt has arranged the lighting himself and was over-illuminated to begin with, but now a further 20,000 watts burst upon the proceedings. I catch sight of my mother and father standing in the wings.

Then a voice comes from the stair behind us, and it belongs to Tilte.

'Henrik,' she says, 'your mother would like to speak to you.'

A female figure now looms into view, this being the Bishop of Grenå herself, Anaflabia Borderrud.

It's hard to imagine some women having husbands and children. I don't mean that in any negative sense. It may be that women such as Joan of Arc or Teresa of Ávila or Leonora Ticklepalate were born to carry out duties too great for them to bother with nappies and parents' evenings. To my mind, Anaflabia is such a woman.

But when, nevertheless, she turns out to be the mother of a child whom she has bounced upon her knee and whose rosy red cheeks she has kissed, it comes as no surprise to me that her child should be Black Henrik. Now that they're standing so close to each other, I sense a commonality in their steely character. And there's a physical similarity, too, a firmness of the jaw, as though it were hammered out of steel plate at the Finø Boatyard.

But motherly love is not foremost in Anaflabia's heart at this moment in time.

'Henrik,' she says, 'is it true what I'm hearing? That you have contrived some despicable bomb?'

The change that comes over Henrik is so profound one can only think that against the feelings even a full-grown man has for his mother, the crusader inside stands not a chance. His body begins to squirm, and what it wants to do is plain: it wants to extricate itself and run for its life.

But Hans has a firm grip on Henrik. And now Anaflabia steps forward.

'Mother,' says Henrik, 'you told me other religions were the Devil's work.'

There's a lump in his throat.

'Henrik,' says Anaflabia, 'you shall switch off that bomb and you shall do so right away!'

Tears begin to slide down Henrik's cheeks.

'It's too late,' he says. 'The timer's been started. It's sealed. Fixed to the box in the vaults. But, Mother, it's only a small bomb. To blow up the heathen treasures.'

Anaflabia stares at him. Though motherly love is unconditional, it may still on occasion stand and gawp.

'Then what are you doing here now?' she asks.

Henrik dries his eyes.

'I wanted to take some pictures for the scrapbook. So I could show the children. Your grandchildren, Mother.'

66

I KNOW WHAT MANY PEOPLE WOULD NOW SAY, TILTE AMONG them. They would say that the present situation is, of course, tragic, yet it provides a magnificent opportunity to consider that all of us at any time may find ourselves in the middle of an explosion with objects flying through the air around us. And if indeed that were to happen, they would say, and if Henrik's bomb should prove to be larger than he himself believes, causing some of us to be lost in such an explosion, all the major religions indicate that the best death you can wish for is when one or more saints are present who can walk in and out of the big door as though it were the swingdoor of the Finø Gentlemen's Outfitters.

Therefore, I am sorry to say that this is not a chance I am prepared to take. Instead, what happens is that my legs intervene. And one thing I've learned from the spiritual pathway of football is that on certain occasions much of one's higher consciousness resides in the legs.

I float down the stairs and fly through the old chapel, slipping swiftly past the security guards. I can tell from their faces they think I'm a choirboy or a novice monk, or a spiritual version of the ball boys at Wimbledon, and then I'm where I want to be, standing in front of Mother.

The events my mother has lived through since the last time I saw her have clearly left their mark. It's plain that she has seen things not even the most effective anti-wrinkle cream would be able to reverse. The furrows that have appeared on her brow are here to stay, provided we survive Henrik's bomb. And now they deepen even further as she sees me standing here before her.

'Mother,' I say, 'there's a bomb under the floor. It's attached to the security box. Can you send that box out of the tunnel?'

The great majority of us will feel compelled to have words with our mothers on occasion. However, it is not often that one must ask one's mother to wave goodbye to a couple of hundred million and go straight to jail for four years with one year off for good behaviour. Nonetheless, this is exactly what I am asking of my mother now, because what she must do is reveal to everyone the presence of soft soap in the tunnel and thereby the plan she has cooked up with Father, and this is a fact of which she is aware, and she stares at me with what I would call a look of panic in her eyes.

'I can't,' she says.

I'll be frank and say that I'm disappointed. After all, what's two hundred million kroner and four years in jail compared to making Tilte and Hans and me and all the world religions happy and saving a billion kroner's worth of glitter, and moreover cleaning up some of the mess she and Father have left behind?

'We'll visit you in jail,' I tell her. 'Father can help the prison chaplain out. And you can play at the services. I've heard they have a new organ at the Læsø High Security Prison. They say some of the prisoners don't want to leave because of it, even when they've finished their sentences.'

She shakes her head.

'It's not that,' she says.

I venture to glance behind me, only to discover that my mother and I now have the full attention of the assembly. It's not just your average sort of attention, this eclipses even what I was accorded when duped into appearing on stage during the Mr Finø contest. And in the brief glimpse of what I see over my shoulder I sense that the assembled notables are naturally curious to discover the state of Danish spirituality, and thus far they have seen Conny, who of course is a delight to any retina, though still only a child star of fourteen, and besides Conny they have seen Rickardt Three Lions, and now my mother and me.

'Haven't you got a remote control?' I ask.

'It's in the rubber dinghy,' my mother says.

I begin to feel dizzy.

'There must be some speech recognition in there somewhere,' I say. 'There always is.'

Powerful emotions surge silently though visibly through my mother's organism. And I well understand her predicament.

'"Monday in the Rain",' I say. 'That's what sets it off, isn't it?'

My mother nods. Despair is written across her face. I can only feel for her. What comes back to her now is of course the trauma of the time Bermuda Seagull talked her into singing that very song in front of the annual meeting of the North Jutland Clergymen's Association.

'On the pathway of spiritual development,' I tell her, 'none of us can avoid making sacrifice.'

As I speak the words, I sense everything falling into place inside my mother. And I sense that the last few days have precipitated a shift in what I think is called the division of responsibility between the two of us.

My mother turns towards the exhibition case. And then she begins to sing.

She performs only the first few bars, and then I feel a slight vibration beneath my feet. Perhaps my mother, my father and Tilte and me are the only ones to notice. But I know for certain that the security box in the vaults is now on its way through the tunnel with Henrik's bomb attached to it.

There's one final concern. How will the sensitive souls here assembled, among them the Pope and the Dalai Lama and the 17th Karmapa and Her Majesty Queen Margrethe II of Denmark, react when the bomb goes off in just a few seconds?

And then an idea occurs to me. It would be too immodest to call it divine inspiration issuing directly from the Holy Spirit. But it's a solid and sustainable revelation nonetheless.

I turn towards the assembly.

'Your Excellencies,' I announce in a suitably loud voice, 'I am from the island of Finø. And there we bid our guests welcome by means of the famous Finø Salute.'

At this juncture I pause briefly to allow the interpreters to catch up.

'Originally, this had military significance. But these days it means *May the peace of God be with you!*'

And then comes the explosion. At first it's a flash of light at the boathouse, then white smoke pouring from its windows and doors. And then its roof is raised a metre into the air, upon which the timber building collapses like a house of cards.

There's a moment of silence in the former chapel. Then comes the applause.

I lean back against the wall so as not to fall down. The next moment, I'm surrounded by security, and I get the feeling they've abandoned the theory about my being a ball boy from Wimbledon and are now more inclined towards the hypothesis that I'm some sort of religious hooligan who needs to be torn apart discreetly.

But no sooner do they grab me than they let go again and step aside, and now Conny stands before me. And though she addresses the assembly, she has placed her hand on my arm.

'Thank you indeed for this marvellous greeting from the island of Finø,' she says. 'And now I would like to present a song about love. I imagine love to be a rather important concept to a conference such as this.'

I raise my head. The nape of Conny's neck is less than half a metre away.

'In all the great religions, love is a keyword. What everyone agrees on is that although it may be hard to find and we must suffer along the way, love is what all of us are looking for. It is the natural state of every human being.'

I look up and she gazes straight into my eyes.

I cannot walk away, because I am unable to walk. I seep away, like some diluted liquid. Behind me, Conny says some more words, and it sounds like she is bidding welcome to heads

367

of state, to religious leaders and to the Queen, but I can't make out exactly what she's saying, all I can do is pray that my footballing legs will carry me into the hall, and my prayers are heard, because when I get there I collapse onto a convenient sofa.

67

HAD THERE BEEN A DOCTOR AROUND, HE OR SHE WOULD HAVE ordered five minutes' rest to get myself together again. But there's no time for that. Because as I slowly come round I see a handful of individuals already seated on an adjacent sofa, and these individuals are Thorkild Thorlacius, his wife, Vera the Secretary and Anaflabia Borderrud. Moreover, Anaflabia has Black Henrik seated on her lap. Next to them stand Lars and Katinka. All wear the empty look of people who have just been reminded that the end of their days may come at any moment.

Katinka rattles a pair of handcuffs. It's obvious they're here to take Henrik away.

Not surprisingly, Anaflabia is the first to recover control.

'Does the Administration of Justice Act allow for sentences to be served at home with Mother?' she asks.

'Maybe the tail end,' says Katinka. 'If the psychiatrists are in agreement.'

Everyone looks at Thorkild Thorlacius, who appears to be less than pleased.

'He was going to blow us all up,' he says. 'The man must be stark raving mad.'

'He's a good boy deep down,' says Anaflabia. 'He got lost, that's all.'

She draws Henrik to her bosom. He rests his head on her shoulder.

'We shall have to discuss the matter,' says Thorkild Thorlacius. 'Take his behaviour in prison into account. There's always a chance.'

His gaze now falls on me. It may be that I am still in shock. But the look in his eyes could almost be confused with kindness.

'Your part in all this is not entirely clear to me, young man. Professionally, however, I believe there to be indications that with time and the proper care you might leave this life of crime and drugs and return to normal society.'

'Thank you very much,' I say.

'The mood in this building,' Thorlacius goes on, 'is rather peculiar. Time has not permitted any thorough analysis, but my feeling is that whatever is going on in that room requires consultation with the upper echelons of the Department of Neural Research.'

I feel I've now regained sufficient strength to advance fifty metres. As I get to my feet, the party is suddenly augmented by the presence of Alexander Flounderblood, who comes staggering across the floor to slump down on the sofa.

'I fear for my mental health,' he says.

It's a fear many would consider to be well-founded. But something has changed within me now. Perhaps on account of my seeing the nape of Conny's neck at such close quarters, or because of what she said, or simply just ordinary relief. Whatever the reason, I suddenly feel a great affection for everyone. And to give you an idea of the scope of this feeling I can tell you that at this moment I would most likely even spare Karl Marauder his life if he were with us. And this affection extends so far as to include Alexander Flounderblood.

'Because of this slime,' Alexander says, endeavouring to remove some of what still adheres to his face, 'my vision is impaired. So when I sat down just before to tidy myself with a napkin I inadvertently elbowed the woman seated on the bench next to me. Whereupon to my consternation she slumped to her side. I addressed her, but received no reply. I reached out to touch her and found her to be dead! And all I can think is that this is the third time in twenty-four hours! Am I stricken by a curse, perhaps? Am I such a person who causes others to wither away at the very sight of me?'

'Alexander,' I say, 'you are not such a person at all. I would say that you are the kind of person whose appearance gives a lot of people a great deal to think about, especially the way you look right now. But the lady on the bench was already dead, as indeed were the others you mention.'

Alexander stares at me.

'I've been thinking,' he says, 'that perhaps I haven't been entirely attentive to the positive aspects, limited though they may be, of working professionally with children.'

I take a step. My legs are rather steadier now. I need some air.

68

THE HALL IS EMPTY APART FROM SECURITY, BUT THEN I detect a movement between two pillars: it's Tilte and Jakob Aquinas, and they haven't seen me.

'Tilte,' says Jakob, 'these past hours have changed me. I have seen things in myself and in your family. I have come to the conclusion that I am unsuited to the priesthood.'

And then Tilte kisses him.

I consider it impolite to remain standing and watch one's sister snogging her boyfriend. What roots me to the floor, however, is that Jakob's rosary has become idle in his hand.

'Jakob,' says Tilte, 'if you want to move ahead to the door, especially if you choose to dive headlong into this secular life again, it's important you keep up your Hail Marys, even when we kiss. Should we try again?'

This time I wrench myself free and steal away.

I cross the courtyard outside. Jakob and Tilte come up alongside me. Hans and Ashanti and Basker are right behind them. Without speaking, we walk over the causeway, pass through the barrier, glancing through the window of the Portakabin to see Finn Flatfoot asleep with Titmouse on his lap, and continue along the lake.

A car is parked on the road. A Maserati. The path leads away into the bushes, then opens out onto a clearing, and on a bench sits Poul Bellerad, the ship owner, with a pair of binoculars. At his side stand the two bald bodyguards, one of whom is drying the ship owner's eyes with a handkerchief, the other massaging his shoulders.

He turns as he hears us approach. His eyes light up hopefully, only then to grow dim when he sees it's only us. He was hoping for Henrik.

'Poul,' I say, 'there's something I want to ask you.'

He stares emptily.

'Finø's undertaker, Bermuda Seagull Jansson. She's a friend of our family and in demand throughout the country, famed for laying people to rest as though they were going to a palace ball. She says only three things can make people draw up truly despicable plans, and those things are religion, sex and money. I can understand religion and sex. But money . . .'

We've got company now. Behind the bench, Albert Winehappy appears with Lars and Katinka. Katinka has three pairs of handcuffs in her hands. She must have a stash somewhere, because the past twenty-four hours she's kept them coming like half-time hotdogs at a football match.

The ship owner gets to his feet. He studies my face.

'You're the one with the flowers,' he says. 'Who are you in all this, anyway?'

'A victim,' I say. 'A victim of circumstance.'

The handcuffs snap shut.

'Money may not be the best of motives,' says Bellerad, 'but it's the purest. Think about it.'

And then they lead him away.

Albert Winehappy remains. He's in the process of unwrapping a dozen open sandwiches from an emergency lunchbox.

'It's no use,' he says.

All we can do is give him a quizzical look. Perhaps he means it's no use eating his sandwiches, because in five minutes he'll be hungry again.

'These arrests. Court proceedings. Prison sentences. None of it's any use. There'll always be others to carry on the work. We haven't got it right yet . . .'

Mostly, he's talking to himself.

'The Queen would like to thank you,' he says. 'I'll give you a lift, when I've finished eating.'

The others walk on ahead. He and I remain standing.

'Albert,' I say, 'I think it's important Tilte and I are afforded some assistance so as not to give too much away to all the journalists who are going to be upon us in a very short while. We might accidentally tell them a story that could give the general public the impression that the police and the intelligence services have been fast asleep on duty and given the runaround by a schoolboy and his sister.'

He stares at me blankly and stops munching.

'What could keep our mouths sealed would be if you were to swear, cross your heart and hope to die, that my mother and father will be let off the hook.'

He swallows what's in his mouth. Then draws an X against the blubber of his chest.

'Cross my heart and hope to die,' he says.

69

FROM FAIRY TALES I KNOW THAT WHEN YOU HAVE THE honour of standing before the Queen so that she might thank you for something you've done, you may ask her to grant you a wish. But right now the only thing I can think of is to invite her to become one of my personal sponsors when I turn professional. Yet in view of our having saved a billion kroner's worth of jewels and Conny having spoken to me about love while gazing into my eyes, such a wish seems rather small-minded, so all I can do is stand there in silence, rocking on the balls of my feet. Tilte, however, goes straight to the point.

'Your Majesty,' she says, 'I have an acquaintance. It's entirely likely that he's nobility without him actually knowing for sure. Could we perhaps provide him with a title?'

The Queen considers Tilte pensively for a moment.

'That would be a matter for the Association of the Danish Nobility and the State Archives to decide,' she says. 'Not the Court.'

Tilte steps up closer.

'Your Majesty's word carries weight,' she says. 'If I were to get my hands on some documents. Printouts of church records, for instance.'

I sense the Queen soften. Tilte has her in her grasp.

'You shall have my private number,' the Queen says. 'Call me at the Palace. We could pool our resources.'

*   *   *

We're seated in the old chapel again. I gaze around the room at the costumes and the hats. And at Conny, who has sat down beside me. In the row in front of us sit Mother and Father. We haven't really looked each other in the eye yet. I lean forward.

'Mother and Father,' I whisper, 'I don't know if we'll ever be able to land this thing. It might not work. There are loads of examples of children being unable to forgive their parents. But we could take a small step in the right direction if we knew whether or not it was a coincidence that Ashanti here was in possession of Hans' number in order that she might book him and no one else to pick her up from Blågårds Plads.'

My father turns and squirms.

'Your mother and I ran into her in the planning stages. We both considered that if Hans should ever have a chance in life it should be with someone like her.'

'I'm devastated,' I tell them. 'By the two of you once again having a hand in it all. But I appreciate your honesty.'

The room falls silent. The Grand Synod is about to begin. So many people gathered, dancing in and out of the door as if it were an open gate. Conny takes my hand. I look around at the people in my presence, at Hans and Ashanti, Tilte and Conny. And at Pallas Athene, who thankfully is seated, because a moment ago I saw Tilte say something to her that clearly swept her legs from under her.

Perhaps it's the mood in this great space. But all of a sudden I see the elephants that reside inside them all.

Beautiful animals, each and every one, though difficult to keep. Requiring much care and attention. Not to mention the amount of food they eat.

I feel the joy of knowing them all. And gratitude for being only a boy of fourteen without an elephant of his own, but with legs made for football and a natural, albeit somewhat inflated, tendency to modesty. Not forgetting a small fox terrier. I stroke Basker's fur.

'Basker,' I whisper, 'Can you feel the door?'

THE FINØ WALTZ

70

WE HAVE NEVER RETURNED TO FINØ.

It may be that we've returned technically to the island, living here, and eating and sleeping at the rectory. But we have never returned home.

It has to do with what I was talking about before, about how when you change inside, those around you change, too, and vice versa.

When we came back from Copenhagen we were no longer the same. And the island to which we returned was no longer the island we knew.

I shall begin with the most obvious changes. The ones you can see with the naked eye.

Alexander Flounderblood has left the island, having taken on a more prominent position abroad, and Einar Flogginfellow has been reinstated as head of Finø Town School, though initially for a trial period only.

The whole school followed Alexander down to the ferry to see him off. And it wasn't to deliver him the final *coup de grâce* that might relieve him of his suffering, it was to wish him a proper goodbye. For Alexander, too, was changed. Following the events I have related to you here, he was never the same again. The last three months of his time at the school he spoke to the pupils as though they were human beings, and often one would find he had begun to daydream, standing at the window and gazing out upon the Sea of Opportunity as though scanning for something he had once glimpsed but which now was gone, something he could never forget.

Moreover, he had brought Vera back with him. She was standing by his side with one foot on the gangway when he caught sight of Tilte and me and came up to shake our hands. It was like there was something he wanted to tell us but never got the chance, because Vera called out to him and he turned and we waved, and then he was gone.

Tilte doesn't live at the rectory any more. In August she moved to Grenå to begin life as a boarder at Grenå High School, which Jakob Bordurio now also attends, and to begin with they lived in student accommodation at the Grenå Kollegium.

But not for long. Only for a month or so. After that, they moved into a swish apartment overlooking the beach.

Reliable sources inform me that it's paid for by Tilte's collaboration with Pallas Athene.

Pallas Athene came to Finø in the summer. Though we are accustomed to the finest vehicles – horse-drawn carriages and golf buggies and Mercedes and Maseratis and Bermuda's armoured wagon – members of the Finø public still paused to stare when the red Jaguar pulled up in front of the rectory and Pallas Athene climbed out in stilettos and a red wig, though thankfully without her helmet.

When she and Tilte withdrew to Tilte's room, I thought at first that I was meant to go with them, Tilte and I having always stuck together through thick and thin. But this time she shook her head, though I could tell that Pallas Athene was surprised, too, seeing as how I was the one who discovered her.

'In Peter's presence,' Tilte said, as though speaking of a person absent, 'one sees the world conjugated in a multitude of ways. Yet there's no getting away from the fact that he only just turned fifteen in May.'

And then they closeted themselves away to speak in private.

When they emerged, Pallas Athene looked like a person who

is fatally wounded just as the sun comes up. She bid us goodbye rather incoherently, climbed back into her Jaguar and drove away.

I stood at the kitchen window and watched her go. Tilte came up behind me. She put her arms around me, but Peter Finø is not for sale, at least not for false displays of affection. I kept my shoulders straight and remained unapproachable.

'That thing she does, putting her heart away in that box,' said Tilte. 'It's no good. Even if it's together with a photo of the kids. I explained it to her.'

Tilte's voice was full of what the Christian mystics call repentance and the desire to placate me. So I condescended to reply. One should never turn a repentant sinner away.

'You want to reschool her,' I said. 'Turn her into a therapist.'

Tilte remained silent. She didn't need to speak. It was obvious I'd hit bull's-eye.

'We've sold that once already,' I said. 'To Leonora.'

'This'll be the next stage up,' said Tilte.

'You want her to get her clients to bring their partners with them. To Abakosh. Where she and Andrik will give them therapy.'

Tilte leaned her head against mine.

'I gave her a couple of soundbites to be getting on with,' she said. 'The two main principles of love. One: always take your husband with you when visiting a brothel. And two: leave your heart where nature put it.'

Tilte has only been back twice since she moved away, and the first time was when we had Svend Sewerman admitted into the aristocracy. Tilte had received a letter from the Palace with a coat of arms on the back, and one from the Association of the Danish Nobility, and together we cycled across to Finøholm. There, we sat in the kitchen with Svend and Bullimilla, and the first thing we did was to give them back their curtains. We had washed and ironed them and folded them neatly. When you're involved with profound personal development, it's important, as far as possible, to return the material world in the state in which you found it.

Then Tilte placed the letter from the Palace on the table with the coat of arms facing upwards.

'Peter and I,' she said, 'are protectors of Finø Football Club. I should like to mention in passing that the club is in desperate need of a new indoor facility, the old one being rather run-down and overbooked.'

Svend Sewerman moistened his lips. And I have to concede that I didn't know quite where to look either, so I chose to stare at the floor in embarrassment.

Then Svend asked what a new indoor facility would cost. His voice was dry, and Tilte replied that the going rate was upwards of six million. Whereupon Bullimilla enquired if the six million included a cafeteria, and Tilte said no, that was just for the basics.

'Svend,' said Bullimilla, 'we need a cafeteria. Think of all the growing youngsters in need of sustenance, and a kitchen's the heart of any building, so don't make this one too small, will you?'

'For seven million,' Tilte said, 'we can do you something that'll last for generations to come.'

Then she placed a document on the table in front of Svend. Mustering all my willpower, I lifted my gaze from the floor. The document was a deed of gift from Svend Sewerman to Finø Football Club. Tilte had drawn it up at home in accordance with all the conventions. It was for the sum of seven million kroner.

When Svend signed it with a look on his face that suggested giving money away ran against his deepest convictions, Tilte opened the letter from the Queen and the one from the Association of the Danish Nobility, both of which confirmed that subsequent to studies of church records as presented by the Parish of Finø Town, the Association found it proven without doubt that Svend Sewerman was directly descendant of the Ahlefeldt-Laurvig Finø family and as such was entitled to bear that family's name, and congratulations were in order, and the Queen had signed it all herself.

Svend fainted. This is the only time I have ever seen a grown man faint. His eyes turned to the sky and he slid slowly to the floor.

Tilte and I did nothing, mostly because we didn't think there was anything we could do. Svend Sewerman is shaped like a barrel and, like I said, used to work digging holes in the ground. He is not a man that can be moved easily without the aid of a trolley. Bullimilla, however, drew him up in her arms as if he were a child. Then she stood there for a moment, holding him upright while looking at Tilte and me.

'When we open the new facility,' she said, 'you can leave the food to me.'

That was the first time Tilte came back.

The wording is intentional. Before the Grand Synod and Mother's and Father's disappearance, I would have said that Tilte had not been home. But I no longer refer to the rectory or Finø as home.

It has to do with the rectory's unexpected guest.

I'll say this slowly, because it's important: Tilte moving out was a greater shock to me than I had anticipated.

I don't know if there are clinics like Big Hill where you can be treated for sister dependency. But that was certainly what I needed. We had returned home from Copenhagen, and Tilte and I insisted on each of us having our own Portakabin in the rectory garden, and that was where we were going to live. We were given what we wanted without delay. That's one of the differences between then and now: since we came back there have been a number of occasions when we have needed to explain to Mother and Father how things are going to be, and now they do as we say.

It's all so as not to be trampled to death by the elephants. We realise that. Mother's and Father's elephants are not the Indian variety that can be taught to sit on your lap and do the crossword puzzle and stand on their front legs and wag their tails. Mother's and Father's elephants are the African species that wander great distances without warning and which you can be on reasonable terms with, but never be certain of. So that was the reason we wanted to live in Portakabins, so as to keep our distance should they begin to wander.

I must have imagined things would continue like that, with Tilte and me in our own separate Portakabins in the garden, but close to each other nonetheless. Even though I'd known for years that she would leave one day. So when it happened, it was worse than I ever thought it would be.

I found out what loneliness is really like.

I'm sorry to have to mention something as sombre as this, now that we're approaching the end. But it's important.

Of course, I had been familiar with loneliness for a long time, perhaps even always. It feels like it's been with me as far back as I can remember.

I don't know how it feels to you. Perhaps we all experience loneliness differently, in our own ways. My mother once told me that for her loneliness is 'Monday in the Rain' playing in the background when she feels like she's all on her own, even though that song also has to do with love and Father. To me, loneliness is a person. It has no face, but when it appears it's as if it comes to sit down beside me, or behind me, and it can happen any time, even when I'm with others, and even when I'm with Conny.

I'm seeing Conny again. Sometimes I visit her in Copenhagen, where her friends stare at me as if I were a puzzle that cannot be solved, and the puzzle is what on earth Conny sees in me. Sometimes she comes to Finø. Very often, being together with her makes me feel extremely happy.

I don't know if you're in love with someone. If you're not, there's something I would like to say to you, and that is that love comes to everyone. All fifteen years of my experience in life tell me that the world is organised in such a way that all of us find someone to love. Unless we work against it. So if you're not in love with anyone but would like to be, you should try to discover which part of you is working against it. And this is founded on in-depth studies conducted by myself and Tilte.

But even with Conny here, loneliness sometimes appeared and sat down behind me, more conspicuous than ever before, and I couldn't understand why. Until one evening in the rectory kitchen.

It was October, the half-term holiday, and Great-Grandma had come to stay with us. Tilte was here too, and she had brought Jakob Bordurio with her. Hans and Ashanti had come from Copenhagen. They live together now in a small flat, blessed with their love, as the hymnmakers might say, and not even the neighbours are any bother, even though Ashanti beats the drums and trance dances and occasionally carries out the ritual slaughter of a black cockerel on the balcony.

Conny was sitting beside me and Father had just presented his roasted whole turbot on a flatbed trolley when Ashanti said: 'I'm pregnant. Hans and I are expecting a baby.'

Thereupon descended the silence of the grave of which I have previously spoken at length, and with it plenty of opportunity to reach inside if one only had the presence of mind to do so. It was a silence that remained unbroken until Ashanti added that she felt certain it was going to be a girl, and that she had already decided on a name. The baby, she said, would be named after our mother, Clara, and would bear the middle name Nebuchadnezzar, familiar from the Old Testament and hot stuff in Haiti. Then there were two family names, Duplaisir and Finø, and furthermore Ashanti had felt her baby kicking inside for the very first time on board the little Cessna during the flight to Finø, and for this reason, and because she wished to modernise the age-old Haitian tradition of giving children names that were far too long, their little treasure would quite simply be called Clara Nebuchadnezzar Flyvia Propella Duplaisir Finø.

We are, as you know, rather hardened to unusual names on Finø, and yet I would say that Ashanti's announcement was followed by a somewhat prolonged pause, during which the only sound to be heard was Basker's wheezing, and even that seemed to be approaching hyperventilation. But then Tilte pulled Ashanti into a corner and told her it was a beautiful name, though a little on the ornamental side, a matter that might make the child the object of unwanted attention from dark forces and the black magic that slumbers beneath the outward Christian appearance of Finø's inhabitants and which very easily becomes jealous of small children with fancy names, so why not make do with Clara Duplaisir Finø, and that was what they eventually decided on.

I have on several occasions drawn your attention to how dramatic events often seem to come in clusters, and this was true of this particular evening, too, because no sooner had Tilte and Ashanti returned to their seats than Great-Grandma cleared her throat and announced that she had something to say to us, which was that she had decided how she wanted to die.

At this point we became concerned. On the most recent occasions Great-Grandma had stayed with us, she had allowed me to stir the buttermilk soup while she herself ran the show from her wheelchair, so when we heard her say what she said we all feared the worst.

'I have decided to die with a chuckle,' Great-Grandma said. 'A hearty chuckle. I've always thought that would be the most splendid way to go. But why, you might ask, am I telling you this now? And the answer is because I don't anticipate any of you being there to witness it. And why not? Because I intend to survive you all, including little Flyvia Propella. And why would I intend to do such a thing? The answer to that is that I have taken a young and athletic lover. And now I should like to present him to the family.'

The door opens and in strides Rickardt Three Lions clutching his archlute, and he walks up and seats himself on Great-Grandma's lap.

None of us saw this coming. Not even Tilte. And I must say quite frankly that a moment passes before we regain our composure and natural politeness and are able to tuck away under the table the questions that crop up in such a situation, primarily, of course, the issue of whether Great-Grandma is now of the nobility.

While everything hangs in the air, I glance across at Tilte and can tell that she needs to swallow this, because Great-Grandma's lap has been Tilte's for as long as anyone can remember.

Many, including myself, would be inclined to believe that we have now exceeded the number of revelations a family can cope with in a single evening. But no sooner have we gathered ourselves than Father makes an announcement.

'I'm resigning from the Church. Mother will no longer be playing the organ. We're going on a pilgrimage. Starting in Vienna, at Knize's, and taking in the great cafés. And when we come home your mother is going to start a small factory. For my part, I shall be writing a cookery book. On spiritual cuisine.'

At this point, Tilte and Father exchange glances. Neither she nor the rest of us are taken in by Father's jovial tone. This is deadly serious.

'I promise you,' Father says with emphasis, 'that my cookbook will contain not a word about the Holy Spirit materialising in the duck rillettes.'

We exhale collectively. I intentionally say we exhale rather than heave a sigh of relief. Because with African elephants in mind, you will understand that when you have parents like ours no guarantee is ever going to accord complete coverage.

And then Father says: 'How about a beer?'

Meticulously he places a half-litre bottle of the Finø Brewery's Special Brew in front of each and every one of us.

I don't know about your own family. Perhaps you were given blackcurrant rum in your baby bottle and served 150-proof moonshine at your confirmation. But in our house, Mother and Father have never once offered me or Tilte or Basker alcohol. This is the first time, and one can well understand why. It's because every time grown-ups crack open a bottle, they hear the roar from the abyss inside them and choose to think that the sound comes from their children. So this is profound indeed. We fill our glasses and say cheers, and all of us know that at this moment we are taking part in a religious rite of quite the same solemnity as the Eucharist at Finø Town Church.

And then I sense that another guest is present, and that this person is seated behind me. The feeling is so very real it prompts me to turn around, only to discover that no one is there, and I realise that this is loneliness. In the midst of good friends, with Basker at my feet and Conny at my side, I still feel completely alone and deserted.

I cannot remain in the kitchen. I stand up without drawing attention to myself and go outside. I walk slowly towards the place where the town comes to an end and the woods begin. The night is dark, the sky sparkling with stars. This is no longer the sky I once wrote about in the tourist brochure. It too has changed. There are more stars now. So many, it's as if they're seizing the firmament. As though the night sky is shifting its weight from the foot that is darkness to the one that is the light of the stars.

Then I put my arm around my loneliness, and I become aware that she is a girl. And for the first time in my life, I stop trying to comfort myself and keep her at bay.

I am looking straight into what I have always feared the most. I am losing them, losing everything. This is what I saw coming in Conny's apartment on Toldbodgade. But now it's stronger and real. Hans is gone, Tilte is gone, and Great-Grandma is gone. Soon the rectory will be depopulated. Mother and Father will be gone.

And now you might say that Conny will surely remain. But at this moment in time, that thought is of little use. Because what I feel is that the loneliness I am now embracing is something not even the person you love can help you with.

It is the loneliness of being enclosed within the room that is one's self. I understand this now for the first time in my life. That the self is a room inside the prison, a room that will always be different from other rooms. For this reason the self will in some way always be alone, and always inside the building of which it is a part.

I can't explain it any better than that. Yet it feels insurmountable.

I walk with my arm around that insurmountability. I hold her tight and do not comfort myself. I can say that quite truthfully. I sense how fond I am of the others who are behind me in the night: Mother and Father, Tilte and Hans and Basker, Conny and Great-Grandma, Jakob and Ashanti, and Rickardt and Nebuchadnezzar Flyvia Propella. All my human rooms.

And then something happens.

In a way, it's like when you're on the football pitch. When the defence is coming at you it's easy to be hypnotised. You see your opponents, the obstacle. You fail to see the opening, the gaps in between.

That's what happens now, all by itself. I shift my attention. From the blackness of the night to the light of the stars. It's my consciousness doing the dustman's trick. My attention is turned one way, towards loneliness, and I go the other. From the feeling of loneliness to what surrounds it. From being trapped within myself, inside the joys and sorrows that make up Peter Finø and which reside like tiny, floating islands adrift within us all, I shift my attention to what those islands are adrift upon.

That's all I do. It's something anyone can do. I change nothing. I don't try to make the loneliness go away. I just let go of it.

It begins to remove itself. She begins to remove herself. And then she is gone.

What remains in a way is me. But in another way, it's just a very deep feeling of happiness.

Behind me, I hear someone approach. Conny. She nuzzles up close.

'We're all rooms,' I say. 'And as long as you're a room, you're imprisoned. But there's a way out, and it's not through a door, because no door exists. All you have to do is see the the opening.'

She takes my head in both her hands.

'Some girls are fortunate enough to be in love with deep and intelligent boys,' she says. 'And then there's the rest of us, who have to make do.'

And then she kisses me, turns and walks back towards the rectory.

I must admit to being rather in a muddle, with one thing and another. So I stay put. There are times when a man needs to be alone.

It's started to rain. Light drizzle. And with the rain comes a sense of gratitude, though I wouldn't know what Denmark's

Meteorological Office would say about that. I am overwhelmed with joy, so intense it cannot be suppressed. Not by my family dissolving. Nor by the fact that when I shared my infinite wisdom with her, the girl I love simply gave me a kiss and one of those comments women make that cause men to lie sleepless in their beds until dawn. Whereupon she floated away, back to the turbot.

I raise my hands to the sky. And then I begin to dance.

It's a slow dance. Nothing that would make the grade at Ifigenia Bruhn's Dancing School. It comes from within and demands my full concentration. Which must be why it takes a while before I notice Karl Marauder.

He's standing in the gateway of their house. I pause. We stare at each other.

'I'm dancing the Finø Waltz,' I tell him. 'By which I express my gratitude for being alive.'

A great many things may be said about Karl Marauder Lander, and many people, myself included, would not hesitate to say them. Nonetheless, he is widely admired for his ability to cope with stress. And that's what he's doing now. His face is expressionless.

'Would that be a private dance?' he asks. 'Or can anyone join in?'

Grace is one of those words that should only ever be handled while wearing velvet gloves, and only when nothing less will do. And yet I must say that I believe it to be the only word capable of adequately describing the fact that life is organised in such a way that even the likes of Karl Marauder may nurture the hope that the natural downward spiral of their lives will one day be halted, and that at the end of the new pathway that appears before them, opportunity lies, delicate, hazardous and refined.

'Just follow me,' I say.

He raises his arms. The rain begins to pour. And slowly, beneath the glittering night sky, Peter Finø and Karl Marauder Lander dance the Finø Waltz.

With thanks to Lisbeth Lawaetz Clausen for the heart piece in the puzzle.

With thanks to the staff of my Danish publishers, Rosinante&Co, and especially to my editor, Jakob Malling Lambert, for insightful, inventive and insistent help in wielding both propelling pencil and scalpel.

Born in 1957, Peter Høeg published his first novel in 1988, having followed various callings – dancer, actor, fencer, sailor, mountaineer – before turning seriously to writing. His novels *Miss Smilla's Feeling for Snow* and *The Quiet Girl* were published to great international acclaim.

Born in 1961, Martin Aitken holds a PhD in Linguistics and gave up university tenure to translate literature. Novels in his translation have been published on both sides of the Atlantic, as well as in Denmark. His translations of short stories and poetry have appeared in book form and in numerous journals and periodicals in the United States, Canada and Denmark. He lives in rural Denmark.